Anneliese and the Geezer

By:

David R. Dye

MAPLE
PUBLISHERS

Anneliese and the Geezer

(Prequel to the book – Cold War, Hot Pursuit)

Author: David R. Dye

First Published in 2024

ISBN 978-1-83538-335-3 (Paperback)
     978-1-83538-336-0 (Hardback)
     978-1-83538-337-7 (E-Book)

Book Cover Design and Book Layout by:
     White Magic Studios
     www.whitemagicstudios.co.uk

Published by:
     Maple Publishers
     Fairbourne Drive, Atterbury,
     Milton Keynes,
     MK10 9RG, UK
     www.maplepublishers.com

A CIP catalogue record for this title is available from the British Library.

Dedication

I wish to dedicate this fictional novel to my grandchildren, Hope, Jake and by no means least, Damian.

Recently, I visited Istanbul to research another book. Damian accompanied me and assisted with all aspects of my research. We found ourselves in a demanding and difficult situation.

His intelligence and strength of character got us through it! I am so lucky and proud to have such wonderful grandchildren.

THIS GREAT COUNTRY IS IN SAFE HANDS!

David. R. Dye

Disclaimer

This novel contains some historically factual events, primarily the capture and deaths of Nazi war criminals. All other events and situations in its storyline have either been modified or are completely fictitious.

The Windrush Generation

I am including this short note as a tribute to Jess who worked on London Buses with my mother. They helped keep London moving throughout the 1960's.

Along with the rest of the 1950's and 1960's population, they worked to put this country back on its feet, following the devastation caused by Word War II.

Jess had arrived in this country on HMT Empire Windrush in 1948. The ship had transported over a thousand people from countries in the Caribbean.

Along with Jess, who was a wonderful character, all the Windrush people have my personal thanks.

David. R. Dye

1

He was coming up to his sixteenth birthday and felt like he was in a living hell. He constantly lived with anxiety, had just recovered from shingles, which his GP said was probably the result of stress. Now, he was facing his final year exams, G.C.E's as they were named then. This was Barry's life in the 1950's.

He was a pretty clever teenager. Academically gifted such that he was in the top tier and always in the top three in his class. But he knew that he had wasted the last year and so far had completely neglected exam revision.

Until now, he repeatedly told himself he would be fine. His testosterone had, for the last couple of years, been at boiling point. His tunnel vision had focused on girls, and going to pubs with some of his mates to search out willing females. But the time to face reality had arrived, so anxiety and stress were intimidating him every minute of the day.

Over the last several years, he had built quite a lucrative business, collecting footballers' autographs and selling them. He had been doing this since he was about ten. He would travel all over to get the most valuable and the greatest quantity possible. Consequently, he had amassed a small fortune, which had dwindled somewhat in the last couple of years as he splurged on fashionable clothes and shoes. And, of course, money spent in pubs and clubs. So now, he was feeling added stress due to his savings shrinking.

Barry knew he was considered good looking, attractive to the opposite sex. He also got girls attention as he was an accomplished sportsman, both cricket and football, and revered for it throughout the local community. He was tall, dark and handsome, a snappy dresser and almost paranoid about his appearance. He had got himself a credit account with a local tailor and had a penchant for brown hopsack or Prince of Wales light grey suits, accented by all the trimmings! Girls found his black hair and long black eyelashes intoxicating so, just like his football, he scored regularly!

From a very young age, his mother had worked, day and night to keep them solvent. She was the best conductress on London buses. When she worked on the late shift, through to 1.30am in the morning, she never knew what Barry was up to. She had taught him to care for himself. Which he did, but mostly, he just travelled on the underground trains to London main line stations to catch up with professional football teams, sometimes even going to their hotels to get their autographs.

The issue that it created was Barry developed more than just street awareness. He was more than street wise. He began to believe he owned the streets. A Dad may have made a difference but they'd not seen him since he was born. Even at the age of 12, Barry was a fit, big strong lad. Travelling around the stations and hotels in London, he began to cross the paths of other youngsters out to make money. Sometimes they thought it was their patch. Eventually, they would meet, disagree, and it would become a street fight. Or bundle as it was known.

Barry didn't seem to be scared of anything. He had learned some boxing in his East London town and his mind had moved into a place where he believed he was invincible. He fought every last one of them. And won! He was starting to believe he was the new Kray Brother.

What was more terrifying for Barry was his exams. And now they were here. He booked in, settled down and did what he could. He had been entered for 8 G.C.E's which, if he got them, would be perfect! Alas, that wasn't to be. Only 3 G.C.E's, which made him angry with everyone and everything. His cruel, vicious streak was beginning to intensify.

In the next few weeks, Barry lived off his anger, brawling and battering other gangs in the area. Most evenings, he would go to Church Youth Club discos and sometimes the Ilford Palais or small night clubs. His anger, which he began to enjoy, spilled out most nights, with somebody getting terrorized or brutalized.

His gang arrived at one Church Youth Club intent on revenge on another gang. Barry started and finished the brawl, attacking the band members with a cosh he had made from a thick metal towel rail. The band were distracted with playing when Barry rushed the stage from the side. His gang joined in the blood bath.

On the way home, he was stopped and searched by police but he had already dumped the cosh in a garden privet hedge. The next day was his last day at school, and it would prove to be the day that determined his future.

2

Down the road from his school, his mum was in the Bus Depot. One of the Inspectors said that the Depot Manager wanted a word. With apprehension, she knocked on his door and slowly entered. The Manager looked up from his desk work and said "Joan, we are having a reallocation of drivers as we have taken on some new ones. I would like you to meet Jess who will be your new driver." Just then, a man who had been standing in the shadowy corner of the office stepped forward, arm outstretched, to shake hands.

Joan had been intent on listening carefully to the Manager and had not even noticed Jess. Now, in the light, she was surprised! He had black skin, although his outstretched hand was very pink in the palm. She'd seen the like before in films; actors like Paul Robeson, a great favourite of hers. But never in the flesh.

Jess was a very tall, thick set, character. His voice, as he greeted Joan, was as deep as the Caribbean, but soft and gentle. His eyes smiled all the way through Joan and she knew she would never forget that smiling gaze.

The Manager, pleased with Joan's obvious acceptance, said "well that's settled then," and ushered them out of the office. They shuffled together into the General Office. Joan appeared tiny alongside Jess and as they took a few steps forward, the noisy General Office became immediately eerily silent. As if someone had flicked a switch and turned everybody off.

The room was full of Inspectors, conductors, conductresses and cashier staff. Every last person stood and stared. The place resembled Madame Tussauds.

Joan, an intrepid, kind and courageous character, was not going to let the silence and stares deter her. Indeed, it made her more determined. She put her right hand in the middle of Jess's back and said loudly, "Jess would you come to a table and help me cash up?" "Well yes Ma'am" replied Jess and they sat at the first empty table in the row.

One of the jokers in the crowd shouted, "We don't say Ma'am here, we say madam." Joan shouted back, "No Joe, that's what we call you!" Everyone chuckled and got on with their work.

Back at the school, Barry was just about to upset the apple cart and partially destroy Joan's vision of a future for him that she had worked so hard for!

It was mid-afternoon. Barry and his classmate gang were walking down the corridor to their last lesson. Barry, the leader, still bruised and with minor cuts from the previous night, was swaggering and enjoying the misguided praise from his mates. Coming towards them was another class gang with one particular lad who had fought for the opposition at the previous day's brawl.

As they got close, none appeared to want a skirmish. However, Barry's psychotic brutal anger got the better of him. He was smiling at the lad and as they were adjacent, Barry, like lightning, threw an uppercut that lifted the lad off his feet. As he started to fall backward, Barry pursued and kicked him relentlessly.

The boy fell through a door into the science lab, knocking tables over, Bunsen burners flying through the air. The science class, which was still in progress, ended abruptly.

Other teachers came running, Barry was hauled to the head's office. He sat waiting until school had finished, then the Headmaster called him in. He spoke in a very caring way to Barry, saying "You are a very intelligent lad but in the last two years, you seem to have lost your way. I've previously talked with your mother. She has worked hard all her life just to give you a good future and now, at the final hurdle, you seem determined to let her down. Barry, in this life, if you do bad things, bad things will happen to you! You now need to beg your mother's forgiveness and hope that your family rally around to help you. It is such a waste and I really hope you can get back on track."

"What do you mean, Sir, please tell me what you mean. I am sorry, I will change!" "No, Barry, it's gone too far for that. I am very sorry but I won't be able to give you a testimonial. You will need to find your own way without a recommendation from the school."

Barry was distraught. He had hammered the last nail into his coffin lid. He knew, only too well, that in those days, if you did not have a testimonial from school, and only a few G.C.E's, you were unlikely to get a job with career prospects.

3

That evening, he explained all to his Mum. He put his own spin on it to soften the blow, but he could see she was in despair. So for the next two days and nights, he stayed, alone, in his room. He was barely able to think about anything other than how he was messing his life up.

On the third day, his Mum entered his room carrying a cup of tea and a cheese and tomato sandwich. As always, he said a polite "thank you," stood and gave her a gentle hug. "Barry", she said, clasping his face in her hands, "I'm on lates' tonight on the 669 down to the Docks and Woolwich. Do you fancy coming for a ride? You can have a laugh and some banter with your uncles and meet my new driver."

Dockers worked shifts, so he was bound to meet the uncles that were working that evening. The more magnetic attraction was that he might meet a teenage girl that worked in the laboratory at the Flour Mills. When they returned from Woolwich, she was usually on her way home.

Barry had travelled with his mum since he was a small kid. Nobody at the Bus Depot or Inspectors seemed to care. Barry loved it, knew all the Inspectors and other bus crews, and even the regular passengers.

As the bus reached Canning Town, Barry was surrounded by three of his uncles, Albert, Bill and Pat. After a bit of banter, with their mates joining in, Pat said, "Your mum told us about your results, so we thought you may like to come to work with us, until you find your feet. Money is great and you could keep an eye on us reprobates for your mum! Uncle Albert will get you a docker's ticket, and drop it round your house tomorrow." "Thanks Uncle Pat" said Barry, although without much conviction. His family had always been Dockers and he really thought he could do better!

When they reached the Woolwich terminal, the bus would be on the stand for about ten minutes, giving the crew a break. Barry got off to stretch his legs, have a few giggles with the people around the local coffee stall and watch the ferries churning up the River Thames as they came and went.

As he stood, one foot up on the railings, peering into the darkness and glittering lights on the south side of the river, someone tickled his side. He quickly turned to see his Mum smiling, alongside a very large grinning, black man. She introduced Jess who vigorously shook Barry's hand. Barry asked Jess, "How do you like the job Jess?" "I love it, Barry, and working with you and your mum is fab-u-lous." "Oh, I don't work for the buses!" Jess interjected saying, "I know, but you have done these trips many times, and Joan tells me you have always been a big help!"

They finished their teas and it was time to set off again. In that short time, Barry had decided that he really liked Jess and hoped they would become good mates. That first meeting had begun to build a framework of friendship strong enough to last forever!

4

The journey back to the depot delivered another bonus. Arriving at the bus stop outside The Sugar Refinery, initially there was no sign of Linda, the girl who worked at the Flour Mill opposite. Jess was just about to pull away when Barry glimpsed her running across the road. "Jess, stop, hang on a minute" Barry shouted. The bus came to a halt, and as she clambered on the platform, Mum was pointing to where Barry was sitting at the front of the bus.

Mum rang the bell and the bus lurched forward. To Linda, this was normal. She travelled on buses every day. She just adjusted her feet and stance and held the grab handles on the top of the seats. She literally fell in beside Barry. She turned, and with a beautiful smile, leaned across and kissed him, a real smacker on his cheek. The bus was quite warm so her face planted against his cheek felt very cold but the feeling was memorable and welcoming.

They chatted, and towards the end of the journey to Plaistow, there were some romantic embraces, but with Barry's mum watching all the time. However, as she looked at Barry, he knew she was pleased for him.

Barry and Linda arranged to meet again, and again, and again. This was turning into a long-term friendship, or rather, more a romance. This young lady was absolutely gorgeous. She was a cockney, but not with an acute accent. A brunette, with scintillating straight long brown hair and long eyelashes to match. She had fashionable dress sense, and to crown it all, had done really well at school, was intelligent, and had found a job with prospects.

Barry found it a real wrench when she had to get off. Then as she stood up, she gave Barry a warm, deliciously smelling, large loaf of bread. She made several each day in her laboratory job. "Think of me when you and your mum are enjoying it," she said.

A week later, Barry was starting a job at the Docks. His cousin, Albie, went with him for the first day. They stood on the cobbles, wondering if they would be selected to work. They worked on a day by day basis, but Uncle Albert was the ganger and did the picking. Albie, Uncle Albert's son, had previously said Uncle Albert will make sure you work today; then it all depends on how you do.

Barry got picked to work that day. And day after day! He was a good worker, a grafter, big and strong. Nothing daunted him. At the outset, he was assigned to a barge gang; seven of them unloading grain ships. It was a dirty, stinking job. By the end of the shift, they were covered from head to toe in corn dust. Worse than that were the rats. Nobody explained, initially, because they thought it funny. But as the corn was propelled from the ships hulls down a chute into the barge, rats came with it. If you hadn't tied your trouser legs up, they would run up your legs and constantly bite you!

Barry got the hang of that, and became one of the best workers. In the meantime, he was earning what, in that area, was fabulous money. Mum was getting weekly income and constant treats. Barry and Linda were out several times a week; both of them were improving dancers and began to enter competitions all over London. Sometimes they would win prize money. They were invited onto Top of the Pops several times to dance in the crowd scenes.

Several months on from meeting Jess, Barry pushed mum into a family party for her birthday. All the brothers turned up. And all their kids and the rest of the family. Linda, looking fabulous with her poise and classic features, arrived and was truly stunning. Jess was one of the last to arrive, and sure enough, there was the usual, but expected, silence and stares. So Barry stepped forward and introduced Jess as his mum's driver and said "Jess was a driver in Barbados in the Caribbean. They have palm trees, sun, sand and parrots there you know!"

The party got back into the swing, and after an hour or so, everyone was dancing. That included Jess, who had been trapped by Barry's auntie Carol. He had some very attractive moves with fluid detail. Most of the family watching commented on his dancing, saying he was sensational!

When the music ended and he took a break, Jess stood by the drinks and got into conversation with Barry and some of the uncles. A torrent of questions flooded to Jess. The main question was "Why did you come here if you have sun, sand and palm trees like we see at the cinema?" Jess did a good job explaining that firstly, the British Government paid them to come, because they were needed to fill jobs that British people did not seem to want. Also, to fill jobs where more people with certain skills were needed, like doctors, nurses and so on. Jess continued, "There were hundreds of us, singles like me, families with grandparents and children, all on a ship called the Windrush. It was really an exciting adventure, but also emotionally difficult leaving our families, friends and especially our homeland. There wasn't much work on Barbados and the pay was less than half what I can earn here."

Everybody chatted to Jess, and Barry and the uncles spoke with him as if he was one of their mates. His dulcet tones, bright whites of his eyes and pink lips had hit the spot with Barry's family and, especially, auntie Carol who followed him around all evening and danced with him into the early hours.

5

B arry worked in the docks for another year. His romance with Linda seemed perfection, but for some reason, he always felt something was missing in his life. He wanted adventure, excitement and a constant adrenalin rush!

During that year in the docks, the need for excitement, adrenalin rushes and something better in his life, had for some reason channeled into aggression. He had always been a bit of a hard man. He was big and fearless. But this mindset had taken him to a different level.

If anyone upset any of his uncles or cousins, he would go after them. And he never lost a fight. Now he was off the grain ships and unloading cargo; his tool of the trade was a docker's hook. He carried that with him all the time, and during fights, had done serious damage to a few people. So now he was becoming infamous. At weekends, when he went to pubs and clubs, pretenders to the throne would come looking for him.

Whenever people tried to lower his flag, they came up against a battalion of family, friends and guys that knew it was best to be on his team! And these people were all guys that thrived on punch-ups.

Barry was now well known around the East End of London. He was still only young, but everyone knew he had brain as well as brawn. At this time, the Krays were in descendency with charges for murder and various other crimes. In consequence, Barry was viewed as the "most likely to succeed". Linda hated how this was developing, but she loved Barry. Wherever he took her, they were treated like royalty, however, Linda's character struggled with this as a lifestyle.

Feeding off knowledge of the Krays business interests, Barry decided he had to make it a priority to find a business. He now had a whole network of people around him that would do anything for him. He had no idea what business! But his mind would explore every possibility.

In his neck of the woods, he earned a nickname. Nobody, other than family, Jess and Linda, dare call him Barry. He was now "Geezer!" he felt he had earned this nickname and it confirmed he was respected, but moreover, feared. So over the next twelve months he used every day to grow and develop this horrific image.

To keep Linda on side and sweet, he booked a holiday for the approaching summer in the Spanish resort of Marbella. This was becoming a fashionable vacation area for Brits, and Linda was impressed and excited by the prospect.

Furthermore, to protect the likeable image that sat with Linda, his Mum and Jess, he ensured that everyone in the community knew that if they informed on his grotesque behaviour, they would have him to deal with.

With the money he was earning in the Docks, he bought a fabulous car which he thought subscribed to his image. It was a Ford Zephyr 6, metallic silver which, probably because of his reputation, had come with a forty percent discount.

Every month he would make a point of meeting with Jess and going for a pint in one of the local pubs. They got on famously. Barry absolutely loved Jess, somewhat because his mum was always saying how good he was to her and such a wonderful person.

6

One particular evening, Jess casually mentioned in conversation that he was going to get a new Routemaster London Bus. The old ones were being decommissioned and sold off. They continued drinking and chatting for a while, then Barry's brain sparked into action.

He asked Jess "How much do you think they want for one?" to which Jess replied, "I think about £600." Barry was now on a roll. "Jess", he said, "What if we buy one and set up a travel company?" Barry had got the idea from the Cliff Richard film, Summer Holiday!

They kicked it around for an hour, with Jess constantly saying "I don't have that sort of money." Barry eventually replied, "Well how much could you raise?" "About £150" said Jess. Barry pushed on, "Do we both think it's a good idea? I can organize and manage all the marketing and advertising: you would just need to be the driver, or help me find a good one!"

Jess was in a quandary until Barry said "I have the rest of the money and more to get the bus checked over and serviced. Jess, you and I could be equal partners. This will get us financially on the move. I have been searching for a legitimate business for months and this is the gift horse. Jess, you know buses, you could test drive it and we can negotiate a deal together."

Jess's white eyes shone bright. He embraced Barry and said "We will be partners, and I will be the driver. When I go to work tomorrow, I will start the ball rolling."

Alongside this entrepreneurial world, Barry's absurd gangster world was growing. His uncles, well really just one of his uncles, had got into an argument with a local scrap dealers family. Barry decided he would fix the problem. Just like the rest of his uncles, you always help your family member that has trouble.

He went to an East London drinking club, The Cactus Club, to meet with a guy. Things were now escalating in Barry's head. This guy was bringing a gun that Barry had ordered. He had decided that he needed to move up in weaponry if he wanted to be superior. He now had many on his team that wanted to be gangsters and were, like Barry, willing to use a gun, if it increased Barry's power base.

The guy concerned was Mick Flick. The nickname flick emanated from him always carrying a flick knife and knew how to use it. His family were Irish with contacts in the IRA, consequently, he had become a supplier to the East End underworld. But he never turned up!

Over at the Bus Depot, Jess was making arrangements with the Depot Manager to pay for the Routemaster the next day. The price was confirmed as £600 which Jess knew was a good deal because he knew the bus well. He'd driven it many times around Forest Gate and Upton Park. It was a 685 that did the "roundabouts," the local route name which circled West Ham F.C, ground. When they were playing at home, it was a very busy bus. Also, it was clean and tidy and Jess was convinced it was totally reliable.

The Depot Manager had grown to like and respect Jess for the quality of his work, timekeeping and happy disposition. Indeed, he was a favourite amongst all the staff. At the last minute, Jess had inspiration. He asked the boss very politely, "Sir, would it be possible to keep the bus at the depot?" The manager George, stopped in his tracks. Dragged his right hand down his forehead and across his eyes. His head bowed as he sat at his large leather topped kneehole desk. After a good 30 seconds, he gradually rose to look at Jess with a wide smile. George said, "I think you will like this, Jess. Yes, if you agree to pay lodgings, it can live here. We will look after it and clean it. The cost of lodgings is...." He faltered seeing anticipation on Jess's face ... "£1 a week! But with a promise! That for at least the next 6 months, you stay here working with us." Jess was stunned, but happily so. "Oh Sir, I want to stay, love this job and will use the 685 in my holidays for some extra work!"

On the way home, Jess called in on Barry and Joan. He wanted to check with Barry that he had all the details of the purchase. Barry exclaimed to Jess "You did a fantastic job" and immediately handed him a carrier bag with the money. At that point, Joan and Linda came in from the kitchen where they had been preparing dinner. "Mum, Jess and I have bought a Routemaster and we are going into partnership in a travel and holiday business." Joan, open-mouthed, looked at Linda. She said, "Fabulous idea, it will be great!"

After dinner, Barry returned to The Cactus Club. He was standing with a good mate, Eddie, at the bar. Another mate, Tonga, was talking non-stop and it was beginning to irritate Barry, but really it was because Mick Flick was due and was late again, which Barry could not stand!

Barry snapped at Tonga. "Shut the fuck up and get me a drink! Eddie, find out where that twat Flick"...there was a loud crack... before Barry could finish. Eddie ran along with almost everyone around the bar, toward the top of the stairs. Barry, trying to appear in control, stayed by the bar drinking.

After a few minutes, Eddie, with a swaggering walk, came back to the bar and stood beside Barry. With an expectant gaze, Barry searched Eddie's face for information. Eddie whispered, with a tremor in his voice, "Geezer, it's all gone wrong. Mick has shot himself in the foot. The Police are on the way. I spoke to him; he won't say anything because he knows what that will get him. Won't shoot himself in the foot twice!"

Barry was furious. The Police arrived with some armed officers. They let dogs in and they were all questioned. However, everybody knew to be careful with anything they said. So after an hour or so, everyone was allowed to leave. Barry remained furious, saying to Eddie "I needed that shooter. Now I've got to find another way. Eddie, pick me up at 11.00am in the morning."

7

Eddie arrived at 11.00am and immediately launched into explaining what had happened. Mick Flick had waltzed in with the gun strapped to his calf, got to the top of the stairs, where several mates were hanging around. Wanting to boast, he told them about the gun. "Well, where is it," they challenged. Mick rolled his trouser leg up, and accidently pulled the trigger. The shooter, a Beretta, shot his small and next toe off. They were rattling around in his winkle picker boot. "Apparently, they got one of these toes, the small one, back on so he may be lucky with his walking ability," remarked Eddie.

Barry could not help but explode into volcanic laughter. "That prick will walk funny for the rest of his life all because he was wanting to boost his ego. Well he managed to blast his ego, and his toes off at the same time. All that said, he's a good guy and he's made me laugh, so tell him he still works for me and I will look after him!"

All through the night, Barry tossed and turned. All his mind was feeding on was the feud and what he needed to do to the opposition. Their crowd was tidy! Well organized, well- armed and always ready to use battering force on enemies. Several times, he woke Linda. They now were living with Joan, but only for a short time. Barry had bought a house for £4500. His reputation had helped force a bargain deal through. Unknowingly, Linda and Joan believed he was gifted with the ability to spot opportunities.

Barry's cousin, Albie, was now his "General". He had proved his worth in several punch-ups, mostly in snooker halls where he spent his time gambling on how he would play. Albie had found two young guys; very intelligent guys, that would arrange advertising and marketing for the bus. He had employed them for a pittance knowing that they would more than prove their worth. Barry was impressed. "Albie, don't let me down on this, I need that bus to pay me back, and a lot more, and I want Jess to do well out of it!"

The next day, Barry, mid-morning, spruced himself up. Wearing a sparkling white button-down collar shirt, striped blue tie and glistening mohair suit, he ventured down for breakfast. Before he sat at the table, in the corner chair, he put on his shiny black winkle pickers with side lace-ups. He was now doing so well financially, he was having all of his clothes made, mostly in Petticoat Lane or the tailors around.

Before he left the house, he checked himself in the mirror. He was satisfied with everything except his dimples. He had dimples in his cheeks and two large dimple creases in his chin. He had always felt that they aged him.

He had arranged for a cohort to go with him. Albie, Mac and Danny. These two were part of Irish traveller families that had settled in the East End. They were both as hard as nails and always ready for a bundle. When they were kid brothers, they lived at the back of Barry in a prefab. They had invited Barry to a party in their home and after a few minutes asked Barry to come and meet their Grandad. He was sitting in the corner in a large winged back chair, wearing a three piece suit and a flat cap. Barry tried to talk to him, but no reply. Then Danny said "No Barry, he's dead, so we are celebrating his life."

Barry knew his mates would be tooled up. He felt in his pocket and found Mick's flick knife that Eddie had rescued before the Police arrived. But that wasn't going to be enough. He checked to see where Linda and his Mum were and then went up to his bedroom. He found it on the top of his wardrobe, and put it in a normal shopping bag. It was his favourite work tool, the Dockers hook.

8

They were going to a pub that the opposition family owned. Barry's plan was to get there just before the doors opened at midday. So not many of their team would have arrived.

The meet was in Canning Town at the corner of Hermit Road. When Barry arrived, his mates were already there, laughing, joking, smoking and seemingly on a high. They had probably been hitting cannabis and purple hearts which Barry always avoided!

Barry strolled up, swinging his shopping bag and stopped a pace away from their huddle. Speaking quietly, he began to say... but Danny, who was clearly high as a kite said "hi'ya, Geezer, we are looking forward to this!" Albie slapped his face hard so his teeth rattled. "Shut your face and listen to Geezer and get your head sorted out."

Barry almost whispered, as people were walking past. "We will go to the front door and, if it's still locked, just knock and wait. If it's open, we go straight in. Once inside, I'll do any talking but there won't be much. His uncle Bert is your problem! Just beat him. If his Mum is there, just get her out the way. We don't hurt women! I will deal with Johnny. Are you clear?"

They all nodded and walked about 200 yards to the White Hart. The door was already open. They stood together a few seconds then Barry said, "Right, let's go."

Johnny was behind the bar, checking stock. They cornered him, Albie at one end of the bar and Barry at the other. Albie ran towards him and he backed up towards Barry. He fought but not for long. They battered him relentlessly. Barry dragged him out from behind the bar and continued kicking him. Then Uncle Bert and Mum, hearing the rumpus, rushed in. Danny and Mac took care of Bert. Mum was thrown back onto the stairs, and just lay there moaning. Then Uncle Bert attempted to make a run for it, through the saloon bar double doors, but Mac managed to grab his shirt collar and hauled him backwards into the bar. A few savage body blows and penalty kicks and he was finished.

Barry said to Albie "grab Johnny's legs" and they lifted him onto a bar table. Barry indicated to Albie to pull Johnny's arms straight out above his head. Johnny was just coming round as Barry got in his face. "You will never ever punch my uncle or any of my family ever again. And if your family ever take us on again, they will get the same."

He pulled his docker's hook out of the bag, stood over Johnny with a callous smile spreading across his face. He swung the hook behind his head as if he were at work, and with force, pierced Johnny's right shoulder joint. The screams were deafening. Johnny passed out. Barry looked at Mac and Danny and with a chuckle said, "He's not keeping my hook," and proceeded to pull hard to extract it from the wound. Then, he carefully placed it back in the shopping bag.

Barry was thinking it was time to go, but it was not finished. Mac and Danny were still either side of the saloon double doors. Barry was facing the doors, holding his shopping bag. A few seconds of noisy commotion and the doors burst open, with Danny and Mac secreted behind them. Albie stood next to Barry.

It was some of the uncles from their team. Four of them charged in, having heard the screams. They were confronted by Barry, ostensibly, only with Albie. They were about to tear them limb from limb, when Barry pulled the docker's hook out of the bag. They stopped dead in their tracks. They sensed Danny and Mac behind them but too late. Danny had sufficiently recovered from the lethargy of drugs, and was now ready to take on the world.

Danny was wearing a dark blue Crombie overcoat and inside, he had a hook where he hung his baseball bat. He pulled it out and went into battle, swinging like he was hitting out of the stadium. Barry was also swinging but with his vicious hook.

In a few minutes, it was all over. Albie, Mac and Danny stood over the prostrate bodies as Barry was putting his bloodied hook back into the bag. Mac said jokingly, "Geezer, should we take some scalps to prove what happened here today." They all began to chuckle, but then Barry heard the Mum, lying on the stairs crying.

He went to her and said, "Are you ok darling, do you want to phone anyone?" She seemed ok, so he continued, "Keep your family under control. Don't let them grass us up because if they do, we will be back and it will be worse. I'll bring you a phone and you can call for an ambulance."

With that, the four amigos strolled off to their cars at the end of Hermit Road. They arranged to meet for a celebration drink in the Black Lion in Plaistow, where Barry had learned to box!

9

They were well known and respected in the Black Lion and the local area. Barry treated his mates all evening, knowing that today would put a massive stake in the ground. He would be revered and feared throughout the East End of London!

Before his amigos got too drunk, Barry took them to one side and said, "I have a great job for you three. I think this is the right time for you to suggest to stall-holders and shops around Canning Town that it would be worth their while to pay us to protect them. Start with the market, and whatever you collect, I want 40% and you three can share the rest." After what Barry saw as a real beginning, he was now going to build his empire!

The two youngsters working on advertising and marketing the bus had been doing a great job. These teenagers were literate but also able to type and put words together on paper. They were Jewish kids, not afraid of work and had spent nights delivering leaflets. They were called Lawrence and David. Both wanted to break into the music industry and were working hard on this project to fund their way in.

So Jess was inundated with bookings. He had scheduled weekends in seaside towns; Clacton, Southend, Margate and Bournemouth. Also, trips to London shows on some evenings when he was working days on the buses. As well as weekend trips on his rest days, he had also scheduled some rest-day midweek trips, to countryside towns and even these were fully booked. He was working like a Trojan, and loving every minute. The money was pouring in, so much so that he needed administrative help. The Jewish lads volunteered, as did Linda. She took on the banking element and was astounded at the money they were making.

She would try to talk to Barry about the Bus Business, but Barry was always preoccupied with building his crime empire. He would listen to Linda, but not really hear! He would tell her, "You and Jess are doing a great job, just keep it up!" in the meantime, he had put time in with Albie extending protection and extortion rackets into Petticoat Lane. This had involved regular fracas and several vicious fights, but he always won and mostly came away with his face unscathed.

The Jewish community around Petticoat Lane were always left in peace. He was a big fan of their skill and work ethic. His tailors had always been Jews and had always looked after him well. In addition, he had fixed in his mind that they had been a brave nation despite the Nazis' attempts to wipe them out.

In a few weeks' time; mid-May, he and Linda would be moving into their new home. A beautiful new semi-detached opposite West Ham Park. Linda was spending all her spare time planning colour schemes, buying fabrics for curtains, bedding and all the usual stuff. Barry always found an excuse, saying it was not his thing. Then mid-June was a holiday in Marbella. Their life was developing into one fantastic journey, as far as Linda and Joan were concerned!

Linda's Dad had a history in the East End as a bit of a lad. He had got himself a business recycling cardboard collected from supermarkets. One day, after a meeting at a supermarket, as he walked out of the door, a car pulled up and blasted him with a shotgun. He died on the spot. This was local gangsters wanting the business. Her Mum had never been the same since, constantly ill and her mental state had suffered. Little Linda was a strong character and had seen how important it was for her to do well. She worked hard and did well at school and now had a good laboratory job.

They moved in on time. Not surprising really! Linda worked on the house every spare minute. She was still working at the flour mill, but as soon as she got home, she would be sewing, painting; even hanging wallpaper. She loved their house and was so proud of what they had achieved. She had no complaints about Barry. He had paid cash for the house and now they were set for life. At least that's what Linda thought.

Barry spent some time helping with the house upgrade, but mostly arranged for mates to come in and do the work. He was out building the business most hours of the day, and evening.

At weekends, they would entertain. Barry's General, Albie would come around most Saturday nights with his girlfriend, Shirley and the four of them would, for that era, attempt pretentious evenings with fine wines, Chinese or Indian food and good cigarettes and cigars.

The day of the holiday leapt out on them. Albie and Shirley were going too. Came the day, the excitement was overwhelming. None of them had been north of Watford before, let alone out of the country.

Eddie was their driver and arrived on time. He was going to be driving Barry's car, without insurance, but that didn't worry anyone. He was known as a good driver, fast but experienced and with an unblemished record.

Then, they were off to Gatwick Airport, Barry with map on lap, sitting in the front passenger seat. The other three in the very roomy rear seat. There was lots of excited chatter on the way, with Barry occasionally shouting "Shut up, I'm concentrating."

Gatwick was quiet so they pulled up right outside the small departures area. Check in was easy and they were accompanied out to the plane sitting on the runway. The flight worried them at take-off. Lots of noises, never heard before. They clutched the arms of their seats, but once in the air, with stewardesses, beautiful ladies, bringing food and drinks, they settled into enjoying the experience.

10

One particular stewardess caught Barry's eye. As she served their food and miniature bottled spirits, Barry asked her name whilst introducing himself. He smiled and said, "I'm Barry, what's your name?" "I'm Rita" she replied with a rather innocent, embarrassed smile. The two lads were seated together allowing the girls, in front of them, to enjoy feminine chats. Barry quietly said to Rita, "Hope we meet again on the way home."

Lately, he was starting to become bored with domesticity and less than adventurous sex with Linda. He loved her more than anything, but testosterone was awakening the animal instincts in him.

The first few days, in a great hotel, between Marbella and Estapona, was fabulous. The girls loved tanning by the pool or walking to the beach and enjoying the bars through the day. So did the boys, except that they found that lying in the sun all day was not enough for them.

In the middle of the week, they met with the tour representative and asked if there were any tours they could go on. She offered several, but the boys set their sights on a boat trip to Ceuta in North Africa; Morocco to be precise. They wanted to be able to say they had been to Africa as well as Spain when boasting to friends!

During dinner that evening, Barry asked the girls if they would like to go on the excursion to Africa. "How do we get there?" said Linda. "It's a boat trip of about an hour from Gibraltar" replied Barry with enthusiasm. "Oh no" said Shirley, "I get very seasick." Linda joined in saying "I can't leave Shirley on her own. You two go and explore. We like just lazing about here by the pool!"

That was Barry and Albie's ticket to ride. They were delighted. A freedom day! Early next morning, Barry found the Rep and paid for their tickets. They would leave Friday at about 8am and be at the ship in Gibraltar by 9.30am.

In the hotel bar during the evening entertainment, the boys got chatting to two Welshmen who were going on the same trip. They both worked as furnace liners and had made a lot of money on their last contract. Their plan was to go to Ceuta to buy gold. Apparently, gold bought in North Africa was much cheaper. The trick was now to get it back through Spanish and UK customs. But they were going to try!

The excursion served to broaden Barry and Albie's minds. Having lived their lives in the concrete jungle called London, now their perspective was of a totally different world. The trip across the Mediterranean with porpoises and dolphins chasing their boat, was almost surreal.

They spent a short while in the bar having a drink with the Welshmen who talked as if they were going to buy the gold stock of Fort Knox. On the way off the ferry, Barry said to Albie, "We can buy a few bits of gold for the girls, but leave it at that. Gold is too heavy to carry and conceal and we won't make much profit on it!"

They had a walk around Ceuta. Barry viewed it as a bit of a grubby place. Mostly it was tourist trinket shops, ceramics and, of course, several gold jewellers shops. Most of these shops were constructed of wood and linoleum. Not the most auspicious shopping centre.

They entered a gold shop to be greeted by Omar and Mustafa. Both men had reasonable English. They both selected a few pieces each for the girls and worked through the bartering time they had been warned about. Mustafa, at the death, was pushing for them to buy a lot more gold, which Barry, in his usual direct manner refused. Mustafa said, "You do not have enough money Barry?" this was a red rag to a bull.

Barry grabbed Mustafa's arm and pulled him to one side. "I have shed loads of money, but I want to spend it on something I can make money on." Mustafa saw the look on Barry's face and intuition took him onto a new path. He began to whisper. "Barry, I can get you smokes. As many as you need. I can get you hashish, cannabis or plenty of other drugs. You think about it!"

Barry responded in a very quiet voice. "So, if I wanted to spend thousands of pounds with you, you could provide good stuff, and not just once…. All the time." "Sure, I would, "he replied. Barry, with piercing eyes said, "Mustafa, I will be back to see you again in the near future."

A few paces towards the door and Barry stopped in his tracks and turned back; got close to Mustafa and asked, "Can you supply shooters?" Mustafa retorted, "All our drugs can be shooters if you wish Barry!" "No Mustafa, not that kind, I mean weapons, you know, guns!" Mustafa's blank look turned to a huge smile. "No, but I have a contact who can, but I must not offend him. So your interest would need to be serious."

"Mustafa, you are good to do business with and I like you. Give me your phone number and I will definitely be in touch soon." The Moroccan wrote on a card and handed it to Barry. They shook hands and left.

They arrived back at the ferry to be greeted by a long line of customs and Spanish Guardia Civil checking passports and checking for smuggling. Barry and Albie walked through the checks and were heading up the gangway when Barry stopped, grabbed Albie's cheeks and turned his head to look towards the check line. Barry laughing said, "Hey Albie, seems I was right." The two Welshmen were being led away by the Guardia Civil to a search area. "Don't look like they will be on our ferry home!"

Barry and Albie talked about the day all the way back. Barry was euphoric concerning the lucrative potential he was visualising. Albie, not so much, probably because he didn't seem to have quite the Barry intellect, albeit an illegal, destructive intellect.

11

It was evening at the hotel when they arrived. The girls were getting glammed up! Barry and Albie were both knackered from the long draining day, but accepted they had to put in one more shift and eat and drink with the girls in the hotel.

Dinner was a fabulous buffet, considering how much they had paid for this holiday. Linda commented that she had never seen, or eaten, so many exotic foods before. The girls were loving the experience, although they, too, were very tired after a tanning and swimming day.

The hotel had a flamenco entertainment evening after dinner, and all four of them entered a Spanish world of culture that made them rapturous. In the interludes, they agreed that tomorrow, they would go into Marbella centre for a glorious Spanish meal.

After a day on the beach and snacks and drinks at a beach bar, they spruced themselves up for a night on the town. The barman, Manuel, recommended they try a tapas bar. The best in Marbella was called El Estrecho. They found it difficult to pronounce, even after several tries, so he wrote it on their bar bill.

They climbed in a taxi at 8pm and set off for the bright lights. A look of surprise on all their faces as the taxi entered a tiny side road and stopped outside a small frontage bar, the El Estrecho.

It was quite busy inside and as they stood at the bar, they noticed the property went back a long way. A very thin long restaurant, many tables and hazy smoke that precluded actually seeing how far it meandered to the rear.

To begin, the order was cerveza for the lads and gin and tonic for the two ladies. The barman, by name Juan, had a glorious smile and quite good English. As Barry paid for the round, he held onto Juan's wrist and, speaking slowly to Juan said, "Take care of us this evening," With that, he pushed a 1000 peseta note into his hand. "Gracia, senior, gracia!"

They all worked hard over the next couple of hours to down as many drinks as their bodies would stand. They were having a great time. Their alcohol increased; so did their confidence. They talked to most people at the bar. Locals, tourists and a few shady characters. Tapas, arranged by Juan, was constantly arriving at their table.

Barry and Albie went to the bar to order more drinks. Two guys arrived at the bar next to them, just as they were laughing, recalling the Ceuta Welshmen. The guy next to Barry, fairly short, wearing a flamboyant large check jacket and a trilby hat, turned and said, "Hello Geezer, enjoying your holiday?" Barry, with a questioning expression, turned and stared into his face. The booze had taken its toll and the difficult side of Barry was beginning to appear. "Do I know you" Barry said with a hint of aggression. The trilby hat guy was a bit knocked off balance by Barry's attitude. "Barry, I saw you in West Ham, you are famous. Just wanted to say hello." "OK, guy, what's your name?" asked Barry. "Oh well, I am Terry and my mate is a local, Jose." They nodded. Barry softened, "This is Albie."

As he was introducing Albie, he glanced across to Linda and Shirley. Both girls had soaked up a lot of sun during the day, and now the food and lots of alcohol was taking its toll. Shirley, in particular, was looking and feeling unwell.

Barry went across to their table and said he thought Linda should take her back to the hotel. Linda agreed, saying it was for the best.

Barry asked Juan to phone for a taxi. As Barry began to help the girls up, he uttered to Linda that he and Albie were going to stay for a while as they were going to arrange some business with Terry and Jose.

Albie joined them and they propped the girls up on the way out. Once outside, Shirley, breathing the night air, immediately threw up over the cobbled pavement with some splatters hitting Albie's highly polished shoes. "You stupid cow," Albie started to shout! Barry slapped his hand over Albie's mouth. "Leave the poor girl alone. They are letting us stay for a nightcap!"

As they helped the girls into the taxi, Barry gave the driver one of the hotel cards with the address and a 100 peseta note. Turning to Linda, he said, "Remind me tomorrow to give you the presents we got for you in Ceuta. I completely forgot today, with the good time we've been having." Linda smiled and he kissed her goodbye!

12

Barry and Albie, now ready to continue to amuse themselves, straightened up and strutted back into the bar. Terry and Jose were at the bar and were now drinking red wine.

Albie turned to Terry and Jose. "Right, you two, let's have some proper drinks. Whisky or Brandy!" He called the barman over and said, "Juan, we would like some large spirits. Barry and I want whisky." Juan said, "Is Johnny Walker black label ok? Y con huella?" Albie seemed to take offence and leaned across the bar getting right into Juan's face. "Hello to you Juan! And I'm not conning anyone "growled Albie. Juan, genuinely startled, replied with a tremble in his voice. "No, no Senor, I am speaking, would you want ice with your whiskies?" "Course we do, on the rocks!"

Albie spun around to face Terry and Jose. "You guys order what you want and I will cough up for it. " Terry plumped for a Brandy with ice and then Jose said, "Ginebra con tonica." Albie thumped the bar, saying to Barry "That lost me, so it better not cost more than our whiskies!"

Throughout several more rounds of drinks, they talked all sorts of subjects, from women to football to the trouble they had been involved in, and many others. Whilst they were boasting about their pasts, Albie, was beginning to get worse for wear. He was developing his glassy eyed argumentative look. He selected Terry as his target. "So what sort of job did you do in the East End that was so dangerous?" "Let's see if you can guess" replied Terry. Albie was now being rubbed up the wrong way, which seemed to amuse Terry. "So give me your best guess," said Terry. Albie, with a glaring stare responded, "Terry, you were an arsehole that couldn't take the heat so you got out of the kitchen, and that's why you're here!"

Terry sidestepped the offensive attack and said, "Albie, what's the time please?" Albie eased his right sleeve up, stared for a second, then squealed, "Where's my fucking watch?" Terry and Jose began to laugh. Terry pulled the watch out of his jacket pocket and dangled it in front of Albie's face. Albie took the watch saying, "so you were a dip," as he tightened the strap on his wrist. All the time, Barry had been leaning back on the bar, sipping his drink and grinning at this amusing episode. However, Barry knew Albie only too well and was expecting horrors!

As Albie finished tightening his watch strap, he delved into his right hand jacket pocket. In the same movement, he grabbed Terry's hand with his left. He slammed Terry's hand on the bar and Albie's right hand hovered over it. In it was a Stanley knife. "Terry, you won't do that to me or anyone else again because I am going to cut your fucking fingers off!"

He stared at Terry for a few seconds and as the knife moved down, Barry grabbed his wrist. Both hands, locked together, trembled above Terry's fingers. Barry was exceptionally strong and squeezed Albie's knuckles so hard, he dropped Stanley!

Barry looked around the bar, smiling as he looked at the faces silently watching. Out loud, he said, "Well wasn't that all a bit of fun. Let's have another drink and everybody in the bar is invited for a drink with us."

As everyone was getting their free drinks, Barry dragged Albie to one side saying, "Listen Albie, these two can work for us and be really useful. Try to get on with them because they know this area and can help us build our own firm here."

Albie was known throughout the East End for an expression he used whenever he felt he had upset Barry. It was so commonplace and well known that young pretenders in cockney land would use it in normal language.

Right now was when Albie would use it. "As it 'appens Geezer, I quite like both these fellas. And as it 'appens I was just 'aving a laugh. As it 'appens Geezer, you are definitely right, they can be a big help to us, as it 'appens."

When the atmosphere had cooled and Albie and Jose were drinking together, with Jose teaching Albie some Spanish, Barry took Terry to one side. He started by buttering Terry up. "I knew who you were Terry. I had heard about you a while ago. You are a legend. 'Terry the Dip'! You are the best in your business. And now we've met, you are my kind of guy. I want to offer you the chance to work for me out here. I am going to invest in this area and I want you and Jose to help me get it underway."

"So how do we help?" asked Terry. "To kick off, it's a simple little job. I want you and Jose to be my recruitment officers. I want to hire the services of 20 blokes… hard nuts who have been around and know the score." Barry went on, "and they need to understand I want loyalty! I look after my people that are loyal! Do any of the guys down here carry shooters?" asked Barry. Terry's lips spread across his jaw, and with his hand rubbing his bearded chin, he slowly replied, "No, not many. But there are a few and mostly they work for a Naples gang that operates out of Fuengirola."

"If you can get any of them to join us Terry, I will pay you double. Without them, it will stand at a thousand quid for the 20. I will be back early September and will pay you then, as long as I can meet them and set up their pay." "Terry, you talk to Jose and if you are both happy with the deal, you will be my first officers down here!" Barry was about to say more, but the bar doors opened, clattered against the wall, as several people entered.

13

Suited and booted, it was the crew from the BEA plane to Marbella. In the middle of the six uniformed group was Rita. Barry's heart rate increased. Her gaze around the bar met his and she smiled as if he had made her day!

She said a few words to her mates and headed straight to Barry. The rest of her team followed. Barry called Albie over and introductions were rapid. They then proceeded to buy drinks for the whole BEA team, with overwhelming banter and conversation all around. Terry and Jose joined Barry at the bar, then Barry whispered to Terry, "Take Jose outside and explain it all to him. I want an answer before we leave."

After a couple more rounds, Rita was now pressing close to Barry. Her uniform was a key fantasy for Barry and now he could feel her suspenders pressing against his legs. He was becoming over-excited and as she was talking, whilst looking into his eyes, he blurted out, "Stay with me tonight?" Different from the original meeting borne in innocence, her reply was brazen. "Of course, darling, thought you'd never ask!"

A distraction which suppressed Barry's horny feelings arrived in the form of one of Rita's colleagues. A very slight blonde chap named Jerome. He made it very obvious, when he spoke, that he was gay. Neither Barry, or Albie, had ever met a gay guy before and were completely gobsmacked.

Jerome was a magnetic comical personality who soon had them all enthralled with his stories. Albie commented that he had never heard the name Jerome before. Jerome, with effeminate voice, explained that he was originally named Richard and was always called Dickie. "I could not take being Dickie all day long, so I thought long and hard, as Dickie would." This brought laughter from all around. "So when I was a teenager going in the pubs down by the docks and then staying out all night, when I got home, my mum would be in the kitchen cooking Dad's breakfast. She would always shout, Yer 'ome then! I heard it so often, I thought that's it. So "Yer 'ome" became Jerome." Stroking Albie's face, he said "and I know you will remember it".

They all appreciated and loved this character. Albie found this a new and likeable experience. So now he had questions. "Jerome, you speak like a toff, even royalty, so where did you grow up?" Rita began to chuckle, as Jerome replied "I'm an East Ender, grew up in Stratford and hated every minute because I felt I didn't fit in." Albie, with Barry smiling all over his face, grabbed Jerome's head, dragged him into the group and said, "We are from the same place and you fit in with us. You get any trouble anywhere and we will sort it out. You are in our crowd now!"

Whilst Albie and Jerome carried on talking, Barry got with Jose and Terry. "Well what do you guys think? Are you in?" Terry, with a nervous smile replied, "Well yes Barry," but Albie heard and interrupted! "He is not Barry to you fellas, he's Geezer. Remember it!" "Sorry Albie, I had heard but forgot." Barry took over. "Terry you had a but." "Well sort of. How's this going to work? Getting money here and keeping things ticking."

"Terry, you seem a clever fella. All the plans are not in place yet, its early days. But I am the best at spotting an opportunity. And I know we will all be at risk from this. You do the groundwork for me and I will look after you. I already have some great contacts and will be back here early September. By then, I will have worked on the details. Terry, you and Jose can begin looking around for a bar with a flat, or a villa, or both, because I think I will move here."

Terry thought for a moment then said, "Don't take this the wrong way Geezer, but 20 fellas is a big crew. There's nothing that size here and it will cost a bit."

Getting close to Terry and Jose's faces, Barry said, "Exactly Terry. We need an army of our own soldiers to make this place our own. I have plenty of cash from my business back home and a massive army that I can bring here if I need to. If we play a good game, we can own Marbella in a year or two. So if you two fellas help me and Albie get it going, you will be the first to reap big rewards."

Albie joined them when he heard his name. Terry and Jose were now becoming excited at their future prospects. Albie bought another round and they all toasted "the future". Jerome joined in the celebrations with Rita, as she caressed Barry's thighs.

Jerome then asked, "Can I stick with you guys and be part of whatever this future will be?" Barry chuckled, then spluttered, "Well I don't know what we can find for you, but yes, I am sure you could be an asset. It's just hit me; with you travelling back and forth all the time, you could be our carrier pigeon!"

Now Jerome was ecstatic. "Barry, I would love that and I will never let you down." Rita was now getting very horny and whispered to Barry, "Can we go to my hotel soon because I want you so badly." Albie, talking to Jerome said,

"None of us call him Barry. In the East End he's Geezer and he will be here! Remember it!"

Jerome in a flustered high pitched voice continued, saying "I find this so exciting. You guys are the type I was always scared of, but not anymore. I know I now have some real East End mates. But what we need is a name. I know, we should call ourselves "The Boleyn Boys". I used to go to Upton Park to watch West Ham and every time I went in the Boleyn pub, I got beaten up. But not anymore!"

Albie said, "Jerome, that is my kind of name! it's great." Barry agreed so that was to be the tag of the future... "The Boleyn Boys". With that, Rita stood up and Barry walked around with her, saying their goodbyes to everyone. Albie was waving but wondering what he would do. Barry stopped at the door and shouted, "Albie, you coming or what?" Albie tripped off behind them to the waiting taxi. As they clambered in, Terry came to the taxi door and said, "so you'll be in touch Geezer, yeah?" Barry was very clear. "I will be back first week of September and so you have loads of time to do your bit. Keep clean, Terry, and don't let me down." "I won't" said Terry as he waived them off!

Rita was sitting in between Barry and Albie. Barry, looking at Rita, said, "We should be able to get Albie a room in your hotel, yeah?" "Certain" said Rita, "I know it's nowhere near full!"

Arriving at the hotel, Rita got Albie booked in, then they urgently dumped him in the bar. Rita said to Barry, "There's a couple of prosy's still in the bar so he'll enjoy himself."

Once in the lift, they were climbing all over each other. Rita left the lift partially clothed, trying to hold everything together. By the time they were attempting to get the key into her door, Barry had become an animal with his hands searching every crevice in her delectably receptive body.

14

Another female, that attracted mass attention, was sitting in a Brussels waiting area. She had secured a lucrative position with a Government Agency named CECD. Anneliese was not long out of a U.S. University in which she had completed a Master's Degree. Her results were acclaimed throughout education faculties in the Western world.

The Americans fought hard and long to keep her, but she had decided that Europe was the place for her due to personal and family reasons. Waiting to be called in to meet her new boss, nerves were absent. She never suffered from nerves. She was a very confident, intelligent individual with intrepid mentality. She had excelled on all the CECD training courses, which were both mentally tortuous but also physically demanding. All she had to do now was to meet the top man, the Commander, to find out what her first assignment would be. This thought excited her because she knew that whatever it was, she would be completely successful!

CECD was an organisation that had been set up by the American and European crime and espionage agencies. This was a first! The Cold war was a threat from Eastern Europe; drugs and criminal gangs were expanding everywhere. The CECD collaboration would attempt to prevent their success and diminish their ability to operate.

The acronym CECD stood for "Counter Espionage and Criminal Deterrent." Essentially it describes the world at that time!! Especially the ongoing Cold War threat from Russia. Espionage by the Russian KGB and criminal activities by the Russian Mafia organisation were rife.

The CECD Commander had only met Anneliese once before. At that time he had been completely entranced by her beauty and intellect. But now she was coming to work for him. She had been chosen by a panel of select, experienced, Government and Military personnel. Now, before opening the door, he reminded himself he was her boss and needed to act with decorum and not allow his mental state to be sensually influenced.

With expectant gratification, he somewhat trembled as he pulled at the door handle. As she entered, it seemed she floated past the Commander. Her poise, elegance and class exuded from every pore of her being.

Gliding across the office, in front of the Commander, he could not prevent his eyes exploring every curve of her physique. In his head, he attempted to remind himself of his pledge. To remain cool, calm and collected.

Anneliese, confidently headed to the single chair facing the Commander's desk, but did not sit. Just stood beside it! The Commander, now more under control, said, "Oh Anneliese please sit. This is just an informal chat, the worst is over; you came through with flying colours!"

As she sat, wearing a figure flattering beige cotton summer dress, she straightened the hem so it sat just a few inches above her nubile silky knees.

The Commander slowly wandered around to his chair behind a large walnut leather topped desk. All the time, trying to contain his thoughts as his eyes explored her fabulous curves. He sat in his large executive leather revolving chair, and almost immediately, his eyes were transfixed by the delta between the hem of her dress and her slightly open thighs.

He began by saying how grateful he was to have her on his team. But then his demeanour became more serious. "I know you have had quite severe training and instruction and, therefore, you are probably already aware. But I have to cover this area again. You are choosing a very dangerous profession. The rewards are great but also is the danger. You may be involved in anything from combat duties, sexual involvement with targets, and if you are captured, even torture!"

"Your first assignment probably won't appear attractive. You will be domiciled in the Red Light district of Amsterdam as a call girl. We want intelligence from your customers, whether they be American servicemen or European politicians. We are close to forming a European Parliament and need to know who we can trust. We also require as much intelligence as we can get concerning drug supply in Europe.

"That won't be for long. We have extensive intelligence on criminal activity and most of it is stemming from Spain; the Costa del Sol. So only a few months, then we want you down there getting us organised to fight them, especially the drug lords and vicious extortion gangs."

"One last thing, you won't be alone. There will be three in your group. Anya, you already know, and is also new to the service. And Frank, who has millions of miles on his clock. You will meet them officially in the next few days. The good news is, and I know HR have already advised you, but I want to cover it again. Your remuneration will be £10,000 per month plus expenses. Have you any issues you want to discuss?"

Anneliese thought for a moment, then replied, "No Sir, I think I am going to enjoy every minute!" That touched a significant nerve with the Commander, and his mind began to imagine things he thought he had under control. It crossed his mind, if only he were 30 years younger!

She stood up and wandered slowly to the door, standing directly in front of the large double doors leading out to the garden. The sunlight stream discovered the gap between the apex of her thighs, and the Commander's gaze became fixated with the splendour of the shape. His mesmerised stare moved to the magnificence of her buttocks, dissected by the fall of her dress into the wondrous chasm.

Anneliese's head turned towards the Commander, capturing his excited gaze and causing a flustered embarrassment. With naturally pouted lips she began to speak, saying, "Well Sir, if that is all." He never heard the rest of her sentence, being absolutely entranced by the innocence and beauty of her features. Her blue green eyes, accented by long dark eyelashes and perfect symmetry of her eyebrows, were augmented by the sheen on her shoulder length dark hair.

The Commander stretched for the door handle, and as Anneliese exited, taking one last look, he said, "We will be in touch in a few days!"

15

In the hot sun of Marbella, Barry, Albie and Rita were sitting by the hotel pool. Rita had to leave in a short while to get back to her job on the flight back to Gatwick. Rita announced she would return in a few days' time as tomorrow was a rest day.

Barry turned to Albie saying, "We need to get back soon and find some bloody good excuses or we are in deep shit." "Why is that?" questioned Rita. "Oh, don't worry yourself, I will explain when you return on Friday."

Barry got up and walked behind Rita's lounger, leant over and cupped her breasts with both hands. She strained to look up at him and he gave her a long lingering kiss. With that, they went back to their rooms, quickly got dressed and were all set to face the partners.

As they walked through the reception area, Jerome came towards them. "Well hello Geezer, may we meet up again on Friday?" "Absolutely" said Barry. "As well as you, I want to see Rita again, so can you bring her to the same bar Friday night. And let her know I really want to see her again." "Of course I will" said Jerome; "Geezer, I won't let you down." Barry handed him a piece of paper with his hotel phone number. "Only talk to me, no one else. "Barry stressed. "And only call if there is a change of plans."

When they got back to the hotel, Linda and Shirley were nowhere to be seen. Albie and Barry sneaked through to the pool area, grabbed a couple of loungers and settled on them fully clothed. The girls eventually found them, both sound asleep; a consequence of their night long, exhausting, sexual activities. Their explanation to Linda and Shirley was that they had got totally pissed. There was nobody on reception because it was late and they could not remember their room number, as the girls had the keys. So they had slept, all night, on the loungers by the pool. The girlfriends were singularly unimpressed with their explanation and indicated so! Barry's usual defence mechanism kicked in. He got angry and said, "It's the truth and if you don't like it, you can lump it, and fuck off!"

The whole day was spent in silence with a very potent negative atmosphere. Barry took it on the chin because, on the one hand, he was guilt laden, but above all, because he was infatuated with Rita. Nothing else seemed important as he recounted, over and over, that night of lust and passion.

Inhibitions were totally absent in Rita. She had schemed throughout the night to inflict supreme pleasure to be shared by both of them. His desire was not allowed to weaken until she dictated so. Then, she had orchestrated lovemaking, and pure trembling passion, to re-ignite and heighten their union. No wonder she had become the centre of Barry's world!

Barry and Albie pulled out all the stops over the next couple of days, taking the girls shopping, lavishing gifts on them and generally ensuring they enjoyed every minute. Barry had spoken to Albie about seeing Rita again Friday night. "I don't know how to get us a free pass, but I have to see her." Albie came up with the answer!

"Tell Linda that we are going to set up business here in Marbella and that we have a meeting with Terry and Jose to discuss the plans. But also, we can tell both girls that you are hoping to buy a bar and maybe, also a villa, and Terry is going to show us some properties. I will talk to Terry and get him to show up here at the hotel Friday evening. Does that all sound as though it might do the trick?"

Barry thought for a moment then said, "Albie, you are a Godsend. It will work, I am sure." Albie had always been close to Barry, but now the bond was strengthening. They both knew they needed each other.

Albie knew that Barry was nervous about Friday. Not due to any reasons of aggression, which Barry could handle. It was the new aspect of a woman that he had to be with! Albie gave him constant reassurance that it would work. Barry loved Linda, but did not want to upset his new love, Rita, or indeed, Linda. Two women on the go was torture!

16

Friday evening, the girls were sat with Albie and Barry loving the exotic buffet food in the hotel restaurant. At 7.30pm Terry and Jose walked in. Not wishing to intrude, they stood a couple of yards back from the table. Terry said, "Good evening ladies" and then turning to Barry, "Are we too early?"

Barry leant forward, gripped Linda's hand and looking straight in her eyes said, "Me and Albie have some business with Terry and Jose." "So what is it now, another night on the loungers?" "No luv, Terry has got a couple of properties for us to view!" "What type of properties, what are you planning now Barry?" "I am thinking of expanding the business down here so I'm going to look at a bar." "Barry, you know zilch about bar work and I'm not going to run it!" Barry stroked her arm, smiled and said, "No but a lot of fellas round here do and will be clambering for a chance to manage it for us. This place is on the up. Everyone in London and Essex wants to visit Marbella, so we could hit the jackpot."

Albie winked at Shirley saying, "This could set us up for life!" Barry shoved his chair back, snatched a langostino and moved toward the door. Just a few paces then he stopped, turned, and excitedly shouted to Linda, "and I might buy a villa as well; we can afford it and make money from letting it, or maybe even live here!"

Linda, hearing those words nearly choked on her paella, then grasped Shirley and gave her a massive hug. The lads scooted out of the door! Terry had a car right outside; all four of them were quickly in and set off. Barry said, "Terry, don't want this to take too long. I'm meeting Rita at the bar." Terry began driving fast, then said, "It'll only take a few minutes and, if you want, I can take you with Linda tomorrow to view a villa. It is fabulous and really cheap because the Essex guy that's selling it, is broke and needs the money!"

The bar for viewing was by the quayside. Terry had the keys and they were soon inside. The frontage was a good size. It had been called Café Del Mar, but they could change it if they wanted. The bar itself was a fantastic size. Past the bar was a massive kitchen and adjacent store room. Barry was very keen, as was Albie. But it all came down to price. To buy it was equivalent to £3000. To rent, it was about £100 per month. This made it sound like a great bargain. Barry looked at Albie then to Terry. "Go and get it tomorrow Terry!" We'll start off renting but need an option to buy at £3000." All of them, totally exhilarated, sped off to meet Rita. As they arrived, a taxi pulled up alongside. It was Rita and Jerome. They all clustered together and entered, receiving a very warm welcome from Juan, who immediately began pouring their drinks.

Drinks were constantly flowing, which generated merriment in everyone. The locals were enjoying the banter and occasional singing. Rita was clinging to Barry like a limpet. Jerome was entertaining, including an attempt to tap dance to some flamenco music. When he ran out of steam, he went to his flight bag, shouldered it and tapped Barry on the shoulder, saying, "Geezer, would you come with me; I have a present for you!"

Once outside, Jerome, leaning to open his travel bag, said, "The customs hardly ever check us, so I've brought you a gift." He delved into the bag and pulled out something wrapped in a t-shirt. Unwrapping it for a few seconds, then it was on show. It was a Colt Magnum. A small revolver. Barry was ecstatic. "Jerome, you are a find." Jerome, rummaging around in his bag, said "But I also managed to get these which are an essential." It was a complete cartridge of bullets.

Barry went round the side of the bar and inserted some into the gun. Then walked back to Jerome, grasped around his neck and dragged him back into the bar. Rita immediately kissed Barry, saying she was worrying where he had got to.

The festivities continued, but Barry was now clock watching. He knew it was impossible for him to stay out all night tonight. He began to explain to Rita, saying that he was with a girlfriend but now wanted to be with her!

She was in love with Barry but the decider was when he told her he was buying a bar in Marbella. She looked somewhat surprised, then said, "Barry, that is fabulous. I will be able to see you on every trip here." Without engaging brain, Barry said, "It's got a flat above it. How's about moving here and perhaps you might consider running the bar!" "Barry, I want to immediately say yes, but I need some time to think. I've got loose ends to figure out but I really do like the idea. It would be an adventure with you and gets me off that plane! I will give you an answer soon!"

Whilst Barry and Rita continued talking, Terry put his arm around Albie's shoulders and edged him to the end of the bar. He was asking Albie where he would get the money to pay the deposit for the bar, which would be required tomorrow. Albie was in the middle of explaining that Barry had enough cash with him when the bar doors creaked open.

17

Two guys, both in immaculate lightweight suits, casually walked to the bar and stood next to Barry and Rita. Juan appeared from the kitchen and seeing these two fellas, stopped dead. The blood drained from his face and as he poured their order, his hands were noticeably trembling.

The mean looking fella in the light blue suit began to stare out Juan with an aggressive exaggerated smile. As Juan passed their drinks across the bar, the fella said to Juan, "It's the end of your month Juan. You must pay today." "It's not been a good month so I can't pay you yet Lorenzo." He grabbed at Juan's shirt and pulled him close, saying, "I didn't hear that, shall we try again? If you want to be deaf, we can soon fix it for you! So I'll say again, it's time to pay up!"

Barry had been watching their every move, he took Rita's hand and slowly, and with demonstrations of affection, led her to Albie. He whispered to Albie and Terry there was going to be trouble so to watch his back!

He slowly turned, smiling all the while. Rita turned to Albie with a questioning look as Barry reached the two extortionists. By now, Barry had his right hand in his left inside jacket pocket. He put his left hand on the shoulder of the blue suit and said, "Hello guy, think we should meet. I am Geezer from London!"

The next action was so fast nobody watching was able to discern what had occurred. Only Albie knew! Barry had pulled out the gun and smashed it with all his might into Lorenzo's face. He slumped to the ground. His partner, with unbelievable ferocity, jumped on Barry's back and was punching the side of his face and attempting to gouge his eyes!

Barry, still gripping the Colt revolver, tried to swing his arm behind to blast the character. Off balance, he missed and the bullet lodged in the ceiling.

Now Albie joined the affray. He already had pulled out his flick knife and the blade was plunged into the guy's right buttock. He screamed out and as he did, Albie attacked the left buttock, this time drawing the knife upward as far as he could.

Lorenzo's partner fell to the floor, screaming in stereo. Barry casually said to Juan, "paper and pen please!" He wrote a note saying this Marbella area was now owned by the "Geezer" and intruders would receive the same treatment. Juan passed Barry a stapler and it was stapled to Lorenzo's jacket.

Barry asked Juan to call a taxi, which arrived in five minutes. Barry, Albie and the other guys, including Jerome, carried the bodies to the taxi; Barry asked Juan to tell the driver to drop them on a beach somewhere, and gave the driver a 1000 peseta note. As they stood in the light streaming from the bar windows, Juan said, "these guys are in the Napoli gang and there are many!"

Back in the bar, Juan was elated but also worried that they and their friends would come back. "I don't think so," said Barry. "They have my note and my reputation will soon be widespread. Juan, don't worry, I will be here next month and my people will look after you in the meantime. I am your protection now. I will do a good job and it will not be expensive for you. You have looked after us so now I will look after you!" Turning to Terry, Barry said, "Don't forget, make sure you look after Juan!"

Rita and Jerome both showered Barry and Albie with affection. Rita now worshipped Barry! He was the man she had always craved. Barry necked his drink, as he turned to Terry saying, "Let's get out of here. Let's go back to my bar to let Rita and Jerome see it."

They crammed into Terry's Seat mid-sized car called a Viento. Very basic, but did the necessary. Barry, as they were speeding along said, "Terry, about bloody time you cleaned the car, the windscreen makes everything blurred." Terry replied, "True Geezer, I can't see a thing!"

They arrived at the Café Del Mar in double quick time. They rushed in, keen to see the bar. Once inside, Barry led Rita and Jerome through the bar, pointing out all the key features and traditional furnishings. They were both impressed, especially with the enormous size of the property.

Then, Terry shouted from behind the bar, but was not in view. He was on his knees, under the counter. He stood, clearly cheerful as he had found some booze. A bottle of Gin in one hand, Rum in the other. Now they all searched for mixers. Jerome found some Coke and Lemonade in the kitchen, so they were about to have an impromptu party.

After about an hour of solid drinking, Barry took Rita's hand and led her to the far end of the bar, out of sight of the others. Opposite the kitchen door was a pool table. Barry picked Rita up and placed her bottom on the edge of the pool table. She was a glorious figure of a woman. Everything about her screamed sensual.

Rita held him off saying, "Wait a minute." She asked Barry to retrieve her bag from the bar and when he returned, she rummaged around for a few seconds. She found what she was looking for, and proceeded to pull her hair back and secure it in a ponytail.

Holding Barry's face in her hands, she pulled him towards her and a gentle kiss gradually exploded into erotic passion. Her legs entwined his waist with a python-like grip. Her breasts were now heaving as he slowly unbuttoned her blouse, ready to ravish her.

He had made a conscious decision to dedicate his whole being to pure loving pleasure for Rita. Tender, gentle massage began the journey to ecstasy. The caresses, touching, kissing, almost overwhelmed Barry. He wanted, indeed his whole body demanded, to accede to his desire. But he resisted the urge and continued with increased vigour to intimidate her body into complete, trembling, orgasms. Several times, over and over again!

Perspiring, but with ultimate satisfaction, Rita slowly regained her composure. Clamping her fingers behind his neck, she straightened her legs. Her body continued to shudder as Barry teased her lips with his tongue. She would now crave the same intense pleasure for the rest of her life!

Cuddling Rita, Barry walked her back to the bar area. Terry, "We have to go now, so drop us at Rita's hotel." As they arrived, Barry said "Rita, I have to get back now! I will sort out my relationship and meet you back here. In a couple of weeks, I will call you! Jerome, you are welcome too, and I will make sure it's worth it.

Rita gave Barry a long lingering kiss, clinging to him as if she wasn't able to let go. Rita and Jerome stood in the hotel doorway waving as their car left.

On reaching Barry's hotel, he said, "Terry, come and find me early afternoon and I will go over the plans with you. " Albie led the way into their hotel and both of them sauntered to the bar to find Linda and Shirley. Barry, somewhat confused about how to declare his infidelity, but also reluctant to hurt Linda, decided his best course of action was to say nothing for now. He would leave it until they were home, which was only three days. He would have time to think it through.

As they entered the bar, Shirley and Linda were behind them. "Well that's better than the last time," shouted Linda. Barry stopped and turned to face them. "Well, from tomorrow darling, we own a bar in Marbella by the quayside." Barry saying this in mitigation, hoped it would quell any arguments.

It worked well. They all enjoyed another hour in the bar. As they were about to leave for their bed, Omar the barman, leaned across to Barry saying, "I heard you speaking about your bar, senor. Sign up quickly tomorrow because there was a Mayor's meeting here earlier and tomorrow they will announce they have approved building of a marina at the quayside; it will be fantastic!"

Barry slid 300 pesetas to Omar saying, muchos gracias. On the way up to the rooms, in the lift, Barry told the others. Albie got very excited, saying this will make us a future. Barry, looking at the girls said, "I must find Terry in the morning and get the contracts done! Don't think there will be a problem as Terry has already walked the contract through the Abogado (Lawyer) and I have paid the deposit!"

Early in the morning, both Albie and Barry tried phoning Terry, but no joy. So they went to reception, hired a car and dug him out of his pit. By 10.30am, they had been to the Abogado and everything was signed, sealed and delivered. Barry was now the proud tenant of Café Del Mar.

18

In Amsterdam it was a cloudy cold morning. Anneliese was sound asleep, dreaming under a very warm duvet. She had promised herself a long lay in, having had a very busy night. The phone rang and being drowsy, she had to concentrate. "Who's that please?" she said. "who, who?"

"It's Lina, I am the Commander's secretary." "Oh yes, Lina, I'm sorry. I have only just woken up." Lina giggled, saying "I'm so sorry ringing you so early, but the Commander asked if you could come to his office for 8.30pm this evening. We will send a car for you. A car will pick you up at 5.00pm."

Anneliese asked Lina "What about Anya...and Frank?" "Yes, they are also required! I was just about to ring them." "OK" said Anneliese. "You make the official calls and I will talk to them later".

At 5.00pm precisely, the car arrived. The driver, an undercover agent, chatted with Anneliese as they drove, only a few minutes, to Anya's apartment. She climbed in the rear seat, embraced Anneliese and as they sped along the E9, girl talk began. After a few kilometres, Anneliese said to the driver, "Where are we picking Frank up?" "At Schiphol Airport" he replied. "He's been on assignment down in Spain for several weeks. In fact, you can blame him for causing this late evening meeting." "Willi, I thought we were leaving too early just to drive to Brussels, but that explains it," commented Anneliese.

They parked in the airport pickup zone, but only for seven minutes. The arrivals main door opened as several people with loaded trolleys exited. Right behind them, noticeable by his usual carefree, casual but proud gait was a male figure. Dressed in a dark blue raincoat, upturned collar and black beret, angled on the side of his head. As he got closer, they could not avoid his wide confident smile. It was definitely Frank.

The Parliament Buildings always appeared drab and uninviting to Anneliese. But then she thought, what do I care, they are paying me well. And maybe someday, they will build a fantastic modern European Parliament building.

Lina showed Frank and the two girls to a leather sofa set against the wall, opposite her desk. Frank stood and began some harmless flirting with Lina. All the while, Lina, unobtrusively, would glance across to Anneliese and Anya. It wasn't that she didn't find Frank attractive, indeed it was the opposite! The fact was she was always fascinated by the beauty and poise of these fabulous female specimens. Indeed, she would try to figure out how such innocent beauty camouflaged massive intelligence, combined with potential ferocious physical force.

The buzzer on Lina's intercom sounded and she flicked the switch. Commander Farrell spoke. "Lina, would you send my visitors in, please." In truth, he was on the edge of his seat as he could not wait to see Anneliese again!

Once inside, with everyone seated, the Commander apologised for the late evening, but said it was unavoidable. He asked if they would like any refreshments but they all replied, "No thank you, Sir."

"Ok, then I will get on with the briefing. Our intelligence people have raised the red flag. They believe that severe criminal activity is about to escalate in Marbella. Frank was assigned down there several weeks ago and has been providing on-the-spot surveillance. Before we get to that, I will summarise the central intelligence information and expectations."

"Marbella is on a very steep incline to become the most attractive tourist resort in Europe. It is already a growth area for the drug trade. Just yesterday, it was announced that a yacht marina is to be built which will attract the rich and famous as well as celebrities from all over the world. "

"Presently, there are only a few gangs drug-running; they are also smuggling arms, cigarettes, booze, gold and anything else that is worth their while. In parallel, with these criminal activities, they are supplementing their income with extortion, insider information on property price growth provided by bent officials, both Government and Local."

The Commander then said, "I will hand over to Frank now to brief you on his findings." Frank, in his inimitable way, looked straight at Anneliese and Anya. "I agree with everything the Commander has outlined. But as always, the devil is in the detail. The only way we are going to get in the underwear of this is with distraction and infiltration of their gangs. And that's where you ladies come in."

"The gangs that exist in Marbella are either small local teams or the Italians. They are the Napoli gang based in Fuengirola, but have never had enough intelligence to increase their stature."

"Now there are a couple of new ones on the scene. A gang from East London are just trying to set themselves up; they are extremely competent. They have achieved wonders in London in the space of just two years. Their hierarchy is essentially two guys. One known as "the Geezer" is the supremo. His cousin, Albie, is his right hand man and appears to be an intelligent, and very loyal character. They both, on the face of it, are likeable young men. But that hides the fact that they are both vicious and without conscience. They are not married, but both live with girls; probably they use them for available sex and domestic support."

"This is where you two ladies can make headway. They are both absolute suckers for women. The Geezer has just met a BEA stewardess and is already head over heels."

"One last thing," continued Frank, "I have noticed some new activity and central intelligence have agreed that it appears that the Russian Mafia are preparing to move in. All these gangs attempting to control Marbella at the same time is a recipe for disaster. That's why Central Intelligence have raised the red flag. However, it also provides us with a major opportunity to crack their defences, cut their supply lines, raid their warehouses and terminate their operations."

Frank turned to look at the Commander. With a nod of the head he said, "Frank, I'll wrap this up now! You three should get yourselves down to Marbella by mid-September. You will have every bit of support you need, especially from CECD Intelligence and our agents. The Spanish National Police Corps and their secret police will also be tracking your every move. Just make sure you pass us every piece of intelligence information, even if you think it is possibly worthless."

"You ladies should use the next few weeks to work with Frank to plan and organise your cover. I would suggest Anneliese and Anya concentrate on infiltrating and securing as much information as possible about the gangs, their people and their processes. Initially, the new London team appear a good target. Especially as the two leaders find it hard to resist beautiful women with superb bodywork."

"They are two young, relatively inexperienced horny guys, who will want to fraternise with you girls. You are our ace card! "Anya and Anneliese, singing from the same hymn sheet exclaimed, "Thank you Commander, we didn't know you cared!"

The Commander replied, with a lecherous smile, and then turning to Frank said, "I know you will do what you are good at. Staying in the shadows, protecting those that need it, and weighing up every tiny episode until you can deliver us a finished article."

"These are just my preliminary thoughts. You three will work it out together, and I know you will make us all very proud of you! I was thinking of naming this operation "The Three Musketeers" . Instead, I am changing it to "the Sex or Tears" Operation. But be assured, there will be no tears!"

19

As they filed out, Frank gave Lina an enticing wink. The Commander shook hands with each of them saying," Someday I will recall this meeting as one of my assignments that proved a complete success!"

With all of them feeling euphoric, they climbed into the waiting car and set off for the Red Light district. On the way, Frank spent a quiet time, thinking. Then he leaned forward and said, "You girls need to finish your jobs by the end of the week. We need to meet several times to review all the latest intelligence. Following this, we should go down to Marbella and get established. I will book you both into hotels in Amsterdam, and then Marbella. We will require some quiet privacy to do all the necessary research. And in Marbella, you two can spend time tanning and beautifying." Anya immediately replied, "So Frank, we look like we need it?" "No, Anya, but you may need pampering before we start work in earnest, so I am giving you the chance to have some female enjoyment time."

Anneliese spoke, "We love you Frank.... But as a brother."

The Crown Plaza Hotel in Amsterdam would be their refuge for the next few weeks. They all met regularly to review the latest intelligence that came through from Central Command. Anneliese gave Frank and Anya her psychological assessments of the various criminal activities and individuals that were featuring in the reports.

Gradually, they formulated a picture of the types of criminal activities that teams specialised in, and seconded other CECD operatives to photograph individuals and the places they frequented. Also, they developed a complete dossier of their criminal records and statistics indicating their lifestyles and routine movements on a daily basis. A complete section of this dossier defined each individual's skills, talents, favoured weaponry and sexual preferences.

During the second week, a new element surfaced. Central Command provided them with intelligence gathered from informants, that another criminal team were preparing to establish themselves in Marbella. This crew emanated from Marseille. They were reportedly a well organised brutal mob that, in the past, had even initiated all-out street battles with other teams, including the French police.

On hearing this, Frank sat down with Anya and Anneliese to discuss this added complication. Their conclusion was that they required more undercover military talent to be based in and around Marbella. They agreed to settle on requesting four ex-SAS personnel who they could call upon if and when the time came.

Frank would talk with Commander Farrell and initiate the request. In his mind, Frank had already selected the people he wanted. He had worked with them all before and knew they were the very best! Although they had been assured of support and back-up from the Spanish and CECD, Frank, Anneliese and Anya, had jointly concluded that on-the-ground, momentary intervention by a crack team may prove crucial.

It took the whole of the following week for Frank to convince the Commander. They had several discussions which moved into negotiating mode. The Commander persisted with the budget argument, constantly saying, "The budget won't stand that amount of extra cost!" He tried using the complimentary approach; "You don't need that much help to deal with these jerks and the girls are very accomplished fighters!" Next, it was a case of numbers. "Frank, two should be enough if they are as good as you say!" But Frank would not relent. He was like a dog with a bone.

Eventually, at the end of a week, the Commander responded saying, "OK Frank, four it is then but it is on your head if you are not completely successful."

These new mercenaries would arrive in Marbella when Frank considered they were needed. And they would only be paid for time at the coal face, as the Commander put it!

When Frank gave Anneliese and Anya the good news, he laughed when he repeated, "Time at the coal face. When they go into battle, they look like miners because they always black their faces up!" They all giggled.

By September 28th they had moved into the Sol Marbella near Estepona. Anneliese and Anya always knew how to enjoy themselves. The first day there, they took advantage of the pampering spa, the poolside bar, the sunshine, and soaked up the attention of all the male nationalities around the pool.

After three days of vacationing, Frank arrived. The girls already had glorious tans, which they were both proud of and continually used sun cream to avoid peeling. To a minor extent Frank upstaged them. He walked out to the pool bar wearing a pair of knee length Bermuda shorts. His body was not yet tanned, and he was a fairly slight character. But every muscle in his body was accentuated and superbly toned.

20

Barry and Linda, by this time, had already been in Marbella a couple of weeks. Before they left, Barry had spent some time with Jess going through the accounts for the Bus business. Barry was very pleased with the earnings and Jess even more so. Now, working full time on the travel business, Jess was becoming legendary in the East End. People loved him, especially the older folks that appreciated his respect and attention to their needs.

He had grown the business to the extent he had invested in two coaches; they were country service Royal Blue coaches and that Company had provided the coaches with a massive discount as he would continue the Royal Blue name. Barry was impressed.

Barry had been considering using the Bus on the Continent, possibly for cigarette smuggling. However, his conscience and Jess's progress negated this idea. Barry decided to let it continue as a legal business.

Jess was ecstatic with Barry being so pleased with their income. Whilst he had been doing so well, he had bought a small terraced house and also had managed to furnish it. Barry's mum was more than pleased because Jess had become a very good friend. Barry knew he could not risk getting Jess in trouble by involving him, even unknowingly, with any criminal activity.

Mum was not quite so happy when Barry announced he was heading back to Marbella. Neither was Linda! But Barry used all his powers of persuasion. The growth of his business with the bar, which was temporary until it was off the ground. They deserved to be rich and he couldn't afford it to fail!

Once back in Marbella, Barry spent a few days making sure that everything was organised. Customers were beginning to appear. Baby steps, but it was beginning to be on the up.

At this point, Barry persuaded Linda to run the bar for a few days because he needed to resolve some business issues in Morocco. To be precise, Ceuta.

Albie went with him, whilst Shirley joined Linda to run the bar. When they arrived in Ceuta, they went straight to Mustafa. He was waiting, having known the time the ferry arrived. Barry had a list of his requirements. Several drugs, Hashish, Cannabis and Cocaine. Also guns, which Mustafa said would take longer as he had to put it through his intermediary. Mustafa would contact Barry to arrange delivery which would involve a boat dropping canisters in the Mediterranean at a specified point and time. Barry opened his case and paid in cash.

Central Command had Intelligence Officers tailing Barry and watching his every move. The information about his whereabouts and dealings with Mustafa were relayed back to Frank and Anneliese. So by the time they arrived in Marbella they were clued up on what Barry had been arranging. As well as the deals with Mustafa in Ceuta, Albie had bought two very fast cars. Also two fast inflatables which had been stored with the Lotus Cortinas' somewhere close to Estepona, on a farm in the hills.

Now it was time for Anneliese, Anya and Frank to get acquainted with Barry. It was late Saturday afternoon. A mixture of Spaniards and tourists in the bar. Probably about twelve in total. It was a hot afternoon. As the Spanish say it was "caliente", about 30C

Frank wandered in and decided to sit on a Marbella Stool at the bar. Linda was managing front of house and was looking wearily beautiful. Shirley was washing glasses and had the same weary look.

Albie and Barry, with not a care in the world, were at the far end of the bar, laughing, joking and downing drinks, at break neck speed. Frank started to chat with Linda. Very polite, very courteous. She asked him, "was he on holiday?" he replied "Well no, not really. I've moved here. Wasn't getting anywhere in Britain so decided to change the scenery!"

Just at that point, Anneliese and Anya arrived and sat at the table at the front of the bar. Barry and Albie's eyes were on stalks. Shirley went out to take their order, which was only drinks. Both girls chose red wine and sat enjoying the sun and one another's company. After about 30 minutes, they arose and wandered inside.

Anneliese went to the bar, saying to Linda that they needed to get into the shade for a while. Then she ordered some more drinks, sitting at a small table about 5 metres from Barry and Albie. They knew their every move was being studied. These ladies were expert at this particular game. Everything they did had been learned and used time and again. Anneliese would smile at Barry. Anya would slowly cross her legs. Then she would accidently knock her drinks mat on the floor, which required her to lean forward towards Barry. Her low cut top provided the necessary excitement!

Now it was Anneliese's turn to exploit the situation. She was an accomplished actress at attracting men into her web. She stood up slowly, put her hands firmly on her hair and pulled it back to place a hair band on her locks. As she did with her back arching, her breasts were dominant. She, smiling at the guys as she went, floated by Barry and Albie. As she headed for the servicios (toilets), her body worked on Barry's imagination. He had lost control. She had gained control.

All the time, Frank was watching every movement of everybody. He was also chatting to Linda and Shirley, his intention being to gradually gain their trust and respect. He knew it would take several visits, but in this type of scenario, he was an expert at using banter, humorous stories and polite charm to gain their acceptance.

It was his usual approach to present himself as a likeable, personable, friendly character, unscarred by life and totally transparent. If only they knew the real Frank.

21

The real Frank had suffered a really difficult childhood. Constantly abused by an unspeakably aggressive father and ignored by a drunken slut of a mother. He had left home, not really any home to speak of, at the age of fifteen. He had slept on the streets of North London until he reached sixteen, then joined the Royal Marines. His achievements in training and then six months in Aden, and then Tanganyika, where their army mutinied and law and order had to be restored, had formed the bedrock of his future.

His prowess as a fighter was respected and he, subsequently, transferred into the Paratroopers. That experience added to his military ability. So now, with all that knowledge and psychological strength, he was gratefully accepted into the S.A.S. It was Frank's dream to reach the pinnacle of his profession. He did this with pride and was one of the best; protecting his country.

In the meantime, Frank's two colleagues were in the middle of implementing their tactics to gain trust and acceptance. Barry and Albie looked longingly at Anneliese and Anya. In their minds, they just saw these two beautiful creatures as normal single ladies in Marbella on holiday. The beauty that these girls were adorned with created a barrier. Barry and Albie could not see beyond it!

What they could not see, behind the façade, was two females with extraordinary intelligence and outstanding physical assault abilities. Anya had been born in Russia and recruited to CECD straight from Volgograd University. She decided that this was her chance to live a life in Western culture. It would provide an escape route from Russian dictatorship! She had excelled at University and was a Jiu Jitsu black belt. At the CECD training camps she had achieved the highest standard in all combat sectors.

Anneliese had grown up in Holland, then attended a private school in Paris. She also excelled throughout her education. She graduated from Ann Arbor University in the U.S.A. where she achieved an MBA. Her results put her in the top 10% in the country.

She had been recruited by CECD directly from University. Having been a U.S High Diving Champion in her early years at Ann Arbor, her fitness carried her through the punishing CECD training camps.

In the existing Marbella situation, this background was completely unknown. Instead, both she and Anya would perform as Bimbo Mayflies, dangling on a fisherman's hook.

Barry and Albie were already fascinated by these two beautiful creatures, twisting and turning in front of them. It may be several days before they take the bait but these girls were well equipped and accomplished to get them on the hook!

Linda and Shirley decided it was time for their break and asked Barry and Albie to take over bar duties. The lads were quick to take over, recognising this as a chance to chat to Anneliese and Anya without the wives suspecting their intentions.

Frank ambled out to a seat on the front patio area. He guessed that was where Linda and Shirley would go to relax. Also, he needed to be away from Anya and Anneliese.

Anneliese, seeing the opening, went to the bar to order. Anya followed and both sat on bar stools with legs on show. Barry and Albie began to chat, mostly getting acquainted chat, leading to banter and disguised compliments.

Linda, seated outside the bar with Shirley, started up another conversation with Frank. "So, what did you do before deciding to give up on Britain?" Frank stood to move his chair closer to the girls. All the while, glancing around at the street and people going by.

"Oh, I was in the army for several years. When I came out, it was difficult to find a decent job," replied Frank. Shirley now joined in. Both girls were beginning to enjoy Frank's company. Shirley asked, "Did you get sent abroad with the army. See any action?"

Frank developed a huge smile. "Not really abroad. Most of the time I was stationed in Ireland. Too much action there! Then I was sent to Germany for a short while, as a trainer. That only lasted a month or two then it was back to Salisbury Plain, again as a trainer. That wasn't enough action for me so when my time was up, I got out. Looking back now, I think it was a big mistake."

A similar type of conversation had been going on with Anneliese and Anya. "How long have you been down here?" asked Barry. "Almost a week" replied Anneliese. Anya said "We really like it here. We were just talking about staying on for a while. We don't have much to get back for."

Albie asked, "So where are you staying?" "Down the coast in a hotel near Estapona" replied Anneliese, with her enticing innocent smile. The lads were just about to ask what the girls did for work when they noticed their partners preparing to return to their bar work.

22

Franks' magnetism prevented them moving away quickly. They both enjoyed his attention and found it hard to leave him. The noise of a car's doors banging shut distracted them. The car had parked directly opposite Café Del Mar. Three characters were striding towards them.

They bustled past Frank and the girls. Just at that time, another noisy vehicle, a quad bike, stopped outside. The driver had stopped to talk to a pedestrian. Frank's eyes were everywhere, following the three guys entering the bar and glancing at the road.

Anneliese and Anya, seeing the three men striding in, realised trouble was brewing. Both girls stood up from the bar stools as the men reached the bar and leaned on it, one with his elbows planted with hands under his chin.

All three guys became agitated. The central figure began to shout at Barry. His face had become contorted and viciously threatening. One of the guys pulled a flick knife out of his jacket and was waving it in Albie's face.

Frank had his moves planned as the fracas increased. He ran to the Quad bike, pushed the old chap off, jumped on and accelerated up the few steps, across the patio to the bar. Simultaneously, the central figure was pulling a revolver out of his shoulder holster. The guy on his right, standing next to Anneliese, was shouting, "Shoot him Luigi, shoot him, kill the bastard!" Luigi couldn't resist waving the gun around first!

The few customers remaining in the bar were diving for cover. Some ran to the end by the pool table. The quad bike engine noise, as Frank powered through the bar, became deafening. Frank had the bike aimed straight for the terror group. Before Frank could strike, Luigi determined it was now or never. Barry had nowhere to go. The gun, being a revolver, would do damage. Just as the bike ploughed through the bar and before Luigi could pull the trigger, Anneliese reacted, head butting the guy next to her as she flung her right arm with tremendous force. Her wine glass sunk, as it shattered, into the side of Luigi's head. He dropped the gun! Anya, quick as a flash, retrieved it whilst back tracking several paces to the rear.

The quad bike powered on with horrific force, into all three assailants. The bar stools flew in all directions. Anneliese tumbled on top of it as it crashed, headlong, into the side of the bar. Frank was thrown off, landing at Anya's feet.

She helped him to stand. He was uninjured and Anya passed him the firearm. Frank stepped forward covering the three assailants using the crouched aiming position. By now, Barry had climbed over the bar and was attending to Anneliese. She, with Barry's help, got to her feet and switched off the quad bike engine, which by now, was clanking and spluttering. This noise was substituted by the noise of sirens, growing louder as they approached the bar.

Anneliese and Frank stood over the three beaten characters. Anya joined them alongside Barry, who began to chuckle! Humour touched him when he noticed Anya was gripping a pool cue in a threatening position. Albie joined them and the laughter grew. He clearly had a fancy for Anya which Anneliese and Frank noticed when Albie put his arm around her waist as they all began to relax.

Linda and Shirley came back into the bar looking very shaken. They were just about to ask questions when the Spanish Special Police began shouting from outside in the street. Although they were using a megaphone, their instructions were in Spanish, "Salga, Salga ! manos sobre tus cabezas!" the few Spanish in the bar led the way out, hands above their heads. Everyone started to follow them.

The police, in dark blue uniforms were armed and ready for action. Anneliese, although bruised and battered, but without physical wounds, looked around and said they should all quietly follow. Once outside, everybody lined up along the sidewalk, Anneliese limping as she went, clung onto Barry.

Another car arrived and parked just up the street. Here, to save the day, were Terry and Jose. The police spoke with several of the Spaniards, then turned to Barry, Albie and the partners. At the side, Jose and Terry were in conversation with one of the policemen. They joined their colleagues interviewing Barry and Albie who were vigorously pointing into the bar. A group of policemen rushed inside and dragged the three assailants out. All of them had quite severe leg and arm injuries, so it required several policemen to get them into the back of the police van. They also collected the revolver for evidence.

All the while, Jose had been getting the complete story from Frank and Barry. He turned to the police sergeant and recounted all he had been told, but with some embellishment that favoured the Barry group. The police were sympathetic, especially when they saw Anneliese.

The police sergeant informed Jose and Terry that the three characters were known to them and had previous convictions. They were leaders of the Naples gang operating in the area. All types of criminal work, but mainly extortion, was their speciality and he believed that this was what they were trying for in the Café Del Mar.

The police carted off the Naples guys. As the sirens disappeared into the night, the area around Café Del Mar fell silent. A taxi arrived for Anneliese and Anya. Frank had already disappeared. Terry and Jose joined Barry and Albie at the bar for a recovery drink. The partners joined them, but just for a moment. Linda had one gin and tonic with Shirley, then as they were heading to bed, both girls looked at their partners and said, forcefully, "We can't live with this sort of violence. You need to get us out of here, and quick!"

Next day, Barry and Albie tried to convince Linda and Shirley that it would not happen again and that it was just some local creeps thinking they had found a soft touch. Eventually the girls said that they would go home and then come back in a few weeks, providing it all settled down and there were no repeat violent episodes. So that was the agreement. Barry and Albie would see them off from Malaga airport the following day.

Terry drove them all to the airport to meet the incoming flight from Gatwick. Barry had arranged that Eddie would meet Linda and Shirley at Gatwick and get them home. The two couples stood in departures; the girls were under an emotional cloud. They embraced, then the girls trudged off through passport control.

Barry and Albie switched their misery faces into gleeful ones. Terry jumped into the driver's seat and they set off. It was their lucky day. As they drove past arrivals, a whole host of navy blue uniforms were coming out of the main doors. Barry shouted, "Terry; stop, wait!" In among the group were Rita and Jerome. Albie jumped out and then Barry and they began shouting and waving. Rita had seen them and came running over. They stood facing one another. Barry said, "Babe, come to the bar tonight." Rita replied, "I will because I have given in my notice and I'm staying!" With that, she lunged at Barry and gave him a mammoth embrace and kiss. "I'll have to go now or our coach will leave without me, but I will see you later."

In their Estapona hotel, Anneliese and Anya were having their own meeting. Their plan to get Barry and Albie on the hook was to go back to Cafe Del Mar two or three times a week. Not necessarily always together. That way they could work out, from the lads questioning, who was missing who. They knew Albie was keen on Anya. Now it needed Barry to need Anneliese.

In about half an hour, they would meet up with the four CECD ex-mercenaries who would provide their backup. They would only be visible when required. They were all ex-mercenaries with light years of experience. They would resemble tourists. Anneliese had even organised paid females, who would occasionally jet in from Amsterdam, to hang on their arms to make them look the part. They would be unobtrusive, and enjoy themselves, until the time came for conflict!

Anya would go to the bar lunchtime tomorrow, to see how the land was lying! About 8pm Rita arrived at Café Del Mar. As she strolled through the patio, with several people seated on the patio, Jerome was just behind. Barry, seeing Rita, came round from behind the bar and led her to the stock room. 15 minutes later, they came out looking very pleased but dishevelled. Jerome had been having a beer and some chat and banter with Albie. These two were now getting on famously. Albie was asking Jerome if he was any good in a scrap. "Don't suppose so", said Jerome, with a meek expression. Albie hooked his fingers into Jerome's waistcoat, pulled him close and with the faces nearly touching exclaimed, "I am going to teach you. Might take a while but I will make sure you can look after yourself."

Terry entered the bar just as Albie was showing Jerome a few moves. Rita joined them, tickling Jerome around his bottom as Albie tugged him here and there.

Barry got Terry a beer as Jose joined them. Terry, looking rather serious, asked Barry if they could have a quiet word. The three of them loped to the far end of the bar by the pool table.

Terry said to Barry, "just wanted you to know we have a team together. Until a day ago, I only had ten. I've done my best. Most of the possibles were already working, mostly for the Naples guys. However, the events last night seem to have impressed many people. So today, three more joined us. They were with the Naples gang but they say last night finished them. Their bosses are going away for a long while and they see you as a good bet. So, I'm sorry Geezer, but we are only up to thirteen." Surprisingly, Barry was magnanimous. "It'll probably grow some more as we get known." Terry, relieved, said "Just two more questions. Could you let me know when and where you want me to get them together for a meet? And do you know who that character was that crushed those bastards with the quad? He may prove very useful to us."

"Take it slowly, Terry. Let's find out more about him. All I know is that Linda talked with him and he said he was ex-army, disgruntled with it and had been out of work for a while." Barry quietened as a few customers came in, and several more took seats on the front patio.

Albie and Jerome stopped fooling around and joined Rita behind the bar. The whole place was beginning to buzz. It seemed everyone had heard about the events of the previous evening. Several of the customers had bars in and around Marbella and they spent their entire evening ascertaining all the details. Probably because they had been paying the gang from Napoli and were relieved that they were now no more!

Terry had, all the time, been worrying about getting Barry's approval of the guys in the team. He took an opportunity to say to Barry about arrangements. "Geezer, there is a nice, out the way, hotel in Estepona. How's about meeting the team there on Wednesday." Barry thought for a moment then said, "Sounds good Terry. But there is one thing that you and Albie can organise. You, Terry, can pick the guys, but we need to try them out. My contact in Morocco has said they will do us a delivery Friday evening."

"Albie will help you, but I need you to pick some guys to collect the drop in the med. If you choose Spaniards, take Jose with you. Are you up for that? It's worth a lot to you and all of us! I will bank-role you and it will need three guys in the powered inflatables to pick up the canisters and bring them back here. I will store the stuff in the bar. Once we have it, we can really get on the move."

Once everybody had left the bar and they had tidied up, Barry, Albie, Rita and Jerome sat talking. Rita made a point of saying to Barry, "I think I am going to like it here." Barry replied, "You were great tonight, babe. All the customers went away happy and there were lots of great comments about you." Rita's expression became more strained. Then she said, "Yes Barry, and I loved the work and the people tonight, but I need some help. I can't handle the whole bar on my own. We need at least two permanents behind the bar serving, a chef and a good waitress." Barry appeared thoughtful for a moment, then gave a clear direct answer. "Rita, I will get you whatever you need as long as we make money. We will start to tackle it tomorrow!"

Jerome, who had been sitting quietly listening to this, asked Barry "Geezer, could I stay and work for you in the bar?" The immediate reply was, an emphatic NO. "Jerome, right now I need you to be my carrier pigeon. If you spend time with Albie learning to fight, you may get the chance to become one of the soldiers. So be patient and work hard at training. Never know, one day you might get to be another General alongside Albie. And, by the way, on your next flight here, bring me another gun for Albie. Don't take risks, but if you can bring one, it will be a big help."

Barry and Albie were beginning to feel that their efforts to build a loyal, cohesive team of key players around them was taking shape! But, in the backs of their minds, they knew they could not forget their partners, Mum, Jess and family back in Britain.

Next morning, with sun beating down, they began to prepare for the lunch time drinkers. Jerome was first up, brewing and making coffee for the rest as they appeared. Barry and Rita sauntered into the bar about 11am. They sat on the front patio with Jerome, catering to their every need. Coffee, toast and a few croissants.

An hour later, customers started to arrive, as did Albie. Jerome was doing his best to keep everybody happy. Mostly just taking drinks to people on the patio. It was a wonderfully warm day, and people came and went for the next hour. Rita explained constantly that they had just opened and food would be available in the next week or two.

23

At precisely 1.00pm a taxi drew up outside Café Del Mar. two legs exited from the passenger door opposite the bar. Another beautiful body came around from the near-side door and the two girls waltzed in together. It was Anneliese and Anya.

Albie left his coffee on the bar and with a pleasant smile and shoulders back, he swaggered out to their table on the front patio. Both girls responded with a sensuous smile. Albie began his chat with compliments. "You were both so brilliant yesterday. You just handled it. How did you get so able with such a vicious attack?"

Anya, using every attractive element of her cute accent said, "Oh Albie, we both worked in bars in Amsterdam and Valencia. Quite often things would deteriorate into gang violence and we learned how to protect ourselves and survive, so now, we can sense it coming. And we both took classes in self-defence. I am proud that I have a black belt in Jiu-jitsu. So if I need to defend us, or indeed, attack anyone, I will!"

Probably his strong attraction to Anya overcame his brain and then his mouth," Hope you don't mind me asking you this, but you were saying earlier that you were staying around for a while. We were having a meeting yesterday. Barry, Rita and myself. We have just got this bar on the road and need more help. We need another barmaid and a waitress. Would you ladies be interested?"

Anneliese, uncrossing her legs as she spoke, said "Oh, I'm not sure Albie. Thanks for the offer but I have a good job, so I will think about it." Anya followed on with a positive response. "Albie, I will accept now! I love the place and the people in it." Smiling directly at Albie!

"Fabulous," said Albie. "I will just go and tell Barry and Rita. "

So, the first CECD infiltration was achieved. In a day or two, Anneliese would wangle her way in.

Barry came out to the patio with Albie. Both guys sat at Anneliese's table. "I'm so pleased you are going to join us Anya. And Anneliese, please think carefully. I would really love you to join our team." Barry was starting to show a strong interest in Anneliese!

Anneliese used every intricate movement in the book to attempt to get him fixated and on her hook! After a few moments silence, with Barry trying not to show it, but admiring every part of Anneliese, Barry ordered some more drinks, on the house!

Rita arrived with the drinks. She said she was so pleased to have help and some female company. Lots of smiles and thank you's, then Rita rushed back to the bar. Anya, immediately said, "It's busy, can I go in and help Rita?" "Yes, of course, if you want but we will arrange some proper training tomorrow."

Anneliese was left with Barry, who by now was becoming besotted. How could he not? He'd never really got involved with her before. Anneliese spoke first. "The police came to question us today. Their questioning had focused on the injuries to the Napoli boys. Despite the attack with the quad bike, the several breaks in the guys' arms and legs did not appear consistent." Just then, Jerome appeared and Barry said, "Come and join us, Jerome." Anneliese and Jerome started to chat with Anneliese asking Jerome how he came to be an airline steward. Barry said he needed to shoot out for a few minutes, Anneliese watched him as he strode off towards the beach.

Barry strolled along the beach front, enjoying the sun and sea breeze, and all the while, thinking! His mind tracked back to the violent events with the Naples guys. Frame by frame, the pictures of what had occurred replayed in this mind. When the police arrived and everyone was ordered to leave the bar, Barry was the last. But he had quickly backtracked, pulled his baseball bat from beneath the bar and systematically and savagely battered the arms and legs of all three of them. The brutal violent streak in his brain had resurrected again!

His mind drifted into possible repercussions. Based on what Anneliese had said, the Spanish police were not as dumb as he thought. So from now on, he had to be very careful. His first port of call would be to the baseball bat. He had to secrete it away somewhere. Next, he would work on Anneliese and get her to give him an alibi. Perhaps he could get her to say he stayed with her all the time, as he helped her out of the bar. Little did he know that Anneliese knew exactly what had happened.

As he walked back towards the bar, his serious expression changed to a smile. The smile was caused by his final thought that the serious fractures all over the bodies of the Naples characters had terminated their activities permanently, and been a severe warning to all rivals!

Over the next several weeks, things began to scorch along. Money had begun to roll in from all areas of the business. The bar was gaining recognition from all locals and, especially, tourists. They had employed a great chef and the bar had a reputation for great atmosphere.... which really meant the bonita's serving in the bar. Regular substantial amounts were being transferred into Barry's Spanish bank from the UK business. Mick Flick and Eddie were doing a good job keeping on top of everything.

Terry and his logistics team had successfully retrieved the canisters of drugs and some small firearms. The drugs were now getting into the market. The local extortion business, replacing the Naples team, had been accepted as reasonably priced. And with that came a bonus of doormen and minders, if requested! Barry had met his new Marbella team and had given them their deals. Everyone was happy!

To crown it all, Jess had been very successful, bought even more coaches, and was beginning to make a mint.

At a personal level, Albie and Anya's relationship had got a lot stronger. Although Anya was deliberately toying with Albie, mostly keeping him wriggling on the hook, but also allowing her temptress scheming to physically enthral him occasionally.

Barry and Rita were now living like man and wife, with continuous rampant sexual gratification. Carefully performing in the background, however, was Anneliese. She knew she had to keep his libido burning with desire. So her approach was provocative but always camouflaged when Rita was around. She would tell Barry that she was not a person to steal a man from another woman. Therefore, nothing would further develop until he was a free man. As she was now working in the bar, most days she was always in Barry's view.

Whenever they could make time, Albie was now making a concerted effort to teach Jerome some boxing, and assault tactics. They had only had a few hours together, but Albie had recognised Jerome as a hard little fella with guts. So now, Albie had approached Anya, asking her to teach Jerome some Jiu-jitsu, Anya relished the idea and would start next time Jerome was in Marbella, which was only a week away! And, of course, Albie would attend with Anya!

24

The special surprise package was Frank. He'd not frequented the bar very often. Possibly a couple of days a week. But he was gradually getting known as the guy that finished that Naples gang. Barry and Albie would sit on the patio, or at the bar, and chat about anything and everything. Frank always had his own look. Wouldn't wear beach shorts, t-shirts and that stuff. He always was smart. Smart but casual in the heat. Casual but in a meticulous way. This impressed Barry and Albie!

Barry and Albie were sitting with Frank on the patio. Barry was feeling stressed. All morning had been questions from everywhere. Terry was finding that keeping control of things was beyond his capabilities. As Barry and Frank talked, it was obvious that Barry had tension eating at him.

Frank looked at Barry and said, "Barry, you look like you need another drink, what do you want? You can have anything, as long as it gets your feet back on ground. Albie, you too; I'm buying!"

After a minute or so of silence, Frank asked Barry, "What's the annoyance? Is it anything I can help with?" Barry wasn't sure how much he should say, so he was guarded. "Well Frank, its several things and they are all coming at me at once!"

"I've decided to put some funds into property around here. A villa that Terry found for me is nearing completion and I'm getting all the bureaucracy to deal with. Of course, it's in Spanish!"

"Then Terry is having a hard time with a new crowd that have had several skirmishes with his people down in Estapona. This team are trying to get their feet under the table and so far, they are doing a good job. Terry keeps bleating he needs some help".

"Then there is trying to keep the bar staff and customers happy, and now my family are wanting to come for a visit. It's all shit stuff, but it has to be dealt with on top of all my other business issues."

Frank turned away for a minute, first looking out to sea, then looking at Albie. "What's ticking in your brain Frank? I can hear it purring and whirring" muttered Albie.

Before Frank spoke, Barry quietly said, "and there's another issue. I have bought some stuff, but it has to be picked up from Seville. So, it's on your plate, Albie; you need to find someone reliable to collect it!"

Frank, in his inimitable quiet controlled fashion said, "Look, guys, I know you are operating what is becoming a big business. I know also that I could help. I would do a very good job for you. I worked for Saints, but that didn't work out. So I think it's time to see what working for Sinners does for me!"

Barry leaned back in his chair, hands behind his head and with a knowing smile uttered, "Frank, I think you may be able to release some of the pressure. We can't talk now, but I will get Terry with us tomorrow morning when its quiet. We can have a proper meet." Albie, disturbed by the thought of getting up early, asked Barry not to make it before 11am. Barry leaned across to Albie, gave him a reluctant cuddle saying," Dipstick, I wouldn't do that cos I know you never see the world before 11am"

The meeting got underway just after 11am. Albie sat quietly, trying to gather himself. Terry had arrived promptly and they were all enjoying some Spanish style coffee. The first thing said was Frank asking if Barry would prefer Frank to call him "Geezer". Barry thought for a moment then said, "No, let's wait a while. I'm giving you a three month trial period, so we can talk again at the end of it!"

In the back of Barry's mind was his intuition about Frank. He had a sneaking suspicion that Frank would turn out to be the best in his team. He had vast military experience, superior intelligence compared to most that worked for him and Barry already had respect for him! So, possibly, he may quickly become a General on a par with Albie, and take a lot of the weight off Barry. However, this was all future speculation.

What came out of their meeting was that, in a few days' time, Albie would partner Frank to get the gear from Seville. They would use one of the superfast Lotus Cortinas' in case they needed to outrun anybody. Secondly, Frank would meet with Terry to develop a plan to subdue the Marseille gang that was causing so much trouble for Terry and his team. Barry wanted to get all this stuff fixed quickly!

They were just about to wrap it up when Barry had an afterthought. Scanning his eyes back and forth to Frank then Albie, he opened up. "I've just remembered that I have an agreement with the Seville warehouse that I can store stuff with them. I need you to take some of the gear that I have stored in the stockroom and arrange with them to handle it on a permanent basis. Our goods will come and go regularly and you two can organise the logistics on a regular basis. Get a price from them and you will pay C.O.D. Are you two comfortable with that?" Frank and Albie both nodded. "And what about you Terry? Can I leave it to you and Frank to suppress, or even, eliminate these French bastards from Marseille?" Terry, opened mouthed, looked across at Frank who replied with a confident smile. "Barry," he said, "I am really going to enjoy this life with you lot! I will get a plan together that Terry will think has fallen out of God's pocket!" The table erupted with laughter and Albie choked on his coffee. Frank appeared not to understand the significance of what he had said. Barry, as he recovered, looking at Frank, said, "Don't worry Frank, I will explain all to you when we move onto the booze!"

During the next week, Barry spent a lot of time thinking about everything. He was an exceptionally good planner and his school education had stuck in the right places. Mathematics was his particular forte which he applied constantly to whatever problem.

He concluded that he had to return to the U.K. to check his business there. Also to show his face and update the fear factor in all the cracks and crevices. The other disorganised element was the females in his life. He, superficially, was partner to Linda. Then there was the local disturbance called Rita. He loved them both. But, the big issue was Anneliese. He was desperate to capture her and engulf her in enthralling passion and love; she was deep under his skin. She was all he was living for everyday! All the rest of it was day to day crap that he had to keep on top of, to maintain his power and lifestyle. Subconsciously, it came second to Anneliese.

In the next few weeks, everything was purely positive. He now owned a beautiful villa and was progressing the purchase of another two. Albie and Frank had executed the Seville trip without any problems. Barry now had a warehouse where he would store his contraband; drugs, cigarettes and even weapons. And Frank had managed with Albie to load enough weapons into their car to inflict serious damage on anyone that challenged their supremacy.

Distribution of their contraband was becoming widespread throughout Marbella and surrounding areas. Cigarettes were the big winner initially, but were now closely followed by hashish and cannabis. The team were working hard to get cocaine off the ground, which would be a big money spinner if it gained acceptance and ongoing growth.

All of Barry's team, the Boleyn Boys, were enthralled with the money they were earning and their elevated status in the Marbella community. But they were not invisible to the CECD. Every individual had been catalogued along with all features of their lives.

Barry, sitting on the apex of the pyramid was feeling he had lost something. The adrenalin rush that he had always experienced from confrontation, was missing. His psyche needed physical assaults, thuggery, brutality, to feed from. This missing element within his life combined with his confused libido, essentially Anneliese, was building a potential ferocious explosion in his mental state.

25

I n contrast, Frank's mental state was perfect, unshakable, controlled and inventive. His mind had been working on how to nullify the Marseille team. He decided to get Anneliese's thoughts. They had a secret meeting on a beach near Estapona. Anneliese understood the issues and asked a myriad of questions. The one that scored was, "Who do you have that may be able to find out where the Marseille characters meet or hang out?" Frank, without needing to think, said, "Terry himself, but more likely, the local Spaniard, Jose." Anneliese suggested that Frank get Jose to visit bars in the area and see if he could come up with anything useful.

Terry and Jose met Frank early the next day. Frank explained that they needed to establish where the whole Marseille team used as their meeting point. Terry looked totally blank as he peered at Frank and then, Jose. It was somewhat understandable to Frank because he had already figured that Terry was not just a dip but also a bit dippy!

With Frank gazing at Jose with a questioning expression, Jose came alive. "Aah, Senor Frank, please thank Barry for my wonderful pay. I love working with you. And yes, that's easy for me." Frank, with a quizzical look, said," Jose, what is easy for you?"

"I know their favourite place," said Jose. "It's down by the beach at Estapona. A beach bar which attracts French people. It's called Playa La Parisienne."

The other thinking and advice from Anneliese had been waiting in the wings. Now Frank brought it into play. She had said, obviously applying her psychology expertise, "You should set a trap for the Marseille faces. One that appears totally innocent but is alluring; giving them most things they desire. Female company, fun, beautiful surroundings, tempting food and plenty of alcohol! And all at no financial cost to them." The conduit to them should be attractive women tempting them to attend. Anneliese had complemented this scenario by saying that, if Frank could set the trap, she would help by providing the female bait.

Frank had the outline. It was time to put the flesh on the bones. He deliberated long and hard. He knew where he wanted to end up, but needed to join all the steps together that would get him there.

The key primary feature was the girls to entice the Frenchmen. His four CECD agents backing him in Marbella had four women on their arms to give them cover as tourists. Two of the females were French. Frank decided they would be used to search out information in the La Parisienne French bar.

The essence of Frank's plan was to arrange a barbeque party in the Sierra Bermeja Mountains, behind Estapona. The girls would leak out details in La Parisienne Bar saying it was a party being organised by some French women. All French people were invited.

Anneliese would supply the hostesses. Frank would persuade Barry to provide food and drink. Jose had told Frank that there was a fabulous waterfall about 5 km into the mountain range, with a natural pool and lots of surrounding cover.... Trees, vegetation etc.

No doubt, when they had seen the girls, the Marseille men would all want to be there. They, almost certainly, would bring drugs with them to get the party in the swing, as well as making money for them. They would then be ripe for an ambush by the Boleyn Boys. And Frank would have the Guardia Civil and Spanish Drugs and Organised Crime Unit ready to take the Marseille gangsters into custody.

The basics of the plan were set. Frank would next arrange to talk with Barry. However, first he would run it by Anneliese who was an absolute guru with this type of operation!

Frank met with Anneliese for breakfast in her hotel. The first thing she told Frank was that she and Anya had rented a flat close to Café Del Mar. Essentially, because it would appear strange paying for a hotel now both her and Anya were on barmaid's wages. After this chat and a second coffee, Frank said he had the basics of a plan and wanted to get Anneliese's thoughts.

"I may have covered this before; but I need about ten of your lady friends from Amsterdam, to come here for a long weekend. I really need most of them to be French. They are the bait for the Marseille fellas."

"The hot spot for the gang is a beach bar in Estapona called La Parisienne. We will get word around in that bar that the girls are organising a party in the foothills of Sierra Bermeja Mountain range. At a secluded spot with a waterfall and a natural pool."

"The girls will show themselves off in the bar just before the event to get the froggies licking their lips. No doubt the Marseille faces will bring drugs and sell some during the party. I will alert the Guardia Civil and Drug

Enforcement Agency to be ready when I give them the "get go". Barry's boys will be secreted around the place. When it's time they can attack. They will be off balance and Barry will win. They will then disappear and I will call in Guardia Civil and Drugs colleagues."

"Anneliese, I would like you and Anya to be there to protect the girls and get them out when I give the alert."

"Frank, you have started with a seedling and must make sure that all the support you will have to give will get it growing straight and tall. Because that is your objective. So in terms of your plan let's consider what you are trying to achieve!"

"The first element of the plan is the bait. All that will work. I know these girls and will make sure that it is perfect. What you are aiming for is the Marseille gang. We want to get them off the scene. They are only minor in this arena. Our major objective is the growing Boleyn Boys operation, both here and in London. Soon, it seems likely they will be across the whole of Europe."

"Your plan, Frank, although nullifying the Marseille boys, may also take Barry or some of his people, out of the equation. When they go into battle, both sides will have casualties. The police will take them all. Furthermore, I have analysed Barry down to the ground. He is a psychopath. I'll explain more to you another time. Therefore, you must keep him well away from this war theatre because he may kill someone and get arrested for it. We would not have much of a chance to get into the details of the business; we need much more time for that."

Frank was now on the edge of his seat. He knew by her assured expression and posture that she would provide the answer. Anneliese continued, "First, you must keep

Barry away from the operation. Get him to the U.K. You had mentioned he was going to catch up with Linda and his family, so that would give us a window. Secondly, have only a few of the Boleyn Boys there as workers. Operating the bar, the food and hospitality. And they would be discreet protection for my girls."

"The next feature is extremely important. We should get the Commander to fund several kilos of cocaine that you would plant to absolutely convince the police to arrest the Marseille team. No doubt they will have their own stash, but the plant would seal it."

"The bottom line is we would have them out of the way and you, me and Anya can get on with the critical operation of tracking and documenting the whole of Barry's business, his assets, his financial framework and his distribution routes."

"If our plan works perfectly, the Marseille team will be destroyed, Barry will be impressed with your work Frank, and extremely grateful. Therefore, he will place much more trust in you! The rest of his team will perceive you as one of their leaders. A massive advance for us, and exactly what we set out to achieve!"

Now, with a huge smile, Anneliese said, "Frank, there is one other plus point. You probably could get the Commander to pull rank and request the Guardia Civil to provide the drug haul to CECD as evidence and for further investigation. The Commander would have his investment returned in full!"

Frank came away from the meeting feeling that all he had to do now was to get Barry to go to the U.K as soon as possible. Once Frank had the date, he would throw everything into organising and mobilising the necessary people. Anneliese and Anya would handle the girls' flight in, and other arrangements for the party.

26

While everybody had been preoccupied with ongoing business, Barry had put a lot of time in, over the last weeks, analysing his business and attempting to plan a new business model which would expand his operation into Western Europe. In his mind he had been developing some firm plans that he could execute in his usual dedicated, precise and resourceful way. He had been researching how to maintain complete secrecy, during the business expansion implementation. His knowledge of Problem Analysis, which he had studied at school, together with his ability in Mathematics, was leading him down a path that would guarantee secrecy. Or, at least, that was his thinking.

It would be a secret coding language that only he and trusted members of his team would be able to decipher. He had already worked out some of the basics and was close to a solution. Then he would need some help with testing it!

With his tunnel vision locked firmly on Anneliese and his new business model, he had neglected Rita. Their sexual relationship had become almost non-existent. The passion had almost fizzled out. Rita had been putting her heart and soul into the bar, hoping that this would please Barry and help resurrect his loving attention. She had also begun to notice little things with Barry's approach to Anneliese. However, she tried not to let her mind gain acceptance, hoping that things would improve.

Barry was about to make matters worse for Rita. He told her he needed to visit his family and his girlfriend, Linda, in the U.K. This hit her hard. She imagined this meant she was about to lose him! She tried to get him to talk but he would have none of it. He made many excuses, constantly repeating this had nothing to do with their relationship. He just had a lot on his plate at the moment.

Two days later, Jerome arrived. He was planning to stay for a week as he had some vacation to take. In his usual way, he was non-stop comical. Albie was really pleased to see his little smiling face. Jerome, almost immediately, went behind the bar to help Rita. Albie sat at the bar so he could continue his catch up with Jerome.

Frank appeared during the evening session. They all sat together, close to the bar, and a drinking session gradually evolved. It was a fairly quiet evening and for most of the time, Anneliese and Anya were able to join in. At one point, Albie was saying that he, Jerome and Anya would do some more self-defence training.

Jerome, looking very proud of himself, stood up and announced that he had used what they taught him just last weekend. "What happened then Jerome" asked Albie. Everybody was now all ears. Jerome took up a comical, hands on hips stance, and with his effeminate tone said, "Keeping a long story short, last weekend I went with some friends to the Marquee Club in Wardour Street. We were at the bar having a giggle. A big prick took exception to us, saying "What are you fannys doing in here? This is a respectable club."

"Without even thinking, I did a twirl, to throw his mind off balance, then punched him right in his Adam's apple. I followed that with an accurate kick in the knackers! He folded like a fan... or maybe a fanny!"

Anya and Albie, following disbelief, broke into uncontrollable laughter. Everybody followed, then stood and clapped their new little soldier.

As the group began to settle again, Barry got up and wandered out to the patio, then out of sight. A couple of minutes later, Anneliese strolled out, and standing on the patio, lit one of her Sobranie cigarettes. Barry had gone to the side of the bar, out of sight. The next thing Anneliese heard was, "psssst Anneliese!" She realised it was Barry and sauntered over to him. "I just wanted to tell you that next Friday I'm going back to the U.K. I will finish my relationship with Linda. You already know why. You have demanded it and I respect you for that. Will I have any chance with you when I return?" Anneliese leaned forward, grasped Barry's hand and kissed him. "You will be, without doubt, in with a chance! I have strong feelings for you but I need to know I am your one and only." He was playing right into her hands!

One at a time, they wandered back inside. Nobody seemed to notice. Albie was at the bar getting another round in. Anya had been upstairs and changed into some very alluring clothes. Figure hugging blue velvet dress and exceptionally high heels. She wobbled, but elegantly, as she arrived and went straight to Albie. She lent all over him limpet fashion. They were now an item and spent much time in the flat above the bar. Albie always had a smile and was in a good place.

That was until Barry said, "When we get home what do you have in mind to say to Shirley." "Oh shit, I'd forgotten we were going back!" The disappointment in his voice related to leaving Anya rather than seeing Shirley. "It's just a week or so" said Barry. "You will survive without Anya for that long!"

They left Friday afternoon, with all their group standing on the patio waving goodbye. Rita stood tearfully waving, feeling as if she was already in mid-air! Where would her life with Barry be in a week's time?

27

Early evening, Frank sat with Anneliese and Anya on the patio. They would be going over the plans for the barbeque party. The Amsterdam girls were arriving Sunday and would stay at the Estapona hotel. Jose would be their guide and go with them to the La Parisienne beach bar on Monday. They would spread the word amongst the customers saying it was a celebration for the birthday of a girl named Elise.

They agreed that only a few of their team would be around, and mostly in the background. Two of the CECD ex-mercenaries, Anneliese, Anya and Jose would be hospitality staff. Frank would be delivery driver for food and drink. Terry would provide transportation back and forth through the foothills, using a tractor and trailer. There would be two more large 4x4 vehicles driven by the remaining CECD ex-mercenaries. Their two French girls had already put the word around about the party, and they now would join the large group of girls.

All the hospitality staff and drivers would wear light blue overalls. The Guardia Civil had been alerted that people wearing these uniforms were not to be apprehended. Frank would be in the centre of things from the start, delivering the food and ensuring that the cocaine stash was well secreted in the food cold boxes.

Wednesday would be D Day. Frank and Terry would be first there, delivering the food and booze to the site. Terry would guard the deliveries until it was time for the girls to arrive.

Anneliese said the Amsterdam girls would head straight to Malaga airport as soon as the ambush was positive. She would pay them off at the airport.

Only Frank, Anneliese, Anya and the CECD backup guys knew details of the Sting plan that involved the Guardia Civil and Spanish Drug Enforcement Agency. All others just thought it was a real party for friends of Anneliese and Anya. French girls they first met when they were staying at the Estapona hotel.

Frank wanted, when it was all over, to give Barry a debrief that gave the appearance that he had planned to take the Boleyn Boys into battle with the Marseille faces. To that end, he had ordered Terry to arrange for all his soldiers to be tooled up and ready to get quickly to the site. But they should only move when they had the "get go" from Frank. When the Marseille gang were ripe for attack!

With this in Frank's pocket, Barry would not suspect any of his own people when he heard the police had turned up before battle commenced. And he would have no reason to suspect the cocaine had been planted!

The Sting site had a raised elevation in front of a natural pool. Beyond the pool was a spectacular thirty foot high waterfall with rocks and ledges either side. Conifer trees and shrub land surrounded the area which was reached by a dirt track road, easily usable by vehicles.

The day arrived! It was exceptionally hot; nearly 40 degrees C. Frank, up early as usual and cool and collected as always; he was looking forward to a perfect execution. He was first at the site, having collected the food from a distributor in Marbella. He would do another trip for the alcohol. He set off for the booze trip, whilst Terry stayed close to the food, with a revolver Frank had given him.

Frank returned and unloaded. Terry was picked up in a BMW 4x4 by one of the CECD ex-mercenaries and went back down the track to collect the girls. They were both excited by this part of the operation. They arrived back about 45 minutes later. A tractor towing a trailer with bales of hay and a multitude of women balancing on them. Another BMW 4x4 with girls, and some of the La Parisienne customers.

This collection of French females was every man's dream. They were all dressed for this exceptionally hot day. Flimsy dresses, tiny shorts, t shirts lacking bras. And so excited when they saw the pool and waterfall.

It was close to lunchtime. The other 4x4 arrived with a few customers from La Parisienne. Everybody was enthralled by the surroundings; the natural pool, and especially the waterfall.

Several people began to strip off. It was such a hot day who could blame them. Even if police had arrived to arrest them, they would have continued. Most of the French girls, by now, were topless. Diving into the pool; climbing on the rocks, beside the waterfall and launching in. The pool was now covered in white water!

Expletives from the French girls were constant. Senor, c'est fantastiques, was a regular call. The men working around were astounded by the beauty they were adoring.

Frank managed to get their minds back on the job. The barbeque was underway. The bar was open and there was a constant flow of French madamoiselles seeking a top-up. The aromas from the sizzling food tormented everyone's palates. It was all going like a dream.

The Marseille team arrived early afternoon. Stepping out of a large black Mercedes bus, ten of the faces swaggered over to the girls by the pool, nodding to the hospitality staff as they went. Within a few minutes, they returned to the bar to order drinks.

They had come dressed for the occasion, mostly wearing lightweight unstructured summer jackets. After a couple of drinks, the jackets were being discarded, along with their other clothes; down to Bermuda shorts. The mademoiselles were making them very welcome in the pool.

Unknown to them all, their every movement was being watched by the secret agents stationed and camouflaged in the trees around the mountains.

Another half an hour and the barbeque offerings, along with a massive pan of paella were ready. Jose turned and shouted to the groups that had formed, "Barbeques are ok, dejeune, dejeune!" They were hurrying to get served. As they did, Frank sauntered casually off toward the Mercedes bus. He, on his knees, slowly opened the front passenger door and pushed a parcel under the passenger seat. Then, strolling in a casual way, he joined Jose to help with serving.

During the next hour, mixed doubles began to appear all over. The girls found the men they liked and the men latched onto the girls they were salivating for! Two of the Marseille faces were wandering around with a small pouch. Packets were being offered and openly purchased. Mostly, the men were buying these as presents for the girls!

This was the time. The Guardia Civil and Drugs Agency knew they had enough evidence to convict with what was around in the site. They advanced en masse. Guns trained on everyone. Loud hailers shocked everyone into static positions.

The police lined everybody up. Most of the girls still in their bikinis. Some of the bar customers were at the end of the line. The drugs agents began searching around. Within a few minutes, the officer searching the Mercedes shouted. Although, it was in Spanish, it was obvious to everyone that he had found a drugs haul.

The police immediately herded the Marseille characters towards two police vans that had just arrived. They were handcuffed as they entered the vehicles. Once they were inside the vehicles, the girls were taken by Jose to their assembly point. The 4x4s' arrived within minutes. They were taken to their hotel to collect their belongings and then off to Malaga airport. It all sounds rushed, but on the way, all they could talk about was what a wonderful time they had enjoyed, and getting paid for it! Sure enough, Anneliese was there to meet them. Bundles of cash were handed over, and Anneliese kissed every one of them. With grateful thanks she said, "I love you all and I may need you again sometime."

Later she went back to Café Del Mar to meet up with Frank. The operation had been a complete success according to Frank. The Marseille team would be off the streets for a very long time. The police, customs and drugs agency personnel were overjoyed. This was the first time they had been able to get them all in one place and nail them. They had all been carrying weaponry, mainly guns, but they were overwhelmed by the authorities' forces. There had been a few attempted assaults on the police, which, on top of everything else would not go well for them. With all the cocaine and other narcotics that were found, they would all be going away for a long time. Frank and Anneliese saw this result as a distinct opportunity to continue their advancement into the underbelly of Barry's growing operation in contraband and illicit narcotics. They knew they needed more time to pinpoint all the personnel involved and the trafficking routes. But they intended playing it carefully, slowly and patiently.

Barry and Albie would be back on Friday. If Anneliese was correct, Barry would place a lot more trust in Frank, which would give them greater access to the business. Anneliese would continue to work her wonders on Barry to gain greater access to the hierarchy. Anya was already totally accepted into Albie's mind and thinking. So, all around, it seemed positive!

28

Friday evening, Barry and Albie appeared. Barry was pleased to see everyone and mostly talked about his mum and Jess and how well they were doing. However, in front of Rita, he was fairly cool with Anneliese.

Anya and Albie planned to spend the night together in the flat above the bar. Drinks were forth coming for everyone and banter and storytelling began. The moment Rita disappeared into the stock room, Barry separated Anneliese from the rest, and said, "Can I stay at your flat tonight so I can explain how it all went?" It was a simple response. "Yes" said Anneliese. The drinking and socialising continued for another hour.

Frank had been biding his time. He cornered Barry away from the rest of the group. Quietly explained the Marseille episode. Barry listened intently to every word. "So the Marseille team are off my patch and will not trouble us anymore?" "Correct" said Frank.

Barry's psychotic side exploded. He grabbed Frank and said, "But that's not what I wanted. I needed them massacred." Grabbing Frank by the neck, he shouted, "why? Are you a fucking pussy?"

Frank had no choice. With all his strength, he grabbed Barry's hand and gave him a fierce glare! "Listen, Barry," he said, "I had no choice! I had all our guys ready to attack, then the police arrived. I managed to get all your troops to safety. What more could I do? So fire me!"

Barry calmed down and went back to the bar looking pretty sorry for himself. Frank came behind him and whispered, "I'm sorry Barry, but I didn't deserve that; I did my best. Got them all there, everything was set to be perfect. Then the police arrived. What was I supposed to do? The end result is they are not in competition with you anymore. You now have a clear run in this area. "All the time Anneliese was listening and watching!

Terry and Jose turned up. They got drinks and began talking with the group. Barry gradually moved himself next to Terry and when Rita moved away to serve, he said, "Terry, I need you to give me a ride soon. Only take a few minutes" Terry smiled.

His next step was Rita at the end of the bar. He held her hand and quietly told her that he had some work to do with Terry and the rest of the Boleyn Boys. "I don't know how long it will take but then, I promise, we will have time together." Rita, knowing Barry, and with a worried expression, said "Barry be careful, don't get hurt!" He smiled and looking into her eyes replied, "I will be as fit as a butchers dog, and just as hungry for you when I get back."

The car journey to Anneliese's apartment was only about ten minutes. On the way, Barry asked Terry about the events with the Marseille gang. "Why didn't you smash those bastards, Terry?" "It was all organised and we were ready" replied Terry. "Frank had done a fantastic job luring them there and all our guys were kitted out and ready to massacre them; then, out of the blue, the police arrived. They were everywhere like ants on a summer's day! Frank did well to warn us all, otherwise we would all have ended up behind bars." Terry thought for a moment, then said, "I suspect it was one of their own that gave the game away because they had been having internal strife. The jungle drums had been saying they were suffering a leadership battle. Or it could have been someone from Le Parisienne bar. But Barry, it worked out really well for us."

Terry dropped Barry outside a bar, opposite Anneliese's apartment. He asked Terry to quietly let Anneliese know where he was. The last thing Barry said to Terry was, "We need to all meet soon to talk about some new business that came my way on the trip to London. Keep in touch!"

Anneliese's shift finished about 30 minutes after Barry had left. She arrived in a taxi and strolled into the bar. She looked stunning. Chic, with sensual movement like a flower gently blowing in the wind! Barry's mind was already besotted with the angelic persona she exuded.

Just one drink, then they strolled off to Anneliese's apartment. As they crossed the road, Barry put his arm around her waist and pulled her close. She pushed him away, whispering, "No Barry, someone may see us and I need to hear what you have to tell me first!"

Whilst Barry and Albie had been in the U.K. they had made time to have a night out in London. To be precise, together with a few of his lieutenants, they all went for a few drinks in Soho. It was Barry's treat to thank them for keeping everything ticking. They finished up in the Pink Flamingo Club in Wardour Street, on the edge of Soho.

A Flamboyant wealthy looking character sat at the bar, with three beautiful girls chatting and laughing with him. As Barry was ordering a round, one of the girls responded to Barry when he attempted some chat. The opulent looking guy joined in and then offered his hand to Barry and introduced himself. He was well spoken; almost the

Queen's English, but with a fairly strong hint of a foreign accent.

Conversation started up in earnest. Barry found him interesting, with stories he had to tell about gambling, in casinos in London and Monte Carlo. In his childhood, Barry had researched Monte Carlo because an aunt of his had been, as a tourist, and brought him back a key ring with the Monte Carlo coat of arms on it.

Mr Flamboyant introduced himself as Igor. He was Russian, but living all around Europe. With the colourful descriptions of Monte Carlo, the Casino and people that frequented it, Barry aligned it with a James Bond adventure.

Barry and the Russian hit it off. Eventually, they were opening up and giving basic details of the sorts of lives they were leading. A level of common trust began to emerge. Then Albie and a few of the Boleyn Boys joined in. Probably the girls were the big attraction and they responded with amorous advances to all of them.

Whilst their partying was growing, Igor pulled Barry aside and asked "So where do you want to take your business next?" Barry responded with conviction. "We are going into Europe in a big way! I have all the facilities and resources and know I can make it happen."

Igor said, "Barry, I have a meeting to go to now, but we can assist one another, so let's keep in close contact. I am a good judge of people and know we can be a success together." They already had exchanged contact details so Barry was pleased with his night's work.

Except, as Igor began up the stairway to the exit, Barry watched a few lads, with their eyes on Igor, follow behind from a safe distance. Barry, due to what had become second nature to him in the East End, suspected they were out to mug Igor.

Barry grabbed hold of Albie. "I need you and a couple of the others to come with me to sort some trouble. It's our new business partner, Igor; looks like he's about to be mugged."

Eddie, Mick Flick and Albie booted it up the stairs behind Barry. When they arrived in the street, nobody was to be seen. But Barry remembered the alleyway a few yards down. As they approached, they heard some shouts and "No, no, why?"

As Barry and the Boleyn Boys turned into the alley, they passed crates of bottles. They all grabbed one. The muggers leader had Igor pressed against the wall and was stripping his watch off his wrist.

This was the adrenalin rush that Barry had been missing. He completely enjoyed his psychotic episodes! They made him feel whole again. The Boleyn Boys attacked the muggers with fearless ferocity. All of them were now on the ground, being kicked relentlessly and beaten with bottles, some broken, but still the assault continued.

Barry made the ringleader his target, first beating him almost senseless with a bottle. Whilst Barry was enjoying the terror they were creating, he wanted to make his mark. He shouted to Albie "bring a crate over." Albie then held the ringleader secure. Barry, with a callous smile said, "You won't chase anyone anymore." He lifted the crate and smashed the guy's feet into tiny fragments!

They left the muggers on the floor of the alley and helped Igor out. As Barry was checking he was OK, he was also putting Igor's watch back on and stuffing his gold wristband and necklace into his pocket. One last comment from Barry to Igor was about the watch." Igor, I can see why they wanted this. It's a Patek Philippe! When you are on your own, out and about, don't wear it! It's a red rag to a bull!"

29

But now, Barry was back in Marbella, almost in the arms of Anneliese. His searing desire constantly tormented him and distracted him from the business. So he had to find a way to get his mind in a calm and settled place, the only answer seemed to be a strong loving relationship with Anneliese. He had to become a one woman man. She had to be his permanent "one and only." And knowing himself as well as he did, he wasn't sure that was possible. Further complicating this was Rita! He needed time to think this through.

Nevertheless, here and now he was alone with Anneliese in her apartment. She, with her back to him was pouring them some drinks, all the time applying psychoanalysis to the situation to determine where to exert pressure or influence.

She asked him, as she passed him a large whisky, "Barry, did you have a good time back home? Was everything running smoothly there?" Barry, looking somewhat stressed, said, "Yes, some of it was fine. Mum was in a good place... well until I ruined it! I had a get together with Linda which ended with us breaking up. I have given her the house and she wants me to buy her a small bakers business nearby. I agreed, then she didn't appear too distraught. But Mum did. She loves Linda and couldn't understand the break-up."

Anneliese felt responsible. She didn't like that feeling one bit. But this was her job, so tonight she would focus on her career! Romance gradually developed. The conversations, with them getting much closer, developed. Barry told Anneliese about the evening in the Pink Flamingo. The Russian he had met and what it may do for his business. The whisky had loosened his tongue and he realised it. Anneliese could read his thoughts, so she pulled him close. "Barry, I know what your business involves. I have for some time, and I am proud of you. You have more guts than any man I have ever known." Barry, with arm around Anneliese on the sofa, cuddled up close to her. With a sad expression he looked at Anneliese and said, "For the second time in my life, I feel I have messed up. I did love Linda, so much, but for some reason it faded. Whatever caused that, I feel responsible. She didn't deserve it! And now to repay me, she is taking revenge by refusing to handle the books for the business. That could build a disaster for me. But I guess I do deserve it."

Anneliese put her hands on Barry's cheeks and turned his head to look at her. "Darling, you are looking at a woman who has spent her life studying to get a business degree. Finance, money, numbers are my hobby now, because I love it. So if you need me to work for you, as well as love you, I am available." Barry's face lit up. She poured some more drinks whilst Barry contemplated his luck!

Barry's careful head; the suspicious head returned. As he snuggled up to Anneliese he asked, "So with all your qualifications why didn't you go to work for one of the blue chip major companies?" "Well, I went for a few interviews and they all told me the same thing. I would start at the bottom, competing with other graduates all doing boring brain-addling jobs. Possibly for years. Anya found the same and we both agreed we could do that anytime. Whilst we were young we should attack life and travel and enjoy ourselves. So that's what we did, and are both pleased with the outcome."

With that, Barry pulled Anneliese closer and said, "! Can't imagine anything better than working with you, seeing you almost every day. However, it's a very complicated business and Linda kept all the books. You will have to study them and work out what it all means. I don't think I could do it, although I was good at school, but I am sure you will crack it!"

"I'm not sure how this sits with you, but Rita will have to stay with us for a while. We can see how it works out. I think I should set you up in an office here and we can meet in one of my villas."

Anneliese replied "It's not my idea of perfection but we have a consensus! "Barry with a questioning expression said, "What's consensus?" Anneliese pulled him close and gave a soft and tender kiss. "It means we can both live with it, for now!"

Anneliese stood and went to the stereo and placed a long playing vinyl disc on. As it began, she took Barry's hand and pulled him up to dance with her. Barry was not in his comfort zone and Anneliese recognised that. One arm tightened around his waist as she pulled him closer and closer. The music was cool, romantic, Frank Sinatra. The first song was, "Under My Skin." Barry was swallowed up by the romantic spell that the music and hypnotic swaying generated.

When the music finished, Anneliese handed Barry his drink saying, "Drink up." She walked to the chair in the corner, picked up Barry's jacket and handed it to him saying, "I suppose it's time for you to get back to Rita."

Barry was speechless; his emotions were in turmoil. This experience was a piece of Anneliese's psychology being applied at the crucial time. It was designed to demonstrate she would always be in complete control!

Just as Barry had recovered enough to speak, Anneliese, laughing, snatched the jacket back, threw it on the chair and pulled him close. "I said you could stay" She uttered, "and I would really love it if you did. Every minute of the day you mean more to me, and I know we will be great together."

Without another word, Anneliese led Barry into the dimly lit bedroom. This would be a night that Barry would never forget; indeed, never want to forget! She had, in her mind, rehearsed this chapter. She would gradually engulf his psyche with tender passion that grew in intensity, until it erupted, overwhelming both body and soul. From now on, he would belong to her!

30

Next morning, Barry felt on top of the world. He had business on his mind because he knew he could handle anything now. He felt super-human. He would see Anneliese in the afternoon at the bar. But now he planned to muster the troops and move the whole business up a gear.

When Barry arrived at the bar, he got together with Rita and Albie. He outlined that he had got some really good business underway with some Russians and needed to get his top team together. "Albie, I want Frank, Terry, Jose and you for a meeting this afternoon." Looking at Rita, he asked, "When is Jerome arriving because I will need him too." "Tomorrow" said Rita. Albie would arrange the meet early afternoon in the back of the bar.

Now, Barry and Albie settled down for a couple of drinks at the bar. After a few minutes, Anya joined them, leaning on Albie as she ordered a drink. She stood between Barry and Albie, then speaking to Barry she said, "I overheard what you were saying about Russians. I am fluent in Russian so maybe I could be of help. Very few Russians are trustworthy, so when you meet with them, I could pretend to be your secretary and sit in the background, ostensibly taking notes, but really listening to any of their chat!"

Albie spoke up. "Boss that could be a great idea. In our business we have to be very careful." Barry thought for a moment, then, looking at Albie said, "Anneliese told me that Anya understood what we were into; is that true? Have you explained it? "Anya interrupted saying, "Yes, but we had worked it out for ourselves. We want to be involved. We want some excitement, and with the quad bike event, I think we proved we can handle it."

Just at that moment, Anneliese arrived. On her way to Café Del Mar, her thoughts had been focusing on Barry. She was beginning to be very attracted to him and couldn't wait to see him again. But as a professional, she was denying it to herself.

Anneliese went to sit with Anya as she said hello to everyone. Anya explained what had been said about the Russian contact and how she could be involved. Anneliese just responded with a knowing smile. They had successfully completed a perfect pincer movement into Barry's organisation.

With his mind in an ultra-clear state, uplifted by his time with Anneliese, Barry had decided he should prepare for the worst, which possibly, he would create. He indicated to Albie that he needed to talk. They went to the pool table and began setting up. Out of earshot of everyone, Barry said he wanted to increase his teams' weaponry. A new shipment into the Seville warehouse was waiting to be collected. Albie would make all necessary arrangements. Barry continued, "I want to be better prepared for trouble, especially if we get involved with the Russian Mafia. And we need to do more to wake people up to our presence, both here and in the U.K. So all our troops should start to be more intimidating, more threatening; more ferocious. You can take the lead on that, Albie. And speak with the guys back home. I want Eddie and Mick Flick to continue as our Generals in East London and Essex. Tell them to get as much supply as the can lay their hands on. And Mac and Danny should hire whoever they need and take on North and West London. They will all get a bigger share of the proceeds."

The extortion racket was going well everywhere. Drug supply and distribution was becoming a massive money-spinner. Cigarettes also were showing dramatic growth and returns. And bent authorities and police were assisting their efforts in the property market, as well as easing the path for almost every aspect of their criminal activities.

Early evening, they all sat together and enjoyed some food and drinks. Afterwards, Barry walked forward with a canvas shopping bag. He called Anneliese over, gave her the bag and said, "These are the books. I think you should go now, and let me know tomorrow if you can make any sense of them!" Anneliese realised Barry was deliberately playing it cool in front of Rita.

That night, Barry slept with Rita, attempting to keep their relationship on some form of distorted course. He was a coward when it came to delivering bad news to women in his world. Rita was happy with the outcome and back in a comforted zone!

Unsurprisingly, Anneliese also was in a good place, even though she had suspected Barry would sleep with Rita. Anneliese was a totally liberated female. She had demonstrated that by working in the Red Light district of Amsterdam. Just doing a job for her boss! Rita did not bother her, because she knew that her own ability to entice and enthral men could not be surpassed!

The following day, Igor phoned. He would be arriving for a meeting on Friday, two days hence. He was driving down from Belgium and looking forward to some warm weather. After the call, Barry got together with Albie and said they should meet, with both Anneliese and

Anya included. It was close to lunchtime when Anneliese breezed in.

She had spent the previous evening micro-filming the books, which Frank had then taken to be collected by CECD Intelligence Officers. It would be subjected to detailed work by analysts at the Central Command Base.

Later, they all sat together at the back of the bar. It was a very hot day and both girls wanted to get onto the patio with the sea breeze. Barry said, "Don't think this will take long, so please bear with me. You two girls are now part of our team and I need us to talk together." Turning to Anneliese, Barry asked, "Did you get any understanding of it?" "Oh yes, I got the whole thing, and I can keep it updated for you." Anneliese continued saying, "But there is an issue. How do I get updated details from the U.K. sitting out here in Marbella?"

They all glanced around at one another. Barry, being a relatively clever sod said, "Well, how did Linda get info from Spain?" Anneliese smiled and said, "that's easy. Marbella was small beer! You gave her details, as far as you had them, when she was here. And she had brought the U.K. data with her. But that finished and it was the end of the road!" They all sat and looked at each other for a minute or two. Anya was the first person to speak.

"Jerome will be here tonight. Could he, perhaps, collect the information from your people in the U.K. He's here every week so it would be easy to keep on top of it." Barry stood up, as did Albie, and both approached her with wide smiles of relief. Barry gave her a very strong cuddle, with Albie watching, with a tormented look.

Barry then began to give details of the Friday meeting with Igor. Just as he was explaining his plans, Frank strolled in. Barry, immediately seeing Frank, waved frantically, shouting, "Frank come and join us." He went straight into introductions. This is Anya and this is Anneliese. Frank, reticent as usual, leaned back in his chair and said, "We have met already, during the quad bike episode."

Ten minutes later, Jerome bustled in with his low slung luggage bag. Anya shouted, "Another one to join us. Come and sit with us!"

It was becoming a large group and the bar was also filling. Jerome circled the group with hugs for everybody. Barry was first to speak, "Jerome, I need your help with a couple of things and perhaps we could talk in a minute. Get yourself a drink first." Then Barry turned to Frank and asked, "Could you do me a favour. I want to get a good car. You seem to know cars, so could you find me something. Expense is no object but I don't want something that attracts loads of attention. Needs to carry four passengers and be fast, if there is such a thing!"

Frank, carefully and slowly responded. "If you want as you describe, it will get some attention. But if you got a car that is not exotic, but still gives you what you want, it would have to be a Jaguar. My preference would be an "S" type. Fantastic car but nowhere near as pretentious as Lamborghini, Maserati or Bentley. And half the price!"

"Sounds good, Frank, could you see if you could find me one. I will pay you a commission!" "No need," said Frank, "I will enjoy searching it out."

Now it was Jerome's turn. Barry held his arm and they wandered to the end of the bar. "Jerome, two things I want to cover with you. First, I need some administration paperwork brought here, regularly. Let me have your address and do you have a home phone?" Jerome, looking pleased to be given this task said, "Yes Geezer." Barry put his arm round Jerome's shoulders and said, "It will be a great help if you could do this every two weeks." He continued, "My two fellas are Mick and Eddie and they will be in touch with you. Also, I will drum it into them that they must treat you as one of my best team and they need to look after you. They are great guys and you can be sure they will never let anyone harm you again. You are very important to me and I am impressed with the effort you have put in to learning to look after yourself."

"I had said there were two things" said Barry. "The next one is; do you fly in regularly to Amsterdam or Brussels? "Jerome smiled as he replied, "Yes geezer, every week to both!" "That's great, "said Barry with a huge grin. "I may need that, but that can wait."

Anya had been listening to Barry's talk with Jerome. She went behind his chair and with arms around his neck, whispered, "Barry, hope you don't mind me offering a suggestion." "No," said Barry, glancing back at her. "What is it?" "If you need something for your business from around Amsterdam or Brussels, I have a very close friend in Amsterdam, who deals with both areas. He knows all the suppliers and dealers covering that area and I could introduce him to Jerome if you wanted. I know he would look after him and it may get us what you are looking for."

Barry thought for a few seconds, then turned in his chair, and looking into Anya's eyes said, "Darling, you are a dream. That may be the leverage I need with or without the Russians. Would you talk to him and then we can set something up with Jerome."

Anya replied, "Of course, Barry, no problem." As she turned away, he tapped her bottom and she gave him a grin.

31

The Friday meeting was next on the cards. He, Barry, spent from early morning with Anneliese in her flat, mostly love-making, then discussing how the meeting should be handled. Anneliese was very clear on how the proceedings should go. "Let him speak, let him rant on, if that's what he wants to do, but don't let him dominate you."

The meet was planned for a small conference room at the back of the Estapona Hotel. Barry's plan was to have Albie, and Anya in the meeting with him. Frank would be stationed outside, watching every move. Frank, once informed, arranged for his four CECD colleagues also to be around the hotel in case of trouble. They would all be in a state of alert with machine pistols secreted in their vehicles!

Their car arrived and two huge characters stepped out of the front. Both wore dark lounge suits. One with a goatee beard and large pointed shoes. The other, with a closely shaved head, opened a rear door. Out slowly stepped Igor, engulfed in flamboyance. He could have been confused with a London Theatre actor. Wearing a bright blue velvet jacket, neatly tied cravat, with his paisley waistcoat sitting uncomfortably on his rotund belly.

One of the reception ladies stepped out to meet them, escorting them down the hallway to the room. The door opened quietly and slowly. Igor was first to enter and with a confident smile, headed straight towards Barry.

His colleagues settled either side of the door. Barry, with a pleasurable expression stood, turned and met him halfway. After a generous embrace, Barry led Igor first to Anya, introducing her as "Annie", his administrator. He turned and introduced Albie. "He's my cousin and we do everything together. Always have and always will."

With that, Igor spoke with perfect English. "Barry, I know you will understand that we have a self-protection protocol. Are you ok with us just checking there is no chance of leaks from this meeting?" "Yeah, if you want," replied Barry.

The two minders went to Anya and Albie. The goatee beard made a meal of frisking Anya for wires and weapons. She kept a false smile on her face as he did his work. Albie was similarly checked and managed self-control. Next they checked the room thoroughly!

They all settled down around a table, with Igor's minders standing either side of the door. A self-service coffee machine was the domain of Anya and she served coffee for everyone. Now it was down to business.

Igor spoke first. "This is a fabulous place Barry. I've never been to Marbella before but I can see why it's becoming so popular." Barry leaned back in his chair, half laughed and gestured to Igor a thumbs up as he drank some coffee. Then. Dabbing his lips with a white linen napkin, Barry began; "Igor, when we talked in London, I told you that getting into Europe would do wonders for my business. You seemed to be saying you may be able to help with that!"

Igor, stroking his chin, gave a wry smile. His expression hardened as he eyeballed first Albie, then Barry. "Very true, but I expect something in return. Let me explain!"

"I have a fabulous level of supply, especially cocaine which has increasing demand in Central Europe. The supply routes are established with the necessary infrastructure. What I need is distribution talent that can grow the European business. If you can find a way to organise it, the distribution business could be yours. Depending on how fast you can grow that element of the business will dictate the share of profits."

"Barry, may I continue regarding another feature I have been giving thought to." Barry, lifting his coffee to his lips again, sipped and with a somewhat gurgled response said, "Be my guest."

"I have negotiated an excellent deal with Colombian colleagues. It gives me sufficient supply to double the level of my business. This means I will have to find ways and means to double the size of my markets. As I already explained, increased distribution in central Europe will go part way towards that opportunity. Another part would be to increase the take-up in Spain and France. They are poor for us at the moment."

"So what I am looking for is a joint venture with you here in Southern Europe. You would need to agree to allow us in and for us to work together, in harmony."

Barry stood up, grinned as he looked around at everyone in the room. He began a low tone giggle and burst out with "I think it's time we had a good strong drink! Annie, would you go to reception and ask if they could send a drinks trolley in with their best whisky, brandy and vodka?" Anya went immediately to the door, giving the minders a glorious smile as she flicked her hair back!

A few minutes later, she arrived back in the room and sat quietly making a few notes. Igor said, "Young lady,

I assume there is nothing in your notes that could be construed as incriminating? Albie lent across and, looking at the page in front of Anya said, "No it's just meeting minutes as if it was a normal business meeting. Cleverly disguised, but a good reminder. You can read it all if you want."

Igor leaned across and took the page, read it, and smiled. "Annie, you are worthy of your position." "Thank you" as he received a seductive lip pursing smile from Anya. Igor continued, "Barry and Albie, if we can make this an outstanding venture, we have the possibility to be the biggest business in Europe." The drinks arrived and as the waitress left, Barry stood once again, and exclaimed, "We will all drink to that!"

The convened meeting was at an end. Everybody had accepted that the strategy was deliverable. With that, Barry invited his guests back to Café Del Mar.

Barry and his small team arrived back first. Igor and his guys had followed. Anya waited outside to greet the Russians. Igor and his two minders followed her in as she wiggled, up the steps, in front of them. Inside, Barry and Albie were already lining up drinks. Anneliese, sitting with Barry, stood up to greet Igor and his men. It was clear that they were blown away by Anneliese's beauty. They each stared, as if mesmerised, as she approached each of them and kissed their cheeks. Igor clearly was a man excited by beautiful women, and immediately turned on his charm.

Next to arrive was Terry and Jose. And the place was beginning to buzz with customers. Drinks were flowing. Rita was becoming overworked so Anya joined her behind the bar. Rita, as they worked, began asking Anya how the day had gone. Once or twice, she called Anya by her real name, so she cornered Rita and said, "While these guys are here please call me Annie. Barry doesn't want them to know I speak Russian."

Barry, all the while was attempting to impress Igor with his people. Just as he'd introduced Terry and Jose as two of his Generals, Frank arrived. As he strolled to the bar and Barry was preparing to introduce him, he was finding it difficult to distract Igor's attention from Anneliese. Igor was caught in her web. His libido was inflamed. He was attempting to maintain his ability to string words together to impress Anneliese, but she had dealt with this thousands of times before.

Frank joined Barry. After some chat, with Albie joining in, Frank with a whispered smile said, "Think I've got you a car you will like." Barry swivelled in his chair and with an expectant expression said "Where is it, what is it?" "It's outside" said Frank. "Do you want a gander?" Barry turned to Igor who was still talking to Anneliese. "I just need to go outside for a few minutes." Igor nodded. Anneliese, looking at Frank with furrowed brow, watched as they hustled out front.

The car was directly opposite the bar. Gleaming maroon colour, with fabulous lines. A 3.8 litre Jaguar S type. Barry was ecstatic. It took his breath away. He'd never even seen such a luxurious, top of the range, car before. As they slowly approached the vehicle, Barry with mouth wide open, walked around it. As he did, Frank followed saying, "Barry, I was so lucky to find this, It's hardly done any miles, has unmarked beige leather interior and Belgian walnut veneer to the whole dashboard. Sit in it and see what I'm saying." Barry, slowly entered the driving seat. As he looked around, fixated with the luxurious interior surroundings, Frank continued talking. "It has an XK engine with twin carburettors, four wheel breaking and

IRS to support fast cornering. For what you require you won't find anything in its league."

Barry turned in his seat to look at Frank; hand on the arch over the driver's door. "What's the price?" were his first words. Frank cleverly replied with a glorious smile, "Don't know yet, I'm still negotiating. But it won't be more than low four figures, and it's worth twice that much."

This immediately strengthened Barry's trust in Frank. He edged out of the driver's seat, put his arm around Frank's neck and said, "Let's go and have a drink to celebrate!" they trundled across the road, locked together with Barry's arm firmly fixed around Frank's neck.

Once in the bar, Barry was so excited he had to tell everybody he had a new car. Igor immediately put his arm around Anneliese's waist and they wandered out to see the new machine. Almost everybody followed.

The car was surrounded by people from the bar. Expressions of delight came from everywhere. Rita clung onto Barry, saying she wanted the first ride in the morning. Albie was in heaven. A real car fanatic who already knew everything about this model. He was the first to notice that this car was left hand drive. He shouted to Barry, "It's a LHD. They've only made a few, so you will almost be unique with this in Spain!"

As the evening wore on, Igor's `two henchmen moved outside onto the patio; almost by the bar entrance, as if they were on guard. Igor bought another round of drinks, then with a light grip on Barry's arm, stood, flexed his eyebrows and said, "Maybe it's time to agree some more business details." Barry, before moving, asked if Anneliese could participate to manage the administration. "Of Course," Said Igor with a look that searched Anneliese's torso. All three departed to the rear of the bar, carrying drinks with them.

Nearly an hour later, business was concluded. Everyone seemed pleased with the outcome, so it was handshakes all round. Igor announced he would be leaving tomorrow as he had many commitments. He had arranged a long-term rental of a villa north of Malaga, with good access to the airport; so he planned to be back regularly.

Igor signalled his henchmen, and 10 minutes later a large Mercedes arrived. Embraces were prevalent for all, especially Anneliese, as they strode to the car.

When back to their bar stools, Barry wanted his top team to get together for a debrief. One at a time, they went to a large table at the back of the bar. Barry, Albie, Anneliese and Anya sat down. Frank, Terry and Jose joined them. Barry whispered to Anya who, immediately, strode back into the front bar, bringing Jerome with her.

32

Barry began, in a quiet voice, saying they were now entering the "really rich zone." "We will have major supplies for Spain and France. Don't know yet how we deal with France, but I will figure it out. Anneliese helped negotiate fantastic prices! Not sure how she did it, but she knew all the current market prices and her mind worked like one of those new computer things."

"Also, we will have sufficient supplies for Central Europe and the Russians will give us help, as far as possible, but we need to get in there and develop a strong distribution network. We need to put a lot of effort into this because we can't afford to have the stock that I have bought sitting in the warehouse for months!"

"Jerome, I'm hoping that's where you can help. The Europe warehouse is on the outskirts of Amsterdam. You said you fly in there every week. So I want you to spend some time finding distributors or maybe even small dealers that can grow with low cost supplies!"

Jerome went quiet; developed a worried expression, probably thinking to himself "I don't know where to start." Anya put her arm round his shoulder as she rode in on her white charger.

"Barry," she said, "I may have mentioned this before, but I worked in Amsterdam for some time and have many contacts. There are more drug dealers and distributors in Amsterdam than there are call girls! I have a very good friend that owns one of the biggest clubs in Amsterdam.

He is not involved in narcotics, but I know he will help us with contacts. So, if you are willing to pay for me to fly regularly to Amsterdam, I will meet with Jerome and we will develop this together!"

Jerome had relief written all over his face. He pulled Anya close and kissed her. "You are all fabulous people and I think that would do the trick." "Ok", said Barry, "I'm up for that plan!" then turning to Anneliese, "What do you think?" "It's a great idea" she said, "Because I know how Anya is accepted in Amsterdam. So, yes it will definitely give us the edge."

There was a further issue. Jerome only had time off in Amsterdam every 2 weeks. The allowance was 2 days free time with a layover.

"That's fine, Jerome, "said Barry. "It should be more than enough!"

The following day, around midday, Anya, Albie and Jerome set off to find somewhere quiet to do more training with Jerome. He now had his own training gear. Loose fitting lightweight cotton clothing for flexibility. Jerome was in his element.

Barry was just about to take Rita out for a drive in the Jaguar powerhouse. Rita was so excited and had asked Anneliese to look after the bar for half an hour. It was pretty quiet in the bar, and just as they were about to leave, Terry and Jose arrived. Barry greeted them and asked Anneliese to get them some drinks.

"I'm just shooting out for a few minutes to give Rita a ride in the new motor. Have your drinks and we'll chat when we get back. "30 minutes later, Rita and Barry returned, both beaming with pride and pleasure!

Rita joined Anneliese behind the bar and Barry commenced general chit-chat about the technical qualities of the Jaguar. Both Terry and Jose complimented the Jaguar saying it was a first in the Marbella area.

Terry had been patiently waiting for a convenient lull to raise an issue. "Geezer, I have been approached by three guys. Now, please don't get annoyed with me. I just thought you should know!"

Barry, with a strengthening frown, asked Terry, "What is it?" "These guys are begging for work with us." "Are they the right sort? Are they capable?" replied Barry. "Yes, very capable," but Terry edged away as he spoke, "So what's wrong? Why are you looking worried?" Barry asked as he leaned forward into Terry's face.

"Geezer, they were members of the Marseille gang. Never got caught up with the Guardia Civil in the French girls' barbeque, and now think you are the best to work for, to make some real money."

Barry stood, turned away and walked to the pool table. He stood, leaning on it for a couple of minutes, then walked back to the bar and asked Anneliese to join him. He walked back to the pool table, with Anneliese breezing along about a metre behind. They stopped alongside the table talking. Mostly it was Anneliese speaking. Anneliese returned first, and joined Rita behind the bar. Barry stayed by the pool table for another five minutes, all the time tossing the pool balls around the cushions. He began to smile as he lingered and caught successive balls.

Turning back towards Terry, his smile increased to a grin. "Rita, get us all a large drink, these guys have arrived with good news and we all should celebrate." Anneliese knew what had made such an impact with Barry. Because she had been doing the steering!

Barry's eyes were glistening as he joined Terry and Jose. "You guys have, I think, brought the answer to a difficult question I have been grappling with!" Terry, with a totally surprised expression, could only ask Barry what he was thinking.

Barry with arms around both their shoulders, pulled them close. "Well, it's like this. We have the chance of some fantastic business in France. But we don't have anyone in France, or anyone that can speak the lingo. It's a massive country, so I took the opportunity. And you may have brought me the seedling that will start it growing!"

"Tell them, that if I like them, they will have a well-paid job. I will meet them the day after next. They have to be prepared to travel all around France, and I will pay their expenses."

Terry was overcome and overjoyed. Anneliese, smiling to herself, enjoyed her successful moment. But she was never one to become complacent with such achievements!

Euphoria never lasts long. Anneliese went to the stockroom and Rita followed. "What is it with you and Barry? What was all that talk up by the pool table?"

Quick-thinking Anneliese immediately concluded this was not the time to give Rita any reason to be upset. That would eventually happen but Anneliese did not need Rita out of the way yet!

So with her professional brain ticking, Anneliese put a comforting arm around Rita's shoulders; but Rita leaned back and brought her arm upwards to brush it away. Anneliese began to speak in a calming voice in an attempt to ease the tension. "It was purely work." Moving closer to Rita, Anneliese continued saying, "I don't know if Barry has told you, but I am looking after his admin and doing the books now. When he broke it off with Linda, she refused to continue doing the job"

Rita seemed less dejected. "It's a big job, "said Anneliese, "So Barry wanted to know how it was all looking. Also, he was telling me about three new French guys that may be joining him and to make provision for their pay. Rita, that's all it was, nothing else! I love the job and he is paying me well, so I won't let anything get in the way of it!"

Crisis over, Rita embraced Anneliese and they walked together back to the main bar. For the time being, Anneliese had concealed her relationship with Barry; designed to allow time to advance further into all aspects of his criminal business.

The CECD viewpoint was that overall, Anneliese, Anya and Frank were doing a superb job. The intelligence information they had already secured was better than the Commander had ever expected. They had comprehensive information on the Boleyn Boys operations, both in the U.K. and Spain. They had evidence and details of the characters involved in illegal supplies from Morocco. They had been able to document every detail of people involved in these illicit activities. They had details of properties that had been purchased with laundered funds. The infrastructure and supply routes, were all on record. The next requirement was to identify the warehousing operations throughout Europe. But by no means least, the Intelligence Special Operations Unit now had a clear and detailed view of the operations of the Russian Mafia.

Thanks to Frank, every detail of Igor's life was being collected. Using his four CECD ex-mercenaries, the Russians had been tailed everywhere. Every movement had been monitored. One excellent result was that they had found his home base near Malaga, in a small beachside village called La Herradura. A hilly horseshoe sea inlet, with plenty of areas around for continued surveillance.

The next key objective was to identify the warehousing for Central Europe and France. Seville was already a key warehousing operation, but the Commander wanted to wait for identification of the structure of the newly proposed areas. And, especially to get undeniable evidence against the Russian Mafia.

So the intelligence work would continue, Anneliese and Anya loved every minute. Frank also, but I suppose he would admit that he preferred physical action! Anneliese was doing a fabulous job, even though this was her first involvement in real action. She was expert at manipulation to achieve success. She had done that in a very short period of time with Barry. She now had his trust and more! But it wasn't completely positive. Her job was to take both him and his operation down. This had to be a 100% commitment. But there was an issue. She had developed some feelings for Barry!

Barry's tentacles were now starting to stretch out all over Europe. But there were a few details that he needed to iron out before it would operate like clockwork. So he spent the next few days moulding and crafting the way ahead. Most of the crafting involved Rita and Anneliese! He reiterated to Rita the story she had been given by Anneliese. It was essential that he invested his time in training the Marseille characters and their advance into French territory. The whole truth, and nothing but the truth, was that he spent from early morning until midday in Anneliese's bed.

He moved on to meet Terry and Jose in the afternoon for a few hours with the Marseille men. This was a key piece in his business jigsaw, but it wasn't without issues.

First, he arranged two cars for their use. Two family sized cars! One a Seat which would be unobtrusive when that was the necessity. The other, a superbly quick Mini Cooper "S" 1275cc up rated engine for pursuit driving.

Terry and Jose took these cars to a quiet secluded area close to the Estapona Mountains. Barry was sitting on the bonnet of the Seat when the Frenchmen arrived. They were seriously late. Over half an hour! Barry had a distinct hate for lateness. First, he became agitated, pacing up and down. The next phase was when his psychosis began to infect his mind. When the French arrived, although Barry was quietly seated on the Seat car, his temper had reached an extremely ferocious stage. Barry was overcome by an essentially deranged state of mind, which he had not experienced for a while, but which he enjoyed and found exhilarating!

33

The three Frenchmen parked their Citroen on the left of the plateau, a few metres from the edge of the steep side of the escarpment. The slope up to the plateau had disguised the extent of the dangerous, near vertical, drop that featured in this escarpment.

However, whilst Barry had paced up and down, and viewed the whole area for several minutes, he had memorised the landscape.

They got out and walked toward Barry. Terry and Jose stood a few yards behind. One Frenchman took the lead. Jose, who could speak some French, introduced him as Claude. Barry said "So you guys would like to work with us!" Claude replied in French and everyone had blank looks. So Barry pointed to the two cars, the Seat and the Mini, saying "These are for you to use. I need you to go to Bordeaux!" Jose tried to help with some broken French.

With that, Claude became aggressive and demonstrably so! They are shit! Why this shit! He moved towards Barry pointing his finger in an angry manner. The other two just stood their ground.

Barry slowly turned and walked to the Seat, but Claude followed. After a few paces, he began to shout, then scream at Barry. All in French, but the verbal onslaught was clearly designed to intimidate.

Barry's psychosis became master; he became very cool, calm and collected. He opened the Seat door, went to the glove compartment and pulled out his revolver. Claude, by now, was only a few paces behind.

Barry turned, pointing the gun in Claude's face. "Fuck off, you useless French fuckers. Get in your car before I kill you all!" With Barry following, the three Frenchies rushed to get in their Citroen. At the same time, Barry shouted to Terry, "Bring the Seat over, quick!"

Where Terry came to a halt blocked the exit for the Frenchies. Barry went to the driver's seat and with Jose and Terry in the rear, Barry turned and said, "I now know why I have always hated the French. We did all that for them in the War and they still don't know how to show us respect."

With his gun hand pointing out of the window at the Frenchies. Big smile on his face, he reversed but then immediately put the car back into first gear. His foot flat to the floor, he accelerated, striking the Citroen and pushing it about ten feet to the edge of the cliff. The Frenchman, Claude; his face twisted and distorted as he pressed it against the driver's door window, was screaming as he closed his eyes, terrified of what may happen next. The two Frenchies in the rear seat had opened their rear door but could not exit as they were right on the cliff edge. Barry shouted "this will teach you respect!" With an evil grin, he waved at them, just flexing his fingers. Then, with one final nudge, it went over, dropping and bouncing some 150 feet.

Barry turned to Terry and said, "Let's get back for a drink; that was all a waste of time." Just as he said that, there was a massive explosion as the Citroen hit the ground. With a callous smile, he said, "That's made my mind up. I wasn't sure about doing business in France and today has confirmed they are not worth the effort. So France is a no go area for us. All other countries are respectful!"

Arriving back at Cafe Del Mar, Barry got out and asked Terry to take the Seat and Mini to the farm property and stash them away with the Lotus Cortinas. "Then come back and I will buy you both a large drink; you deserve it!"

Anya was serving behind the bar. Rita had gone for a sleep in the flat upstairs having completed a long shift. Anneliese was waitressing, delivering drinks to a few customers. It was early evening, so fairly quiet!

Anneliese joined Barry at the bar. With loving eyes, she said "Will you be over to see me in the morning?" Before Barry could reply, she looked around then stroked his face. "I love your dimples. They are a feature of your face that excites me. I can't wait to see them in the morning." As Anneliese finished speaking, Barry appeared distracted. "What's up Barry, what's going through your mind?" "Oh, you know I was planning to get into France. And I've bought the supplies for it. But I met with the Frenchies today and it didn't go well. They were arrogant bastards so I have decided to drop the idea. We'll stay with what we've got and concentrate on expanding into Central Europe."

Anneliese did not ask another question. She already had been informed by the CECD agents that had maintained surveillance throughout the episode with the Marseille characters. They could arrest Barry and most of his team now; but they were targeting the whole shoal, not just a few big fish!

Terry and Jose strolled in saying, "Geezer, it's all clear." Albie joined the group and drinks began to flow. Spirits had been low but gradually lifted. Barry described all the events of the afternoon to Albie. He absolutely loved it. "I'm fucking proud of you guys. Let's stick with Spain, not the French lot. My Dad died in France trying to help them resist the Nazis who bombed our family out of their home in Canning Town. So why did we let our troops get massacred in France?"

Barry, back into work mode, said to Anya, "Could I get a few minutes with you." Just at that point, Rita arrived. She rushed around the bar and with both hands on either side of his face said, "Barry, did it go well?" as she kissed him with a long lingering kiss. "No, not really" replied Barry. "I was thinking of working with the French, but they are not our sort of people. So I've kicked it into touch! Good riddance to those arrogant, rude Froggies. But, Rita, now I've done the deal with Igor, I must get something on the move up in Amsterdam or I'll be in deep shit. And for that I need a while with Anya. Do you mind because this is important for us both?"

As Rita slowly moved away, she ran her hand down Barry's arm and gave him a smile of acceptance. She went off around the bar, checking that all the customers were happy.

Barry grasped Albie's arm and said, "I'll need you for a few minutes." He broke away from Terry and Jose and Barry gestured to Anya. They tripped off to the quiet area near the stock room.

Anya, being inquisitive, was first to speak. "What is it Barry, what's up?" "Nothing! Just need to organise something. When is Jerome next in Amsterdam? Now France has fallen flat, I think we need to get the rest moving."

Anya thought for a moment then said, "I think its next week when he is there with a couple of lay-over days." "OK, then I need you to meet him and get something organised with your contacts. I have lots of gear now. More than I want. So can you two get that arranged." Albie jumped in! "So where do I fit into this?"

Barry first glanced at Anya then across to Albie. "I want you to go with Anya, to back her up and make sure she has some protection. And it will give you a short holiday, new surroundings, different people and lots of beautiful women!"

Anya was provoked by this. "Barry, I don't need protection. I can beat Albie in a fight any day of the week. And he doesn't need beautiful women!" Albie began to smile and put his arm around Anya. She accepted and smiled back at him. "I know you are very capable," said Barry, " But just you and Jerome worries me. He is still an infant learning to survive. The three of you are more secure and you can have a bloody good time. Right now, I wish it was me coming with you! So, can you guys get it organised? You, Anya, said your friend Marco, would help and we have lots to splash around, so I will look after him!"

Next morning, Barry left Anneliese to go to the bar. He was in a more vibrant mood, now feeling like he was walking on cloud 9. As he arrived at the steps, his right hand brushed his jet black hair off his forehead. The bright sunlight glistened on his hair and eyelashes and as he ambled onto the patio, he was attempting to read Rita's expression. His psyche was now constantly reminding him of the guilt he carried due to his infidelity.

As his stare intensified, Rita saw him as she looked up from clearing a table. She immediately gained a look of delight, which substantially eased Barry's guilty feelings.

Rita, looking fabulous in a white blouse and skin tight leather trousers, gave Barry a long sensuous kiss on the lips and then went behind the bar to pour him a drink.

They sat and chatted as Anya and Albie came to join them at the bar.

Whilst fragmented conversations continued, all Barry could think about was spending time with Anneliese in the morning. He would spend this night with Rita and then leave early morning to join Anneliese in her bed! Occasionally, he would purse his lips for Rita to see, and between sips of his beer, give her an amorous wink. All designed to maintain her confidence in their relationship.

Anya, in a micro skirt and skimpy top, arrested Albie's gaze and attention. They talked incessantly about their romantic weekend in Amsterdam, envisaging a luxurious time with continuous lovemaking and Albie's favourite indulgence, shared showers!

They had opted to drive to Amsterdam, and Anya had arranged to meet Jerome in Dam Square for lunch. The next stage of the plan was to visit Twirling Club to meet with its owner, Marco. Anya had worked there previously and Marco thought the world of her. She had been his star performer and had made him a massive amount of money.

Next day, driving to Amsterdam was very slow at various points. So they had taken a tourist route, off the main highways, and stayed overnight at Bordeaux. It was a small quaint hotel in a village on the outskirts of Bordeaux. Their room looked out on a square, and below their second floor room was an old fashioned, typically French, bar.

34

Around the square were a few benches, all with old Frenchmen who seemed to have squatted there since the end of World War II. A few bicycles leant against building walls with a generous fountain, almost central, which leaked water onto a small grass verge. It was late afternoon but a few accomplished players were continuing to relish a game of Petanque on a sand pitch in one corner of the square.

The sun streamed through the panes of the large segmented window at the front of their room. Albie drew the curtains and their fine linen dulled the sunshine, marginally. He began to undress; first his short sleeved light blue shirt. As he stood top-half naked, his muscular body was extremely well defined and toned. His daily workout routine had gradually gifted him this superb physique which was his, and Anya's, pride and joy!

As Albie began to pull down his trouser zip, Anya entered from the bedroom. Albie had recently spent time on his tan which, in the dim light, enhanced the strong definition of every muscle. Anya was unable to resist. She walked towards Albie, arms outstretched as she clicked her tongue several times. Small globules of sweat began to form on Albie's skin as Anya's crimson painted finger nails trailed over his torso.

In a heartbeat, Albie relinquished the rest of his clothing. Anya was completely fascinated by the suntan lines around his buttocks. Her mind was thrown into mental gymnastics, leading her fingers to skim his tan lines and upwards, over his chest, to the back of his neck. She stroked his thick brown hair, tenderly inserting her fingers to brush it back from his forehead. Scrolling across his crown, slowly down his neck to his shoulders, she commenced a firm shoulder massage. After a few minutes, with Albie now putty in her hands, she was again, drawn by the magnetism of his tan lines, back to his buttocks. The rear of her right hand lightly skimmed back and forth across the tan lines around his bottom, then with both arms, Anya grasped around Albie's waist, turned him and took his hand. She whispered in his ear and he nodded his head slowly. They were both trembling with anticipation as Anya led him towards the shower in the corner of their bedroom.

The romantic element of their trip up through Spain and France had reached a soul searching crescendo in Bordeaux. They moved ever closer to becoming pure soul mates, however, every so often Anya reminded herself that factors beyond her control may snatch this away from her at a moment's notice!

It was a very dark and misty drive into Amsterdam; fairly slow at various points despite it being a Sunday evening. Feeling extremely tired, they had an early night, enjoying the luxurious comfort and continuing romance in the hotel Anya knew best; the Sonesta.

As they arose in the morning, Anya realised she was feeling very at home. She had many good friends in Amsterdam and now the environment surrounding her brought into sharp focus how much she had missed them all. As they strolled past reception, out of the main entrance, the canal with its tour boats full of tourists, sunshine glistening on the rippling waters, pounded her emotions.

Fighting back against this emotional turmoil, Anya gripped Albie's right arm and swallowed to try to quench her quickly drying throat. This did the trick, stemming the near flow of tears. Her mind, almost immediately, moved to a different gear as she remembered the wonderful times she had shared with Anneliese. She was her female soul mate who had always been there for her, and Anya prayed they would remain together forever! They had a tough job, but together, nothing was insurmountable!

With Anya's head leaning on Albie's shoulder, they ambled along beside the canal. None of the girls in the Red Light shops had arisen from their slumbers, so their walk to Dam Square was without distraction.

The sky, by now, had completely cleared. The cotton wool clouds had drifted on and the sun beamed down through the branches of the trees lining the canal edge. As they entered Dam Square, standing alone in the middle was Jerome. Wearing his dark blue flight attendant's uniform, very tight fitting trousers and his long blonde hair tossing around in the breeze; he wore an expression that said he felt exposed.

As soon as he saw Anya and Albie, exuberance overcame him and he began star jumping on the spot. They both ran to Jerome and as they embraced, he stumbled over his single travel bag lying on the floor at his feet. He looked up from his kneeling position, his boyishly pretty face feathered by his tussled blonde hair. He momentarily clasped a flat hand over his eyes. He was sincerely embarrassed to be staring up into the glory under Anya's micro Ra-Ra skirt, as it floated in the breeze. As she reached down, putting her hands under his arms to help him stand, he uttered apologies over and over again. As he slowly arose, Anya, as she giggled, could not resist saying "Jerome, I am flattered that a guy of your persuasion even noticed. It raises the question, or maybe even something else, regarding whether you are completely homosexual." She pulled Jerome close, and with a teasing lascivious smile continued, "Perhaps my girlfriends in Amsterdam will get to the bottom of it!"

Albie now stepped into the situation, helping Jerome with his flight bag. As he did so, Jerome said, "Albie, please help me to be careful with my bag as I have some updates for Anneliese on the UK business. Mick Flick and Eddie visited me for the first time last week. I was apprehensive at first, but they were fabulous. They took me out and everywhere we went, we were treated like celebrities. We went to a restaurant called Simpsons and then on to the Lyceum Ballroom in the Strand. They knew almost everyone, and we ended up on the dancefloor dancing to a new, sort of, Spanish song, called La Bamba. I had the best time of my life and got several people's addresses. And then to crown it all, they took me all the way back to Stratford in a taxi. My Mum couldn't believe it when I was already home for breakfast in the morning and she didn't need to say "Well you're 'ome then!"

With that, all three of them set off, arm in arm, walking in time to a restaurant in the corner of Dam Square. After a relaxed enjoyable lunch, having consumed just a few glasses of wine, they began an, initially wobbly stroll, to the Twirling Club. Anya led them as she was the only person that knew how to find it, and as Anya strode ahead in her summer blouse and Ra-Ra skirt, it was threatening to rain.

Much further south in Marbella, the afternoon heat would have been ideal for Anya's outfit. It was the type of weather that lifted the spirits. But it wasn't so for Barry! He was consumed by the thought that it would not take the Guardia Civil long to ask questions all around Marbella. They must have found the Frenchies in their burned out car, so their investigations would be intense. He just hoped that nobody cracked and gave them information that led to him, Terry or Jose.

His worrying was a foundation for anger. This had always been one of the features of his psychosis. The growth of his anger developed the usual deranged bravery. He wandered around the pool table, tossing one ball after another against the cushions. All the while, he quietly talked to himself. "Those bastards in the Docks, those in the Cactus Club, those Frenchies.... I beat them all. And I will continue winning everywhere." With that, he strode back to the bar and leaned across to whisper to Rita. "Darling, I need your help with something. If the Police arrive, tell them I have been here in the bar with you all day." Rita put her arm around his neck and pulled him close. "Have you been naughty again?" she asked. "If I do this for you, will you be naughty with me tonight?" Barry knew he had to say yes, and really wanted to! Rita responded with a slow sultry smile.

Barry, relieved, said he was going to the flat upstairs to do some work, but she should let him know if problems occurred.

Once in the upstairs flat, he decided to take his mind off things by continuing his work on his encrypted code. He was 90% to achieving something that would work for them. It would be based on published books. The book choices would be secret but he had not chosen yet. Indeed, he'd never been an avid reader so he thought he would ask Anneliese to choose. His code would use numbers. First, the page number, then the line count from the top, and lastly, word count in from the line start. For example, firstly the word to be used is chosen. It may be on page 31, line 5, word count in 8, i.e. 31.5.8. This code could be developed for multiple words. The book to be used as the basis for the code would be changed regularly and only those that needed to know would be advised at the necessary time. There would be five books in the select library and they would each be given a number between 1 and 5. The book chosen would be the last number in the code.

Barry, pleased with his effort, planned to review the system with Anneliese during tomorrow morning's visit. She would be key to book selection. Although Barry was not aware of it, she was also the Trojan Horse that would be key to the downfall of his encrypted code!

35

Whilst Barry had been imagining himself as a "code maker" to rival the best "code breaker" brains in wartimes' Bletchley Park, Jerome was adapting to the pole dancing delights at the Twirling Club in Amsterdam. Initially, he timidly viewed the whole scenario with trepidation. Anya and Albie recognised this and quickly took him under their wing, to put him somewhat at ease. Anya was engulfed by her girlfriends and a few of the male employees and regulars. She introduced every one of them to Jerome and Albie, with an emphasis on Jerome to boost his ego.

After a while, she pulled Jerome close and forcefully reminded him that he was there as an important business man with exceptional qualities and needed to exude confidence. Her penetrating words that made a significant difference were "you are an actor in an actress's world, so behave like one and you will have everyone in the palm of your hand."

Just as she finished speaking, Marco strode across from his office, both arms outstretched to greet, first of all, Anya. She then introduced Albie who took the British way of smiling and shaking hands. Although last, it had given Jerome time to prepare. As Anya began introductions, Jerome stood, puffing out his chest and clasping Marco in a gentle bear-hug. With a gracious smile and his eyes penetrating Marco's, Jerome said "Marco, you have an amazing club, thank you so much for seeing us; would you care for a drink with us?" Anya and Albie were gobsmacked at his professionalism. Jerome went on to order drinks for them, while Marco continued, with a glorious smile on his face, to chat to Anya and Albie.

Anya's advice and coaxing had worked wonders with Jerome. In the short time they had been in the club he had grown massively in stature. So now, it was obvious his mind, self-confidence and paradigms were expanding, just like his athletic prowess and physique. It was almost unbelievable how quickly he had developed.

The drinks arrived to underpin about an hour of socialising. Scantily clad girls came and went throughout, mostly to chat to Anya, but occasionally with questions for Marco. He was always very generous in the way he accepted their interruptions, often calling the bartender to get them drinks.

Marco's demeanour and appearance were both mesmerising and pleasurable. He presented a strong build with an impressive barrel chest. His dress sense could not be criticised, wearing a three piece double-breasted grey suit which wrapped neatly around his chest. Facially, he was close shaven, with a strong chin. His eyes and smile were ingratiating features that were almost hypnotic. Dark brown eyes, to match his strong dark brown lashes and eyebrows. His hair, although slightly receding, was slicked back with meticulous care. Marco's surprising feature was his soft voice which seemed to infiltrate and command any and every conversation!

After an hour or so, Marco suggested they should retire to his back room. As they entered, Albie noticed one of Marco's doormen arrive to stand guard over their room. Quickly getting down to business, he detailed that he had done his best, following Anya's call to him. He passed a sheet of paper to Jerome saying this was a list of contacts. He went further, saying" It's an extensive list but mainly they are small fish. The big fish will be here in a moment. If you can do business with him, you will have captured the essence of business in Holland and Belgium, and possibly even wider afield!"

At that very moment came a knock on the door. Slowly and proudly, a suave guy entered as the doorman held the door open for him. Marco stood, and Anya's team followed. Marco introduced him as Paulo. He spoke as he embraced Anya, saying "My last name is Lopez. I don't usually offer it unless I am dealing with people that have a strong recommendation, and you certainly have that from Marco." He shook hands with Albie and Jerome following with gentle embraces; then sat in a large wing chair facing all of them.

Marco said "Please excuse me as I have to ensure that everything is working fine in the club." As the door closed behind him, Paulo uttered, "Marco is not involved! He has left us to get on with our business, but we all need to show him the greatest respect and loyalty!" Looking across at Anya, he continued, "Marco has fantastic respect for you and that is the only reason I have come here today."

Anya stood, as she had noticed a small drinks bar in the corner of the room. They all stated their tipple and Paulo, surprised them all by asking for Malbec red wine. Marco had stocked this for Paulo because it, like Paulo, was from Argentina!

Anya played hostess as they got into the business detail. But just before, Jerome spoke. "So you are from Argentina. It seems a world away from us. All I know about Argentina is that you love horses and you are the best horsemen in the world! Paulo's face showed his pleasure, "Why yes,

Jerome, I am what Europeans call a horsey person. I love them. In my early years I was a Gaucho, I loved the life but it didn't give me enough to live on !" Jerome was fascinated by Paulo and wanted to know more. "You also have the finest polo players in the world. I once was invited to watch a polo match at Windsor Great Park, near London; it was the most fabulous spectacle. The ability of those horsemen was beyond belief."

That was it! Jerome and Paulo had already clicked. This created a very positive atmosphere which, combined with Paulo's kind words to Anya, set a massively favourable tone for the business discussions.

Paulo relaxed with his drink, leaning back in his chair. His appearance was, to say the least, eye catching! Most people would have viewed him as a South American aristocrat or upper-class ranch owner. His black hair, slicked back into a short ponytail, shone under the fluorescent light. His eyebrows were thick and distinctive. Although around 40 years old, hardly a line graced his handsome face. His clothing was definitely expensive. A hounds tooth grey jacket accompanied by navy blue trousers with stepped bottoms and two small buttons to add an elegance. His black crocodile leather shoes were chisel points, noticeable as he sat with one crossed leg. The whole package demanded the utmost respect!

It quickly became obvious that Anya and her team were enthralled by Paulo. Indeed, the highlight came when Jerome decided to lead the discussion. He opened with "Paulo, our boss is known as Geezer and he sends you his regards and respect! In essence, the message he wants us to impart to you is with regard to the supply for your business."

Paulo had been studying Anya's thighs, but he awoke. "Jerome, I already have a good supplier, but being honest with you, I do need to expand, so I am open to offers. The cocaine market is increasing, almost geometrically, so an alternative supplier would be beneficial."

Anya interjected. "Our supply would be from a local area. No delivery costs. We would match your present suppliers price and offer a 5% discount if you take more than the minimum quantity of 3kilo per month. We can also supply any other offerings if you require."

Paulo half laughed and then his jaw hung loosely. Rolling his eyes, he looked up from Anya's thighs, took a deep breath and in a soft voice said, "You guys offer a very enticing deal." Anya's team all sat in limbo! Paulo leaned forward in his chair, became expressive, waving his right land in the air, then saying "Yes, it's good, we will do it! We are now in business together."

Jerome was first out of his chair, firmly shaking Paulo's hand, followed by Anya who said to Paulo "Please come to visit us in Marbella. It's a spectacular place and much warmer than Amsterdam."

Paulo, his eyes searching Anya's face replied "I will! I am only accustomed to Argentinian sunshine and Marbella would give me a break I think I deserve." The inference in his voice, the slow and deliberate way he spoke, really said he wanted to see Anya again!

Albie then stepped forward, shaking hands with Paulo. But he wasn't intending to be left out of the business. Still gripping Paulo's hand, Albie asked, "What about all these other small local distributors that Marco gave us in a list. Can we still sell to them?" Paulo said, "Yes, if you wish." Then thought for a moment! "I am your solution "said

Paulo. "I will order on their behalf. They will be happy with that and I want them around because they are supplying to small pockets of demand. And most of them are my friends. Would you be happy with that?" Still gripping Paulo's hand, Albie smiled and said, "Absolutely Paulo, it's been great to do business with you. Would you care for a drink with us in the club?"

Paulo's manicured hands moved to his ponytail to correct a wisp of hair that had drifted onto his cheek. Completing this task, he exhaled, placed his right hand on Albie's shoulder and motioned with his left towards the bar. In a hushed voice he uttered, "You are a very fortunate man to have a beautiful, intelligent woman as your partner. You should look after Anya and treat her well." Albie with a proud smile, nodded his head slowly saying, "Paulo, mostly she looks after me!"

36

In the pre-dawn darkness of Marbella, Barry slipped out of the bar's side door and gently opened the Jaguar and slid into the driver's seat.

Arriving at the magnificent villa; definitely magnificent compared to the small, two up two down terraced house he had grown up in. Barry went into the garden and stood beside the pool, staring at the glorious moonshine reflecting on the water. For a full ten minutes, his mind drifted back over his early years; nostalgic thoughts trickled back, softening his emotions, as they had done several times recently.

The guilty thoughts regarding Rita brought him back to reality. As he quietly inched up the stairs an innermost thought repeated over and over in his mind. Love is a battlefield, and I am in the thick of it! Just as my life has always been! I must find a way out!

Standing beside Anneliese's bed, he became almost fearful. She looked so serene; hardly a breath passed her soft moist lips. He must never lose her. She had become his "be all and end all."

Anneliese turned towards him, opened her eyes and they both smiled. Just waking, she ran her tongue along the edge of her lips, then reached out and locked onto his hand. Pulling him towards her, they kissed passionately and Barry slid in beside her. From that moment, their desire became hypnotic, without thought, simply pure passionate love.

About two hours later, slumber retreated and they gradually arose and prepared breakfast. As they sat in the near midday sun by the swimming pool, Anneliese, without a word, stood and with two steps to the edge of the pool, executed a faultless dive into the clear blue water.

Barry watched with pride as Anneliese eased through four fast front crawl lengths. She exited with the agility and poise of a gazelle, grasped a towel, then leaned on Barry's back, tossing her hair to drench his warm body.

Her power-house of a brain was now acute and ready for anything. Barry sensed this and as she sat down at the table, he asked if she would mind giving his attempt at the encrypted code the once over. "Barry, of course not. I'm sure you have done an excellent job". Barry had been sitting on the file, so it was slightly damp.

He pushed it across the table and she got straight to it. He had bullet pointed the steps and how it would be implemented. As she read through the whole piece, Barry explained that he needed her help selecting the five books. Whilst reading, her lips, with their slightly upturned corners, broadened into an exhilarated smile!

Barry was not expecting her reaction. She jumped up out of her chair, saying, "It's amazing. So simple, but as a code, so impossible to break. You are so clever. No, clever is not the word! This is brilliance." She sat back down. Barry was lost for words! So, maybe those years at school had not been a complete waste of everyone's time!

Anneliese continued, I will give you five, not so famous or important books, that nobody would ever guess. It will be perfection. We can write messages on paper or even those new computer things. You can be confident this will be secure!"

Barry was elated, more because he had impressed Anneliese than the fact that this would work for his business. "A business, your type of business, needs secure information, and you have found a way" commented Anneliese.

Anya and Albie returned from Amsterdam late afternoon the next day, Tuesday. A day with good news and bad news! Barry had followed the usual pattern with an early morning visit to Anneliese. They sat at the bar with Rita serving them drinks. Rita appeared indifferent to their approaches, especially Anneliese's attempts at friendliness.

Albie, with his cockney style, was explaining to Barry that they had got a great deal with an Argentinian who was a major player in the Dutch and Belgium business. "He is going to come here for a visit to meet with you, Barry." Anya joined in, telling all the specifics of the deal. Barry, in a thoughtful mood, began to appear pleased until Anya said "and we have a star in the making."

Barry's gaze became questionable. "Why, what happened?" "What happened "said Anya "was that Jerome came out of the clouds. He was confident, convincing and took charge. Paulo engaged with him and clearly appreciated his approach. Paulo was obviously a man of experience with negotiations, but once Jerome got into full flow, Paulo developed absolute trust in all of us. Even more, he liked the elements of the deal being offered. So we have a new and very important ally."

Barry placed his hands on the edge of the bar, bent over and shook his head. His grin widened as he turned his head to look along the line at Anya, Albie and Anneliese. "The deal you guys achieved is fabulous. It's sort of made my day. But what has really, properly, made it is the performance of Jerome. What did you two do to his brain when you were out there training him to look after himself? It's almost a miracle. Sounds to me like we now have a supremely clever, confident member of the team. I am over the moon for him and us! You just wait until we get him back with us. We will have to surprise him with a celebration party. Sounds like he deserves recognition."

Both Anya and Albie were somewhat surprised by Barry's reaction. It wasn't all about business or all about winning! But they also were enamoured by Barry's appreciation of their protégé. "Oh Barry, that's a fantastic thought, and he really does deserve it" said Anya. "He will be back next weekend, and I will get in touch with Marco and ask him to invite Paulo down to meet you, if you're ok with that?" "Super idea Anya" and turning to Anneliese he continued, "And are you up for that, love?"

⊷⊶⊷◆⊶⊷⊶

37

That was breaking point! The word love! Rita with an anguished look, strode around to the front of the bar. As she did so, anguish turned to anger! Rita, having worked all day was somewhat less than glamorous, but still a beautiful pure virginal face, with eyes that could not be ignored. She pushed her way between Barry's legs as he turned on his bar stool to face her. "We need to talk. No, I'll correct that; I need to talk. Barry, for some time now your bollocks have done the talking. Mostly to Anneliese." She turned her head to shoot an angry glance at Anneliese. With her voice almost breaking with emotion, she continued, "You have been having an affair with Anneliese. I asked several customers to watch out for you early morning. None of them knew anything, until a customer's wife saw you entering the villa where Anneliese has been living. For days she watched you both come and go! Barry, I am leaving you and want you to pay my air fare back home. Is that another good deal for you today? If so, I will go and pack."

As she moved away, she said, "I want nothing else. Other than this." She grabbed Barry's private parts. She didn't let go and tugged so strenuously, his bar stool followed her for a whole 12 inches. With eyes still watering, Barry sat silent for a good five minutes, as did the rest of the crowd. Anneliese wanted to console Barry, but knew Rita would return any minute.

She appeared momentarily, just as a taxi arrived at the front of the bar. She walked to Barry, dragging her two cases behind and stood still in front of him, eyeballing him, and then, holding her hand out. "How much do you need?" asked Barry. "About 20,000 pesetas" said Rita, "and you need to pay me a month's wages, so in total about 150,000 pesetas.

Barry pulled out the money from his wallet and with a guilty enigmatic smile, passed the bundle of notes to Rita. As she commenced to drag the cases out to the taxi, Barry dropped off the bar stool and handled the baggage. At the taxi, with cases loaded, he got close to Rita. "I am so sorry," he said. "I've got no excuses and I will always remember you as a wonderful lover that I would have stayed with forever if things had not taken me on a different course." "Please forgive me." She stepped into the taxi to disappear from his world forever.

Anya sheepishly stepped off her bar stool and, head down, quietly shuffled behind the bar. She stood sadly, looking at Barry and, occasionally, glancing at Anneliese.

Barry sat staring into his whisky glass for three or four minutes. It was as if he had been battered by a tornado and was now left floating in the aftermath as the tornado disappeared in the distance.

Then, suddenly, he sat up straight, rolled his eyes and shouted "Anya, give me that bottle of Scotch and a jug of water please!" Anneliese wanted to go to him to comfort him but stopped abruptly as Barry stood, clapping his hands loudly. Then, with a huge grin on his face, he filled his scotch glass to the brim and shouted "Everyone please have a drink on me!"

Barry, Albie and Anneliese, joined together in an enthusiastic drinking session, as did most people in the bar. The recovery session grew in intensity, and after about an hour, they were all boisterous. Barry was now, with Anneliese's direction, also downing lots of water with his Scotch; but by now was glassy eyed. He leaned across the bar, took Anya's hand and kissed it gently. "Come round for a second and talk to me and Anneliese" he slurred.

She trotted in a jovial way, passing Albie, patting his bottom as she did so. "Hey Albie, your Anya is a little wonder. I want to give you something. Those two Lotus Cortina's are something special. I want you and Anya to have one for your own use and business as it arises. And with what you achieved in Amsterdam, there will be more honeymoon trips up there for you two." "And Anneliese" Barry continued, "I want you to have the other Lotus. You three are now all supremo's in this business. You have proved your worth, and together, we will be the best there is!"

Barry went back to sipping his scotch. All three of them Anya, Albie and Anneliese, recognised that his emotions had become confused by the alcohol and hurriedly crowded around Barry, arms entwined with simultaneous kisses on his cheeks.

This managed to resurrect Barry's spirits and Anneliese stayed close and comforting. Anya turned to Anneliese, quietly saying "There was another plus point for Jerome. He brought you those papers. They are in the Lotus. So I will give you them tomorrow, after we collect the car from the farm." Anneliese just nodded as she smiled.

There was a new arrival. Frank strolled in saying, "You guys look as though you have had a great day. Barry jumped off his stool, slightly wobbling as he put his arm around his neck. "Have a drink on me, Frank and we will tell you all about it!"

A small group of Spanish Flamenco singers and dancers had arrived and were set up in just a few minutes. The music began and gradually customers were getting up dancing. As heels clicked on the wooden floor, Barry was enticed by the mood. Although severely inebriated, Barry stood upright and was clapping, flamenco style, in time with the music. Anneliese joined in, probably in case he needed some physical support.

Anneliese, after he had enjoyed the clapping and sat on the bar stool, spoke to Frank. As the evening ended, Frank asked Barry if he could drive him back to his villa. Barry began to argue saying he was going to drive. He was quite capable and he was taking Anneliese too. "Come off it Barry; you would be a danger to yourself and Anneliese." Frank went on to say "Let me be your chauffeur and have a drive of that super special S type. Remember, I did get it for you!"

They managed to get Barry into the Jaguar about 1.00am. He was paralytic and commenced an abusive tirade against Rita as Albie and Frank shoved him into the passenger seat. Anneliese clambered into the rear seat and as Frank pulled away, she leaned forward, placing her hands on Barry's shoulders.

With only a ten minute drive, although on some unlit Spanish winding roads, they arrived at the villa. Lurching and almost tumbling through the decoratively tiled archway, they piled through the Moorish carved, generous front door.

Frank and Anneliese struggled to get Barry up the stairs and onto the king size bed. He moaned and groaned as they removed his shoes, socks and then his trousers. His summer T shirt and boxers were left on to simmer in the heat of the night. Lastly, Anneliese placed a white enamel bucket beside the bed, thinking it may be necessary!

They both breathed a huge sigh of relief, as they headed outside by the swimming pool. Anneliese put some music on. A Tony Bennett LP, with the stereo sound system loud enough to drown out their conversation.

Neither of them wanted alcohol; instead it was Anneliese's favourite iced tea. Both spoke quietly. Anneliese first, saying that today, with Rita, was the part of her job she found very difficult. However, she had always known that Rita was an obstacle that had to be removed.

With his usual calm demeanour, Frank said, "Anneliese, you are relatively new to this work. The best advice I can possibly give you is to make it your top priority to remain remote from emotion. This is a life and death business. So ensure you are always well removed from anything that may lead you to the death end of the business."

"Our Secret Service Intelligence Agents have followed and documented every element of Barry's business, including his new associates. All of them are very big fish and we are approaching a time when this case will be finalised. We have photographs of everybody involved and tomorrow, Anya will give you Barry's interests in the U.K. Another piece of concrete evidence in this scenario."

"Also, you should know that our Intelligence Analysts have assigned an exemplary profiler. You were trained initially in that discipline and studied with him; his code name is Mark Dart. He has generated substantial information about both Igor and Paulo. We need to be very careful with those characters, because they appear to have varied allegiances and alliances. Their every move is being tracked and analysed!"

Frank continued, "I understand Anneliese, that there will be a party next weekend for our young naïve Jerome. Be on alert because there is some intelligence floating around that Paulo will visit. If so, that same intelligence indicates that MOSSAD, the Israeli secret service, have some interest in him. so, all I would say is, be ready for anything. They are an absolutely professional outfit that do not take prisoners."

"I'm going to go now, but I will pick you both up at mid-day and get you to Café Del Mar." With a wide grin, and tapping Anneliese's arm, he said, "It's my duty as a Good Samaritan!"

As he eased into the S Type, he turned, smiling at Anneliese. With a low, almost apologetic tone, he whispered "I'm sorry you found today difficult. Just keep remembering you and Anya are doing a superb job, and it will help the world keep these drug dealers at bay!"

As arranged, Frank picked them up at 1.00pm. Anneliese and Barry, particularly Barry, tottered slowly to the car. Barry was wearing the obligatory hangover sunglasses. Anneliese was her usual elegant, sophisticated self that would grace any man's arm.

Barry, having tripped up both steps into the bar, was greeted by both Anya and Albie. Anya immediately passed a bag to Anneliese with the all-important U.K. papers. Carefully, so nobody noticed, she passed them to Frank who took them out to the car. They were too important to have hanging around.

Albie took charge of Barry. "Have a hair of the dog mate. It's the only way to de-coke your engine." "No, I couldn't face it" said Barry. Albie got tough! "Barry, do it or the alternative is raw eggs in tomato juice."

"Ok", replied Barry, "but just a beer." Albie smiled a knowing smile. Anya pulled a small beer and then a scotch, encouraged by Albie. With both placed in front of him, he sipped them intermittently.

As if the mausoleum door had been opened and he had been resurrected by his friends, he brightened and became apologetic to Anneliese. She sat for a moment looking into his eyes. Then pulled his head to her's and eased into a slow, tender, loving kiss.

There was not much routine to Barry's life except a phone call to his Mum, Joan, once or twice a week. As the afternoon drew on and blood began to liven his brain, he told Anneliese he was tripping to the upstairs flat to phone his mum. Anya and Anneliese sat chatting across the bar. Albie was playing pool with one of the customers. Frank had been sitting quietly on the patio, watching the world go by.

He strode in, saying to Anneliese he was leaving and she should remember the papers in the car when leaving.

She nodded as he sauntered out and sped off in his new acquisition; a Spanish Jeep with a quirky boxy shape! Barry returned to Anneliese after about 15 minutes. He bore a tormented look and sat, without speaking. Anya with a quizzical look on her face, glanced at Anneliese.

"Is everything ok?" said Anneliese. Her voice, soft and coaxing caused Barry to shift from his stool, stand tall, arching his back, as if he had stiffened. "Yes, its fine," he replied. "But can we go back to the villa. I fancy a quiet night by the pool and perhaps a bit of tapas." "Of course; Barry, sounds delightful!"

On the way back, Anneliese said she had checked with Anya and Albie that they were ok to manage the bar. Anya had said "You should take as long as you need and hope you feel better soon."

Anneliese was careful to take the UK papers in and stash them in an upstairs cupboard. Tomorrow she planned to take them to her flat, to work on them; and document summaries to pass to Frank.

Barry sat quietly on the front of the floral patterned settee, his elbows resting on his knees with his face in his hands; staring at the long beige shag pile carpet. For just a few moments, Anneliese stood on the other side of the room, without speaking. Her psychology training was having to work overtime.

38

Slowly lifting his head, Barry said, "Let's get some drinks and go outside by the pool." "You go and I will get the drinks" replied Anneliese with a soft, caring tone.

Barry sat on a luxurious settee under a canopy at the corner of the patio. Anneliese brought the drinks and sat beside him. After just a few seconds, she said, "What is it Barry? You seem really disturbed. I thought today, after Rita, you would be happy. You had got what you wanted. At least, I thought I was what you wanted. I definitely want you and now we have that chance! Instead, you appear depressed."

Barry slowly opened up, although he was finding it difficult to describe the complicated thoughts that had been building over several weeks.

"Darling, I am going to find this really difficult to explain but I will try. For years, I have suffered these aggressive episodes that, to be honest, I enjoyed. I did some really wicked, evil things. In my mind I was rewarded for those violent events, with adulation and worship! That led me into this evil business. I wasn't brought up like this. My mum is the kindest loving person so I am ashamed. I can't even bring myself to tell her what I really do. My thoughts keep trickling back to my early years in the East End. I'm having flashbacks all the time. I yearn for my years riding that bus with Mum and Jess. Meeting Linda. The pleasure every weekend from playing football and the excitement of the crowd when I scored. My family, my uncles, all meant so much. But now, even they are fearful of me."

"It's not a business I have developed. It is some grotesque money making machine that has totally consumed me. I have to find a way out of its influence over me."

Anneliese was absolutely and totally lost for words. This had never figured in her psychological assessment of Barry. She had strong feelings for him, but his cruel streak always had directed her mind to her ultimate objective. To destroy his trade!

"Barry, you are suffering from mental stress and pressure. You are extremely good at what you do, but now you feel it is all getting too much and taking over you. I understand your feelings and I will do everything I can to help you, whatever you decide."

"Since I found you Anneliese, all I crave is happiness and contentment spending my life with you. I am so in love with you, the darkness that descended before every one of those wicked times has left me. I am terrified that those horrors will return. If I remain in this business it seems a certainty that the violence and horrific behaviour will descend on me once again. Worse than all that is the terrifying fact that I am putting you, every day, in harm's way."

Anneliese, without saying a word, stood and slowly walked to the drinks cabinet. As she pulled out the top drawer, she inhaled a deep breath, and pulled out a packet of her Sobranie cigarettes. Turning to give Barry a tender smile, she said, "I've stayed away from these for weeks, but I need one to help me think!"

She gently placed the cigarette on her moist bottom lip. Then lit the cigarette with a swan shaped lighter. Drawing on her black Sobranie, her neck imitated the swan's curve, and she puffed the smoke towards the ceiling light.

This extremely clever secret agent was churning through all her psychology education and training. Not to harm Barry, rather to help him with his mental anguish.

She wandered around the room for a minute of two, enjoying the cigarette, then stood in front of Barry. With him, expectantly looking at her, she said "I want to tell you what I think is real, and what I think may help us both with our relationship." "OK", said Barry with a slightly concerned look.

"I believe, Barry, you have suffered most of your life with a condition, a psychotic condition, which is stimulated by a further condition known as dual personality disorder. This may all sound Greek to you but don't worry because the good news is that you are in remission. The grey matter in our brains is so complex and is not understood enough to explain what causes a condition like yours! But you're thinking may be correct. We have found each other and your mind is now at peace!"

"So, from this moment, if you begin to feel tormented with anguish, I want you to imagine this. We are on a raft, floating in the warm sea of the Mediterranean. We can have a swim whenever we want. No sharks around! The skies are bright blue with constant warm sunshine. We have plenty of food and drink to last forever. The tides are just drifting us along. The wonderful thing is we are together. We are loving every day and know that sooner or later, we will reach a glorious tropical island."

"Barry; that is the equivalent of our reality. We have what we have at the moment and it's pretty good. And sometime soon, we will reach that tropical island and, when that approaches, you will be able to take me off the raft, and get us both into a better world. But for now, it's not so bad!"

He looked deep into her eyes. "Thank you, so much. You have helped me understand everything and I will never forget this time."

Barry, with a warm smile said, "I'm feeling great now, so what's next." Anneliese, in a heartbeat replied, "We have to live for today. No pressure, but we need to work with Anya on the party for Jerome. Also, keep our finger on the pulse of the business. It's going great, and we will need the direction that you always bring to the business. But simply remember, if you feel tormented just keep saying to yourself the word RAFT! That will be the trigger that brings you back to the reality that we are fine together, on that raft, and a tropical island will eventually appear.

With a finality in her hushed voice, Anneliese motioned toward the staircase, and said, "May I take you to our bed now?" Barry's melancholy expression surrendered and as he followed her up the stairs, he breathed in her perfume and was now in a brand new world!

Next morning, after several exhausting attempts to sever contact, they enjoyed a shared cooling shower, had some breakfast then drove to the bar. Both were in an ebullient mood. Barry had returned to the world where he treasured every moment with Anneliese and his friends, and as they walked in it was obvious to everyone that the old Barry was back!

Albie had relief written all over his face, purely because he was not just a cousin, not just a friend; he cared for Barry and would do anything for him.

After a rapturous beginning, and a few cervezas, the girls joined, but only drinking Tinto Verano. An hour or so later, Frank arrived and stepped in amongst the group. He always had this fabulous way of participating but remaining aloof and alert.

Barry transitioned into business mode, saying would you guys mind having a short meeting. His attitude and tone had mellowed. It was no longer assertive and autocratic. They all smiled and strode to the back bar by the pool table.

"Anya, the first thing is Jerome's party, so would you take the lead?" asked Barry. "I've done some work on this already", she replied. "I recommend we have it here on the Marbella beach. We can move enough of the bar stock out there and we will still be close to this bar. We can do some of the food, but being one down on staff, I have asked Juan to prepare us stacks of tapas. Also, he has arranged for a guy to barbeque sardines in a small boat stationed on the sand. Jose has found us a company to erect a multitude of string fairy lights. And I will probably think of some more things as we head towards Saturday. One more thing! I have booked a Spanish Pop Group who are renowned in this area and will play the whole time." Barry was impressed. "Anya, if you need any help just tell me." Anya's response was as expected. Gripping Albie round the waist, she spoke with sincerity in her voice. "Jerome is our protégé. But he's much more than that and he deserves this party. So, yes I will ask for your help if it's needed, but I am on a mission with Albie to give Jerome a night to remember!"

Barry bent forward in his chair, raised his eyebrows as he blinked several times. He then clasped his hands together and with them in a reverent pose, said "Anya and Albie, he could not have better mentors. You should be proud of yourselves."

He smiled at everyone then, immediately said, "We have a couple more subjects to deal with. Frank and Albie, I'm hoping you can deal with this. I need a couple of long range, high frequency radios for contact with Paulo and for us to use as required. There is a guy up in Malaga that supplies them and will set them up. Can you organise that?" Frank responded, saying, "Of course, sounds easy. Just a short visit up to Malaga."

"The last subject concerns Igor. I don't want anyone inviting him or telling him about the party. If he got into conversation with Paulo he would, no doubt, quickly figure out that we are just middle men. He would cut us out and deal directly with Paulo. If by any chance he turned up, we would need to keep them completely apart. Is that clear?" Everyone nodded and mumbled yes Geezer!

Friday arrived, as did Jerome. He arrived mid-afternoon and was immediately collared by Anya and Albie. Some of the preparations were already taking place, and they wanted to keep him in the dark. The whole team were together in the bar about 7pm and party time was raising its head. Jerome was becoming suspicious with all sorts of objects being moved out onto the patio. Anya surrendered. Turning to Albie she said, "I think it's too difficult to conceal. Let's tell him!" They grasped Jerome's hands saying we need a minute, as they led him onto the patio.

As they wandered outside, with people seated all around, Jerome appeared perplexed, imagining bad news.

A strong sea breeze struck at that moment, and Jerome's long blonde locks blew and covered his face. Anya's hair followed his lead. Both of them stood brushing hair off their eyes and lips, while Albie smiled through his unruffled college boy haircut.

Anya cuddled Jerome, explaining the plan for tomorrow. "You are doing all this for me," he exclaimed. Anya replied, "Everybody here agreed we should do it because you deserve it. So it's not just Albie and me that love's you."

The customers on the patio waved and applauded with approval, as Anya led Jerome back to the smiling group in the bar. The party atmosphere grew and everybody became more excited as fairy lights were installed on the patio and across the bar frontage. The contractors would do the same on the beach in the morning.

Later on, Anya cornered Barry as he walked to view the outside lights. "Barry, I had a visit early this morning. A young Spanish lady asking for bar work. I liked her personality and she seems competent. May I offer the barmaid's job to her, because we really need someone now I am going to be helping Albie. Barry thought for a second, then said, "Great, well done. Now I'm busting for the toilet. It just hit me, but please call her and make the arrangements!"

Next in line to talk with Barry was Jerome. As Barry stood, glass in hand, admiring the light show, Jerome said, "Please excuse me Geezer, but with all the excitement I have only just remembered I have a couple of letters for you. One from Eddie and Mick Flick and another from Jess". He timidly offered them to Barry. In a flash, Barry put his arms around Jerome, saying "Well done mate, you've done great." He continued to cling on to Jerome, stuffing the letters in his back pocket.

As they began to head back to the bar, Anneliese appeared at the door. As she watched them, with her right hand high on the door frame, she joined in, gripping Jerome's waist as they stepped into the bar.

With her thoughts clustering in her mind, a very strong scenario gripped her. Picking up the pieces that she had experienced throughout the day, one truth was obvious. The pointer on Barry's psyche had moved away from malevolence into personable. Maybe only slightly, but he was changing!

It is said that some things, good or bad, come in threes. During this evening, Anya had found a new barmaid, Jerome had delivered two, probably important letters. Barry had accepted both with geniality!

39

A taxi arrived. The passenger door slowly opened and the occupant emerged. The third was Paulo! With leisurely steps, he sauntered up to the patio. His dress sense would have singled him out at the Cannes Film Festival. It was immaculately exotic; carried with a presence that could not be ignored.

Anya was the first to see him, and hurriedly went to meet and welcome him. On the way she whispered to Anneliese. "Paulo is here!" He kissed her on both cheeks and they both wandered to the bar. Everybody at the bar had relinquished their stools and were ready with a warm welcome. First Paulo chose Barry to embrace, although Barry was seen to wince at the cheek kisses. Both Anya and Anneliese were in the wings, waiting to be next.

No, it wasn't to be! To everyone's surprise, Paulo, with arms outstretched and with an enamoured expression took Jerome's hand and embraced him for, what seemed, an eternity. As they eased away, Paulo whispered, "You are morning dew on a brand new day." Jerome stood back, staring into Paulo's besotted face!

Anneliese and Anya, gleefully looking into one another's eyes, nodded as if to say "This could be the start of a fine romance!" Both girls then embraced and welcomed Paulo, as Albie poured them all some drinks. The girls had concluded that Paulo enjoyed both men and women!

Progress through the evening was enjoyably conversational. Paulo was staying at Anya's favourite hotel in Estapona. Through the evening, he ingratiated himself to Barry and Albie, with special attention to Jerome. The girls were almost ignored by him, but they had already worked out why.

Only one business issue was raised. Albie mentioned the intention to buy long range radio transmitters. Paulo attempted to bat the subject away saying, "Please, no work tonight," but Barry intervened. He said "Listen Paulo, it's a clever security thing. I am buying you this transmitter so we can communicate. And I have a code that I will explain before you leave. With what our business is developing into, we need extra security."

Paulo was impressed. "You guys are thinkers. I like that! I appreciate your efforts and we can go through the details before I leave. Once again, gentlemen, thank you so much!" As he uttered those final few words, he grasped Jerome and pulled him close. "Barry, this guy is a gem. He was so impressive at our meeting up in Amsterdam, that I value him above all else. Your organisation will succeed while you have people of his quality."

Jerome's response was dominant. Clasping his arm around Paulo's shoulders, and speaking to the whole group, Jerome said, "These guys, especially Anya and Albie, deserve the credit. Without their support you would not be seeing the person you see now. They have given me the confidence to enter a universe I never imagined was there for me to explore. Barry and Anneliese also have given me the chance to recognise opportunities. So I want to thank all of you, over and over again, and even that's not enough!"

Everyone crowded around Jerome, most saying, "Just enjoy your party tomorrow!" The evening seemed to go on for an eternity. Paulo left in a taxi about 3.00am. The only sensible ones left around were Barry, Anneliese, Anya and Frank! Terry had provided transport for those staggering around; Jerome, Paulo and a few others.

In the morning, the sunshine was so strong it woke everybody early. Their hangovers did not help, but they all knew they had a busy day in front of them. The body clock was in charge. So Barry and Anneliese woke early. Normally this would be their time for passion. But Barry explained that he needed recovery time. So it was a simple, quiet breakfast with a bit of an Anneliese massage followed by several aspirins!

They arrived at Café Del Mar about 9.00am. Nobody had risen before them. But as they let themselves in, Anya appeared. She gave Anneliese a warm cuddle, saying "I'm so glad you managed to get here early because there's a lot to do and I want it to be a special day for Jerome."

As they were talking, with Barry trying to shake off rigor mortis, the new barmaid appeared. She strutted in, full of life, and Anya greeted her.

Taking her hand, Anya led her in the bar to introduce her. Barry greeted her first saying, "Encantado." One of the few words he had learned. Anya introduced her as Carmella but they could call her Carrie. Anneliese joined the throng and the three girls went behind the bar to explain some of the work!

Anneliese, standing back from Anya and Carrie, was very welcoming, saying, "With you two senoritas standing together it is dos bonita senoritas." Carrie uttered "Gracias" with a gracious smile. Turning to Anya and with a sideways glance to Carrie, Anneliese motioned with fingers to her pursed lips and as she flicked her fingers away said, "The men have double ecstasy with you two around."

Carrie's English was relatively good. She understood, and looking at Anya, she responded with a gentle blush and "thank you." She raised her head slowly and turning to Anya asked, "What do you prefer me to do in the party?"

Anya, using slow diction, said, "I think we should work out at the bar on the beach together. I am also new to this so we will learn together!"

The party was due to begin in earnest at 3.00pm. By mid-day men were beginning to dominate, inside the bar. Albie was coping with Jerome, enjoying every moment, working together.

The excitement was building. The contractors were just finishing installing the string lights around the beach bar and for about 100 feet along the beach area.

Other guys had arrived and were setting down an area of wooden panelled flooring, but nobody seemed to know why! The band arrived but decided to head to the bar for refreshments. After about another hour, one of the band members felt the need to express his music. Sitting on a chair in the corner of the bar, he became one with his guitar and began to play flamenco music. This enhanced everybody's enjoyment, with several Spaniards joining, with hand clapping and foot tapping!

By now, Barry was fully recovered. With a release of energy he now was grasping Anneliese around the waist as they treasured every moment. The guitar player stopped for a moment, sipping his drink. Just as he did so, there was a loud shout from the patio doorway. "Don't stop please. That was fantastic. "It was Paulo! Barry, Albie and Jerome sprinted to greet him. Lots of embraces, especially for Jerome, as the guitar player struck up again. This time a romantic Spanish song, "Guantanamera."

There was a surprise in store for everyone in the bar. Paulo broke away from the embraces, strode up to the guitar player and began to sing. His voice was amazing. People came off the patio to listen. Every note of this beautiful romantic song was perfect. His voice was a mellow baritone that would have graced the Westminster Cathedral choir. But the passion in his singing showed his love of music.

As it finished, the room went quiet, but for just a few seconds. The anti-climax was superseded by loud applause, people standing and cheering and overall euphoria.

Paulo, after shaking many hands and embracing many people, with a happy smile walked back to Jerome.

After Paulo got a drink, Anneliese took charge. I think she was intent on getting the band and the men away from the bar and out to the beach. The party atmosphere took hold around the beach bar. Anya and Carrie had the initial wave of customers to serve, and Barry and Albie provided the fetch and carry support.

Juan had set up his tapas stall, ably assisted by a couple of senoritas. Attendance continued to grow until about 8pm. People were moving onto the small wooden dance floor, relishing the bands interpretation of many American artist's songs.

It would remain light through to about 10pm when it was planned to switch on all the string lights around the bar and beach. Anya and Albie had done one hell of a job with the organisation. At approximately 9pm came another surprise. A set of Flamenco dancers arrived. Anya and Juan greeted them and as they prepared, the wooden dance floor was vacated.

Jerome, Paulo, Barry and Anneliese were in conversation at the bar while Anya and Carrie were on a mission to keep everyone happy with bar service.

The Flamenco began and the whole area around the beach became silent. Three ladies and two Senors commanded the small dance floor. It commenced with one of the men, on the edge, playing flamenco slowly, but with increasing velocity. The senoritas, elegantly dressed in white tops and scarlet floating skirts, took to the floor. Heels stamping and clicking in perfect time to the music. The remaining male dancer eventually stepped out performing, as if a matador. The girls scarlet skirts swished around while he performed a statuesque proud, foot stomping matador imitation. Lots of clapping and cheering from the audience added to the intensity.

The male guitarist downed his guitar and took centre stage. With two bolas and drumming provided by his colleague, the beat began slowly. He swung the bolas as if he were an Argentinian gaucho and as the beat tempo increased, the wood balls at the end of the two ropes, the bolas, struck the wooden floor in time with the drum beat. He twisted and turned, all the time completely in unison with the drumming. A fantastic spectacle that brought applause from everyone. They bowed and waved to everyone, with flashes from cameras all around!

Paulo was overcome. He had not seen this dance since he left Argentina several years ago. He clasped Jerome and Anneliese explaining that the sector they had just experienced was the national pride of the Gauchos in Argentina. Originally learned from the Spanish conquistadors but now endemic in Argentina's culture.

40

It was nearly 10pm and as the conversation continued around the bar, a motor launch slowly appeared off shore, about half a mile out. This was nothing unusual but it added to the panorama as sunset created an orangey glow backdrop.

Whilst everyone had been distracted by the Flamenco, some uncaring individual had parked his bicycle against the front of the bar, making it difficult for customers. Anya wanted it moved. She and Carrie were pulling it out from under the bar top when Paulo joined in to help. The handlebars were stuck, but that was not going to prevent them moving it. As they were struggling with it, Anneliese walked up, and asked "Has anyone seen Frank?" "Not seen him for half an hour or so" replied Anya. Just as the handlebars released from the notch under the bar, the string lights came on. Everybody cheered! As everyone quietened, Barry beckoned to Anneliese; wanting to talk. Nobody heard a sound until, just as Barry was saying he'd had two letters, there was a loud clanging noise, as the Cruzcampo beer pump tilted sideways and fell on the floor. At exactly the same time, Anya gave a piercing scream and fell backwards into Paulo's arms. Seconds later, as he bent forward to prevent Anya falling to the floor, a metal tray leaning on the back of the bar, jumped two feet in the air and fell on the floor!

Frank appeared as Anneliese and Barry knelt down beside Anya. With his eyes scanning around, Frank shouted

"Take cover, it's a gunman. Barry, call an ambulance!" To everyone's surprise, Frank grabbed the bicycle, mounted it as he sprinted away, peddling like fury along the road by the beach.

He stopped as a speed boat was beaching; ran to it and jumped in. The owner, taken by surprise, was pushed backwards into the surf. Frank hit the accelerator, straight to top speed, heading out to sea. The chase was on!

The target was the motor launch that Frank had monitored during his surveillance of the area around the party. He was totally convinced that the two shots emanated from that boat.

He was in pursuit of a fast modern craft, but his sleek speedboat with its powerful outboard engine was gradually gaining. The motor launch was turning past the headland where the sea grew rougher. Frank, at this point, edged closer still and although the bow waves and spray were drenching him, he could discern, clearly enough that only one man was on board the motor cruiser.

Now in a small bay, the assailant drove his craft, at full speed, straight at the beach, ploughing into the sand, until forced to a stop about 20 feet beyond the water's edge.

He clambered out and ran hell-for-leather up the beach. Frank, being 50 yards behind, did the same manoeuvre, and gave chase. As he sprinted through the sand he was memorising his target. Bald head, stocky and just over 6 feet tall. The back of his neck, reaching to his cranium, was covered in a large tattoo.

Frank had not managed to get any closer; obviously this guy was a very fit character. Once at the top of the beach, and across a small unmade road, he entered a village. Typically, Spanish narrow cobbled streets which criss-crossed like a zebras stripes.

He jogged around the whole village for almost half an hour. But he'd lost him. Frank was not one to concede, even checking out bars as he went; but eventually, decided to withdraw.

Having memorised the name and maritime number of the vessel, he climbed in the motor launch and did a search. He found nothing in the bridge cockpit or cabin other than a bottle of orange and remains of a sandwich. However, in the stern was an important find. Laying on the floor was what he recognised as a Russian made SVD sniper rifle, complete with a PSO 1x4 scope.

Frank grasped it with gratitude! A slightly slower passage back to the Marbella beach; returned the speed boat to its owner and trudged back to Café Del Mar, now crawling with Guardia Civil.

Frank entered the bar and slumped at a table. Anneliese and Barry, followed by Jerome and Paulo came in from the rear of the bar, followed by Anya, with her arm in a sling, and Albie. Frank stood, and walking as if on eggshells moved towards them saying, "Anya, how are you doing?" They all sat around a table. Anya explained it was a flesh wound, only slightly worse than a deep graze. "You look awful Frank" said Anneliese. "Why did you need to go for a cycle ride, Twisting her lips into a wry smile, she continued" Suppose you needed to escape the action!"

Frank coughed to clear his throat, then leaned forward with his elbows resting on the table. "The sniper fired from that motor launch anchored about half of a mile off the beach." He was about to say more but Paulo interrupted, asking "How do you know it was a sniper? That makes him sound professional." "Oh, he was" replied Frank as his right arm searched around behind his chair, dragging the rifle from its wedged position between his chair and the wall, he placed it on the table. "That is a sniper's rifle!"

Everyone around the table looked at Anya in disbelief. "It couldn't' have been meant for you" said Jerome with a sad but poignant tone. It must be a mistake!"

Seeing the gun lying on the table, the Senior Guardia Civil officer, came to the table. Frank took him out on the patio to explain what had occurred. Secretly, they knew of Frank and he agreed to go to the station in the morning to give them more details. Meanwhile they took the rifle as evidence, and asked Barry not to move anything at the beach bar.

The dissection and analysis of the events went on into the early hours. Before he left, Frank whispered to Anneliese that he should meet with her and Anya for lunch at the Estapona Hotel.

As people drifted away, Barry spoke with Carmella. She had been shaken by the events but assured Barry that she was ok and would definitely continue to work at the Bar. She was one of the last to leave, and once she had gone, Barry drove with Anneliese to the villa.

Next morning at their breakfast table, he knew it couldn't wait any longer. "Anneliese, I tried most of yesterday to tell you this but it kept eluding me. I have had two letters from Jess and my UK guys. Jess is doing great but has had an offer for our travel business. Mick and Eddie have had a lot of trouble piling on their plate and are begging for my help. I don't want to, but feel I need to go back to the UK for a week. And being totally honest with you, I would love to see my mum!"

Anneliese, with a gracious, understanding smile, said "I will miss you, but of course it's ok." Barry, with an urgency in his voice replied, "Why not come with me?"

She had been walking towards the kitchen, but as Barry spoke, she stopped abruptly. Turning to gaze out of the window as her thoughts developed, she swivelled on the balls of her feet and began to express her feelings. "Barry, that's a wonderful thought, but I think we should wait for a while. Perhaps your next visit." With a slightly nervous laugh, Barry asked "Why? I would love you to meet my family, and it will have to happen sometime."

"I think it needs time. Time is my only concern! You have told me before how much your Mum thinks of Linda, and it's not long since you broke up. That all needs time to heal. We should do it when we are both comfortable that all the pieces have been picked up. So I believe it will be best for all of you, Barry, if you face them alone!"

Barry thought carefully for a few seconds, then nodded as he winked agreement. "Anneliese, you always come up with the best answers." He lovingly uttered "I will miss you so much." "While you are away, I will work on the coding system and do some test runs with Paulo. It will keep me occupied." In the back of her mind, Anneliese knew this would progress her work for CECD!

It was now time for Anneliese to head to her meeting with Frank and Anya at the Estapona Hotel. She made her excuses saying she was meeting Anya for a girly lunch and to make sure she was in good spirits after yesterday's episode. Paulo had departed so now Barry wanted to spend some time with Albie, Jerome and a few of the others, talking business at the bar.

Frank arrived first at Estapona and having checked around, decided they should meet on the hotel patio in the gardens. It was a quiet peaceful place where they would not be overheard. Anya and Anneliese arrived on time and were informed by reception that Frank was on the patio. They would come out soon to take their drinks order.

Just nods and smiles rather than embraces and Frank got down to it. "First, I want to tell you all I know about yesterday's events. I had been watching the whole area from under the first beach canopy. When I saw the motor launch I began to use high visibility binoculars, but had to switch back and forth to keep an eye on the beachfront. It wasn't easy to get a clear view with the vessel so far out and bobbing up and down in the waves."

"Here's what happened. The first shot hit the Cruzcampo bar pump, ricocheted off the steel pump, and hit Anya. I was watching you and Paulo, struggling with the bike, and there couldn't have been more than a foot between you. The second attempt was made exactly at the time Paulo was trying to support you, Anya, as he bent to lower you to the floor. Once again, both of you were so close; less than several inches. But, significantly, if the shot had been a second earlier it would have shattered his skull. Instead, as he bent over it struck the metal tray on the back of the bar."

"So what do I make of all that. Well, playing Devil's advocate, I think I can confidently say he was attempting to assassinate one of you. Having said that there was another variable. His launch was rocking up and down in the waves. Do I think that was why he missed either Paulo or you, Anya? No I don't. The rifle I found, the fact that he was shooting from so far away, indicate he was an experienced sniper! So Anya, it's between you and Paulo. So what is the likelihood we should consider? For you Anya, could be your cover is blown! For Paulo, with the game he is in, he probably has many enemies. But we don't know enough about him yet."

A waiter arrived to get their drinks order. As he left, Frank said "Only a couple more things. We all need to be on our guard because if word gets passed around, we could all be targets. And we must be especially aware of the possible dangers for Anya." "There is another possibility, but I think unlikely. Carmella was behind the bar, but close to both of you!"

Anya chewed her lips as she looked at both of them. Frank continued, sitting up in his chair with both hands gripping the edge of the table. "Our target is a brute of a man. Big, over six feet, stocky, bald and very fit. But none of that helps much with identifying him. There is one thing that does. He has a tattoo covering all of the back of his neck up to his skull. I couldn't see what it was, but lots of blue ink; I've given all this information to CECD Intelligence and they are pouring through all their data to find him. Now, this is just my thinking; nothing yet from our Intelligence people. I have a strong suspicion that he is a Russian. He looked a Russian. But I have no idea why Russians would be involved!"

"The last point to make"... and he stopped as the waiter arrived with a bottle of Rioja and three glasses. The waiter only had eyes for the girls and made a very slow exit. Frank got back into his stride. "Early this morning I sat down with the Guardia Civil Senior officers and took them through the whole episode. Every detail. They will leave us to make progress but will always be watching and will support whenever we need it. I have explained that we are closing in for arrests here, and all over Europe and the U.K.

I laid it on a bit thick saying that I expected they would receive the kudos, but that after yesterday they needed to stay close to avoid any embarrassing political situations. I think that hit a high note with them."

Anneliese thanked Frank for all that detail. Then said, "Anya you are ok and so am I, and we are doing well with our work. The sun is shining and we are in a fabulous place. We are the best team anyone could imagine, so let's just continue enjoying life." They finished their drinks; Frank went off to his unusual Spanish Jeep, and the girls to their two superb Lotus Cortina's.

41

nya and Anneliese returned to Café Del Mar. Despite only having one capable arm, Anya hurried behind the bar to assist Carrie. Anneliese also joined in with the bar tending. Carrie had spent the morning with Barry and Albie, clearing the bar equipment from the beach and generally tidying up. The Guardia Civil had given them the all clear after studying the bar and agreeing with Frank's view on the attack.

With a look of discomfort in his expression, Barry told Anneliese he planned to fly back to the U.K. that evening with Jerome. He was due to work on the evening flight, so Barry thought he would take the chance to have some company. However, Barry was uncomfortable leaving due to the uncertain circumstances.

Albie wanted to go with Barry, but thought it best to join him in a few days to help with Danny's problems!

Up in a quiet secluded area of Calahonda, Frank was meeting with several CECD Secret Service agents and Intelligence Analysts. They talked through every feature of the previous day's events. Frank was accompanied by his 4 ex-mercenaries, to glean any information they had collected. It was an intense affair, trying to determine who was behind the attack, and if Russians, why?

Before they left for Malaga airport, Barry phoned Igor to say he would not be able to meet with him during the week, as he had a crisis to deal with back in the U.K. Igor was congenial, saying all his business with Barry was doing very well, so their meeting could wait until he returned.

The flight to the U.K was uneventful, Jerome was discretion itself; not indicating he knew Barry, but making sure he was very well looked after! Before Barry checked in, Jerome said he would be in Marbella in a week's time and in Amsterdam the following week.

Barry was picked up at the airport by Eddie, who took him directly to his mum's house. Seeing him, she cupped his face in her hands and attempted to choke back the tears. As they moved into the kitchen, mum filled the kettle to make Barry a cup of coffee. They sat at the kitchen table, leaning toward each other as they held hands across the table. As mum got up to take the boiling, whistling, kettle off the gas hob, suddenly the door opened. Framed in the doorway, stood Linda. Not a speck of animosity in her eyes. Indeed, the opposite; rushing towards Barry she was fighting to control her tears. Barry, overwhelmed by her spirit of generosity, clasped her tightly, first kissing her cheek, as she twisted her neck and drifted her lips to his. As they relented and relaxed into their chairs, Barry, with a nervy edge to his voice, said "I have missed you both so much" The outlook for the week could not be better! All the small talk led Barry to say he would love to meet with Jess the next day. Following that, it would all become more difficult with the business with Eddie and Mick Flick.

Frank was now back in his apartment in Estapona. He paced around, thinking about all the information he had gleaned from the meeting; which did not get him very far. Then he began to go over the whole event again. As he stood with his hands gripping the top of a chair, he became incensed, with himself. He could have done better, a lot better! If he had caught him, things would be different! His hands tightened on the chair; so tight his knuckles turned white and he swore to himself that he would find a way to recover the situation.

Essentially, the intelligence information available at present gave them nothing, however it was early days. Fingerprints from the gun, the boat, the orange drink bottle, were not on record. The assailant's description, including tattoos did not show up on records. The vessel had been stolen from Fuengirola. They had not intercepted any messages that indicated any form of link. Nothing, nothing, NOTHING. Frank decided it was time to sleep on it. Most of his best thoughts and ideas came through in the form of his dreams!

Next morning, his anger had subsided. He resolved to be less emotional. His years of training had instilled in him the need to stay calm and objective. He reminded himself to return to a steady state. His sleep had provided the ways and means to get back on track. Sitting alone, sipping his hot black coffee, it was now obvious that playing the lone ranger would not get the results they needed. So the first part of his plan would be to get his money's worth out of his four CECD agents.... The ex-mercenaries. He would meet with them and instruct them to work the whole area from Marbella to Almunecar... all along the coast. They would interview the motor launch owner and everyone in the vicinity to try to find any clues to the assailants' identity and whereabouts. There was a third element for them to execute. His dreaming had helped with this.

Although, until now, nobody had given any credence to Igor, the Russian, being involved, there was a slim chance. He is Russian, and despite him being in business with Barry; as Anya had said earlier, you can never trust a Russian!

Frank knew that coincidences, more often than not, identify the answer to all evils. So his team would watch Igor's every move, maintain 24hour surveillance on his house, and track anybody he met or associated with.

Barry, on the other hand, seemed to be having a much better time. He felt he had stepped back in time, several years, which was alluring to his newly developed genial mind set. His whole temperament treasured his meeting with Jess. Just like his mum's smile, Jess awoke his soul!

They sat in their local grubby pub. In the corner an old guy was tickling the ivories'. For Barry, this brought back the world that he had missed so much. He was back in the days when he had family love, and friends. And not friends that feared him; real friends!

Pulling his right ear lobe whilst chuckling and boisterously nodding his head, Jess eased to a gentle smile. Then with a fixed stare into Barry's eyes, Jess, with a gleeful raised voice, said "My best mate, you have done so well; been so successful and made me successful! We are all so proud of you. Joan is in ecstasy and talks about you all the time! She deserves to have a wonderful son like you!"

Those last few words downloaded the feeling of guilt Barry had been trying to ignore for several weeks.

"Jess, you have been more than a Dad to me and I will always be grateful for how you have cared for Mum. I'm just so sorry I have been away for so long; but I needed to try to make my own life." "Yes, and what a life you made, and for me as well!" Jess added with the widest grin, "But now I want to talk about the future."

With a slightly more serious expression, Jess reached across the table and clasped Barry's hand. "I'm sure you remember how much we paid for the Routemaster. A whole £600! Well Barry, we have received an offer for the business." Barry gripped Jess's hand tightly saying "Jess if you want to sell, go ahead and you should keep the proceeds. You put in so much hard work, it's well deserved."

Jess fidgeted in his seat; thought for a few seconds as he stared at the sticky carpet. "No Barry," he said as his face lifted to look at the ceiling then back to Barry's eyes.

"Please let me finish Barry because I am going to find the next bit very difficult." Barry's expression now filled with uncertainty. His eyes appealed to Jess to relieve his increasing concern.

Barry listened intently; his jaw hung loosely. Jess continued, "You, Barry, masterminded the business. I just did the menial work. But now, a man I trust, is offering us a life changing sum. I know we spent more than the £600 with the extra vehicles but not more than double. The offer on the table, Barry, is £35,000."

"Barry, I don't even know how many noughts in that figure!" Jess's expression exploded into raucous laughter and Barry joined in, leaning to Jess and smacking his arms.

However, there was more to come! "Barry, still easing down from the laughter, developed a partial frown. Jess, in a soft voice, whilst clasping his hands together, said, "Your Mum and I want to get married!" he stuttered into the next part; "and we both want to ask for your blessing. " Jess's eyes searched Barry's face.

There in the non-descript "Earl Derby", cockney back street pub, Barry's epiphany appeared. He was ecstatic at the thought of his Mum finding happiness, and that he had now been granted a Dad! One he had enormous love and respect for and, moreover, one he wanted to emulate!

"Jess, I'm so happy for you both. Of course you have my blessing! I know its early afternoon, but this is the East End so we have to have a party. Now! "Barry jumped out of his chair, went to the bar and asked Charlie to get everyone a drink. Throwing several notes across the bar, he asked Charlie, "Can I use the phone?"

He called a few numbers which got the jungle drums involved. Barry sat back down, looking at Jess as both of them sipped large whiskies. The pianist's loud vamping increased in volume as everyone around started raising their glasses, shouting "To Joan and Jess."

All the signs were that this would turn into a stag night. The uncles were first. Then a few cousins, followed by a host of Barry's henchmen. Mick Flick and Eddie were obviously pleased and relieved to see Barry, and all the time drinks flowed. Next came a pleasurable experience for Jess.

Just across from the pub, in the house on the corner, lived some people who were from the Caribbean. They were friends of Jess. They had several different occupations. Some were nurses and doctors in the local maternity hospital. So now the party included them; indeed they were the "life and soul."

They all came to embrace and congratulate Jess. Then straight to the bar and began partying. Some, after a while, began to dance, as Charlie plugged a record player in to play some modern music.

Barry glanced across at Jess; he couldn't help noticing that there was moisture, born out of pleasure, under Jess's eyes. Barry walked around behind Jess, and with everybody's eyes on him, grasped him around the neck and kissed him on the side of his head. A lengthy embrace that said everything!

The party was a fabulous evening. The uncles had always worried about Joan. She was the youngest of six. So now there was a lot of relief! Jess, with uncles either side of him, wobbled out of the door. For a while, they could be heard singing "On a bicycle made for two" and as that gradually ebbed away, Barry decided it was time to go home to Mum!

He edged to the door, shaking hands on the way. Mick Flick and Eddie decided they should go with him in the taxi. On the way to Joan's house, he agreed to meet his men on Thursday, giving them all time to recover. Danny and Mac were also to be there.

42

At the street door, he fumbled around for the key and eventually got himself through the door. He was disappointed to find Joan had gone to bed. On the other hand, he knew he sorely needed his!

Joan was first up in the morning. Barry about an hour later. The smell of bacon cooking woke him and he edged down the narrow staircase. As he reached the bottom of the stairs, pushing the soft latch door open with his knee, the first thing he noticed was the gas lights on the chimney breast wall. He stood for a minute or two, remembering how Joan had taught him to turn on the gas lamps and even replace the mantles if they broke. He recalled he must only have been six or seven when she spent ages with his training. First a chair to stand on and then a box of matches to light the mantles after turning on the gas. He quickly had become an expert!

But now Joan had electric light in her house, but had retained the gas lights. Just at that point, she walked in with a full breakfast for him. "Barry, I was just about to call you." "Mum, it's been some time since I've had an English Breakfast. You have made my day!"

As they both tucked into breakfast, Barry leant across the table and clasped Joan's wrist. "Mum, Jess told us the news last night. I couldn't be more pleased for you both. He is definitely the right man for you!"

Her angelic face always seemed to bear a calm expression. That was still there, but her eyes sparkled through some happiness tears that slowly trickled down her cheeks. Barry leaned forward to wipe them away. Joan said, "I was so worried you would find it difficult to accept." "No Mum, I love the bloke; he is my best mate and loves you!"

The emotional stuff was not in Barry's repertoire so, trying to change to a more light-hearted subject Barry asked, "Mum why have you still got those gas lights. Jess has helped you modernise with electric light and I got you a telephone. So why not get them taken out?"

"Barry, the reason is simple. Well it is to me! Modern is good if it helps us through the day. But life is not about just living for today. Your whole life is built on memories! I come down in the morning and see those gas lamps. I see you learning to use the chair to turn them on and off. I still feel the heartache as I remember going to work at night and having to leave you to look after yourself."

"Barry, they were really tough times for both of us, but they made you the man you are. And now you have worked hard and given us all a much better life." Barry smiled at her, but behind the smile was anguish. The life his Mum thought he had was total fiction; a complete and utter lie!

Mum was the most important person in his life, so he vowed he would not let this deception continue. He swore to change and find a way out!

Tomorrow he would meet with Danny, Mac, Eddie and Mick Flick. He was sure that meant they would be expecting him to lead them into some violent confrontation with the North London Boys. For the next 24 hours, his mind searched for an escape!

The day of reckoning arrived. They sat in the quiet lunchtime bar of the Greengate Pub. All the talk was almost a whisper. Mac described what had been going on. They had pushed ahead in North London and had taken several areas from Hackney, north. Customers liked them… much more than the Northies. But regularly, their people had been ambushed and sustained severe casualties. "How many?" asked Barry. Danny, who had endured the best education answered, "We have lost about 30% of our guys." But then quickly, following that, saying that the Northies had lost as many. "We gave us good as we got!"

"Ok", said Barry, "Let's stop there. I get the picture." "So where do they have a regular meet together?" Mac answered, "Tottenham Royal Disco, Saturday night, Most of their firm will be there."

Barry leaned forward with elbows on the small glass topped table. "Ok, this won't be too difficult. I would like you to get the maximum number of bodies there. Independently, time spaced, using the underground or buses. I will travel with you fellas to get there about 8pm as the dancing is beginning. We head in but no one, repeat no one, attacks until I say so." Eddie and Mick Flick looked at one another, a bit surprised. Then Mick Flick asked a crucial question. "Should we tell them all to come tooled up?" "Mick, of course," Barry replied, "We need to protect ourselves."

Barry patted all of them on the head as he stood. Shook their hands and his departing shot was "You guys are doing a great job," "I've got to shoot now lads. Got to sit down and start working on the Wedding arrangements. You will all be invited, so start thinking and planning your suits. Go to Manny Rosen in Forest Gate. He's the best!"

❈◆❈

43

Without Barry, the Marbella scene had seemed to enter a limbo period. The contrast was Frank. He spent every hour trying to find something that confirmed his suspicion about the Russian, Igor. But although he was receiving truckloads of information from Central Intelligence, nothing had any whiff of uncertainty about the credibility of the guy. None of the surveillance and research by his four colleagues had turned up anything. But Frank was absolutely certain that he was involved in the attack on the Jerome party and never gave up searching. As luck would have it, next day, a small chink of light appeared. Intelligence had intercepted a call from the Mayor's office to Igor. The Mayor's end of the call could not be distinguished as it was scrambled. But Igor was heard to say, "It is not wise to call me. Please make this the last time!"

That was all Frank had, but it was a lead. A fragile lead, but then why would the Spanish Mayor be calling Igor? Frank was sure this was a good lead and immediately left his apartment to find Anneliese.

They met and strolled along the beach together. Frank gave Anneliese, word for word, the exact intelligence information describing the phone call. They stopped and sat for a minute. Anneliese stared at the surf for a moment then began tapping her left knee as if trying to force her thoughts into the light! Looking sideways at Frank, she said, "Ask yourself this. What activity is easy for a Mayor to become involved in, have substantial influence in, and have access to every piece of necessary information? And, therefore always susceptible to temptation and corruption. My money would go on land sales, developments, property and construction."

Frank, tugging on his earlobe, uttered, "You reached a conclusion which I had considered, and I agree it's top of the pile. But where I can't make it hold together is when I try to align it with the sniper attack at Jerome's party. The shots were either for Anya or Paulo. I'm pretty definite on that, but I can't find any potential link to the Mayor or the property angle!"

"Neither can I, Frank, but let's not concede before some more investigation. I will talk with Central Command; their best intelligence analysts. I'll get them to research every commercial property deal, land sale and construction in the whole area. They may find a link to the Mayor or Igor somewhere! And, a tail on the Mayor as well as Igor won't go amiss either."

Whilst these two had been applying their brains, Barry and Albie were lining up the brawn. Their team, well-spaced out, entered the Disco and unobtrusively mingled. Barry and Albie were chatting and laughing as Albie described how, when he arrived at Shirley's she was with a new bloke. Albie smiled, saying he wished them the very best!

Danny, wearing his trade mark Crombie, was standing the other side of Barry. The expression on Barry's face hardened. The dance floor was clearing and his vision picked out a line of fellas forming on the other side of the dance floor. The Boleyn Boys, as if by magic, appeared from all over, forming their line to face and eyeball the Tottenham Boys.

Barry's eyes turned to a questioning look as he stared at a red haired guy standing in the middle of them. His expression changed again; gradually the corners of Barry's mouth turned upward into a wide grin.

Barry, with arm outstretched, pointing at the redhead, began to walk forward, still smiling as he said to Danny, "It's Billy Murdoch!" Then some of the Boleyn Boys followed, as if dragged along in his slipstream.

Barry had always figured that "latecomers" always caused a problem! This night was no different. A very young, fresh faced impetuous Tottenham "death or glory" lad arrived behind the Boleyn Boys. Seeing his boss across the room, Barry pointing and heading towards him, he decided on glory!

With his knife gripped to plunge deep, he rushed past Danny and Albie. The saviour was Danny, who reacted with a knee flexing flick, tripping the young assailant. Losing his balance, he careered into Barry; the knife, slicing down the side of his upper arm.

Several punches began to be thrown all around, as Danny pulled out from his Crombie the trusted baseball bat. Ready to batter the kid and all of his cronies!

By now, Billy Murdoch had run across to Barry and was supporting him. They both screamed out, "stop you lot, back off, this is not going to happen!" The room quietened as Billy Murdoch led Barry to the bar area.

With everything now quiet; the bouncers, keeping their distance, just considered themselves very fortunate. The bar filled with both Boleyn and Tottenham boys, and enjoyment, rather than engagement, became the name of the game.

That evening in the bar, Barry and Billy Murdoch became good mates once more. They had lost touch, but reminisced about times training together and playing against one another when both of them were trying to build a career in football. Danny also knew Billy. Like most footballers that don't make it, both Danny and Billy had ended playing for an amateur side called Cubitts Town FC from the Poplar area. Billy now had two good mates to resurrect his earlier life.

Just before it was time to leave, contact details provided, Barry said, "Billy, let's get together in this business. You are good at it and so am I. And if you like the idea, think about the details and then come down to Marbella for a holiday with us." Billy's expression changed. "Where is Marbella?" "It's on the Costa in Spain." Replied Barry. "If you will come, I will pay for your holiday."

Billy was gobsmacked. Embraces were the order of the day, and nobody was in intensive care! Mick Flick and Eddie were ready in the car, although somewhat inebriated. Mick, concerned about Barry's arm, took a close look, and with a smile said "It's healing already." Eddie, pulled away slowly, as Barry began to explain.

Barry, although somewhat excited by the story he had to tell, but also feeling very tired, said "the leader of the Tottenham boys is a fella named Billy Murdoch. A red haired tough looking geezer."

Barry still smiling said, "I first came across him when I played for the West Ham boy's team. He was playing for Tottenham boys. Then West Ham sent us to train at Tottenham. In the changing rooms the atmosphere was pretty stiff. Then the local cleaner came in, ordering us all around to keep the place tidy. He was aggressive, but was only small so we gave him respect. By that I mean, me and

Billy. Most of the others were shit heads that continually messed up and gave him a hard time."

"Our nickname for this little man was Popeye because he looked like him and had massive forearms. If the other fellas gave Popeye a hard time, me and Billy gave them a roughing up! Then we did training together at a place in Stepney. Indoor, mostly 5-a-side, with a Tottenham First team player called Tommy. Smashing fella and brilliant player. Then the last time we met was in an A Team game at the Spotted Dog. It had been a West Ham training ground but then Clapton took over"

Through these teenage football years, Barry and Billy had become close friends. But football had left them both behind; they both felt dumped! So now with animosity driving their thoughts, both had been trying to build criminal lives.

During recent stressful times, Barry's psychosis had been tested to the limit. However, Anneliese had given him tools to manage it. Over the last 24 hours, he had relied on that special word.... The word RAFT. It was proving to be a superb method to prevent those horrific psychotic episodes. The events in the Tottenham Royal had given him positive confirmation! Possibly, Anneliese had given him a way to prevent these nightmares.

44

Now, with everything on the up, all he could think about was returning to Anneliese in Marbella. Danny and Mac were now calm and comfortable about working with Billy Murdoch and his team. Jess and Mum needed time to plan the wedding. All Barry's uncles were in a good place, having met with Barry; and relieved about Joan getting married. So, it seemed there were no outstanding issues that needed Barry's attention.

He, therefore, decided he would return to Marbella next day, a day early!

At breakfast, whilst Barry was getting his mind in some sort of order, Joan was cooking, talking, and generally enjoying having her boy around. She had been up for hours, wanting to prepare a grand East End fried breakfast for Barry.

During the next hour or so, Barry was fed, watered and most of all, pampered by Joan. He was in the middle of explaining that he needed to get back to Marbella today to handle some business, when the kitchen door opened. Linda stood in the doorway, sunshine all around her, creating a stunning silhouette. She smiled a smile that caused an emotion in Barry. He genuinely still had love for her, but not with the romantic sensual strength of Anneliese.

The gentle conversation with Mum and Linda essentially involved the wedding. Barry asked that they keep him up to date and Linda promised to help with everything. Barry, almost overcome by Linda's sincere sentiments, said if they needed anything paid for, he would handle it. And to tell Jess to enjoy every minute of the build-up to the big day!

He arrived at Malaga airport about 2pm. His Jaguar S Type was parked at the airport and he couldn't wait to get down to Marbella. He sniffed in the aroma of the leather as he settled in his seat, looking around at the instruments and wood panelled dash board. As he roared away, once again he was overcome with thoughts of where he had got to; it all seemed like a dream! Albie was asleep in his own dream!

He booted it all the way down the Costa del Sol to Marbella, desperate to see Anneliese. He enjoyed every moment, every fast cornering moment. The car behaved as if it knew where it was going! The journey was exhilarating then as he slowed into Marbella, down by the quayside, he skidded to a halt outside Café Del Mar.

Barry stood leaning on the car roof, admiring his surroundings. As he took off his Ray-Bans and began to carefully place them in the case, there was a squeal from the doorway. Anneliese was floating down the steps toward him. With her right arm outstretched and left hand preventing her skirt blowing in the sea breeze; she ran straight into Barry's arms, clasping him around the neck, as she kissed his face.

They strolled up the steps together, with Barry rubbing his eyes to temper the strong sunlight. In the bar, everyone was pleased to see him back again. Barry sat with Anneliese, Albie and Anya recounting events of the last week. Anya, opened with one new piece of news. The work on the Marina was beginning. Early days, but with some noise during the day. Jose had told her that in the next few weeks, cranes and dredgers would appear to begin the difficult ground-works in the harbour.

Barry, with great pleasure, told them about his mum and Jess tying the knot. Barry looking around the table, said "Once I know their plans, we will get ourselves organised. New outfits for everyone!" With that, Barry stood to take off his white linen jacket. Anneliese was first to notice his arm. "Barry, what happened, that looks awful!" The bandage and tape covering it had not been able to prevent the constant leakage.

Both Anneliese and Anya surrounded him, looking closely, saying "That bandage needs replacing!" Albie, the usual joker, laughed as he said, "It could have been worse!" The girls, with concern on their faces, never responded. Just then Carrie, seeing the wound, came round from the bar. "Senor Barry," she said with concern reflected in her dark Spanish eyes. "Let me clean it and dress it for you. I have learned First Aid." She turned and looked at Anneliese and Barry. They both smiled and nodded!

Carrie went off to the stock room to the first aid box. She returned in a moment and led Barry to the back of the bar saying, "Don't think our customers want to watch us!"

As she worked on Barrie, Anneliese appeared. Carrie, speaking with a serious tone said to Anneliese, "We must be careful with this, it is deep and really required several stitches. If it does not improve in the next couple of days, we must take him to hospital."

Anneliese smiled and nodded, as she clipped his ear like a mother would do, saying "Barry what have you been up to now?" Glancing at Carrie, then Anneliese, Barry said "It's a long story, but I think you'll like it. I will explain tomorrow."

They hustled back into the main bar, just as Frank appeared. Looking at Barry's bandaged arm, Frank couldn't resist saying "Barry how did you manage to get a love bite on your arm. Was the girl short sighted?" All around began to giggle as Frank, with a huge smile, shook Barry's hand saying, "We have missed you!"

Barry stayed that night with Anneliese. She explained that in the morning she had to go into Marbella town to buy some ladies products. The truth was she would have a short meeting with Frank.

Anneliese met Frank at their usual secluded part of Estapona beach. Frank gave the first feedback. Central Intelligence had not turned up anything new on Igor, but they were continuing delving into all areas of his life, and continuing surveillance. Igor had met "off piste" with the Mayor twice. But the meetings seemed just sociable. Intelligence personnel were now putting more effort into Paulo, although they seemed to be coming up against a brick wall. The suspicion was that, for some reason, MOSSAD were protecting Paulo's details.

Anneliese then detailed her plans for Barry over the next few weeks. She would cajole Barry into testing out the coding system with Paulo. "Maybe some more information about Paulo would slip out somewhere."

Anneliese arrived at Café Del Mar early afternoon. They spent the rest of the day enjoying the delights of Marbella. Later on they left the bar community and went for a walk along La Playa. Shoes off, they trudged down to the water's edge and eventually sat on the warm sand at the top of the beach.

Barry turned and gripped both of Anneliese's hands. "You asked for the story about the arm wound." He began by relaying all the stories from Mac and Danny, about the constant trouble with the Tottenham Boys. "What was strange was that none of it got me angry. The more thought I gave it, the more my mind wanted to side-step those psychotic episodes. I used your trigger word, RAFT, constantly. And before we even arrived to face them, my mind had decided that I would do my best to convince them to work with us, rather than carry on with bloodshed."

"The bottom line was extraordinary. We faced across from each other, and then I recognised their leader. And he recognised me! We had been good mates in the past, so now it was all about to settle down. Except, there was an accident. A young upstart had arrived late and imagined it was all about to kick-off. He fell over as he stabbed me and the Tottenham Boys pulled him away."

"Anneliese, the most fantastic thing was that my psychosis never appeared. This, I am sure is all down to you. You have changed my life, and now I can begin to prepare for both of us to leave this distorted world."

Anneliese pulled Barry close. With his head resting on her shoulder, she spoke with a soft gentle tone. "Barry, I can't believe this is happening. It's amazing, but you need to be certain you want to step into a different life, and be sure that your recovery will be long-term."

Barry could not see the perplexed look on Anneliese's face; her mind was pleased for Barry's renewal, but concerned for her work situation. In a split second, she decided that there was only one thing she could do, and that was to humour him!

That night, Barry's lovemaking was tender, gentle and mesmerized Anneliese's body and soul. This is an enthralling transformation, she thought, as they rolled back onto their pillows and sleep engulfed them.

Next morning, she sensed that her affection for Barry was becoming uncontrollable. As they sat across the breakfast table, Anneliese was resisting a feeling of adoration for him. She clamped down on those thoughts, by getting into work mode. "Barry, can we do a couple of hours work on the code and then set up some tests with Paulo?"

When breakfast had been cleared away, Anneliese brought out the five books. She began, with Barry, by writing a few messages that Barry composed. She explained that she thought they were too long. "They need to be brief and staccato!" "What does that mean?" he asked. "Well, short, sharp with clear direct meaning!" Another half an hour of this training and Barry held Anneliese's wrist, saying "Anneliese, this is not my thing. Never was good at written English. Could we try it this way? When we need to send a message, we can agree what's to be said, you can put it together and do the necessary with the books. I'm sorry love, I can handle and enjoy problems, but I am not a person that can manage writing!"

Anneliese smiled graciously, all the while knowing that Barry's secret messaging system would be completely visual to her. She would provide all information of importance to Central Command Intelligence, and would also share, as necessary, with Frank and Anya.

Over the next three or four weeks, they all enjoyed the Garden of Eden that was Marbella. Business continued without a hitch and gained ground throughout the region. Anneliese did several test and dry runs with the coding system, using the long range radio. She involved Barry on most occasions to give him confidence that he was in charge!

45

The doubts surrounding Igor seemed to gradually drift away as Paulo became the focal point. So Barry was now more at ease with having another meeting with Igor. The business in Central Europe was growing rapidly and Igor would have seen that from the supply orders. But the negative he had to bring into the open was France, and also the patch of Spain that Igor would find acceptable.

They agreed to meet mid-August. Igor was flying in that day so they would drive up to Malaga and join him in one of the airport hotels. It was a roof-top bar that looked across the airport. Noisy at times when planes were taking off and landing, but that lessened the chances of being overheard.

Barry had his agenda, but Igor spoke first. He was rapturous concerning the growth of business in Central Europe and Spain. The two henchmen that always seemed to accompany him sat on a separate table. They never uttered a word and maintained a fierce looking stare.

That seemed to unsettle Albie, but then Barry launched into his agenda, taking Albie's mind off the fearsome two Russians. "First Igor, I am pleased you can see we have been working hard. But there is an issue. I've decided I don't want to work the French regions. You can have it, and if you need any help I will attempt to provide it."

"Next is your focus on Spain. I would think the two best areas for you to approach are Cadiz and Alicante. Both are developing tourist spots which I have been working towards myself. That whole Cadiz region is offered to you. Instead, I will continue to work up the coast from Marbella. How does that sound Igor?"

"Let's have one more drink while I consider your offer," replied Igor. He sat with his legs crossed, sipping his Rioja. All the while his resting leg swung loosely up and down. His leg stopped moving as he leant forward placing his glass on the table top. "Barry, I like your offers so let's go with it and see how we get on!" Barry smiled. Then leaned across the table to shake hands.

Igor gripped his hand as if he would never let go. "I have to go now Barry, but there is one other small item. When you return to your Utopia, you will find you are missing a barmaid. The one you hired recently. She works for the Spanish Secret Service which is a dangerous thing for both of us. We tried a short while ago to eliminate her threat, but failed." As he spoke, he glanced across at one of his henchmen. "Be more careful, Barry, with people you let in!"

The three Russians headed out the door glancing back at Barry and Albie as they left. Both Barry and Albie spotted it! The last Russian's neck was decorated with the head and wings of an eagle.

Barry, with a concerned expression said, "Albie, think we need to get back." As they drove, Barry, as if talking to himself said, "They planned this when they knew we would be out of the way." Albie with a furrowed brow, said "Carmella and Anya were alone in the bar when we left."

The road before Café Del Mar was blocked off by several Guardia Civil Police cars and an Ambulance. Albie and Barry pulled over about 100 yards from the bar and sprinted along the side of the road. They were prevented from entering the bar by one of the policemen at the entrance. Barry showed his ID and stated he was the owner. They were allowed in. The furniture was a bit of a mess with three tables upturned and chairs knocked over. In the corner, sitting on a chair was Anya, being attended by two paramedics.

Barry and Albie went directly to her. She appeared generally ok but with a few minor wounds; a large gash in her ankle, a swollen wrist which had been bandaged and a graze down the right side of her neck. She appeared dazed, as Albie faced her and stared.

One of the Guardia Civil Officers came across to Barry and Albie. He was accompanied by an English Interpreter who began to explain what had happened. He only managed a few words when Anya snapped out of her aftermath haze.

Apparently, early afternoon, Carrie and Anya were in the bar alone. They were just doing some cleaning with Carrie cleaning behind the bar and Anya cleaning table tops. Three stocky guys, all wearing black masks burst in. As Anya was, after a deep breath, going to continue, Anneliese walked in. Initially a picture of elegance, her poise fell away as she dropped to her knees in front of Anya. Cupping her face gently in her hands, with emotion in her voice, she asked Anya, "Who did this; what happened my darling?"

Anya continued her descriptive commentary. "Three guys burst in. I thought they were thieves, but all of them chased around the bar trying to catch Carrie. She was unbelievably agile, throwing herself across the bar and began to run down to the back of the bar. They attempted to jump the bar, so I attacked and fought them. One grabbed my throat, so I whipped round and punched him so hard he fell down on his knees. The third guy was only interested in chasing Carrie and as he leapt off the bar, I kicked his leg so hard, I split my ankle. I fell on the floor with the pain, and they all managed to chase her out of the back door. She had her car parked out the back so I think she managed to get away. One thing I noticed was that all the pool cues were lying across the floor, whether she used them to defend herself, or whether she just pulled them over to slow them down, I don't know."

The Guardia Civil Officer said there was no more they could do, but would go away, put out all the necessary alerts to see if they could find Carmella. Anya had said she thought they had used a Citroen Van, but it was parked across the road. So nothing definite!

The usual group sat at the bar, and after about an hour, customers began to arrive. It was as if these events had a magnetic effect and customers wanted to be in the thick of it.

In the quiet of the Men's toilets, Barry asked Albie not to mention to anyone what was said by Igor. "Of Course not," replied Albie. "Because, if you did, it may involve us two and not sure where that would lead." Barry continued, "We need to stay out of this one if we want to keep a clean sheet!"

Anya and Albie went to their flat early. Anya had been very quiet since the attack and also was probably concerned for Carmella. Terry and Jose arrived saying they had only just heard. They had been out with some of the other Boleyn Boys pursuing business up in Fuengirola.

After Barry explained what had happened. Jose volunteered to use his local network to find any trace of Carmella. Then Terry said to Barry, "Geezer, you look like it's been a long day. Why don't you and Anneliese get off and we will look after the bar. There's only a few customers, and when they leave we can close up early!"

Barry knew he could trust these two characters. Their loyalty had proved impeccable. He was extremely grateful and placed a marker in his mind to ensure he repaid them in some way.

Neither of them were in the best of spirits, but once in the door of the villa, their mood brightened. Anneliese went straight to the bar and opened a bottle of Rioja. Barry, simply holding his glass of glorious red wine, seemed to relax. Some music from Elvis, the "King of Rock n Roll" completely suppressed the solemn atmosphere.

The progress to the second glass of wine was as fast as the lifting of their spirits. Anneliese spoke, as her tall statuesque figure eased off the settee. "Barry, I'll just go and make us some small tapas. It will only take a couple of minutes."

For a short while, Barry now very relaxed, continued sipping his drink. The Rioja aroma found a sensitive spot and overwhelmed his emotions. He had to be close to Anneliese! That was all he knew. He strode into the kitchen where she stood, curvaceously chopping something! He edged close behind her and grasped her around the waist. Her head slowly leaned back and he kissed her neck, time and again! Barry, with a choked stutter voice, slowly spoke. "That Carmella was a lovely person. I was taking to her." Anneliese turned her head, looking straight into Barry's eyes. "No, nothing like that; not an attraction. She just seemed to want to do the best for everybody. She worked hard and got on well with all of us. No woman should ever be attacked or abused! I will never forgive that bastard for it. What goes around comes around!"

Anneliese, swivelled immediately to face Barry. "What are you going on about? What bastard?"

Barry, with guilt in his face, and sadness in his eyes, began to explain. "As Igor was leaving our meeting, he turned and said, when you get back to the bar you will be missing a barmaid. The new one you hired recently! She was Spanish Secret Service and dangerous for both of us. My anger psychosis never kicked in! I wish it had, because all I am feeling now is guilt and sympathy for little Carmella.

Anneliese spent the rest of the evening pampering Barry. She was acutely aware of how Barry's mental state had changed, which continued to negate the negatives and, without her realising it, increase her devotion.

Next day was a new day. Barry had decided he would get his mind back on the business. So had Anneliese! Barry left for the bar and Anneliese would catch up with him midday. Her time, until then, would be taken up with feeding this incriminating information to Central Command Intelligence.

She, almost immediately, received a call from Central Command. The boss wanted to meet with her, Anya and Frank urgently. They should get themselves to Granada for a 2pm meeting tomorrow. They would receive details of the location in the morning and would need to invent a cover story. One suggestion was that Anneliese and Anya wanted to research skiing in the Granada Region, as they were approaching winter.

Anneliese set off for Café Del Mar at lunchtime to give herself time to get this organised! Before she arrived, it was all planned in her mind. She just needed to be patient and pick the right times with Barry and Albie.

Early lunchtime the bar was quiet. Anya and Anneliese sat at one of the bar tables on the patio, chatting as ladies do! Anneliese whispered to Anya that in a short while they would pretend they had just come up with the idea. Five minutes later, both girls jumped up, and with excited expressions ran into the bar.

Barry and Albie were seated on stools at the bar. Anya and Anneliese, with deliriously happy faces, cuddled both of them. Albie with a knowing frown said, "Barry its trouble; they want something!" Both girls giggled then Anneliese, caressing Barry's neck, said, "We have a request. It's not too difficult and won't cost anything. " "Ok, that's all the soft soap, now explain!" Barry's approach received an immediate response.

"Anya and I love skiing and its coming up to winter." Anneliese stopped as Barry began to chuckle. "Darling, you won't find much skiing around here unless you mean water skiing!" "No, my own little geezer, you are wrong. Granada is famous for its winter resort facilities. It's only an hour away and Anya and I would like to drive up there tomorrow and do some research, and perhaps make a booking. We could all go and have our Christmas there. After all the sunshine, it would be a superb end to our year, especially as it's such a close venue and such a contrast!"

Barry and Albie were lost for words. "Anneliese, are you sure about this? It's 35c today and you are telling us we could be in a snow capped resort that's only an hour away." "Yes, yes, yes" squealed Anya. "It's so exciting! It will be a real Christmas to look forward to!"

Barry and Albie, still doubting what they were hearing, looked at one another and then to the girls. Barry took Anneliese's hand and said, "Of course we agree. So what is the timetable?" Anya had it all worked out. "We will leave about 8.00am and be back here about 6.00pm. That should give us plenty of time." Anneliese asked, "Will you boys be ok with the bar? It's a very quiet period at present so I think you will have a relaxing day." So, the cover story had been perfectly executed!

At precisely 8.00am, the girls set off in Anya's Lotus Cortina. The arrangement with Frank was to meet him on the outskirts of Malaga, at a services. It was about half way, and they could get coffee and a breakfast. From there, he would shadow them at a distance in his Jeep. After the meeting, Frank would go his own way to meet up with his surveillance operatives who had been keeping tabs on Igor.

46

As they entered Granada Centro, Frank closed in and flashed his intention to overtake and lead the way. The CECD office, was close to the Catholic Cathedral and the Alhambra Palace. Frank pulled into a small courtyard on the Calle de Gomerez. It was a very scenic area. They stood in the courtyard, shaded by palm trees. However, they were not precluded from a view. Both the Alhambra Palace and the Cathedral were to be seen, towering in the distance.

As they sauntered towards the two storey office building, both Anneliese and Anya presented exquisite and enthralling female forms. Despite a lengthy car journey, both girls appeared as innocent pure waterlilies floating across the courtyard.

Frank, who never ever seemed to notice, strode ahead, leading the way to the access point. A security guard checked their credentials and showed them into the Commander's transit office. All was very quiet. The offices seemed vacant, other than two men they noticed climbing the stairs as they entered the Commander's inner sanctum.

The Commander gave them a generous welcome and invited them to sit. Anneliese and Anya were, clearly, a bonus he had been looking forward to! After a few polite references to the journey and the weather the Commander continued. "I have taken these offices to be closer to you. The stuff you are dealing with is high on the agenda. The people you have identified are very big fish in the narcotics pond, and possibly, the business of de-stabilising our democracies. The Russian, Igor, has significant backing from the Kremlin. The Argentinian is under surveillance by the Israelis. We have not got to the bottom of that yet, but he is playing in the big league."

"I called this meeting, because we need to talk about the recent information you gave me, and how we should react. You guys are very accomplished. You know that, right now, there is a whole basket of people that we could arrest. The Boleyn Boys all over Europe; The Moroccans; people all around Amsterdam and Brussels; The Russian, the Argentinian and their Columbian partners. But Igor is only susceptible to drugs charges. I think that, if we are patient, there is a lot more we can get on him. The information from Anneliese concerning the meeting with Igor and Barry was an eye opener. We have done more work on that!"

"Igor, said she, Carmella, was Spanish Secret Service. That was her cover within Spain. Indeed, she was an agent, but not for Spain. I have been over and over it with the Spanish. she was not with them. Our research says she was working with the Israelis. She is MOSSAD. Her name is a giveaway. Carmella is of Hebrew origin! We still do not know why or what they are trying to achieve, but eventually we will."

"In the meantime, ladies and gentlemen, we should just carry on. Our Intelligence Specialists are constantly in touch with MOSSAD and are beginning to establish a rapport. They appear desperate to find their agent, Carmella, so they can recover any intelligence she had not already passed on. Somehow, they had managed to infiltrate Spanish Secret Service administration and had planted documents that gave her access to their files. So

MOSSAD must be searching for someone or something! Now they are pre-occupied with rescuing their agent and establishing what she knows!"

"Lastly, we should not, under any circumstances, move in on Igor or, indeed anyone else at this stage. We will keep Igor under surveillance, and I will liaise with MOSSAD concerning our information about Carmella, at the appropriate time! And your team must find a way to prevent Barry or Albie spreading this information. I am relying on your ingenuity!"

The Commander's closing shot was "We are close to finalising this assignment and, therefore may need to meet again very soon. You now know that I am close by and will support you in any way I can!"

Anneliese and Anya arrived back at the bar late afternoon. Having had a long day, they slowly strolled into the bar, expecting to have to answer several questions about their day researching the ski resorts. Instead, Barry wide-eyed and grinning, rushed to meet them.

Barry stopped in front of them. For several seconds, he seemed lost for words. Anneliese and Anya, open-mouthed, waited for him to say something; anything! Albie appeared, and whilst attempting, comically to flex Barry's cheeks and lips; said "Well should I tell them?" This initiated an excited response. Barry just blurted out, "Mum and Jess are getting married at the beginning of October.... Only two weeks away! We are all invited and so we have to start getting ourselves organised."

An hour or so later, after the wedding talk had been exhausted, Albie asked Anya how the ski resort reconnaissance had gone. Both girls gave the appearance of being excited. Anya began by saying they had visited

Pradollano in the Sierra Nevada. There were many ski hotels and lodges to choose from; none open for business yet. Anneliese continued "We went to a small bar for lunch and struck up a conversation with a lovely couple. They said the highest peaks, usually with the best snow, were the Mulhacen and the Valeta. They recommended a ski lodge named the Vista Nevada and thought they would probably start taking bookings in October for vacations in January."

Anya began prancing around saying "Can we go, please can we go!" Anneliese edged toward Barry, slowly sliding her arms around his neck, "Barry, we want to go back in October to view the Vista Nevada Ski lodge. Apparently it has slopes both for novices and the more accomplished, like Anya and I. So all four of us could enjoy New Year in the snow!"

Barry, with a grimace dictating his expression, nodded his agreement. Albie, said, "But we are not promising to ski. Instead, we may start in the bar and go downhill from there!" Barry chuckled, then said "My agreement is on condition that you take on some of the tasks to get this wedding trip arranged!" " We will start tomorrow and it will be a true pleasure," announced Anneliese.

The next week flew by. They had all put effort into ensuring the wedding arrangements were totally reliable. They would travel a week before the day so that Barry, Albie and the girls could have time in London to select their outfits. The girls couldn't wait for this element.

Frank had agreed to manage the bar with Jerry and Jose's assistance. The Commander had concerns as they were close to finalising the operation. But Frank had convinced him that nothing would evolve in the short time Anneliese and Anya were away, and it would appear very suspicious if they attempted to find excuses in the circumstances.

Barry's contribution to the arrangements had involved him spending most of the week telephoning, mostly his mates. He had invited them all, including the latest associate, Billy Murdoch. Anneliese had advised Barry that they would be staying in a posh hotel in London. Close enough to Bond Street for the girls to find fabulous outfits. Barry had used Danny to organise some special things. A Registry office full of flowers, a white Rolls Royce, presents for Mum and Jess, as well as paying for a co-op Hall, Disco and buffet fit for a Queen! Barry even managed to get Eddie to invite Jess's Windrush friends who had decided on a Caribbean dress code and Reggae music!

47

It was to be a Friday wedding. They arrived in London the previous Sunday and spent the evening enjoying the delights of their posh hotel. They planned to do their shopping Monday and Tuesday. The girls were excited and set off into Bond Street and Soho early on Monday. Albie and Barry went to Manny, their East End tailor. They agreed to meet early evening, at The Ritz. Barry and Albie stood at the door as Anneliese and Anya jumped out of the taxi, smothered in classy shopping bags.

They entered The Ritz. All of them were overcome by the grandeur of the place. Reception stored their bags and they were invited to the restaurant, which the girls could not resist. Their evening was more than enjoyable, with some dancing, with all eyes on Anya and Anneliese.

Later on, a couple of young, posh Chelsea upstarts could not stay away from the girls any longer. They sidled up to the table. Looking at Albie and Barry, they asked, "Gentlemen, would you mind if we asked these ladies to dance." Anneliese and Anya, glancing at them, seemed amused.

Albie began to stand, but Barry grabbed his wrist and pulled him back down. The lead guy turned to Anneliese and asked, "May I have this dance beautiful lady." Anneliese, her smile gradually extending to the corners of her mouth said, "We are so flattered that you have asked, but we are with MEN, so I think you should cut your losses and find some young girls that appreciate posh boys!"

Having said a polite "thank you" they turned and strode off across the floor. Anneliese looked at Barry. He glanced a return smile. "You definitely have changed, Barry. You were astounding!" Anya pulled Albie towards her and said, "That's how to behave. You have nothing to worry about with me!" Then those few words that are inescapable emerged. "Albie, I love you so much."

The second day of shopping, Tuesday, was Anneliese's and Anya's day of pure excitement. They returned, early evening with dresses they had selected at Derry and Toms. Both dresses had required minor adjustments and both carried the exclusive "Balenciaga" label. The girls couldn't wait to try them on for the boys to see.

They looked stunning. Knee length and with tops that were not cut too low, but still retained attractive femininity. They both reflected utter class!

But the true excitement came when they modelled in front of Albie and Barry. Anya's dress was maroon with light blue edging. Anneliese's dress was light blue with a maroon neck and arm edging. These girls had done their homework.

Barry, for a full minute, could not speak. He turned to Albie and their speech was completely synchronised. "They are wearing West Ham dresses!" Albie screamed, "C,mon you irons" and both of them rushed to the girls, gushing "thank you, thank you."

The next stake in the ground was Wednesday evening. They would all go to meet Joan and Jess.

Anneliese and Anya could sense the boys were nervous about them all meeting Joan and Jess. They needn't have been, Joan and Jess were their normal selves. No airs and graces. Short welcoming embraces were followed by

Joan putting the whistling kettle on the gas hob and Jess offering Barry and Albie a beer. They all chose to have tea, and sat around the kitchen table as Joan, set up the best tea cups, as she took off her pinnie!

There was an almost magical affinity between the girls and Joan, especially Anneliese. She got up and went to help Joan with the teas, all the time chatting, probably about the wedding. They all bonded throughout the evening.

When it came to time to depart for their hotel, Joan embraced each of them. Barry and Anneliese received special attention. Joan clung onto their hands and looking into Barry's eyes said with a lovingly proud expression "You have found your treasure. Anneliese is your holy grail; I knew you would find her one day!" Scanning back and forth both their eyes, Joan's voice quietened almost to a whisper. "Please care for, and love, one another, every minute!" Glancing at Jess, she continued, "I've got it and pray for the same for you two."

Jess put his arms around Barry and Albie as they wandered towards the street door. Anneliese and Anya hugged Joan and, as they went to their car Jess, with a Caribbean dialect tone, shouted, "See you Friday, and don't be late!"

Essentially, Thursday night started the wedding celebrations. The lads went out on another Stag night. The girls all joined Joan at her home to celebrate in the girls' way. Joan insisted she wanted her bed at 10pm so all the ladies showed respect and went around the corner to finish their evening in the grubby local. By 11pm, closing time, all the fellas had arrived and the cockney knees up began in earnest. Anneliese and Anya had never seen so much expressive exhibitionism, in both young and old.

When they left, despite most being inebriated, there was no sign of a bad mood anywhere. Almost everyone came out to wave goodbye to them as they set off for the only hotel nearby... in Stratford.

Albie, for once, was up early. He got everyone else up to have breakfast together. Although there were a few sore heads, they all managed to become partially alive by mid-day. After a few lunch time drinks in the Stratford local, The Two Puddings, everybody seemed back in the real world and ready for the 3.00pm wedding.

They all arrived at the Registry Office in East Ham Town Hall in plenty of time. The fashion on show was extraordinary. Especially, Anneliese, Anya, Barry and Albie. Compliments from all and sundry had them glowing with pride.

But then the bride and Jess arrived. Nobody could match their attire. Jess was wearing a vivid light blue three piece suit with winged collar shirt and maroon bow tie. West Ham United appeared again!

Joan upstaged everyone, she stepped out of the car wearing a gloriously colourful Caribbean outfit. A smock dress and turban so colourful not even the bright sunlit afternoon could compete. Two young Caribbean children followed her, also in dresses full of colour.

As they led the guests' into the Town Hall, smiling and chatting to everyone, Joan stopped at Barry and gave him a motherly kiss. Jess shook his hand, and at that point, all the guests began to clap and cheer!

The service was faultless, with quite a few tears shed by guests. The evening entertainment in the Co-op hall was exceptional and constant. Early evening a disco, followed by a superb buffet provided by the wives of Joan's brothers.

After the service, when they first arrived at the Co-op hall, Barry sat quietly with a melancholy expression. Anneliese knew something was eating at him. She got close and asked "What is it Barry, you seem sad." "Oh nothing," he replied, "Just tired." "Barry, I know you and can read you, please tell me."

Barry, very quietly said, "It's stupid, its years ago; almost a different life away." Anneliese, with a questioning gaze, took his hand. "Please don't laugh" he said, "It's so long ago I don't know why I still remember it." Anneliese continued staring into his eyes, with a quizzical expression.

Seeing Mum today and realising I have a new, wonderful caring Dad, my early years came back. Like a sore that just won't heal." Anneliese stopped Barry. "What do you mean, what came back?"

Barry, his eyes beginning to glisten, said, "When I was about 12, I wanted to be like my friends. I wanted some nice clothes, some nice shoes and not be laughed at. Mum said, your real Dad should pay maintenance so if you can get him to pay it, you can have the money. He should pay it into East Ham Town Hall, but never has. You could go there and talk to them to see if they can help."

Barry, by now, doing everything to continue to appear manly, took a long breath and leaned back in his chair. He leaned forward again, resting his head in his hands. Slowly he looked up at Anneliese, who smiled and said, "Barry its ok, take your time."

"Well, they did try and I went back to see them week after week, but nothing, even though it was a court order! " Barry continued, "Anneliese, this is all shit that you do not deserve; it's a load of crap from my early life, but walking into that East Ham Town Hall today brought it all back.

From this day forward, I promise you it won't bother me and I will blot it out!"

The evening people gradually began to arrive. Most of Barry's Boleyn Boys congregated around the bar. Barry and Albie introduced the girls to them and their girlfriends and, sometimes, wives.

The Chinese whispers were soon all around with everybody enamoured with Anneliese and Anya and full of admiration for their dresses. Evening entertainment commenced with chart topping records playing as the buffet was placed along one wall of the hall. Most of the men carried on drinking, snatching buffet food occasionally.

As the booze settled inhibitions, Barry's entourage gained in confidence. Soon, he was surrounded by his best mates and the worshippers. Laughing, joking, paying homage and enjoying being part of his crowd.

The double doors into the hall swung open and noisily clattered against some chairs. The lads went silent, probably expecting trouble. Standing in front of the doors was Billy Murdoch. He was a big, red-haired fella with a face that would have intimidated Genghis Khan. He stood, proudly gazing around the hall.

In contrast, next to Billy was a relatively insignificant individual, but with attractive, ingratiating features, and a persona to match. It was Jerome!

Barry, Albie, followed by Anya, rushed the whole length of the hall. Barry, with his arm clenched around Billy Murdoch's neck, patted Jerome's head as he passed him and dragged Billy to the bar. Albie and Anya almost lifted Jerome off his feet as they all headed back to the bar. Anneliese, jumped out of her seat and kissed Jerome on both cheeks. He was now, clearly a real favourite with them all.

The music was about to change. A group had arrived and would keep the entertainment going for most of the evening, but with a break half way through. They were a group from Ilford called "Jimmy and the Teens." As they were setting up, Barry was involving Billy, although most of the Boleyn Boys seemed concerned.

Barry got everyone a drink then turned to his Boleyn Boys. Poor old Jerome had no clue as to what was going on. The Boleyn Boys all strained to listen to Barry as he spoke. "You all met Billy at the Tottenham Royal and you all had a good time. He's here because I invited him. He's on a strange patch and has had some guts coming. So we will all include him in our crowd. Remember, this is my Mum's Wedding! And he's my mate. "

"Jimmy and the Teens" were fantastic. Lots of Beatles and Searchers with a few others thrown in for good measure. By now, Anya had Jerome up dancing. They were jiving and he was so accomplished he was gradually teaching Anya some extraordinary elements such that guests were starting to congregate to watch. Anya, a really good dancer, was enjoying every minute and Albie was also amazed by the spectacle.

Barry, meanwhile, called Anneliese to his side. With his arm around her waist, he called Mick Flick over and said, "Get Eddie, Danny and Mac to come over for a chat." It was short and sweet. First looking into Anneliese's eyes then turning to the four of them, he said, "You guys have done a fantastic job. If you want it, you can have the business here. You don't need to send me any more income. It's yours. You can have the whole thing! I've got enough on my plate in Spain and you have proved you can go it alone.

I will always help you if you need it, but I know you won't need me!"

They were all astonished. Barry looked at their faces and knew this was the right thing! "You guys talk about it over a drink and let me know before we leave tonight."

Billy Murdoch had just bought a round. As he passed Barry and Anneliese's theirs, Barry leaned across and tugged Danny closer. Standing between Billy and Danny, he turned to face both of them as he leant back against the bar. "You fellas are ok with working together?" "Danny, I don't want to interfere," said Barry, "But if Billy takes the lead, you could grow North and West London into a fantastic business. Billy has already done all the groundwork and knows the territory inside out." As Mac arrived and joined in, Billy said "I've known Danny for some time, back to our football days in Poplar. We will be great together. Barry is right, because he is cleverer than me, and has chosen you two; his best guys to work with me!"

Barry had worked wonders, Billy, Danny and Mac formed a huddle and continued their celebrations.

It was the time for the band to take a break. The record player, connected to several loud speakers, began to play Reggae music. An exotic sound that most people in the room had not heard before, swept the hall. Then the surprise. Three beautiful Caribbean ladies, in colourful exotic dresses and head-dresses swayed and stomped to the music. Three of their men joined them, dancing in perfect time. From that point, the only way was up! Jess led Joan out onto the floor. Barry and the family knew that Jess had fabulous moves. They had seen it at a family party. But Joan was a really special treat. He had never seen his Mum dance before. She had worked through a hum drum life, and while Barry had been around, never had the chance to do exciting things in her life. But, with Jess, that time had arrived; their dancing was spectacular and, clearly, fed their souls, and everyone's.

Barry could not believe what he was seeing. When the music finished, Joan and Jess came straight over to Barry and Anneliese. Anneliese was the first to say, "You two are superb together; that is an indication for your life together." Joan thanked Anneliese, alongside Jess, who was grinning ear-to-ear.

Billy was standing just a few feet away along the bar. Barry circled Mum and Jess and reached out to Billy saying, "Come and meet my Mum and my new Dad." Anneliese took a step back to let Billy in. But Barry made Anneliese the first introduction. She offered her hand as Billy just stared. He spent a good 20 seconds trying to get some words out. Before he did, Anneliese leaned forward, saying "So pleased to meet you, Billy," then gently kissed his cheek. She turned to face Mum and Jess. Now Barry said, "And this is Jess! You have already met my Mum, Joan." Billy and Anneliese shook both their hands. Joan stepped forward and gave Anneliese a lingering embrace. Jess, looking towards Barry and being the gentleman that he was, in his Barbados brogue, fervently blurted out, "Barry, this lady is so beautiful! And Joan tells me she is also very intelligent." Anneliese grasped Jess's hand and blushed as she said, "Thank you, Jess."

Following smiles and a few silent seconds, Joan said, "Come on Jess, lets enjoy the music, "and they stepped back on the dancefloor.

Linda arrived at the bar beside them and got into talking with Anneliese. Barry stood back with embarrassment, but Billy stepped into the action, turning Barry back to the bar to have a drink with him. "Barry, your girlfriend is mind-blowingly beautiful, she is breath-taking. When she was talking to me, I totally lost control,. I felt as if the universe was tilting and I was falling off!" "Billy," Barry interjected, "Keep your voice down, please. Anneliese is talking to my ex-partner and I don't want things to boil over."

The arrival of Albie and Anya, who had been dancing and needed a drink, stopped them in their tracks. The small talk got underway, until both Barry and Albie began waxing lyrical about Marbella. Then Barry brought the talk to a conclusion, "Billy, please come down to us in Marbella. Soon! We are going back this weekend, so the following week or the week after. We will book your flights and a hotel nearby."

Billy thought for a minute. Gradually a smile appeared. "Yes, I will." He said. "The week after next. Now I've got Danny and Mac, they can look after things." Anya spoke, saying, "We will look after you." Billy, with emotion in his voice said, "If there are any girls as beautiful as you two in Marbella, I will be in heaven!" Anya couldn't resist saying, "There is a girl out there for you and you will find her!" "I'm not the best, looking fella" replied Billy, "But a beautiful, caring woman, like you two would always be safe and looked after by me!" "That's settled then," said Barry, "We will go ahead and make the arrangements. Billy, you will love it. We will have a fabulous time." Just then Jerome joined the throng. Barry, pulling him close, asked, "When are you down in Marbella next?" "Next Friday week, "replied Jerome. Barry explained about Billy's visit. Jerome agreed to accompany him on the flight and they would come down to Cafe Del Mar together. Billy had never been out of the country before, so this would be an exciting adventure!

The wedding had been a tremendous success. Memories for Joan and Jess that would last throughout time. Barry also, along with all family and friends.

The white Rolls Royce, covered in ribbons and rattling tin cans, reminded the whole community that Joan and Jess had tied the knot. And as they drove away, the sound of singing rang in their ears. "Show me the way to go home" and "Bubbles" were the outright winners!

Next morning, the rain was falling in torrents, but whilst hangovers persisted nobody seemed to care.

Around mid-day, Barry, Albie and their ladies checked out of the Stratford hotel. Eddie drove them first to Joan and Jess to say their goodbyes. Standing outside their house, Anneliese, holding onto Barry, paused for a moment, her face pointing skyward. "Do you know Barry, I'm loving that feeling of rain on my face. It seems an age since I last experienced it. "Anya copied Anneliese saying, "You're right, it's a lovely feeling that I had almost forgotten."

They didn't stay long, but long enough for strong embraces and some emotion. "Mum, you know I will be in touch every week," said Barry as they all headed to the car. Anneliese shouted, "Yes, and I promise we will visit often."

Eddie got them to their posh, last night, London hotel; The Berkeley in Chelsea. They settled for a while, then went for a walk along by the Thames to blow the cobwebs away. The girls were fascinated by the colourful houseboats moored along the Chelsea embankment, but the lads were hungry and got them back to the hotel in time for dinner. Next morning, after a leisurely breakfast, they packed.

48

They flew back to Marbella, arriving just around mid-day. After the weather in London, the heat as they stepped off the plane seemed intense but welcoming. Terry was there at arrivals to meet them. "Nothing to report Geezer," was his aside as he loaded the cases into the car.

All the talk on the journey was about the wedding. Barry and Anneliese spoke continually to Anya and Albie about who, where, what and when. Terry smiled as he listened, occasionally chuckling at what he was hearing!

They all had that coming home feeling as they pulled up outside Café Del Mar. However, there was a distraction. The tremendous amount of construction work going on in the Marina. There were dredgers everywhere, cranes and vessels full of materials.

Frank, Terry and Jose had been doing a wonderful job. As they entered the bar, it was greetings and congratulations from all around. The place was full! Frank explained that the chef had left and he had hired a new one. His name was Pedro and he was a known master with Tapas. Word had got around and the customers, at times, had been queueing. They had all been busting a gut to keep up!

Barry, hearing this, got off the bar stool, strode around the bar and clasped Frank's hand. "You guys have gone way beyond what I could have expected, so I will make sure you are given a big bonus." With that, Anneliese swapped places with Barry saying, quite loudly, "Thank you for looking after everything so well." As she kissed his cheek, he whispered, "We have to see the Commander. We'll talk tomorrow."

The following day, whilst Barry and Albie were getting barrels from the stock room, Anneliese surreptitiously, ambled onto the patio and stood close to Frank's table. As she took a Sobranie cigarette out of the tin, and began to light it from her small maroon Dunhill lighter, Frank whispered "We need to get up to Granada this evening." Without hardly moving her lips, Anneliese replied, "Can't". She dropped her Sobranie tin close to Frank's table and knelt to pick it up. "Frank, we've only just returned; it would look suspicious." As he looked away from her, he quietly said, "Ok, I will go alone and debrief you later!"

As Anneliese walked back into the bar she smiled at Frank and went to join Anya behind the bar. As they stood together, Anneliese said, "There is something going down. Frank has been summoned to Commander Farrell tonight. He'll debrief us tomorrow. But I want you to help persuade Barry and Albie that we want to go up to Granada soon, to book the skiing. This will give us a backup plan in case we have to meet with the Commander!"

During the afternoon, the girls in their break, sat on the patio. They used a similar approach again; with a spring in their step, they hit the lads with their sucker punch. "Barry, in the next week or two, would you mind if Anya and I went back to Granada to arrange the skiing?" Anya, turned to Albie and said, "We shouldn't leave it any longer or they may become fully booked!"

Barry completed a full turn on his bar stool; looking back and forth at Anneliese and Anya for a few seconds. "Are you serious about this skiing holiday? The nearest me and Albie have been to skiing is sliding down the sewer slopes on a tin tea tray! And that was about 15 years ago."

Anneliese put her face in her hands and was giggling as she placed them back on her hips. "Barry, you and Albie will love it, we will look after you every minute! And it's not all about skiing. There will be amazing après ski parties with more music, food and booze than you can imagine!"

Albie and Barry stared at one another as Barry reached for a napkin to mop his brow. "We are not going to win this one," said Albie with a hefty sigh! "Oh, I suppose so," wittered Barry. Anneliese couldn't resist the opportunity. Picking up a tin tray off the bar she said "I promise to take this with us to the slopes!" Anya in a flash, grabbed the tray and clattered it on Albie's head. Striding away, she looked back over her shoulder, saying, "it's not strong enough Albie, you've dented it!

The following morning the girls said they needed to go shopping for underwear, but would be back in time for lunch time service. Barry and Albie were cleaning the Jaguar, including the engine! Barry, with his head deep under the bonnet, grunted a muffled, "Yes, ok."

They met Frank at the usual secluded spot on the beach. Anneliese said they didn't have a lot of time so Frank got straight to the point. The Commander had met with his Intelligence Officers. They had been through every property development and the Analysts had interrogated all financial backers details. They have incriminating evidence against both Igor and the Mayor. The Commander believes they have enough to put them both away for a very long time. Igor has been laundering drug and criminal funds through numerous projects, particularly the Marbella Marina and several large scale housing developments.

The bottom line is he believes he now has all the ducks in line, with sufficient evidence against all the gangs, both here, in Central Europe and the U.K. We should, therefore, be ready in the next few weeks to support and enforce the search and arrest warrants that are under preparation.

Anneliese and Anya both appeared to have taken silent pills. Frank continued, "As soon as I have further information, we will begin to plan the mobilisation!"

"I know the implications are going to seep in gradually. You have been here for some while, so this feels like home. You have made friends and built relationships. But the reality is that this was just work. You are both relatively inexperienced in this business, so I expect that, now the time is here, it will be a bit of a shock to your system. It was always in the cards that we would, eventually, reach this point. So I am saying this with utter respect and sincerity. If you find this too difficult, please talk to me. Neither you nor I can afford things going wrong for emotional reasons. When the balloon goes up, I will be relying on you two, as you will be relying on me! Don't, in any way, underestimate what we are heading into. In this scenario, it will compare with the allies pushing on into Berlin to finish the war!"

"There is another angle I need to cover. Carmella is safe and sound! She is an Israeli by birth and is here shadowing Paulo. She works for Israeli Intelligence and escaped when the Russians attempted to abduct her. We are continuing to work on why she is pursuing Paulo. And we don't know why the Russians were trying to abduct her, other than they thought she was a Spanish Secret Agent. There are two things I do know! She is a very experienced, adept agent and we will eventually ascertain what is going on. The Commander is having regular, routine discussions with MOSSAD and he assures me he is establishing a strong relationship. Indeed, this has got to the point where he is receiving communications from the head of Israeli Security, Moshe Dayan."

Frank, probably feeling like a Dad who could only afford to put fruit in his kids Christmas stockings, did not want to labour the subject any longer.

He attempted to gaze into the eyes of Anneliese and then Anya. But both were transfixed, staring out to sea. "Snap out of it, girls," he shouted. "You girls are professionals, here to deal with vicious criminals who are killing people, thousands of people, every day of the week!"

"I'm relying on you, because if you think that this change in your happy, comfortable, well-paid lives is bad, the violence that we are heading into could make the Belfast troubles look meek and mild."

Anneliese gave Frank a thoughtful gaze, then said, "It's time we got back. We won't let you down, but I know you will understand why we are not enamoured with your news. Both Barry and Albie are trying hard to get out of their business. They are basically good fellas. They had a hard time growing up and have now recognised the error of their ways." Both girls waved goodbye and strode along the beach, leaving Frank with a totally empty feeling.

The next several days were largely uneventful. There was quite a bit of sunbathing on the beach when there were quiet times at the bar. Anneliese took every opportunity to swim in the sea to build her fitness, in order to increase her readiness in the event of an imminent alert. She powered through the waves, sometimes managing a swim of about two miles.

Anya also spent as much time as possible working at fitness, but mostly with running and Jiu-Jitsu training on the beach. Albie occasionally would attempt to assist her practise but seemed to spend most of the time on his back.

Not to be outdone, Barry had bought a set of weights and was body building every chance he got. As his mirror began to reflect improved muscle definition, the more his repetitions would increase. His thighs, especially, had always been muscular, but they were beginning to be the focus of attention from most females.

A week later, Anneliese and Barry arrived at their villa, close to midnight after a full day at the bar. Having poured a glass of wine, they both began to relax. But the pressure rose again when the radio transmitter bleeped its high pitched signal.

Anneliese ran up the stairs to receive the coded message. Ten minutes later, she returned with a puzzled expression. "It's a message from Paulo, Barry. I've decoded it and it reads as follows: Urgent, need two out of Europe via port. Can you help? High value - - Mars A..

"It's a strange message, Anneliese. What do you think? What's he up to. All our business, so far, has been from a distance. Not really had much to do with him but now the message almost makes it sound like he's in deep shit and wants me to help get him out. And what does high value mean. I would want to know more; if he means he's offering to pay me well, just to get someone to a port then how much is it? I think I've worked out the Mars. A. But if it's the port why not just spell out Marseille?"

Whilst Barry was talking, all the warnings from the Commander and Frank were skimming around in her mind. Overshadowing those thoughts was what was heading towards him. She just couldn't let him get in deeper trouble than he was already in. But her conscience would not allow her to warn him! But nothing would prevent her from using intellectual thoughts to dissuade him from making a disastrous mistake!

"You were clever working out Mars. A. It didn't strike me straight away. The obvious thing is that possibly, being Argentinian, he doesn't know how to spell Marseille." Anneliese continued as she saw a smile creeping across Barry's face! I think the more likely reason is that he could not find the word Marseille in the book we are using. His next issue could have been the spelling problem!"

Both of them saw the funny side and began to chuckle. Anneliese was about to use some of her methods but Barry spoke first. "Darling, I'm trying to find a way out of the business I am in. We don't need money, and if we ever do, I will get a 9 to 5 job while you keep the bar running. I really don't want to get into another sordid business. It sounds like human trafficking or assisting an escape. I don't want to be part of that sort of thing. What I've landed myself with is bad enough!

Anneliese, totally relieved, went to get them both a drink. As she sat on the settee, placing the drinks on the lounge coffee table, she pulled Barry towards her. "I really care for you, so much! Sometimes with all you have going on, it is so intense it hurts".

Barry, searching Anneliese's face, said, "You own my soul, my whole being. Paulo was offering money. Perhaps lots of money. But it can't buy me what I've already got. And, best of all, you have brought me peace!"

49

nneliese exclaimed, "I know how we can get the best of all worlds! At least I think I do. I really need to get some sleep but just give me a couple of minutes, Barry. "She took and lit a Sobranie then sauntered out around the pool, blowing smoke upwards as she stared at the moonlit clouds. She wandered back in.

"Listen Barry, I think you can avoid upsetting Paulo and the European dealers. We don't have a clue what he's up to but he wants to pay you well for it; this is my idea!"

"Frank has told me he is on his uppers. He had to find his next six month's rent and he's paid for that Jeep thing. He's probably the most capable and adaptable guy you've got and therefore, best placed to handle this unknown job. Why not offer it to him on a 50/50 basis. You don't get involved but you do collect 50%!"

Now it was Barry's turn to visit the garden. Barry's practice football lay near the path. He took a step to the right, then tickled the ball with the outside of his right foot. It rolled three feet away from him. He took two steps and struck the ball with his right foot. From his knee down to his toes was as straight as a cricket bat. The power was ferocious. The ball flew three feet from the ground into the wooden back fence, which splintered into pieces, flying in all directions.

Anneliese came running out. "What was that, why did you do that?" she questioned. Barry smiled as if pleased with himself. "I needed a release" he said, as he pulled her close. "I love your idea but I felt as if I needed to do something on my own that I'm good at. In the past, all I have been good at is getting in deep. If I take half the proceeds, I am still in deep, still involved. But what we could do, if Frank wants the job; let him have it all. I will stay out of it completely, and I promised him a bonus so what better way to play it!"

She took his hand and they went upstairs to bed. As she was undressing, she was consumed by the thought that this was turning into the perfect scenario. Barry would not aggravate his situation, Frank and the CECD would have every chance to understand what Paulo was involved in and, therefore what MOSSAD's interests were. Her thoughts drifted on. Possibly the Commander would advise MOSSAD which would gain their confidence to work more closely with CECD.

Once in bed, Anneliese rolled towards Barry and clasped his face. "I am so proud of you, "she said. "I am now beginning to believe that you are now in your new world. And be assured that if that is what you want, I am with you every step of the way. Leave me to talk with Frank tomorrow, to see if I can get it organised with him. Then I will message Paulo!"

In the morning, the sun was unrelenting. Whilst at breakfast, Anneliese suggested Barry go to the bar while she tried to get things agreed with Frank. She spent over an hour on coded messages with Paulo. He was clearly under pressure to get this off the ground. He wanted it to go ahead in the hours of darkness. The pickup was arranged for the bridge over St Michaels' river in Ghent. Two people with limited luggage.

Frank had accepted willingly. This was a gold nugget find! The drive was pretty simple, down the A7. About 12 hours. The Commander, hearing the news was overjoyed. He wanted to understand MOSSAD's endeavour and, more importantly, he knew that establishing a rapport with Israel was a key element of both European and US strategies to maintain peace in the Middle East. This could be a major feather in the Commander's cap!

The clever bastard that Frank was, and that's not derogatory, had led him to arrange a vehicle.... from the Commander's fleet. It was a Singer Gazelle, fast but not too noticeable. The Jeep would have taken twice as much time and Barry's cars would have implicated him. That was the key thing that Anneliese had intended. Not to implicate Barry.

He set off early morning, having worked out that he should get his passengers to the Marseille freight docks by midnight. He had planned in detail. He was carrying his small Beretta revolver and had a machine pistol taped on the side of the luggage compartment. Covered in soft grey material, it blended with the interior.

Next morning, Anneliese and Anya were becoming concerned. No Frank, no news. Barry and Albie sensed the concern. Barry said, "He'll be ok; you know Frank, he's dropped them off then decided to get some shut-eye in a B&B." Both girls looked at him in disbelief. They knew Frank much better than Barry ever would. But although his heart was in the right place, they were correct. They should be concerned!

About 5pm, the bar had only two people sitting eating on the patio. A car pulled up outside the bar. Three people, slowly, and somewhat mysteriously, edged out of their doors. The car was a large gleaming dark blue BMW. The driver and front passenger stood by their doors, their eyes searching every bit of the surroundings. Both were wearing black T shirts; around 6 feet tall with lean, rather thin torsos'. The driver, with dark piercing eyes, continued scanning up and down the road as the rear seat passenger exited.

The third person was a complete contrast to the other two. Fairly short, no more than 5 feet 6 inches, and for a hot day, wearing a strange wardrobe. A royal blue linen jacket that sagged and gave the appearance of dropped shoulders. The jacket had been matched with denim jeans, but the most extraordinary thing was the face. It could not be seen! Dark sunglasses overshadowed by the peak of a dark grey trilby hat. Other than the jeans, the look was almost pure Gestapo!

As the third person led the way into the bar, the last two customers were paying Anya on the patio. Anya had already prepared herself for trouble as they marched past her into the bar. Anya followed closely.

Once inside the bar, with all the rest watching, the leader threw off the trilby and sunglasses, turned to face Anya, then rushed towards her. Anya didn't need to think. By now, this came naturally. It would have been a Geoi-nage shoulder throw and then pounce. But before it got that far, she screamed "Anya, it's me, Carmella." She grasped Anya and pulled her close, kissing her cheeks.

Anya was overcome! Looking into Carmella's eyes she welled up. "Oh, I am so pleased to see you safe". Carmella, interrupted saying "Anya, you saved my life and took a beating for it. I had to come back and let you know how much that will always mean to me." Anya took Carmella's hand and led her to the bar. "Let's have a drink and talk about what it was all about."

Barry stepped forward, went to the doors and closed up. The closed sign was clear to all, but he knew that if any of his guys needed to visit, they would just knock and show their faces.

They were all overpowered by Carmella's entrance. So pleased she had survived such a vicious attack. So now, Barry, Anneliese, Anya and Albie waited for the details.

Carmella, seeing this in their expression said, "While I explain, would you get my colleagues a drink. They protect me day and night, which is not easy. I think you now all know I work for MOSSAD, the Israeli Secret Service!" Barry and Albie showed appreciation in their expressions. Anneliese sat quietly listening, hoping to gain more information concerning MOSSAD's work.

Carmella continued. "I had been assigned to shadow Paulo. That's why I came here. We had information that said he wanted to be involved in the Marbella area. I love you guys, and really came to say thank you!"

"But I came to tell you more than that. You are probably all concerned for Frank. You don't need to be. He was arrested with the two Nazis' that Paulo was trying to get out of Europe. MOSSAD have the two Nazis' and we are overjoyed with that result. Frank will be released soon."

"However, it got better. We raided Paulo's apartment in Amsterdam and it has given us substantial evidence and information. Paulo has been working for Nazis' arranging their transportation to safe havens, mostly to South America. He has been very successful, and has been receiving riches, jewellery, art work, gold and museum pieces that the Nazis' looted from all over Europe. After the War, the Americans documented approximately 20,000 Nazis' that should go on trial. Most disappeared and escaped. There are about 100 that we are searching for, with immense support from the Jewish Community. One in particular, Simon Wiesenthal is a past master. He is leading people known as the "Nazi Hunters" and we are working with them!"

"We have to leave now but if you agree, I would like to visit again. I am certain our work will be concluded in the next couple of weeks, and I would really love to spend a celebration night with you guys." Anneliese, with pride in her eyes, replied, "We would love that. You are welcome here anytime."

The three Israelis' went to their car, with everybody watching from the patio. Several minutes went by and the car had still not moved. Barry went to them, and as he got nearer, he could see they were talking on a radio. As he got close, Carmella jumped out of the car and with excitement written all over her face, blurted out, "Paulo is under arrest. He was captured trying to board a ship to Genoa. So now we have more chance of catching the Nazis' that were relying on him to get them to safe havens. Barry, I am delighted. My assignment is concluded until I'm given the next one. So I may be seeing you sooner than you think."

With that, Carmella jumped back in the Mercedes, and with massive smiles from all three occupants, sped off out of Marbella.

50

Jerome and Billy arrived mid-afternoon Friday. Barry had been impatiently waiting. As the taxi arrived, Barry rushed out to meet them. Billy stepped out with a look of disbelief on his face. He appeared totally mesmerized by his surroundings. The warm climate he'd never experienced before and the extraordinary landscape and exotic vegetation were astonishing.

The excitement created by this new environment, and friends all around, washed a torrent of adrenalin through Billy's veins. After an hour of drinking with the usual crowd, Billy began to look worse for wear!

Anneliese nudged Barry saying, "He should be getting off to the hotel to get booked in." Billy slurred a few reluctant sentences and held an expression of disdain until Barry spoke up. "Anneliese is right, Billy, you've had a long day today and you will have an even longer and more exciting day tomorrow!"

"I'm going to take you to your hotel in my Jaguar. Want to give you a ride to enjoy! Then I will pick you up around 11.00am tomorrow." Jerome asked, "Can I tag along too, Barry?" "Yes, of course. You are both in the same hotel so you could help Billy get settled!" Jerome said his goodbye's and set about getting their luggage to the car.

Billy was over whelmed by Barry's Jaguar "S" Type. Turned out he was a real petrol head ! Then when he saw the hotel, his reaction was as if he was entering paradise.

The two lads, with their luggage, stumbled into the Estapona Hotel with Barry shouting "See you in the morning!"

When Barry walked back to the bar, Anneliese was at the bar chatting to Anya whilst she served. Albie had moved to the back of the bar and was, in a moody way, thumping balls around the pool table.

Barry sat on a bar stool next to Anneliese. She quietly, as she placed a comforting hand on Barry's knee, said, "this will sound bizarre but Albie and I have just had words." Barry's expression stiffened as he glanced down the bar at Albie. "Why, what's got him riled?" asked Barry. "All I said, and Anya agreed, was that Billy seemed a nice fella. Albie got arsy saying "He's from that shit area of Northie Land. You can't trust them!" and with that he stormed off to the pool table."

Barry stood, straightened his shirt and strode off to the pool table. "What you up to mate? I'm told you had words with Anneliese and that Billy coming here is worrying you!" Albie walked away from Barry to the opposite side of the table. "Well yes, it is worrying me. He is a Northie, and we don't mix with them. So why are you giving him so much attention?"

Barry slowly walked around the pool table and stood beside Albie. "Please trust me, Albie. I've known him for years and he helped me avoid lots of trouble with the Tottenham Boys." His arm rolled up Albie's back and encircled his neck. "Albie, if this is anything to do with you thinking I am going to get stitched up, I can assure you that won't happen. You have known me all my life and so you know I am too clever for that. If you are worrying that he is going to become more important to me than you are then, you need your brains tested! You might be my cousin, but

I think of you as my brother. You are family, but more than that. I love you with every part of my being. Nobody will ever rise above that!"

"Billy Murdoch has stood side by side with me in lots of tough situations. He's never let me down, and like you and me, his early life was difficult, so I'm pleased we have got back together and I think, if you give him a chance, you will trust him. I want to help him and I'd like to think you would work with me on this!"

They walked back to the front bar, with Albie now gripping Barry's neck, and just as they got to Anneliese, the door swung open and Jerome strutted in. Albie rushed to him followed closely by Anya. "Why did you come back Jerome?" "Well I didn't want to spend the evening alone in the hotel. Billy went to his room and must have gone straight to sleep because I knocked on his door and there was no answer. And as I'm only here for two days, I wanted to spend it with you lot!"

The evening was spent wading through nostalgia and comical stories, mostly from Jerome regarding his journeys and eccentric passengers. They all planned to meet up around mid-day after Barry had picked up Billy and Jerome.

During the drive back to Café del Mar, Billy spent the first five minutes waxing lyrical about the luxury of the hotel, the room and the sumptuous buffet breakfast. Then, in a lull, Jerome asked Barry, "What do you need me to do in Amsterdam next week?" "Jerome there is nothing for us up there anymore. Paulo has been arrested and possibly extradited by now." Billy leant forward, all ears. Barry continued, "It seems he had a separate business evacuating Nazis' to South America. He will serve a long stretch for that." Billy became incensed. "What a bastard thing to do, he deserves whatever they throw at him. Those Nazis' executed 10 Million people, 6 million were Jews but they went much further. Gypsies, homosexuals, disabled people and that's without the thousands of our soldiers and civilians they bombed."

Jerome peered at Billy and gasped, "Wow Billy, you know so much about all that." "Yes, and we need to keep it in the front of our minds forever. I have read a lot about the Nazi Hunters, and I just wish I could be one of their crew!"

As they pulled up outside the bar, they saw Frank entering. Barry turned to Jerome and asked if he would remind him to ask Frank to collect their gear from the Amsterdam warehouse.

Just as they began to exit the Jaguar, Billy said "I can't believe how wide you have spread your wings. Spain and into the rest of Europe." Barry piped up "Don't forget Africa." "You're kidding me" exclaimed Billy. "The closest I've got is the Africa section in London Zoo!"

Billy continued taking in all the surroundings as they all climbed the patio steps and entered the bar. All Barry's crowd came to meet them, with Albie leading the group. The previous reticence had disappeared, as if blown away by the warm sea breeze. Albie gripped Billy's right hand and grasped him round the neck, as they trundled to the bar. Anya had joined Jerome as Anneliese kissed Barry.

Frank, standing at the bar, was the only person that had not met Billy before. Barry soon eradicated that issue and Frank, generously, bought everyone a drink!

The afternoon wore on into the evening. Barry had spoken to Frank about collecting the remaining stock. Albie and Billy had been playing pool, and all the while the

Master Tapas Chef had been supplying wonderful exotic tapas.

About 4.00pm, Barry announced that he would be taking Billy on a tour of the coast in a grand motor cruiser that he had hired, and all their crowd were invited.

Everybody, and I mean everybody, was excited. Only a few hundred yards walk and they were all climbing aboard. This was a fabulous modern cruiser. Barry had arranged for it to have a well-stocked bar. They sailed past a couple of coves up towards Fuengirola, then dropped anchor and swimming began.

Anneliese, sitting next to Barry, declared, "Barry, I love you so much. You've done all of this for Billy and also the rest of us." Barry turned to Anneliese saying, "I had to do it. Billy has not been anywhere before. I had to let him experience a different world." Anneliese caressed his face and in a whisper said, "I can't believe you are mine!"

They arrived back at the bar about 6.30pm. The tapas was continuing to be delivered to the tables and, of course, everybody was ravenous. From the moment of their arrival, there was some disturbance. Men began walking in and out carrying equipment and instruments. It was the Spanish local group that had provided the musical entertainment at Jerome's party.

By now, everybody had consumed lots of booze. But this had been somewhat alleviated by the mountains of food and all the exercise with swimming.

The group struck up about 7.30pm and their crew and the customers became very alive. A mixture of Spanish music and flamenco followed by Pop music.

51

At 8.00pm, through the open patio doors, came an angel in disguise. This time in a figure flattering dress and very dark hair, that reached down her back. Even the band's rendition of La Bamba softened as she coasted across the bar floor towards Barry's group. This was Carmella, with no work strings attached!

Only half way across the bar floor, originally swaying to La Bamba, she stopped dead in her tracks. Everyone watched and wondered why. Billy's eyes had met Carmella's across the room. When her eyes met his, it was total magic. Billy was not a very confident, forward person but the intoxication of this was something he had to pursue. He stepped off that barstool and walked across to meet Carmella. It was the same, exactly the same, for her. Across a crowded room, she had found her soul mate!

All those at the bar were speechless, and intrigued by the spectacle. As they moved closer, Billy's arm stretched out to Carmella. They began to slowly dance in a smooth smoochy way. The band, seeing this, quietly joined in playing, in a Spanish style, "I've got you under my skin." The music moved on to "Blue Moon"; the buzz went around the room "Have they met before?" "They must know each other!"

The contrast between Carmella's ebony hair and dark features, and Billy's red hair and pale skin, created a fascinating picture!

The music softened as Billy took Carmella's hand and led her to the friends in the bar. Billy was trembling as he lifted his drink. The girls, Anneliese and Anya, were embracing Carmella. Barry, smiling at Billy, excitedly said, "Blimey Billy, didn't realise you were so good at pulling." "Oh, I'm not" replied Billy, "never have been and, hopefully, I will never need to be." With that, he turned to Carmella, grasped her hand as she, willingly, moved in close and put her arm around his waist. "This is the girl of my dreams. Never thought I'd ever find her, but as soon as Carmella walked in and our eyes met, I knew she was the one. Carmella, with a blushing smile, leaned her head on Billy's shoulder.

Barry gulped his whisky saying, "Billy, it was the same for me and Anneliese. We met here in Marbella, and I had the feeling that something special would happen for you, here in the same place!" It was Anneliese's turn to move close.

It was a fabulous evening of entertainment and enjoyment, and as it came to a close, Billy and Carmella went to sit at a table in the far end of the bar. They were engrossed in conversation for around 45 minutes. In the meantime, Barry had closed the bar and now it was a small private party.

Most of their conversation was romantic, but Carmella knew that eventually Billy would hear about her job and previous episodes. She explained that she had just finished her present job and could stay around all week with Billy.

They returned to the group and gave them the news. Billy, clearly was ecstatic. Barry and Anneliese congratulated them and Albie gripped Billy's hand and almost shook his arm off. Anya embraced Carmella and kissed her cheek saying, "We always were a great team, and now we have more team members!" Smiling at Billy, she moved onto Jerome with a warm motherly cuddle.

Barry looked around and then gave Albie a contented gaze that confirmed the strong feelings he had for him. "Albie, since we moved here we have had constant good luck. And now we've had the luck to gain another good mate. Let's raise a glass to Billy. No I'll change that! To Carmella and Billy!"

Jerome couldn't contain himself any longer. He could never resist shows of open affection. He strode across the bar to the microphone. "Please forgive me for changing the words slightly but I think this song captures what we are all feeling."

It was a total surprise. His voice was soprano like most rock singers. It enthralled them all as he sang without backing. He la-la-la'd the intro, then with total confidence, began. "If paradise is half as nice, as heaven being here with you, who needs paradise, I'd rather have you!" He sang the whole song and everyone joined in to the chorus. It was a fabulous end to the night and he received loud applause from the small proud group!

Billy, Carmella and Jerome were all staying in the Estapona hotel. Carmella was giving both fellas a lift. As they left, Barry whispered to Anneliese, "Would you mind if I loaned Billy the Lotus Cortina, if and when he needs it, this week. We've got the Jaguar and I just thought it may make things easier for him and Carmella." "No, of course not" she replied. Waving at Albie and Anya, they made their way to the Jaguar. "I will tell Billy tomorrow."

Carmella arrived first; about lunchtime, saying Billy and Jerome would be about an hour later as they were waiting for the alcoholic mist to lift. Barry immediately said, "Would you like some lunch." "No, no" replied Carmella. "I had a wonderful breakfast a short while ago."

"Come and have a drink with me at the bar then, because I would like to ask you a couple of things." Barry had a pleasurable expression, but Carmella appeared quizzical! Seeing her expression, Barry said "It's nothing to worry about. I just wondered if you and Billy would like to borrow the Lotus Cortina this week."

Carmella replied, "Yes, I would be extremely grateful. The Russians know my car, so I'm always concerned that they may be tailing me." "Ok" said Barry. "That takes me to the last question; does Billy know anything about your job, the events with the Russians and is there anything else that you think he should be aware of?"

A sadness appeared in her eyes. "Barry; that is a dilemma I have been struggling with. No, I've only known him a very short while, but I must not lose him! He already means everything to me. He's the man I have always dreamed of meeting. We only talked for about an hour, but that time with him confirmed what a sensitive, caring, lovely person he is. I totally refuse to let him see difficulties with our relationship."

Barry sat for a moment peering into Carmella's eyes. He nervously coughed to clear his throat, then gently held her hand. "I've known Billy for years. He has a fairness in his make-up that I wish I had. He is never pretentious and he's never been very confident with women. He is brave, strong and able to protect himself and anyone he loves. I am a recent testament to that. Add to all that the fact that he detests cruelty and the grotesque things that the Nazis' did in World War II; he is the man that would be with you every step of the way in the dangerous commitment you have made to bring those evil inhuman creatures to justice. Carmella, only yesterday, this subject came up in discussion. Like me, Billy lost several of his family in the war. But he had researched the details and spent time yesterday explaining what the Nazis' had done to the Jews and many other people. He finished by telling me and Jerome that his ethos and conscience would demand him to be a Nazi hunter!"

Carmella clearly treasured this insight into Billy's values. She tightened her grip on Barry's hand, then said, "Barry, I can't thank you enough." Where did you gain that ability to be so clear-thinking and expressive?"

"It was an East London school' a depressed area but the teachers were incredible!"

Just then, Jerome and Billy sauntered in. Anneliese arrived just behind them, and a few minutes later, Albie and Anya appeared. Tapas began to arrive and everyone joined in.

Mid-afternoon, Barry suggested they go down to the beach, by the beach bar. Anya said, "You go, it's a quiet period in the afternoon." But then Terry and Jose arrived. You all go," said Terry; "Well help yourself to drink," said Barry.

Sitting on the beach with Billy brought it all back to Carmella. The assassination attempt. The attempt to capture and abduct her. The question in her mind that may define their future worried her. Should she explain her work and these events to Billy?

Nestling close to Billy, feeling his heart beating against her breast, she decided that, for the time being, she would avoid the issue!

Her mind moved into more enjoyable thoughts. "Billy, should we plan some things for the rest of the week or would you just prefer to take it as it comes. I know this whole area, and as Barry has loaned us the car, we could drift around for a few days and I could show you the sights."

Billy, with gentle hands, turned her face toward his. He was about to speak, but a yearning inside him took over. He was drawn to her lips. With a strengthening passion their lips mingled. They withdrew abruptly as whistles, shouts and cheers erupted on the beach around them.

They both drew back smiling, then giggling at the show of genuine affection from the Café Del Mar community. As it subsided, Billy said, "Lets mix the two. A few days sightseeing and then just drifting along when that suits us."

So that was how it went, until Friday. They had an amazing time visiting tourist spots and loving each other's company. Reluctantly, Carmella told Billy that she had heard from her boss and he needed her in work Monday, which meant she would be leaving Sunday. Reality hit Billy right between the eyes. Immediately, he began asking, "So how will this work; I must see you again."

Carmella had not dared think about it before. But now that awkward question had to be addressed. She said the first thing that came into her head. "Can you stay another week?" Billy became elated. "Yes I can; I've nothing to get back for. Well, nothing that compares with you." "But Billy, you have to understand, I can't say when I will get back to you. Right now, I'm sitting on a rainbow, but in my job a storm can move in at any time. But, be sure I will be with you the moment I get the chance. Can you be that patient?" "Absolutely" replied Billy, "but you sound pretty secretive about your work. I don't want to put you under pressure, but can you give me a clue?"

Carmella's expression turned thoughtful. She needed time to think! She bent forward with her face in her hands. Her long black hair fell over her face and hands, and she appeared as if she was in hiding.

Billy never said a word, just stroked her hair back from her face. She gradually raised her head and looking straight into Billy's eyes said, "Ok, it's a long story, but before I explain can I ask you something?" Billy nodded but with a concerned expression.

Carmella said, "Billy, this is the big one for me. It's make or break. We've only been together for a short time. But do you think we were meant for one another? Is this our destiny? Will you want to stay with me, whatever I tell you? And do you believe we will always stay together, whatever happens?"

Billy didn't even need time to think, "its yes to all those questions. I have been waiting for you, and now I've found you, its forever." "Ok, Billy, the story goes like this."

"I was born in Israel. I am a very proud Jewess. Most of my family were lost to the gas chambers of Auschwitz, Buchenwald and Dachau. I can't even talk about forgiveness. There is no such thing for the cruel, deranged animals that did those things."

Billy's jaw was dropping, almost to the floor, as he listened. Carmella, now with tears in her eyes, continued; "I did well at University and was immediately given the opportunity to work for Israel's Secret Service. It's known as MOSSAD."

"I am here in Europe working with MOSSAD and civilians of Israel, known as the Nazi Hunters. We have ongoing work having just captured an organiser that helped Nazis' escape to South America. But there is a lot more to do and I will be given my next assignment on Monday."

Under normal circumstances, when Carmella's assignments came to an end, the protection squad were stood down until the next assignment. However, due to the Russian attacks, her Captain had retained her "shadows" who were sitting, unobtrusively, a short way along the beach.

Although unnoticeable, they had been close to Billy and Carmella all week. Billy was always alert, and as he rolled over onto his side, his vision pinpointed them. Now directly lying facing Carmella, his view across Carmella's neck allowed him to focus on them, without his stare being obvious. As he moved closed to Carmella, he whispered "don't move to look, but there are two fellas just down the beach that I have noticed a few times before. Don't get worried but I think they may be tracking us!"

Carmella sat bolt upright, laughing, "Billy, you are full of surprises" as she gestured for him to sit up with her. Billy shook his head as if to say, what have I said now, something ridiculous I suppose.

"No Billy, no, I am not making fun of you. You are correct, they are tracking us. They are my protection squad. Until I get my new assignment, they will be following us. I'm sorry if I didn't tell you that before, but they are great guys and I need them."

52

"I didn't want to scare you but this is a dangerous, very dangerous, job. But I have to do it. I really believe in what I'm doing. Those deranged beasts must face their maker in War Crimes Courts. I say the Hatikvah every day to increase my chances to get help from above, but now I know I've been given it! It is you! I laughed because it hit me that you are so perceptive. You will provide my protection from now on and we will be a force to be reckoned with!"

Unknown to Billy, Anneliese also had received instructions for Monday. She, Anya and Frank were required for a meeting in Granada with the Commander. Frank would travel alone as he needed to meet with his ex-mercenaries to establish if they had anything new. Anneliese and Anya would drive up in the Lotus Cortina and they would all meet in the Commander's office.

Anya and Anneliese had given notice to Albie and Barry. Monday was a quiet day so they would use it to go up to the ski resorts to make a booking. That was the fiction, but realistically, Barry and Albie could be looking, depending on the Commander's plan, at very lengthy prison sentences.

Similarly, Carmella had no clue where Monday's meeting would take her. She was pushing it to the back of her mind. Her faith in Billy as her destiny made for comfort but, an uneasy comfort. Her answer was to distract her mind from those disturbing thoughts.

She tugged Billy's face towards hers saying, "Let's do something special tomorrow." Billy, with a massive grin, said, "Good idea. You have driven me around all week so I think it's time I took a turn."

"So what destination do you have in mind?" quizzed Carmella. "The Rock of Gibraltar," answered Billy, "I saw a news report about the place, at our cinema, when I went to see "From Russia with Love", the James Bond film. I'd like to see the place for myself, visit the baboons and have a luscious lunch with you in one of the rock restaurants!"

Carmella grimaced slightly as she thought to herself, wishing he hadn't mentioned Russia! They began to stroll back to Cafe Del Mar, then Carmella asked "Are you OK with driving on the right?" Billy thought for a moment, then with a mischievous smile said "I might as well get some practise because the U.K government have announced we will soon be changing to the right, to be in line with Europe! Cars will move over next year and trucks the year after."

Carmella's expression became strained, as she thought it through. With a resounding smack on Billy's arm, she exploded into laughter. "You are making fun of me, Billy!" She pulled him close, giggling as she clung to his waist.

As they walked up the bar steps to the patio, Billy casually explained that, when making fun of someone in Britain, it is usually called "pulling their leg." It was now Carmella's turn. "So you wish to pull my leg. Which one do you like the best?" "No, Carmella, I didn't mean…." She put her hand over his mouth, saying, "I'm just making fun of you!"

They set off very early next morning. Billy was in his element, driving a fast car, but in essence, driving sensibly. Carmella's protectors followed discreetly in a powerful black SAAB.

It was a constantly romantic day. When they returned in the evening, the holiday spirit continued with Billy describing the whole day in detail, and Carmella laughing with everyone about the Baboons antics with Billy. Apparently, they were fascinated by his red hair; Carmella admitted to Anneliese and Anya that she was entranced by his red hair, so the Baboons were not alone!

Sunday afternoon arrived much too soon for Billy and Carmella. Billy became melancholy as he sat with Carmella at a corner table. The others began to sense their feelings and soon moved to join them. Drinks were coming thick and fast, and amusing stories and laughter.

The bar was relatively full, with banter exploding all around. Next, three big fellas entered, followed by Carmella's minders. They stood at the bar, ordering drinks, with the protectors immediately behind. They also ordered some drinks, listening and watching the newcomers every move.

Their group quietened as Anya, then Carmella, stood. A very drunk Albie also stood. Anya gripped Albie's arm and quietly said, "Let me go first. I will quickly know if they are the Russians." Anya and Carmella wandered slowly to these new customers.

With that, Barry stood. But before he moved, the girls returned. Anneliese had stepped alongside Barry with an expression on her face that was analysing every possible development.

Anya, laughing said, "False alarm! They are contractors working on the Marina. And better than that, Barry, they are English from West Ham." Barry got excited and rushed to the bar. "Give these guys two rounds of free drinks. Terry, they are West Ham lads."

The excitement was over and their group assembled again. Billy had been bewildered by all this. But he had picked up on something! Everyone seemed worried for Carmella due to Russians. As she settled next to him, he asked, "So what is all this with Russians, Carmella?"

"Ok, Billy, this was a recent event. I didn't want to worry you because we had only just met, and you were still in the dark about my work. A local drug baron got the impression I was working for the Spanish Secret Service. His informants had gained access to Government files that had been doctored by MOSSAD in order to allow me to work freely with the Spanish.

The first episode was here on the beach at a party. A sniper tried to eliminate me. The next episode was when they attempted to abduct me, but Anya helped me escape! Both events had been orchestrated by the Russian drug baron."

Billy was stunned, mostly because his beautiful Carmella was not perturbed or unsettled by these horrific incidents.

Sunday afternoon was soon upon them. Carmella set off for with her two minders. Their embrace had been slow and loving. Billy was reminded several times by Carmella that she would be back soon. Hopefully, it was just an initial meeting to review her next assignment.

Anneliese and Anya would leave early Monday morning and return the same evening. The boys; Billy, Barry and Albie, would have a free day together!

Carmella set off first, feeling somewhat under a cloud. Her meeting was in Malaga, close to the airport. Her Captain, Avram Ben Simon, sat behind his desk, dressed in casual clothes. But his appearance did not convey his direct, autocratic approach. Within five minutes, he had explained that Carmella was to go immediately to a meeting with CECD to determine if they could work together to achieve the MOSSAD objectives. This had been directed by Moshe Dayan personally. Their belief was, it would substantially increase their success rate.

Carmella arrived at the transit office of CECD Commander Farrell. As she entered the building, she sensed a presence behind her. She looked back over her shoulder and was very surprised.... It was Frank.

53

Frank, usually controlled and confident, appeared slightly flustered. "Carmella, it's so good to see you, but are you sure you are in the right place?"

Carmella, being an extremely perceptive lady, worked it out, immediately, "I could ask you the same thing, but I guess, after the work I saw you do on the beach, we are in the same business!"

"Well yes, I think you are correct, "replied Frank. "it's more than I could ask for.... Having you, a friend, working with us."

The invitation to enter the Commander's office came very quickly. The Commander spent the first minutes explaining that CECD thought that closer work with MOSSAD would benefit both organisations. Towards the end of that monologue, the Commander asked, "Where is Anneliese and Anya? They should have been with us 15 minutes ago!"

Carmella, surprised hearing their names, looked at Frank. "Commander" he said with concern in his voice. "I am beginning to be worried. They are never usually this late." The Commander checked his watch, and then stood. As he began pacing the room, he looked at Frank and said, "I'll give them another 10 minutes, then we will action a top priority search and rescue!"

20 minutes later, a helicopter landed in the forecourt of the offices. It was tight, but had been previously planned,

as possibly, a future necessity. Frank and Carmella climbed in and they were off!

The rotors only took about 30 seconds before this small, agile craft lifted off the ground and, once up, banked steeply. Frank was in the front with the pilot, while Carmella was in the rear with a reconnaissance camera. Frank suggested to the pilot that they follow the A92 as far as Malaga, and if nothing turned up, to widen the search. They did exactly that but, nothing unusual was seen. They turned up towards the Sierra Nevada, flying over the A395 towards the Quentar Reservoir Dam.

Carmella spotted something. The pilot banked around as Carmella said to Frank she thought she had seem some flashing lights. She had! It was a police car, which they followed. At the Quentar Dam was a lay-by or viewing area. Trees shaded the area and the police car pulled in; the pilot took them down as Frank and Carmella strained to pick out anything. The trees blocked the view, so they landed. Frank clambered out and sprinted to the police. Carmella, not far behind Frank, then glimpsed what Frank was seeing close-up!

It was their Lotus Cortina. It had crashed through the wall surrounding the viewing area. Almost half the car was hanging over the Dam retaining wall. Frank, with Carmella's help, said a few quick words to the police. Anya and Anneliese were nowhere to be seen.

Frank grabbed Carmella's hand saying "Get back to the helicopter; looks to me like they were rammed into that wall."

Back in the air again, Frank took hold of the radio handset to speak with the Commander. It was short and sweet. An all-points bulletin was to go immediately to airports, the coastguard, navy ships in the vicinity and the four ex-mercenaries. They should meet him back at Marbella. The Guardia Civil Services should set up road blocks, especially on the coast road and check all movements in and out of marinas.

With Frank's direction, they were now heading back to Marbella. As they flew, Frank asked the pilot, "What is this little chopper? It's a fantastic piece of equipment. I need you to stay around Marbella because I may need this agile little monster." Although Spanish, the pilot replied in almost perfect English, "I will sir. I will be at the ready."

As they closed on Marbella, Frank took to the radio again. "Commander, nothing yet, but I'm going to the Russian's villa. For that, I need a Super Frelon chopper with a rescue hoist. Please, in the next 15 minutes if possible, with a stock of 5 H&K sub machine guns and two 7.62 heavy calibre machine guns. They can land on the beach, as close to the marina construction as possible."

Their chopper landed so close to Café del Mar, the glasses in the bar almost played music. Frank and Carmella were inside in an instant. No sign yet of his team, the ex-mercenaries.

Barry, Albie and Billy, by now, were pumping adrenalin at macro speed. "Frank, what the hell is going on?" "Can't find a way to make this easy for you. Anya and Anneliese had an accident, but I think it was caused by an ambush, most likely by that Russian." Frank stood quiet.

Carmella grasped Billy. "I'll explain everything later but now we have to find them!" Frank took over. "My guys will be here soon and we have a chopper on its way to use to find them, and if necessary, tackle the Russians."

Just then, the bars glasses started to rattle again, but now so severe they were raining down; smashing on the floor. The Super Frelon chopper had arrived; landing on the beach 50 yards from the bar.

Frank walked to the door and turning to Barry said, "Where the hell are they? I need them now." "No you don't," replied Barry. "I'm coming with you." "No you're not," said Frank, as Albie and Billy joined. "Yes we are; work's one thing but we love those girls. We are fucking good fighters and you take-off with us or not at all."

Frank chewed his lips then turned saying, "Ok". As they climbed into the Super Frelon chopper, the radio was requesting Frank to talk to the coastguard. "I was told the main target area was between La Herradura and Almunecar. If that is correct, a motor yacht is a mile out between the two, just off the town of Cotobro. We will try to block any attempt to exit. Oh, something new is now going on! There is an IRB motor inflatable heading out from the beach to the yacht. If you want to apprehend them, you need to be here soon!"

Next was a call on the radio, again for Frank. It was his ex-mercenary team. The guy began to speak but Frank shouted him down. "Get yourselves to Igor, the Russian's villa. Arrest anyone and search the villa."

"Listen you lot!" Frank was shouting to be heard over the engine noise. "Barry, dish out the weapons from the armoury just behind you. And the floodlights and flashlights." The pilot shouted to Frank to test the winch.

It was dusk, and soon would be dark. As they entered the Cotobro bay area, they flew over the coastguard. They could see the outline of the Motor Yacht about a mile away. As they closed on it, they could see the inflatable approaching the yacht. Their yacht was a Mercury in original black paint, making it difficult to see in the dark.

Frank, still shouting, said they would go down on the hoist two at a time. Frank and Barry first. Albie and Billy providing covering fire. Carmella shouted, "No, I will go, not Billy!"

It was almost pitch black, but the sea was calm. Frank knew this craft. It had a 30 foot deck at the stern. They would drop there! The coastguard had moved closer and turned its floodlights onto the yacht.

54

With one foot placed in the winch cord loop, Frank screamed, "Let's go!" Billy started the motorised winch and as Frank lowered, Barry clambered on above him, with his feet on Frank's shoulders. About 10 feet above the deck, Frank dropped. Barry had no choice but to follow.

Both began to scramble to their feet as two of the crew rushed them. In a split second, a red fury engulfed Barry. He went berserk, wielding his machine gun like a club. Two more Russians ran from the bridge. Carmella, seeing them, simply pointed a machine gun in their direction and with just one burst of fire, left both lying on the deck.

Frank had one bent over the side-rail and was brutally punching his face, with both fists. Billy, seeing his chance, jumped to the winch cord and slid down. Dropping the last ten feet. He sprinted to assist Frank. Both pounded the Russian. Then in unison, gripped his legs and tipped him backwards into the sea. Barry, having beaten his attacker to a pulp, began a high pitched scream as he sprinted around the yacht. The screaming terrified two others, who ran towards the bow, to escape Barry.

These two Russians, standing with their backs to the bow rail, looked ready to surrender. Instead, realising Barry was alone, they figured they could take him. Definitely a wrong move! As they approached, Barry threw himself into the air and did, what can only be described as a footballers overhead kick. It was slightly side slanted and struck the jaw of a Russian with such power he fell to the ground unconscious.

Barry, lay on his back, his machine gun on the floor, a yard a way. The second Russian saw this as his chance, powering ferocious kicks into Barry's body and head. Nothing was going to shake Barry out of his insane rage. Despite the vicious onslaught, he reached inside his jacket and whipped his Beretta revolver out of the holster.

Frank and Billy arrived as Barry began to stand, and pulled the trigger, one, two, three times. The Russian was thrown backwards into Billy who stepped aside, letting him slump to the ground.

Barry, still engulfed by his rage shouted "Frank there's more" as he sprinted towards the steps to the cabins. Frank shouted back, "Barry, there will be at least two more." Breathless, Barry screamed "I'll kill the bastards. I need to find Anneliese!"

Albie had been the last to jump to the winch; Carmella lowered him to the deck. He joined Barry on the steps to the cabins. Frank and Billy went to check the rest of the craft.

There were four cabins. Barry slowly opened each door. The last door was locked. Albie took a couple of backward strides as Barry stood behind him, revolver in his hand. Albie rushed forward and the door lock crumpled.

In full view of them was Igor, pointing a pistol at the two girls. They were tied to chairs in the corner of the room. Igor with a nefarious smile creasing his face, stretched his gun arm out, almost into the girls' faces. "If you come any closer I will blow these bitches away. You two guys are going to help me leave here and they are coming with me. If you do not do as I ask, you will be scraping their brains off your clothing."

"Now, what I want you to do is...." He never finished. Anya's Jiu Jitsu was about to save her life. With a forceful, accurate kick she booted Igor's gun into the air. In an instant, Anneliese dived forward, still with arms tied to the chair, and head butted Igor in the stomach. As he fell to the floor, Barry pounced.

"You fucker," Barry screamed as he thrust his beretta in Igor's mouth. "No, no" screamed Anneliese. "Barry, please, for me, don't harm him. He will get what he deserves! We must take him back!" Frank, by now was just behind Barry. "She's right, Barry, we have to do this properly." Barry eased back with a disconcerted expression.

The transfer to the coastguard boat was relatively simple. The sea was completely calm. The coastguard got his vessel alongside, so close it was just a hop, skip and jump and they were in.

The minute Igor was dragged across the small gap, the coastguard took over from Frank, Barry and Albie. While they held him, the coastguard snapped handcuffs on and left the cord tie in place. Barry bundled Igor into a corner, all the time doing everything possible to make it painful. He pulled on the handcuffs, pretending to check they were secure, but so ferociously, Igor screamed. Barry had not yet exited from his psychotic state. It had erupted when his mind thought he might lose Anneliese.

The journey back to Marbella quay only took about 40 minutes. The coastguard and his three crew tried to give them some comfort. Blankets were provided and hot drinks. Billy sat quietly thinking about the events. Carmella had returned in the Super Frelon chopper. Billy could not think of anything other than her!

15 minutes into the journey, Barry was recovering. Frank was with Anneliese and Anya on the small deck at the stern. They had both wanted fresh air, having been locked in that small cabin for hours. Barry slowly approached them, dropped to his knees in front of Anneliese saying, "I'm so sorry for wanting to rip that bastard apart. It was because it was about you. I know I will get over it!"

Anneliese took his face in her hands. "Barry, we were just talking with Frank about that stuff. You were absolutely fantastic! We would not be here if it had not been for you. If that's how much you love me and want to look after me, I will find a way!"

Barry was beginning to be in a better place! But now wondered what "I will find a way" meant.

They arrived at the Marbella quay. Police and Guardia Civil were everywhere. What was noticeable was military type people in flak jackets. The place was crawling with them. Once on the quay, several of those uniforms spoke with Frank, then led Igor away. Barry watched as he walked with Anneliese and Anya. Frank caught them up just outside the bar.

Barry had been thinking everything through. All that had happened. All that had been said. Barry stopped just before the Café Del Mar. He turned and grasped Frank's arm. As Barry was about to speak, another person appeared and stood beside Frank. Anneliese took hold of Barry's arm. She turned and looked towards Anya, following with Albie. The group stood looking at each other wondering what would come next.

55

The new person's appearance was central. He looked very official in his three piece suit and groomed appearance. He, out of the corner of his mouth, said "Frank, get this over with." Frank steely eyed, looking at Barry and Albie, said "I am arresting you for drug dealing, drug supply and several other offences."

Barry and Albie looked astounded. They were led away as the Commander began to congratulate Frank. Anneliese ran after Barry and stopped him in this tracks. His escorts, two of the CECD Special Forces, continued to drag Barry along. Turning his head to peer back at Anneliese, Barry shouted, "What's happening Anneliese, what's this all about?"

Albie tried to cling to Anya, but all she could do was to stand motionless, with arms down by her sides. She stared up at the sky with a helpless expression as tears began to trickle down her cheeks. Albie followed Barry, pushed and pulled by the Special Forces personnel, his mind consumed by the abyss they were staring into!

The Commander was calling it a day. He began to stride toward the Westland Wasp helicopter parked on the beach, saying to Frank "I will meet with you three in my office at 11am. Now the balloon has gone up we need to catch up on events as they unfold. I will send a car for you!"

Anneliese broke away from Barry and his guards and sprinted after the Commander. "Sir, please wait, I must talk to you." The Commander stopped and turned to face her,"

Oh Anneliese, great job and I am over the moon that you and Anya are safe!"

"Sir, I must have a meeting with Barry. A chance to talk to him, because if it hadn't been for him and the other lads, I would be dead. And I must meet with you soon because there is a lot I need to explain."

"Well, young lady, I've informed Frank that we will all meet tomorrow. Then we can talk about you seeing Barry." The Commander stroked Anneliese's arm, saying "see you tomorrow". He then stepped up into the "Wasp" and whirred up and out of sight.

Their group, Anneliese, Anya, Frank, Billy and Carmella met up in the bar. It was a pretty solemn affair. Carmella approached Anneliese and Anya. She spoke quietly to them saying, "So it appears we are all in the same business!" Anneliese nodded. In an even quieter voice, Carmella asked "They don't have anything on Billy, do they?" "No," replied Anneliese, "He's not been under the CECD spotlight." Carmella's concerned expression eased!

Anneliese strode over to Frank. "I want to ask a question, Frank" She said. "Why do you think Igor and his chums tracked us and then attempted to kidnap us? It doesn't make sense unless it was some demented reason, such as sexual gratification. I had seen in his eyes that he was seriously attracted to both of us, but that would be extreme!"

Frank, running his fingers through his scalp began to explain. "Our intelligence analysts came up with the answer. The Commander informed me before he left that an informant had blown your cover. The informant was in the pocket of the local Mayor. As you know, we determined a while ago that Igor was in league with the Mayor, laundering drug money through property."

"The informant, who was in the pay of the Mayor, was a senior Spanish Police Officer. He has been arrested and will stand trial alongside the Mayor and Igor." Smiling, Frank finished by saying, "Goes to show you can't trust anyone nowadays!"

Carmella was requested to attend a meeting with her Captain early next morning. Carmella had agreed that Billy could go with her to Malaga. But he would have to wait in the car!

As Frank, Anneliese and Anya were attending a meeting with the Commander, they would shut the bar for the day.

Before Anneliese and Anya went to bed, they sat together and drafted a reminder document that they planned to use with Commander Farrell. Essentially, they intended appealing on behalf of Barry and Albie, for leniency.

Carmella was at her meeting at 8am. Her Captain, Avram Ben Simon, set the parameters for the day. But the first element was her next assignment. He gave her great praise for her work on the Paulo case. The sting in the tail was that her next assignment would be in Argentina. She, working with a team, would follow the trail of Nazis' that had escaped to South America, with several having been assisted by Paulo. The trail would still be warm so their chances of finding them would be better. The second element was that Carmella would accompany the Captain to a meeting with the CECD Commander and some of his undercover agents. Avram had discussed this strategy with Moshe Dayan who thought it would be a tremendous way to strengthen relations with the Europeans and North Americans.

Carmella never uttered a word, not an argument, not a question. She had decided to wait for the outcome of the meeting with CECD. The Captain said they needed to leave soon to be in Granada by 11am. Carmella, excused herself saying she needed to go to the ladies room before their trip.

She quickly crossed the foyer and ran across to where Billy was parked. Two minutes and she had explained all. She would tell the Captain that Billy was her driver, as she had injured her foot in the previous night's events. He would follow them and wait in the car whilst they met with CECD.

Carmella re-entered the Captain's office and explained. The Captain said, "Am I correct that he knows nothing and is not involved in any way? "Yes sir," she replied firmly.

On the way up to Granada, they chatted for a while. Then the Captain asked, "How was it you got involved with the CECD rescue of their agents."

"Sir, these were the Russians that tried to kill me. They had abducted two CECD agents and at the crucial time, CECD did not have enough qualified personnel to mount the rescue. Their organisation, CECD, had put everything into finding the Russian aggressors. I could not stand back when they needed help!"

"Carmella, when we are in company you should continue to show respect and address me as Captain. However, I have utter respect for your efforts and performance, so please, when we are alone, call me Avram. Your work has been exemplary, and has been mentioned to Moshe Dayan. You have put our brigade into a very favourable light and, I thank you for that!" Carmella's expression, initially was one of disbelief. That quickly turned to euphoria!

They arrived in the courtyard to the Commander's office at 10.55am. Carmella and the Captain were first to arrive. As they were helping themselves to coffee from the gurgling coffee pot, Anneliese, Anya and Frank arrived. There were embraces for Carmella and handshakes all around.

56

The Commander opened the meeting, with a heartfelt thank you to Carmella for assisting his troops in a very difficult rescue. He continued by passing the baton to the MOSSAD Captain. Avram Ben Simon explained that the capture of Paulo was a magnificent advance for MOSSAD and the Nazi Hunters. It had also given them a change in their mind set. They now believed that working with CECD, the joint pact between Europe and North America, would provide extraordinary advantages.

The Captain cut to the chase. "I have already spoken with Carmella and asked her to take on a new assignment in South America. Argentina to be precise, because we know that is where most of the Nazis' we want to bring to justice, have escaped to. But we want to work with you on this!"

Commander Farrell, looking directly at his three agents said, "I need you three to work with Carmella and bring this to a very successful conclusion. The world would applaud us for bringing Nazis' to justice and it would do a tremendous amount for relations between Israel, Western Europe and North America."

The three, Anneliese, Anya and Frank all looked, pensively, at one another. Anneliese was the first to speak. "Commander, I need to talk to you about some of the people that were arrested last night. People that put their lives on the line to rescue us." The Commander, looking at the Captain, said, "I don't think we need you for this section of the meeting, so I just want to say how grateful I am for your input."

As Carmella and the Captain were leaving, Carmella stopped abruptly at the door. Looking back at the Commander she said, "Those guys, Barry and Albie, were fantastic last night. We need more of their type in our service!" The Captain gripped her arm and led her out to their car.

"Now we are alone" uttered the Commander, "I want to debrief you on the series of raids and arrests that have severed most arteries supplying drugs to Western Europe and the U.K. We have almost 150 suppliers and dealers in custody in six different countries. And we have closed down 5 warehouses, and apprehended most of their personnel. Also, the supply line from North Africa has been closed." "You have distinguished yourselves throughout! The intelligence you provided enabled our agents, police and troops to systematically amputate the tentacles of ruthless businesses run by several drug barons. And in concert with that effect, the capture of Paulo has cemented an alliance with Israel. A superb feather in our caps!"

Commander Farrell took a step towards his three secret agents. "In summary, you are the toast of all our Governments!"

Although the Commander was beaming a smile at them, Anneliese, Anya and Frank were clearly grappling with agonising thoughts. "Well let's continue" remarked Commander Farrell. "Anneliese, you said you needed to talk to me. You all appear somewhat disconcerted, so, please go ahead and tell me what's on your mind."

Anneliese slowly stood, her gaze fixed on the Commander. "Hope you don't mind me standing and possibly walking. It helps me to think clearly, and I must perfect what I'm going to say. I must influence your thinking!"

Taking a very deep breath, she slowly strolled to the corner of the room. As she turned she said, "This concerns Barry and Albie. You know Anya and I have lived with them for several months. Both these guys are as hard as granite and completely fearless. They grew up in a tough place in a tough time. In the events of yesterday, Barry was the hero of the day. He saved our lives! He could have been killed in the process, but his loyalty and love for us were never in danger of being compromised. And you will never find more bravery in a team than the one that rescued us yesterday." As Anneliese said those words, she glanced and smiled at Frank, her eyes saying a thank you!

"Barry is a very accomplished fighter, but he is also very intelligent. You saw the coded message system he designed which reflected his intellect."

"Barry and Albie are courageous individuals and are totally loyal and committed to one another. That was demonstrated yesterday." Anya now stood, walked to Anneliese and gave her a paper, pointing at something written on it. It was the Reminder List.

As Anya sat, Anneliese continued, "Commander, Barry has suffered an intermittent psychosis illness since he was a child. In the last few months it has begun to dissipate. He has become more congenial and his violent episodes have almost totally regressed. He, in consequence, decided a while ago he wanted to exit all criminal activities. Indeed, in recent months he has relinquished every part of his illicit business. Albie has given him total support in their endeavour to put new structure into their lives. Finally, I would add that they both have loving families and they love them in return…. Up to the hilt! And just to add to that, and you probably have already guessed this…. We are in love with them, me with Barry and Anya with Albie."

The Commander, with a knowing smile, nodded. Anneliese continued, "Sir this is our plea for Barry and Albie. The assignment in Argentina would only be possible for me if Barry could accompany me. And I know the same applies to Anya. These men, Barry and Albie, would strengthen our team an inordinate amount. They work well with Frank and he could mentor them. And the icing on the cake for you, Sir, is that they would provide natural protection for Anya and me."

Frank, recognising the interlude said, Commander, I agree with everything Anneliese has said and support her plea. As you know sir, I have been in many battles and yesterday those guys were the best I have ever fought alongside."

"Ok", said Commander Farrell, "We will close now. I will sleep on it and would like you all back here tomorrow at 1pm. I will then let you know of the arrangements for you to see Barry and Albie."

Heading towards the door, Anneliese spun round and asked the Commander, "Are you able to tell us where Barry and Albie are being held." "Well, as you are travelling back to Marbella in one of my cars, I think I can be confident you won't attempt to break them out!" Chuckling as he finished the sentence, he announced, "They are very comfortable in the Seville Penitentiary. The only negative is that Seville is very hot at the moment."

The Commander's driver whisked them to the bar in double quick time. As the secret three approached the steps, Carmella and Billy rushed across the road to meet them. They had been waiting for their return as the bar was closed. Carmella put her arm around Anya saying, "I couldn't leave without seeing you and hearing how it went."

Frank opened up and went straight to the bar to pour drinks. They all needed them and after a few sips were relaxed and grateful. Carmella and Billy sat close together, appearing like Siamese twins. Billy was ecstatic with a grin from ear to ear.

Carmella couldn't hold on any longer. Gripping Frank's hand as her smile widened, she turned towards Anneliese and Anya. "Billy is coming with us to Argentina. We are both so excited. But as she looked into the girls faces she realised they were not on her cloud nine. Frank tightened his grip on Carmella's hand. "We are uncertain if we will be going with you." Before he could say another word, Billy clambered off his bar stool saying, "You must be with us. You mean the world to us!"

Frank took on explaining Anneliese and Anya's plea for Barry and Albie. "So what do you think of the chances?" Carmella, sensing Anneliese' pain leant over to cuddle her. "Your boss seemed a person with a heart." Anya stepped into the arena. "You are right! He's a great boss but we don't think he has enough authority to over-rule the courts. They have been arrested, so will appear in court before anything else!"

❦

57

armella now became agitated. "No, no, I think it's different in Spain. I have lived in Spain for years, and some senior officials, may have authority to decide a penalty. I studied law at University so there is some knowledge behind what I am telling you!"

After a few minutes, while Carmella's words sunk in, the mood lightened. Anneliese kissed Carmella and smiles began to re-appear. As the evening wore on, tiredness was taking its toll. Billy and Carmella were thinking of retiring to their hotel, but they had both had several drinks. Anneliese, feeling grateful to Carmella, turned to Anya and asked "Would it be ok with you for Billy and Carmella to stay in your flat upstairs tonight. And you could stay with me at the villa? I don't really want to be on my own tonight!" So that was all settled!

Frank had already gone on his way. Anya and Anneliese were preparing to leave, helping Billy to close up and make the bar secure. Carmella just wanted Billy all to herself. But just as Anneliese and Anya were about to leave, Carmella said she was going to bed.

Billy turned to Carmella and with a mischievous look exclaimed, "Carmella, I am going to be living in a bar tonight. A bar with lots of booze and a pool table! I will come to bed in a couple of hours." Carmella's fierce temperament took over. "Billy, you will come to bed right now!"

Anya and Anneliese were laughing all the way to the other Cortina!

In the morning, nerves were jangling. They all met at the bar at 10am. The atmosphere was fraught, except for Frank. He couldn't tell the others, but he already had given counsel and options to Commander Farrell. Frank's assessment was that things might not be as dismal as they may have been.

Carmella offered to tend the bar with Billy. Frank was attempting to lift Anneliese and Anya's spirits as they set off in Barry's Jaguar. On the way, Frank did everything he could to avoid talking about Barry and Albie. He spent most of the time, speaking to nobody listening! Mostly about the Jaguar S Type, its features, attributes and almost every car he'd ever owned.

Frank figured they would arrive too early, so he took a detour to find a place to waste some time with breakfast. All through the meal, the girls continually checked their watches. Conversation was noticeably absent and then, when Frank indicated it was time to leave, both girls' expressions showed relief.

As Frank prepared to pull away, Anneliese said, "Frank, wait a minute. The Commander is going to arrange for me to see Barry. But what do I say to him? It's crucifying me!" she gasped and placed her hand on her mouth. "Oh, that expression is smack on. I was a Judas and there are no excuses!"

Frank turned in his seat to look directly into Anneliese's eyes. "You're asking me, a man that has messed up every relationship he has ever had. All I know is, and I'm saying this to you both, Barry and Albie have never had it easy, but they've always found a way. They are survivors. They will appreciate the truth and will relish you telling them about your feelings for them."

"That's as much as I know, because, as I said, I've always messed up my relationships. It's the reason I'm in this job. My motto has been the same for some years now; Make war, not love!"

The last few words brought smiles to the girls' faces. Frank turned and grasped the steering wheel as they pulled away.

As they drove along the bending road that climbed all the way up to Granada, Frank reduced speed, and as they slowed, with no other cars around, Frank spoke. "Just want to say one other thing to you girls. We have worked together now for quite a while, so I'm hoping that what I say, you will see is said with sincerity. Whilst I was going through a difficult time with a relationship, words of a song I heard stuck with me. They are always true. The words that I treasure are "heartaches you face alone!" May sound strange for me to say I treasure them, but is the truth. I know, that in your case, you will come out of your heartache better than you expect, and better than I ever did! And look at me. I'm still here, alive and kicking, because life will go on!"

They arrived, right on time, at the Commander's offices. As they entered several Special Forces squaddies could be seen, milling around at the end of the corridor.

They sat quietly waiting for the Commander. He arrived a couple of minutes later, shuffled some papers on his desk; then sat in his large leather executive chair. With a welcoming smile, he started to ask if their trip had been acceptable, commented on the heat of the day, then relented when he was consumed by the sadness in Anneliese's and Anya's eyes.

He began to ask, "Do you ladies have any...."but Anneliese couldn't wait any longer. "Sir," she said, "With the greatest respect, and I am so sorry for interrupting, but when will we be able to see Barry and Albie?"

Commander Farrell looked at them with a serious expression, which gradually and slowly changed to an understanding gentle smile. He sat pensively thinking for a few moments, stood, walked round his desk to stand just in front of them. Looking swiftly sideways at Frank, he took Anneliese's hand and then Anya's hand. "Well, if you really want to see them, I will take you to them. We can do it right now. They are waiting just down the corridor!"

The Commander led the way. Albie was in one office and Barry in the next. Special Forces soldiers stood guard at the doors. As the girls entered, the Commander quietly said "good luck."

Anneliese, standing just inside the door, stood looking at Barry. He had his back to her but turned, and with a look of surprise, seemed rooted to the spot. Emotion smothered his mind as he rushed toward her. They both couldn't wait to feel their arms around each other again. A few seconds later the tide of emotion ebbed. Barry led Anneliese to a small settee by the window.

Barry, driven by his feelings, tried to speak first. Anneliese placed her hand over his mouth, saying, "Barry, I love you, so please let me explain. My boss has given me 20 minutes with you. I am a government secret agent working for a counter-espionage and criminal deterrent, government organisation." I took the job before we met and you were my first assignment. In the early days, before I really got to know you, I fed lots of information about your activities to my bosses. But as we travelled further down the road together, I fell in love with you. That is the truth, and nothing but the truth."

"From that point I didn't know what to do, where to turn. The only way I can explain it is that I was caught in a tube, a long pipe. If I tried to escape from one end I would have to accept that you would be arrested. I couldn't get away from my job, and stay with you! If I stayed with my job, you would be arrested based on the earlier information I had provided. So I buried my head and stayed with you hoping something would turn up and get us out of this mess. It's roughly been the same for Anya."

A knock on the door came. Barry smiled at Anneliese. As they walked to the door, he said, "Its ok, we'll get through this together!" The guards escorted them to the Commander.

58

They stood in front of the Commander. He began by saying, "Make yourself comfortable. We've got a lot to discuss." As they sat, he looked to Barry and Albie. "I've heard a lot about you two from Anneliese and Anya." "The first thing I want to do is thank you for your bravery and unselfish efforts to rescue my operatives. Anyone that helps my people deserves recognition."

"Having said that, I don't suppose you have any clue why you are here. Well, I'll explain it in short simple terms. If you go to court you will get at least 20 years in prison for your offences. Anneliese, Anya and Frank have appealed on your behalf."

"Under Spanish, and new laws applying to my organisation, I am, authorised to decide your fate. So the alternative offer is pretty simple to understand. You can accept a position with us as an agent working for CECD. You would be required to work in a team with Frank, Anneliese and Anya. Your cousin Albie," the Commander nodded at him," will also be expected to accept!"

Commander Farrell was relishing the way it was going. He continued, "The bottom line is that you will be stationed in Argentina for five years. Our existing agents, Frank, Anya and Anneliese may return at any time, after completing their two year assignment. But you two, Barry and Albie, will be required to stay for 5 years. You will work with MOSSAD and civilians hunting down Nazis' that escaped after the war."

The Commander seemed to have finished; he looked around the room. Barry, not aware of etiquette advanced to the Commander. "Boss, I have always wanted this type of job, and I swear I won't let you down. " As he stretched out his arm to shake hands, Albie followed, saying, "Thank you Sir, you won't regret it."

Anneliese and Anya rushed forward, embracing them both. Commander Farrell stood as Frank joined the group. As they composed themselves, Barry asked "So Boss" but he was stopped in his tracks. Anneliese said, "Barry, to be respectful you can say Commander or Sir." "I'm sorry," said Barry. "Do we not have to go back to prison tonight?" "No," the Commander replied. "Get yourself back to your bar and have a celebratory drink on me." "Wow, Sir, there is no way I can thank you. You have given us the chance we have always searched for. And if we do well, may we return to the U.K. after 5 years without fear of being re-arrested?" "Correct Barry." Replied the Commander.

"Just one more thing" said Commander Farrell. "You will report to Frank. He is your boss. He is also your mentor. And if you attempt to escape, or go absent without leave, Frank and my best operatives will hunt you down, and be assured you will be captured! However, at Frank's discretion, you may be given chances to talk to, and perhaps even visit, your family."

"Right now, I want you to leave and begin preparations for your assignment. You will leave for Argentina next week; dates and time will be provided shortly!"

They all, silently, walked across the foyer and out the main door. A couple of the Special Forces soldiers shouted goodbye, but they could only wave. All of them were almost paralysed with disbelief. All except Frank who snapped them out of it saying, "Well that was a result!"

Those few words kicked Barry and Albie out of paralysis into euphoric glee. They both ran around the car park, jumping and punching the air, followed by laughter and warm embraces. Anneliese and Anya joined them, both girls tearfully in raptures.

Frank congratulated the boys as they entered the Jaguar. Frank said he had better drive because he was the only sane one amongst them.

They laughed, giggled and recounted the whole thing over and over again. All Barry repeated constantly was that every piece of the jigsaw fitted perfectly. He would then move on to explaining that phrase." We can be together, we will work together, we've been given an exciting job, we will be Nazi Hunters and it will all be an adventure in a new country, Argentina!"

Frank, as he drove, started to chuckle. "You are missing a piece of that jigsaw Barry." "What have I missed Frank?" "Well, you will be pleased to hear we will be working with two new agents in our team, Carmella and Billy!"

59

With joyful expressions on all their faces they entered the bar. Billy and Carmella immediately started preparing drinks. They all sat together at the largest table in the bar. Initially Carmella was apprehensive, but as she searched their faces for a sign, a realisation set in. "Barry, Albie you are here! Why are you here?" Carmella exclaimed! Anya and Anneliese burst into laughter, jumped out of their chairs saying, "They are free and will be working with us in Argentina."

Carmella, with Billy, trickled around them; all received strong embraces and kisses. "How is it possible?" screamed Carmella. Frank decided he would answer that question. Leaning back in his chair, he clasped both hands behind his head. With a look of complete and utter pleasure on his usually stoic face, he said, "It would appear it is totally true! Love really does conquer all!"

The whole group spent every minute of the evening in conversation about the upcoming assignment in Argentina. As they began to tire, Frank decided they should finish on a productive note. A meeting next morning at 10am required their attendance. Albie's expression was dubious, until Frank remarked "You will have to get accustomed to working a full day!" Frank continued, "We should use the meeting to summarise concerns and issues so we can tackle them before we depart next week." "Great plan," Said Anneliese as she pulled Barry towards the door. "See you all in the morning."

Lying in bed beside one another, Barry was quiet and thoughtful. Two things were rattling around in Barry's head. He turned on his side to face Anneliese. "Darling, I'm starting to think about what we need to do next. You know I'm a person that plans everything, but I keep bumping into the thought that none of this is real and I'll wake up soon and find it was all a dream." Anneliese stroked Barry's ebony hair from his face as she said, "No Barry, it is all absolutely real, and we will wake up in the morning to the reality."

"So Barry, what's the second thing?" "My Mum, my family, how to explain why I'm going to live in Argentina!" "Well, that's simple, so simple; we will deal with it in the morning." As Anneliese said this, she stroked his face, moved close to him, saying, "At the moment you only have one priority …. to kiss me!"

Barry and Anneliese sat on the patio in the warmth of the early morning sunshine, having breakfast. As Barry breathed in the pure Marbella air. Anneliese's fragrance enthralled his senses. He felt more alive than he had for years. Over the last few months, his life had been transformed. Tensions had drifted away and he was consumed by a calmness.

"Right darling, shall we get started on our new life together." As Barry finished speaking, he took a last sip of his coffee and they set off for Café Del Mar.

As Barry drove, he began to reminisce. "I've done a full journey, from rags to riches and back again. All the money, property and valuables I acquired during my previous crazy life have gone. They've all been confiscated, and you don't know how relieved I feel." A glorious smile settled across Anneliese's face. "We will be fine, with more than enough to live on, doing an honest worthwhile job! And the most precious thing you still have is me," giggled Anneliese.

The team were already in the bar as Barry and Anneliese entered. They took their coffees and sat at the large table again. Frank, with a grin said, "I would like each member of our new team to introduce themselves."

Carmella spoke first. "You are having a little joke with us Frank, yes? But I do need to inform you of something. I have been instructed to attend my Captain's office tomorrow. He will review his plans for me in Argentina and give me necessary information. Primarily, a list of Nazis' to be apprehended including initial intelligence." "I believe I will also meet colleagues that will work with us, and possibly some civilian Nazi hunters that will provide extra support and intelligence data. Finally, and I'm not certain about this, but after the meeting in Malaga, the plan may require us to fly almost immediately to Buenos Aires. Obviously, Billy will come with me! I will aim to give Frank feedback after the meeting."

There was a stunned silence throughout the group. Frank took up the reins again. One after the other, Frank asked the team if they had any concerns, issues or questions. Barry was the only one. "Sorry, Frank but I have several. I will take them one at a time and will speak for Albie as well." Barry took a deep breath as Anneliese gave his hand a squeeze. He was in the starting gate when the bar door clonked open, pushed by someone using his back as a battering ram. The character was grappling with a large travel bag. He twisted and turned to get through the door. It was a tussle haired, red-faced Jerome!

Anya ran over to help him; smothering his cheeks with kisses, she screamed; "We are so pleased you are here because things are moving fast." Jerome pulled a chair over and joined the group.

Frank, once again attempted to get them back on track. "Jerome, please bear with us until Barry has finished, then I will explain everything."

Barry, with a sad tone, explained that he needed to find a way to see his mum before they went. His voice juddered with emotion. "And I am really struggling with how to explain why I am moving half way round the world to Argentina." Jerome gasped!

Frank, with his usual directness said," There can only be one answer.... Honesty is the best policy." Anneliese interjected. "Frank is bang on, but there are some tunes you can play to make it easier. Just begin with the true fact that you have taken a new job which gives you the chance at a fantastic career. Don't mention anything about your previous life. It is not necessary and you will not be lying. Explain it is a career chance that you could not turn down. An important Government job. I know your Mum. She will be so happy for you! And don't forget, she's not alone now. Her heart is also attached to Jess!"

"Fabulous answer," said Frank. "Now the answer to the other half of the question. How to get to see your Mum and Jess. I will ensure the flight arrangements will take us first to Heathrow." Jerome then asked Frank if he could say something, "is it relevant Jerome?" "Yes, I hope so, Frank." With a nod of the head, Frank gulped his coffee.

60

Jerome said, "If the flight plan could be organised like this; I book a hotel on the doorstep of Heathrow for the night before your departure. Rooms for all of us, including Barry's Mum and Jess. We could make it a farewell get together. I will take on the job of getting Mum and Jess to the hotel. I'm guessing they would love to spend time with all of you, and it would give Mum and Jess something to talk about and remember for the rest of their lives. Also, Albie's Mum and Dad could be there. I will even pay for the whole thing if you would let me!"

Frank took Jerome's hand and shook it like he was trying to kill it. "Don't know what you think, Barry, but I think it's a superb suggestion. And as I hold the team's budget, I will happily ensure that CECD pick up the tab." Barry stood, and with eyes glistening said, "I need a drink. How about the rest of you?" Billy began filling glasses.

Once they had all settled, Barry said, "I have a couple more things." With a questioning expression, Barry looked at Frank. "Terry and Jose, Frank; do you know what is happening with them?" "Yes, I do. They will both be out on bail tomorrow. None of the CECD or Guardia Civil intelligence had picked them up. The Spanish Police insisted on going back through their files, but nothing damaging has been found that could be used in evidence!"

Barry spoke. "That's a relief. They have been loyal and worked to help us through thick and thin. Frank, could you get a message to them? I want a chance to talk with them. I want you all to know that this bar is mine and is not being confiscated. I plan to offer it to Terry and Jose, and the cars! They have earned it, several times over!"

Frank peered at Barry. "Does all of that get rid of your concerns?" "Yes, boss!" With a smile on his face, Barry followed that with "That's the first time I have called you boss, and it's a start with getting me used to it."

They were all feeling in a much better place. But then Barry thought of one more thing. Everyone had begun to drift to the bar. Barry shouted to Billy, "Leave that, come round here with me. "Barry wheeled Billy towards Frank. "Billy, I know you will be in Carmella's team, but we are all working together on this. Do you have anything you are worried about that we can help with?" Frank looked up at Billy, saying, "Yes, if we can help with anything, in any way, we will. If you have any U.K. issues, tell us and we will try to help."

Billy, a big statuesque guy looked surprised that anyone cared! "I've never been asked that type of question before." He stopped and cleared his throat. Frank interrupted just as Billy was about to speak. "Billy, we have not known you long but we now have the utmost respect for you. And, adding to that, you are taking on a difficult job down in Argentina. Do you have family in the U.K. that we can help with?"

Billy walked away. All the way down the end of the bar and stood by the pool table. He slowly walked back to the bar and poured himself a very large rum and black. Glass in hand, he stood in front of Frank and Barry, but looking straight at Carmella.

His face turned back to Frank. He gulped his rum, took a breath, and waited a few seconds. "Frank, no is the answer. I have no family. Never have had. I grew up in St Bartholomew's children's home. Had a few times, later on, in homes with nuns' looking after us. They were all great. Fed and watered us. But I've never had family!" He stepped and turned away, and as he did, pulled a checked handkerchief out of his pocket. He turned back, pushing the handkerchief in his pocket, whilst staring at Carmella. Understandably, the powerful emotions overwhelmed her psyche and tears welled up in her soft brown eyes.

Billy continued, stuttering occasionally, "Frank, I have always done everything on my own. I was a good footballer but that was down to me! Everything I survived was down to me! But now I have found someone; Carmella; that wants to spend her life with me! And I couldn't ask for anything more. But both of us now have a family. It's you lot! I've never had anything like it, but you lot are better than anything I could ever expect!"

All the emotion in the room gradually eased and enjoyment took its place. In the meantime, Jerome, having been extremely patient; found a way to get Albie and Anya's attention.

Anya began to explain all the recent events. Jerome listened intently, initially with a poignant expression, which developed into disbelief, then acute shock. Anneliese joined them, firstly apologising, followed by an outline of the roles of Frank, Anya and herself. She moved to the complications caused by their relationships and then the decisions made by her superiors.

Jerome sat quietly, open mouthed; stunned by the complexity of the tapestry Anya and Anneliese were describing. However, with hearing details of the new assignment in Argentina, his mood lifted into pure excitement.

"You are going to do a fabulous thing, "he uttered, as his fingers tapped the table with exhilarated tension. "My Dad has told me of all the awful, depraved things the Nazis' did. He and my Mum were born in Yugoslavia. They escaped to England as the Nazis' began to send Yugoslavians to the concentration camps. My Grandfather died in Auschwitz along with 20,000 other Yugoslavians. The Nazis' also killed thousands of homosexuals, just because they were different. And you all know, I am homosexual, and I've experienced how terrifying it can be to be threatened just because of the way you are!"

"Sounds to me like we should ask if you would want to come with us?" Anya grinned, but before she could continue, Albie interrupted. "You, my gay little treasure, are the only gay mate I have ever had, and both of us would love to have you with us!" "I would do anything to be given the chance," said Jerome. "I would work my nuts off if it would mean I could stay with you. And I could wreak some revenge for my family!"

Albie, first checking Anya's expression, scratched his stubble. "You understand it's by no means certain" he said, "But I will try to persuade Frank." Albie got with Barry and Anneliese and recounted the Jerome conversation. They all got drinks to have a hopeful celebration. Later on, Albie and Barry drew Frank away.

Seated on the patio, Albie spent a minute or two telling Frank how intelligent, brave and physically fit Jerome was. "I only had to explain things a couple of times and he got it." Anya found the same with Jiu-jitsu. "He's a good, brave fighter now."

61

Frank became serious. "I'm guessing you are building up to ask if Jerome can be part of the team" "Yes, boss" said Barry, holding his gaze directly into Frank's eyes. "He doesn't have to work on the front line. He could be our gopher. He could be more than that! He could do research, communication. He's very good with all that intelligent stuff. He could be our backroom. We are going to need that!"

Frank stood and did a turn around the patio, thinking all the while! He then said, "I'm just going to have a word with Anneliese." When he returned, he sat and eased into the table. "I've discussed your request with Anneliese and we agree that, it may be possible. But I don't have the last word, the Commander does."

"Anneliese and I have mentally structured an application. We are proposing he be classified as Civil Service Administration, responsible for research, analysis and documentation. His salary will be within a Civil service grade. Not a fortune, but more than enough to live on. Depending on his results, he may be considered for promotion into a higher grade, or indeed into a CECD Secret Service Agent's role. He will have to sign the official secrets act, as will both of you."

"Well, what do you two think?" Barry and Albie smiled at Frank saying, "Sounds great, we all deserve a drink." Frank, now in work mode, said, "Leave me out for a moment. I'm going to have a word with Jerome and get this as far as I can tonight."

At the bar, Albie suggested to Jerome to go and have a word with Frank. As he swivelled round to Barry, Terry and Jose charged through the door, shouting "Geezer we are buying!" Barry had the broadest smile, and with arms around both of them, he loudly announced "Ladies and Gentlemen, meet the new owners of Café Del Mar." Terry gasped, "What are you talking about, Geezer?"

"Well, it goes like this Terry. I am going away for a while." "What, prison?" replied Terry. "No, I'll explain later, I won't be allowed to tell you much, but it will be enough." Barry continued, "I am offering you and Jose the bar. No charge and it's a great money-spinner!"

They were both lost for words as Anneliese joined in. "Great to see you two. Hope recent days haven't been too punishing." She embraced both Terry and Jose, saying, "we are really grateful for all your work and help you gave us."

Terry, having got his breath back said, "Well, we are grateful in return. It's fantastic; Jose, we are bona fide business men!"

Barry, now enjoying a large scotch, pointed outside and said, "There's that other little bonus." "What now Geezer?" before Barry could say a word, Anneliese said, quite loudly, "From now on its Barry. No more Geezer!" They all broke into rapturous laughter and applauded!

Jose was first to be correct. "Senor Barry, what is outside? What were you saying?" Barry, rather choked as he explained, "When we leave, only after we have gone, you guys own that fabulous Lotus Cortina outside. And another that's being repaired at present. Then there is my fantasy car, the Jaguar S type. It's yours as long as you agree to chauffeur us when we come to visit!"

The euphoria was building at a supersonic rate. Next it was Jerome. He rushed to them, saying, "Oh, we're going to Argentina." He grabbed a drink from Billy and downed it before you could blink.

The mood was about to become sombre. Carmella had been checking around and collecting hers' and Billy's stuff. She joined everyone at the bar, with Billy continuing to serve. "We have to leave soon. We may see you again before you leave, but probably not! In which case, we will meet you when you arrive at Buenos Aires airport."

Billy came out from behind the bar and cuddled Carmella. He could see emotion was reaching her. Carmella, trying to distract herself, began to phone a taxi. Terry, immediately said, "No, I will take you in the Cortina." "No, Terry, no, "she exclaimed. "Carmella, please let me," replied Terry, "I just want to drive that car again."

The bar became extremely quiet as everybody embraced. At the door, Billy and Carmella stood for a moment. "We will see you all soon and we can't wait." Billy strode back into the bar and grasped Barry's hand. "I can never thank you enough mate! This is even better than the hat-trick I scored against you!" Barry clipped his ear as he walked back and stood beside Carmella.

As they edged out onto the patio, Carmella shouted, "We are going to be a sensational team. I can't wait to work with you all on this assignment! No, that's not completely true. I just can't wait to be with you! We love you all so much! Don't cry for me Argentina"

The rest of the night was dedicated to ecstatic enjoyment. All of them had reasons to feel that life was good. Frank got together with Jerome again, trying to tie up a few loose ends. How much notice did he have to give BEA?

Only two weeks! Did he have any criminal convictions? No, none! How many previous jobs? None! According to Frank, it all looked good. Then Jerome remembered he had several weeks untaken holiday. So his notice period could be less. It was looking really good for him. Frank informed Jerome he would talk with his boss tomorrow and possibly be able to give him an answer the same day.

They all carried on enjoying the relief after an extremely difficult period. On this day, the time they had all spent together had been completely jaw dropping!

62

Jerome had to return to his airline steward's job Sunday evening. In the morning; Saturday morning, he sat on the patio in the sunshine waiting and hoping to hear from Frank. He arrived about 11am. Most of the others were milling about in the bar, but Frank went straight to sit with Jerome. "I'll get straight to the point, Jerome." Just at that moment, Anya brought Frank a coffee. Anya hung around to eavesdrop!

Frank glanced towards Anya, and smiling said, "Yes, you're in; you got the job. I'll give you all the details in a minute. But first, I have something more urgent to discuss. How quickly do you think you can start?" Jerome looked at Anya who now had been joined by Albie and Barry. "Well working it out last night, with my carryover vacation, and it's a short term contract, I think I could terminate tomorrow and start with you Monday." "Fabulous" replied Frank.

Now Anneliese arrived and they all craned their necks to listen. "It's like this, Jerome. Your first assignment will start on Monday. I need you to fly to Vienna. Carmella and Billy will meet you, and you will all go to meet a Mr Wiesenthal. This was a direct request from MOSSAD to the Commander."

"Simon Wiesenthal is a freelance Nazi hunter that has a mountain of information. He has commited his life to bringing Nazis' to face the courts. He is an expert that works constantly with MOSSAD. He has already proved his worth with the capture of several high ranking Nazis. Most notably, Adolf Eichmann."

Jerome obviously knew the name. He gasped! Frank, turning away, then back to Jerome, said, "All you need to do is listen as he talks with Carmella. Document what he says and record as much as you can. This information will give our team a fast start in Buenos Aires. You will then fly with Carmella and Billy to Heathrow for the family get-together. We will meet you there on Thursday. I will get the travel arranged, and tomorrow, give you the equipment for the job. Jerome, can you handle it?"

He ran his fingers back through his hair, then rubbed both his temples. "Frank, I will do a perfect job! It's my type of work! I won't let you down! But I'm finding handling the excitement really difficult!" Bursting into laughter, he glanced around the others. "Two days back and I'm heading into the greatest adventure of my life!"

Anneliese spoke directly to Frank. "This is a marvellous tactic. I've read about Simon Wiesenthal's work. You're right, he is the world's living expert on everything to do with Nazis'. He pieces together every minute piece of intelligence, even the most unobtrusive information and finds a way to make something of it. He may be able to teach Jerome and Carmella ways that we can use to help ourselves!"

The rest of the day evolved to be a day of information. Mostly for Jerome. Frank, Anneliese and Anya spent time explaining the work of CECD; its objectives, Counter Espionage and Criminal Deterrent. Work with the CIA, MI5 and MI6 and Western European Secret Service Agencies. As Albie pointed out previously, Jerome absorbed and understood information very quickly.

On Sunday, Frank would deliver all necessary documents and equipment. The CECD version of the Official Secrets Act would be reviewed and signed by Jerome, Barry and Albie. Then it would be "all systems go!"

After a completely exhausting day, Saturday evening, they all enjoyed some Spanish delicacies and booze; Jerome was still bursting with pride and excitement. At one point, when the lads were all together at the bar, Jerome quietly spoke, out of the corner of this mouth, "Frank, do we all get issued with our own personal packet of cyanide pills?" They all chuckled, then Frank replied, "Why Jerome, do you feel like you need one?" "Well, you may all think I do, because the arrangements for Mum and Jess have not been made and I'll be away!" They all developed anguished expressions. Frank's deep giggle commenced once more. He looked around them all and announced, "Don't worry, I booked everything last night, and this morning. We will all be in the Skyline Hotel and one of our Royal Marine drivers will pick them up. Anneliese gave me Jess's number and I called him last night. He will explain all to Joan.

Sunday was a packing, checking and relaxing day. And not just for Jerome. The rest followed his lead, even though they had a few more days.

Terry and Jose were at the bar early. It was a real pleasure to see their efforts to please everyone. Pampering, freebies and even a local band. The whole team and the customers perceived this as a change in owners and going away "party". It was so busy, by early evening people were even on the beach dancing…. Some just in swimwear.

Barry and Anneliese, along with Albie and Anya, were in their element. The excitement of the forthcoming adventure and relief from the stress of the previous days, intensified the romance swirling around them. Both couples were dancing, which became close, very close, dancing.

It was an extremely hot evening, and as the romantic tension increased, all the watchers, the customers, quietened. After a minute of the song "Have I told you lately that I love you," everybody was feeling the heat. As the music slowed and the singer whispered the final words, they all stood and applauded, whistled and cheered.

Anneliese and, especially Barry, looked embarrassed as they left the dance floor. Anya and Albie responded, waving to the crowd. But romance was in the air, probably initiated by the thought of a new life together!

Very early Monday morning, Frank arrived to take Jerome to Malaga airport. He was borrowing the Jaguar to take Jerome so he could go over everything again. What he wanted him to do; where he would meet Carmella and Billy, and the plans through to the party with Barry's Mum and Jess. He handed him a page he had written with hotel addresses and important phone members. And lastly, a bundle of Austrian currency. "Wow," said Jerome as he accepted the notes. "It is called "Schilling." Sounds like our shilling!"

63

There were no problems on the journey for Jerome. He knew all the tricks of the trade, and as he wandered out of departures, Carmella and Billy were right there waiting. After handshakes and embraces, a large Mercedes taxi took them to the hotel in Vienna city centre. As they arrived, the Austrian driver said in broken English, "Hotel Danke Vienna yah! Ist a wunderbar historic hotel." Carmella paid him saying, "Danke, Danke."

Once inside the hotel, all three of them were overawed by the decadent splendour and ambience of the interior. The furniture, decoration, wall and floor coverings, and, in particular, the gilt framed works of art were dominated by the Austro-Prussian War period. Characters that ruled the Kingdom of Prussia and battle scenes of the "Seven Weeks' War" surrounded them!

Later, they met in the bar and, initially, all the talk was about how sensational the hotel, and their rooms, were. Carmella inched them into the present world, but as she did, piped music began. Carmella, obviously a student of classical music stopped speaking to listen. She looked at Billy and Jerome and with an excited expression said "This is one of the things, an important thing, which Vienna is famous for. The dance, the Waltz! This music is from the famous composer Johann Strauss. He composed over 500 waltzes and we still love them and dance to them today!"

Billy and Jerome sat looking uncomfortably imbecilic as Carmella drifted off with the music, into an ecstatic state! Whilst the boys sat quietly drinking and chatting, Carmella remained in her own rapturous world for over ten minutes.

The piped music was interrupted by noise from a small ensemble that were setting up in the corner of the bar. Eventually, with quiet flute, violins and cellos drifting together, they played. As they began, the piped music was terminated. Carmella, straining to hear the ensemble's music exclaimed, "This is Brahms, another Viennese composer. He is my favourite."

As the violinist stepped forward, and began to play, Carmella said "Oh how wonderful, Violin Concerto Number 3" She leant forward and gripped Billy's hand. "Billy I want this as our wedding music." Billy nearly fell backwards off his chair!

Jerome thought he would try to bring these two back down to earth. "Brahms has always been part of the cockney repertoire. And he had a mate called Liszt. Most people in the East End of London, talk about them on a Saturday morning after a heavy drinking Friday night. We all talk about having been Brahms and Liszt!"

Jerome jumped up saying, "Let's have another drink, let's get Brahms and Litzt! "Billy explained all to Carmella. When Jerome returned, Carmella peered at both the boys. "I'm sorry, but this mustn't get out of control. Frank and my bosses have been very generous, but we are here to work on a very serious subject. So now I want to take you through a couple of things. "She pulled some papers out of her small carry-case and handed one each to Billy and Jerome.

She explained that her supervisors had compiled this list of Nazis' that, intelligence indicated, may be in South America. It was a long list, around twenty or more. Carmella went on to say that in their visit to Simon Wiesenthal, they should attempt to get any information to increase its usefulness. But, more importantly, to get his evaluation of the Nazis' that rated the highest in terms of their atrocities, combined with the best information that may lead to their whereabouts. The top three should be the objective!

Billy and Jerome had been forgetting the essence of their trip. Carmella had brought them back into the real world! They agreed they would finish their drinks and be more than ready in the morning to have a successful day with Simon Wiesenthal.

Daybreak arrived and they were all ready. A fast coffee and a pastry or two and their driver arrived. It was a short ride to the "Documentation Centre of Jewish victims of the Nazi Regime." A small office property in the Vienna old town.

Simon Wiesenthal was at the door to greet them. He was an imposing father-like figure with a partly bald head and greying feathery hair above his ears. The bags under his eyes were noticeable, probably caused by the long hours he spent amassing paperwork on Nazis. He was very smartly dressed in a grey, wide lapelled, double breasted three piece suit.

They all sat in an office surrounded by filing cabinets. Initially, some gentle chit-chat, and then he was direct. "MOSSAD have given me complete detail on your assignment." Looking at Carmella, he said "Young lady, we are all very proud to be working with such a brave Israeli girl. This is a difficult and dangerous assignment, but after I read your history, I could see that failure was not in your vocabulary. I thank you from the bottom of my heart.

Indeed, I thank you all for having values sufficient to drive you into this!"

They moved directly into the important topics. Wiesenthal began by announcing that he had detailed files on hundreds of Nazis. He had been working at this for years and had even spent time working with the Americans, for the OSS. Then he stepped into the arena that Carmella had as her priority.

"If you are going to have any level of success, you cannot take on the task of reviewing 100s of Nazi files. I would suggest you start with a top three."

Carmella smiled and said, "That was exactly our thinking. We have been given a list of over 20, but we have already agreed to ask you for the top three we should be hunting." Wiesenthal wiped his hand across his mouth and smiled. "You have just got over the first hurdle! This is a one-at-a-time job. I have proved that to myself and my colleagues time and again. So, next to the crucial point. Who are they?"

Wiesenthal stood and walked to a tap and sink in the corner of the room. "Would you like water?" All three of them said, yes, please. The excitement was drying their throats.

He brought their water, sat and was just about to speak when the door opened and two guys walked in. Wiesenthal stood, shook their hands, then did introductions. "These are my two best operatives, Ezra and Immanuel. As you know, we are all civilians, well not quite true! I am now working for MOSSAD. These gentlemen speak a little English, but I expect that by the time they finish this assignment, they will be fluent." As the three musketeers showed questioning expressions, Wiesenthal said, "Yes I am pleased to say they are coming with you to Argentina!" They know our targets and the files of hundreds of Nazis, inside out, and should prove invaluable to you."

Simon Wiesenthal walked across to his men and herded them to meet Carmella, Billy and Jerome. Then, turning to them all, said "We have worked past lunchtime, but Ezra and Immanuel will go and organise some sandwiches from the delicatessen a few doors away. Is that acceptable?" Billy now hit the forefront. "Simon, no, we can last until this evening. It's so interesting we could carry on!"

Wiesenthal leaned back on a table behind him, one cheek of his bottom edging to sit. "Billy, I am overcome that you are enjoying this, But, to be honest, I am starving. I spent years in several different concentration camps, so now all food is a luxury that I can have. So, please let us buy you some sustenance. If I could, I would ask for manna from heaven, but that may take a while and I am really hungry!"

Ezra and Immanuel were laughing as they exited! Simon Wiesenthal continued, "Whilst we wait I will give you the three that are top of the "must be captured list." Josef Mengele is top of the pile. A brutal, sadistic pervert. Next is Franz Stangl. And the third is a female, although she would probably be termed an animal, Hermine Braunsteiner. We know all three are in South America, and have intelligence that takes us much closer. Where we need to be careful is that travel between South and North America is relatively easy."

Lunch arrived. As soon as the food was set down, Wiesenthal attacked it as if it may never be available again. Carmella, watching him eat, stopped and gripped Billy's hands. He turned to her but realised he shouldn't say a word. Tears were edging down her cheeks. She was visualising her family members that had suffered in concentration camps.

As Simon Wiesenthal was finishing his simple sandwiches, Carmella was continuing to picture the horrendous atrocities in the concentration camps. The continuous beatings, rape, and then the finality and relief, the gas chambers. Wiesenthal as he moved away from his plate, sensed her emotion. He focused on the three of them, looking back and forth, but then centred on Carmella. "You are feeling what I have felt since those days, and I know, when you get yourself together, we will use those tears as a force to be reckoned with. "

"I have prepared three dossiers; one on each of those inhuman war criminals. This afternoon I will walk you through each one. I have included some excellent facial photographs. I would suggest you study them closely, indeed, stare at them and memorise every feature, every line, every blemish, until you are certain you would recognise them in a crowd."

"To help you to form a picture of two of these brutal creatures, I will refer you to the nicknames given to them by inmates of their camps. Mengele was called "The Angel of Death." He would select prisoners, as they arrived, and performed unspeakable unscientific operations on them. He particularly seemed to enjoy performing this torture on children."

"Braunsteiner was labelled the "Stomping Mare." She was given this name due to her propensity to kick her victims to death. The third, Stangl, does not appear to have been given a title. The reason probably comes from the fact that, in the camps he commanded, so few people survived. He alone, oversaw the deaths of over 900,000 people."

The rest of the afternoon and early evening involved detailed information about each of the three. Possible sightings, their characters in terms of addictions, perversions, sexual persuasion and preferences, smoking, drinking, health issues and so on.

All possible and potential leisure haunts. Bars, restaurants and clubs that were known to sympathise with neo-Nazis' and fascists, and were willing to provide meeting rooms.

Wiesenthal finished his afternoon of tutoring by explaining that all this navigation information would become much clearer and more defining once they were actually in Buenos Aires and could see it for themselves.

As they were about to leave, Simon Wiesenthal said he would be there to support them in their assignment, every step of the way. Not physically, but MOSSAD were very accomplished in communication!

"Tomorrow", Wiesenthal said, with a fatherly smile, "We will go back to school until lunchtime. I know you are leaving to fly back the day after tomorrow but you will enjoy my teaching and then you will need some time to yourselves. We will study maps of Buenos Aires and embroider them with information about areas Nazis' have been known to frequent. I will include information that has been extracted recently from Paulo. It will pinpoint areas in Buenos Aires that he and others used, for safe houses for Nazis'."

As they approached the door, Wiesenthal put his arms around Billy and Jerome, Saying "You British people have always fought for us, welcomed us, and now work with us to right the wrongs. There is no way we can ever repay you!" He swivelled around to face Carmella, took her right hand and gently leaned forward and kissed the back of her hand. "You, my dear, are an example to us all and will one day feature in history books!"

64

Back at the hotel, they went straight to the bar, needing a drink. It had been an intense day! They sat relatively quietly for a while. Billy needed to give Carmella affection, so moving close, they huddled together. Jerome's mind had been drifting along a lonely road, with all he had heard during the day. But then, seeing the hurt in Carmella's eyes he had to change the mood!

He stood, glass in hand and looking at Carmella said, "Here's to doing something worthwhile. Do you know until I listened to Simon today, I thought my life had been difficult. But the difficulties I have faced are nothing compared to what we heard about today. So I am going to propose a toast to There is always someone worse off than you!" He sat down and, smiling, said, "Here's to Brahms and Liszt!"

Carmella came out of the doldrums and Billy leaned across and grasped Jerome's hand for a second or two!

Out of the blue, Brahms seemed to appear. Unnoticed, the small ensemble had organised themselves in the shady corner of the bar and they began to play. Once again the violin led them in a soulful rendition of "Concerto Number 3" which then quickly transitioned into a light-hearted version of the Strauss Waltz, "The Blue Danube."

Hearing this, Carmella was inspired. She stood and applauded and others in the bar followed her. Carmella was elated!

Ezra arrived early morning to drive them to meet Simon Wiesenthal. He explained, with great difficulty, that they were going to Wiesenthal's home, and that he would give the reasons.

They had not driven long when Ezra pulled up outside a dull, almost ugly, tenement building. Wiesenthal's apartment was on the first floor, up one flight of stairs. Ezra tapped on the door and within seconds he appeared.

He, with a warm welcome, invited them in. He began to say they would be more comfortable here, rather than the office; just then a lady appeared. Wiesenthal introduced Cyla, his wife. An attractive, middle-aged lady, surprisingly, with striking blonde hair. She stood beside Jerome, and with the same colour hair, could have been his relative.

Cyla, with fairly good English offered hot drinks. Everyone opted for coffee, as she led them into the living room. It appeared a very modest apartment with a large bay window to the front.

All were seated and Simon Wiesenthal, being a confident speaker said "You are only with us for the morning and you already have all the necessary information. So I wanted to invite you to our dwelling and have you meet Cyla. We will still do the tutoring but my impression is that you are all very intelligent people that will quickly adapt to your challenging occupation!"

With that, Cyla appeared with the coffee. As she distributed them, she said, "Please excuse me because I am going out to meet some friends. You wouldn't want me around as I always seem to distract Simon. But I will be back before you leave."

Simon stood in the middle of the room, turned and glanced out of the window to watch Cyla striding down the road. Still with his back to them, he started to speak, as he gradually turned. "There are two things I want to start with. Firstly, you may be surprised to hear that Argentina has a massive German population. My guess is that most are escapees from the war. They provide help and support to the animals we are hunting. And there are numerous, active, neo-Nazi organisations that are nurtured there."

"Secondly, you should be aware that the Argentinian Government and its officials are not excited by the prospect of Nazi hunters in their domain. They will suffer you, probably due to U.S. pressure. But don't expect too much assistance. You may find a similar attitude in other South American countries."

Wiesenthal decided he needed to continue. "I'm so sorry, "He said. "I wanted to tell you two things, but there is another. A very important third that you should impart to your colleagues."

"Originally, the War Crimes Commission set an expiration date of 1965. After that it would not be possible to bring Nazis' to trial. Thankfully, the deadline has been extended 5 years. Probably, your superiors know this, but it's important that you guys leading the charge are aware that we now only have until 1970, to initiate War Crimes charges!"

Carmella was clearly impressed by the platform that Wiesenthal had just constructed for them. "Thank you, Simon. That information is invaluable and will encourage us to turn over every stone as fast as possible."

Wiesenthal moved to a large cabinet, opened a drawer and pulled out a large map which he placed on the dinner table. "Come and look with me," he said.

Jerome, Billy and Carmella, each stood at a point around the table. "I will show you, on this map, the areas of Argentina that are always in our focus. Most are around or in the centre of Buenos Aires. I have coloured and numbered the map. The numbered areas and colour chart show you the most prolific areas and where they may congregate." He took them through each area explaining what it depicted and how important it seemed to be.

After two hours of this viewing, with questions and answers, Billy asked, "but Simon we can't remember all this." Wiesenthal chuckled as he stared into Billy's eyes. "No, I wouldn't expect you to; I have a packet for each of you. The packet contains photographs. You may need a magnifying glass for some of it, but you will be able to capture all the information I have given you today."

As they were preparing to leave, Carmella spoke for all of them. "We will never forget this day with you. We just hope we can help in some way."

As Ezra opened the door, Cyla arrived. She joined Simon Wiesenthal in thanking them for what they were doing and hoped they would all meet again.

Ezra soon had them back to the hotel. They stood just inside the foyer saying their goodbyes. Ezra said he would fly direct from Vienna to Buenos Aires with Immanuel, and MOSSAD would give Carmella their address. His English was already becoming sufficient!

They really enjoyed a couple of drinks in the bar. It had been an intensely studious day-and-a-half. The rest of the afternoon was spent relaxing and showering in their rooms. They planned to meet for dinner in the hotel restaurant at 8pm.

Jerome was 15 minutes late, having fallen asleep. His apology was graciously accepted and the dinner began with a bottle of Mosel wine. Then a glorious dinner which finished in style with a desert the waiter recommended; blue Danube berries, summer fruits and Alpine cream.

All through the meal, the conversation focused on Simon Wiesenthal. They had all been completely enthralled by his work. But along with his work, the stories of his personal bravery in the various camps he had been incarcerated in. The number of times he had escaped the gas chamber. The number of times he had found ingenious and inventive ways to escape the clutches of the Nazis'. He had lost almost all his family, over 60 relatives to their brutality! No wonder he had sworn to continue hunting them throughout the rest of his life. Throughout the talk, Carmella and Jerome both were thinking about their families that they had never had the chance to meet or, indeed, get to know.

As they were finishing, and about to leave for their rooms, Carmella said, "When we get back to England tomorrow, we will have several hours of nothing, whilst we wait for Barry's Mum and Dad to join us. I would like to offer Frank and the rest of the team a couple of hours at school with us. We definitely won't do as well as Mr Wiesenthal but we can do our best to impart some of the knowledge he has given us. What do you think?"

At 10.30am they were on the tarmac at Heathrow. Both Jerome and Billy had applauded Carmella's idea, but then said they thought Carmella would do the best job of presenting the detail. Carmella put her foot down, with a firm hand, saying "experience is one of the best ways to learn, so we will all take part! No arguments" she said, with a mischievous smile!

The first person to see them as they entered the Skyline Hotel was Frank. "How did it go," he said. Billy answered, "Simon Wiesenthal blew me away. So clever, and explained everything in a way that I understood." Carmella, looking around, said, "Frank, what a fantastic hotel." Frank pointed to Jerome, saying, "You have him to thank. An airline steward's job is not too bad then Jerome, is it?" Jerome's expression was accepting.

As they walked towards Reception, Carmella held onto Frank's arm and pulled him to a halt, "This day is relatively free until Barry's parents arrive. What time will that be?" Frank pondered for a moment then said, "I expect about 6.00pm."

"So we have the whole afternoon free." "Yes," Frank replied. Carmella said, "Frank, Wiesenthal gave us so much useful information, we all thought we could give you and the rest of the team as much of that intelligence as possible. Frank, you know we are not professionals at this sort of thing, but I have agreed with Billy and Jerome we are willing to give it a try."

Frank's face lit up. "Carmella that is absolutely fabulous. It's time I got them off their arses and into work mode. I will arrange a conference room for 2.30pm and we can get started."

Frank found everyone and spread the word around. About 1.30pm they all gradually met in the bar. Lots of chatter, embraces and pleasure from getting together again.

65

All in the conference room at 2.00pm, Carmella opened the show. She began explaining how modest Wiesenthal had been. And then explained what he and his family had suffered. Billy joined, detailing all the information and telling the audience that they had been given photographs and intelligence about the possible whereabouts of the "Most Wanted" three monsters that Wiesenthal recommended they should hunt.

Jerome was next up. He walked them through the knowledge he had gained from the maps. But, more than that, he emphasised the enormity of the German population in Argentina; the areas that should be targets contained a wealth of bars, mostly with cellars. These places are prime areas for neo-Nazi and Fascist meetings and celebrations.

With questions and answers, the event went on until nearly 4.30pm. Carmella drew a halt to proceedings saying that they did not want to encroach on the evening visit from Barry's family.

Whilst Frank had them all together, he decided to cover a few things. Firstly, he asked that they all dress smartly, out of respect for the visitors. The men should all wear their business suits. With a straight face that developed a hint of a smile, he said "I know it comes naturally to you ladies to take pride in your appearance so, perhaps, you could motivate the gentlemen! Secondly, I have arranged a room here on the ground floor where Barry can meet privately with his parents.

About 6.00pm the area around the hotel foyer appeared as if hosting a Civil Service convention. Two cars drew up directly, outside the main entrance. Both of them were gleaming as if they had just rolled off the assembly line. The first, an Austin Cambridge A60, followed by a pristine Ford Zephyr Zodiac. Both cars were shining through their pure black metallic paintwork.

A Royal Marine stepped out of the driver's seat of the first car and marched swiftly around to a rear door. Out stepped Joan. She stood on the concourse as the Marine escorted Jess around the car to join her. She took his arm, the Marine saluted, as they slowly entered the hotel. It was similar with the Ford Zephyr Zodiac. The Marine opened the doors and escorted the passengers to the main door, just behind Joan and Jess. It was Albie's Mum and Dad, Albert, and Dot----two good old Cockney names!

Barry, Anneliese, Albie and Anya bustled to the door to greet them. As they entered, their eyes were searching their surroundings. They were overwhelmed by the palatial experience. As embraces took centre stage, Jess glanced to his right. The rest of their team were standing smiling and watching the family greetings. Jess, meanwhile, had noticed the hotel's centre piece. "How fabulous," he screamed. "It has a Caribbean bar in it! " Jess had spotted the ground floor swimming pool, decorated to resemble a Caribbean island. Palm trees and luscious exotic plants all around. He was finding it difficult to contain himself; and not dive straight in!

Barry and Albie were glowing with pride, but in the middle of the distraction caused by Jess, managed to ask if they would like to go with them to their private room. Anneliese led the way with the mums'; the fellas' followed.

They were all in the same room. It was luxurious with three paisley patterned settees and a stocked bar in the corner. Barry and Albie got everyone drinks as the conversation and general polite chat developed. Joan, talking with Anneliese, explained that she and Jess were back working on the buses; on the same bus, and they loved it!

Albert, Albie's Dad, said he was still in the Victoria Docks working as a "ganger". A very well respected man that picked the gangs each day. Albert began heading towards reminiscing. "Hey Barry, do you remember when you started?" Before he could continue, Anneliese astutely passed Albert another drink and looked at Barry, saying "I'm sure you're Mum and Jess want to hear about your new job."

Barry took the cue and confidently stepped forward. He began by saying, "This is not just what I'm doing, but Albie also. We have been selected to work for Governments. It's a secret job so I can only tell you the basics. It's the type of job we've always wanted. Well paid, well respected. We are Civil Servants working for the Crown." The expressions deserved photographs! He continued following the script that Anneliese had practiced with him. The parents were absolutely lost for words! Their boys had achieved so much. At the end Joan asked, "Well how long will you be in Argentina? When will we see you again?" Barry said, "It depends on how this job works out. If I do well, it won't be long. Mum, I promise I am going to do better than anyone expects, so it won't be too long. Mine and Albie's contract is five years and Anneliese and Anya are coming with us. There are phones there these days so you will hear from us regularly."

The whole room was more than satisfied with the way it had gone. The parents, especially, were so proud of their boys. They were then asked by Anneliese if they minded going back to the bar as the rest of their team wanted to meet them.

They moved out of their private room with everybody clutching each other as they strolled towards the bar. On the way, Joan whispered to Barry, "We have to leave at 9.00pm because me and Jess are on earlies." Barry began to say, "Oh Mum!" she stopped him in his tracks. "Barry, me and Jess have to do our job. You have given us so much in these last years and now tonight! You will only be half the way round the world, not the whole way! And in the scheme of things, five years is a short while. You have made a great life for yourself, and I pray, every day, that you and Anneliese will always be devoted to one another."

There was some swimming back and forth to the bar. Jess borrowed some dark green trunks and splashed about with the rest, enjoying every moment.

However, the time to separate came all too soon. The Marine drivers arrived and stood quietly in the main entrance. Leaving was so very hard to do! Barry held his Mum for an age. Both had tears welling up in their eyes. Albert and Jess were stoic, quietly moving around the group shaking hands and putting on a brave face.

Everybody stood together at the main entrance waving them off. As they, with heads bowed, trudged back across the foyer, Frank said, "I think we all need a drink; I'm buying!"

In the main bar, with everyone assembled, Barry, grasping his glass, turned to face them all. Putting his arm around Albie, he spoke, initially with a slight quiver in his voice. "I want to thank you all for your support this evening." His arm tightened around Albie's shoulder. "We are both extremely grateful for such a wonderful leaving do. And now I would like to make a toast!" As he took a deep breath, he glanced at Anneliese who pursed her lips and returned a knowing smile. "The toast is to us all, and our great adventure in Argentina."

Everyone raised their glasses and loudly toasted "Argentina." Happy chat resumed in the bar. Jerome, with excitement in his voice proclaimed, "We are flying tomorrow in a Boeing 707 jet. It's a long flight. With re-fuelling it will take us close to 20 hours, but it will be enjoyment all the way."

Frank entered the flight talk, saying they were flying KLM with re-fuelling in Lisbon. Taking charge of proceedings, he continued, "Jerome is correct; it will be a long day tomorrow so I would like us to finish up now and go and get plenty of shut-eye. I will see you all at breakfast. We will meet at 7.00am so don't forget to arrange a wake-up call with reception."

As they were finishing their drinks, with some heading to the lift, Jerome politely asked Frank if he could assist with ensuring everything went to time in the morning. "I will get to reception early to oversee the calls to all our team." Frank replied with a few complimentary words. "Jerome, that's an excellent idea, as it will avoid any hotel mishaps. If you keep this up, you won't need me and you can take over!" This accolade would constantly resonate in Jerome's mind!

Sure enough, it worked like a dream. Not a single person was late. Jerome was taking his job very seriously. Even to the degree that he toddled around, with gay abandon, helping everyone to get their luggage to the store behind reception.

66

After breakfast, they all mustered in the reception area as their taxis' arrived. Jerome, by now, was on a mission! His previous life as a steward came into its own. His efficiency left nothing to be desired. He helped each of them with their luggage, escorted them to the cars, opened and closed doors for them, and over all, lifted their spirits to excitement level!

Heathrow had been alerted to treat them as important Government personnel, and so their passage through passport control was hardly noticeable. Their flight was due to leave at 10.00am and at 9.45am they had all selected their seats and were getting comfortable. In that last 15 minutes, Frank wandered around them explaining there would be no other passengers as CECD had arranged this flight just for them. They had the whole 110 seat plane to themselves, so they could wander around and make themselves as comfortable as necessary.

Just over 3 hours later, they landed in Lisbon; re-fuelling was over in about 45 minutes and they took off again. Now they were facing the long haul; sleeping through the night. Jerome had decided to work with the cabin crew; and went around asking if they needed anything. Eventually, Frank grabbed his jacket and pulled him next to him. "Jerome, you have done much more than any of us could expect. Please, take a break and join us as a passenger. You don't have to prove your worth to me. You have done that time and time again. So relax and sit and enjoy the flight."

After a superb airline dinner, everyone, following their wine, began to mellow. They were snapped out of it, by Carmella. She stood in the aisle way facing them all.

"Sorry, but if you have not finished eating or drinking, this won't take long." Anya, downed her knife and fork to listen. Carmella went on to explain that they would be met at the airport by Argentinian Special Service agents. "So please, remember to be nice to them. As I've explained before, Argentina is assisting us, under pressure from the U.S.A. MOSSAD have arranged properties for us in a suburban area called Martinez. About half an hour from the centre of Buenos Aires. It's a beautiful place, and then when you wake up tomorrow, I will find you and we will get our business moving.

They arrived at Buenos Aires International, named Ministro Pistarini, at around 2pm on Saturday. It was reasonably quick getting through passports and customs, and four Argentinian agents met them at the gate.

Carmella, with her fluent Spanish, spoke to each of them, then they were off in two large American Galaxies, with bench seats. One of the agents stayed at the airport to do some more work with Customs. Two were in the first car with Carmella, Billy and Jerome. The rest were in the second car.

On the way, Carmella gave Jerome 6 copies of a document detailing the addresses they would occupy; two houses, one with a large office area. Frank and Jerome were assigned to the office/house which would predominantly facilitate the group's headquarters. The other was a four bedroomed luxury property.

They arrived at the two adjacent houses which were gated properties in a tree-lined avenue with aristocratic buildings. Carmella explained that the small cabins they had noticed driving along the avenue were manned by 24 hour security personnel. Clearly, this was a prestigious neighbourhood.

Carmella took them in and whisked them around, showing them their domain. Jerome handed out the address and information documents. They were in an area called San Isidro, part of the Buenos Aires borough of Martinez.

Carmella continued showing them the white goods, heating, ventilation etc. but she informed them that, although heading towards Christmas, it was the start of summer. Last but not least were phones. Several in both properties.

They could be used normally, but also had direct lines to the MOSSAD Command Centre, the CECD Command Centre and the Buenos Aires police. Looking at Jerome, Carmella said "All of that contact information is in your jurisdiction." He stood, proudly puffing his chest out. "Lastly, at the bottom of your document is my personal phone number," said Carmella. "You can phone me any time, even if it's just to ask how to operate the washing machine!"

Carmella continued as she moved towards the door. "I suggest we get together in the morning to get organised. I will be here about 11.00am." Albie, looking at Anya, appeared relieved. Billy took her hand, as he smiled, winked and waved goodbye! None of them knew where Carmella and Billy were going to be staying. Indeed, they knew not to ask. She would tell them the moment she had clearance to do so. From what she had said, all they were privileged to was, that she and Billy would stay in a MOSSAD safe house, with two MOSSAD Intelligence Officers and the two Wiesenthal civilians, Ezra and Immanuel.

For the next stage, Frank and Jerome were shuffled out by Anneliese to get unpacked and organised in the office/house. She then pressed the buttons on the rest, to get them into an acceptable state in their house.

Once that was done, it was still early evening. Anneliese and Anya had decided what they wanted to do next. Anya said to Barry and Albie, "We are going for a walk. Just down the end of the road, Just a stroll, do you want to come?" Albie gave Barry a glance which had "yes" written all over it. Barry thought; we've been cooped up for the whole of the last 24 hours. His response was "Yes please, love to."

Unlocking the gates was a bit tricky, but Albie got them open. As they strolled along, they loved the warmth of the early summer's evening. It was reminiscent of Marbella, but nearly Christmas. As they continued, Anneliese was enthralled by the trees along the avenue. "They are so large, so green and imposing." Turning to Barry, she commented, "I suppose they are like that because we are close to the rain forests of Brazil."

As they walked past a security lodge, the guard waved and spoke saying, "Hola, como estas?" Anneliese immediately responded saying, "moy bien, muchos gracias!" Barry, as they got out of earshot, said "Well done, love." He had learned the words but was still lacking confidence!

67

When they reached the end of the avenue, they were at the junction to the main road into Buenos Aires. Both left and right were lined by shops, bars and restaurants. But, there on the corner was an ice-cream parlour! They all looked at each other. Barry said "Shall we?" "Yes let's" said Albie leading the way.

They were thrilled with the ice-cream, and the parlour itself. It was bright inside with three round tables. The walls were light blue tiled and everywhere was spic and span. But the epitome of enjoyment came from the ice-cream. Both Anya and Anneliese had tubs with small wooden spoons. Barry and Albie had large cornets and, very quickly, had ice-cream almost from ear to ear. Albie and Barry both commented that they had never seen anything like it in London. However, Anneliese said there was an ice-cream shop in Amsterdam, but not as splendid. Everyone agreed that this place had the best ice-cream they had ever tasted and it would become a regular haunt.

In the warm, humid, darkening evening, they sauntered back to the house. The kitchen had been stocked with food and they ended the evening well-fed. It was around 10.00 when Jerome and Frank decided it was time for bed. After the long journey, they all were becoming bleary-eyed so it soon was lights out for all!

Breakfast in the morning was a fairly quiet affair. Frank was the first to comment. "I think we are all suffering from jet-lag, but don't worry, it will ease. For some of us, it may take another day and night." With a straight face, Frank joked, "No doubt it will be longer for Albie as he needs more sleep than someone with catalepsy!"

They all chuckled. Albie placed both hands on his chest saying "What me? Not me!" Just as the laughter gained pace, in concert with Albie's innocent expression, the doorbell rang.

It was Carmella with Billy, Ezra and Immanuel. After coffee, they all moved into the office area next door, Carmella took the chair. First, she explained that her team of four had been assigned to work jointly with the CECD team. Billy would be the equivalent of Jerome, providing analysis and administration. As Ezra and Immanuel were German speakers, they would take assignments that involved interaction with Germans, but also assist Billy. She, Carmella, would operate as a distinct MOSSAD Secret Service Agent, especially where a fluent Spanish speaker was required. She moved on, saying we need to agree how we are going to get this off the ground. Anneliese, the thinker, sat quiet. She was never ever a glory seeker! She slowly looked around the group, as she placed a paper in front of her. From her expression, everyone sensed the need to listen intently.

She opened with the ice-cream story, how they had enjoyed a couple of hours in one another's company, teasing and tempting their palates, during a beautiful warm summer's evening.

But, she continued, "We are not here on holiday or vacation! You can choose either word, as long as you remember that whilst we are here, we must all constantly remember we are here to right horrendous wrongs. I've done some work on how we should be assigned, to make good progress."

"Initially we have three targets. Franz Stangl, Hermine Braunsteiner, and the greatest monster that ever lived on this planet.... Josef Mengele. As you know, having met with Simon Wiesenthal, we have a massive amount of information and data. I know, that as a team, if we get this right, we are capable of apprehending them.... All of them! And MOSSAD have provided operatives to assist as we move on through this assignment. And I am not saying this to disturb you, but you must, you must remember this is an extremely dangerous job! I know you all so well, and love you so please don't get into violent situations that will cause me distress!"

"Now, I will go on to my work plan; the teams and assignments would be as follows;"

"Billy and Jerome are our intelligence analysts and will operate the centre for communication and administration."

"Myself and Barry will hunt Franz Stangl"

Anya and Albie will hunt Hermine Braunsteiner"

Carmella, with Ezra and Immanuel as support, and Frank will target Josef Mengele."

"That's as far as I want to go right now. But I would like to continue in the morning at the same time. Is everybody in agreement with my proposals, so far?" The room was quiet for half a minute as they all looked at one another. The outcome was nods of agreement all round. Carmella came to Anneliese to thank her.

Carmella then called Ezra over. He was carrying a very large, thick folder, which he had just retrieved from his car. Carmella said that Simon Wiesenthal had prepared a detailed dossier on the three "most wanted" and asked Ezra to deliver it to her.

Ezra then tried to explain, needing some help from Carmella; "Wiesenthal had recent information on Franz Stangl. It is detailed in the dossier and may develop into an urgent chase down in Brazil. Wiesenthal would update Anneliese frequently, as it may eventually mean a rapid visit to Sao Paulo!"

Carmella, smiling at Ezra said, "He is excited at the chance to work with you guys. And today, he and Immanuel have parked two cars outside for your use. They deliberately look decidedly old and decrepit, but they are reliable and go like the wind. They will not attract any attention in Buenos Aires." All the while, Ezra smiled and nodded as Carmella explained.

Now Ezra nudged Carmella, saying, "Aeropuerto" and held both arms out like wings. She patted him on the back, saying "well done Ezra." "I nearly forgot," continued Carmella, "Both Ezra and Immanuel were pilots in the Israeli Air Force. Now, although civilians, they have offered to fly you anywhere domestically. Essentially, anywhere throughout South America." Ezra smiled a huge smile as he peered at Anneliese.

Anneliese stood and clasped, then embraced Ezra saying, "That is fabulous." She turned to Carmella and did the same. At that point Immanuel appeared. For a minute or so, Carmella explained all that had been said. Immanuel stepped forward, took Anneliese's hand saying, "Shalom und danke."

As they left, Carmella said they would attend the morning meeting. Billy, standing in the doorway, gripped Carmella's hand and turned to Jerome, who had just appeared. "I really miss you lot, but I can sense this is going to get better and better for all of us!"

The things they had spoken about oiled all the gears in Anneliese's mind. She called Jerome over, then Barry. "Sit here with me for a minute. I've been given a definitive, detailed dossier on Stangl. Simon Wiesenthal sent it with the message that it may soon turn into an urgent chase situation."

"I want to ask you this. We are all gradually escaping jet-lag and by tonight we should be free. After dinner, would you both sit with me and go through, word by word, the Stangl dossier? I want us three to have knowledge of every detail. We can discuss it and use each other as sounding boards. All I am asking for is your full attention, from say, 7.30pm to 9.30pm. I think it's paramount because Simon Wiesenthal has indicated that finding this moronic criminal may become urgent." Both Jerome and Barry seemed excited by the prospect that there may be an early lead. Both nodded and said, "Of course Anneliese, let's go for it."

68

They settled down together at 7.30pm. Huddled together, the three, looking at the papers, listened as Anneliese slowly read. In the early sections there was descriptive text concerning how Stangl oversaw the deaths of over 900,000 people; the atrocities and cruelty that he initiated and became involved in.

He was an escape artist! He had been in U.S. detention for two years, but remained unidentified as a war criminal because so few witnesses had survived his camps. He escaped from a roadwork detail in Linz. He managed to secure a Red Cross passport and fled to Syria. Then, cleverly, he organised the immigration of his whole family to Brazil.

From this point, Wiesenthal's people and MOSSAD had raided several addresses, but each time Stangl escaped and moved to another property. He obviously had substantial help from the local people, especially supportive Neo-Nazis'.

Anneliese placed her hands on her hips and leaned back in her chair. "Jerome, we will take five minutes break. Would you get us some coffees?" Once re-assembled, Anneliese with a thoughtful expression, turned to Barry and Jerome. "I think I have an outline plan that will have to remain flexible. It's only about six weeks to Christmas," she said. "Wiesenthal has listed several addresses where Stangl may be hiding or where he is receiving support.

Also, he has given us the address and details concerning Stangl's son-in-law."

"Barry, after Christmas, you and I will head down to Sao Paulo. I suspect Stangl now believes the chase has been given up. We will resurrect it in earnest! From now until Christmas we will work with the others on developing strategies' from the intelligence provided by Wiesenthal on Braunsteiner and Mengele. Meanwhile, Jerome, I would like you to concentrate in Argentina. You can make a start with Public Records and Companies Registration information.... ownership, directors etc."

"If we take this approach, we should be able to get the other teams some clear solid tracks to follow, while Barry and I are away in Brazil!" Looking deep into Barry's eyes, her fixed gaze reflected intense purpose." Barry, we will use every minute whilst there to make sure we find that animal and destroy him! He will not escape us!" Barry grinned, recognising her intense certainty!

Next morning was perfect. Sunshine, pure blue skies but very high humidity. Carmella and her team arrived about 10am. Anneliese and her group had decided to have breakfast by the swimming pool. Barry, who never seemed able to sit still for very long, had the pool net and was skimming leaves off the water surface.

After the usual greetings, they all filed behind Anneliese into the house. It was steaming hot outside, but Jerome quickly went round switching on the ceiling fans and several static floor fans.

Anneliese and Frank sat together at the end of the large dining room table. Anneliese took the Chair. "It's a bit crowded in here, so if you want, we can move into the office next door. Would you prefer that?"

Albie, as he gradually glanced around, sparked into life. "No, Anneliese, we will be ok in here. It's good with the fans on!" With a wry smile, Frank said, "Well I am surprised Albie. Must be down to that Oaty mess you had for breakfast. Keep it up."

Everyone was getting accustomed to Frank's banter with sleepy Albie. As the chuckle muted, Anneliese explained the outline plan she had developed with Barry and Albie. She went into quite a lot of details regarding Stangl and progressed into the strategies for the other two inhumans. But before she'd gone far, Ezra put his hand up. Anneliese nodded to him to speak. In somewhat fractured English, Ezra said he would fly them to Sao Paulo after Christmas.

Carmella, attempting to help Ezra, explained that MOSSAD had provided them with a Lear jet and a small Cessna 172 Skyhawk. Both were based at the Buenos Aires domestic airport, Aeroparque, only a few miles away.

"That's fantastic, "replied Anneliese. "Thank you Ezra. We may take up your offer, but our plan will remain flexible for a while yet."

Carmella asked Anneliese if she may continue for a few moments more. "Go ahead, Carmella," "I now have clearance to tell you where we are staying. Well it wasn't the original plan, but we have ended up in the Israeli Embassy in Ricoleta. Stricter security has been applied due to the growing unrest in the Middle East. That is why I could not tell you, or anyone, of our whereabouts until we had official clearance from Tel Aviv. But we are settled and comfortable now!"

Frank suggested they take a short break to stretch their legs. Carmella and Anneliese wandered out by the pool together. Anneliese sensed that something was worrying Carmella. Your worried expression is a giveaway, Carmella. What's up?"

"The tensions in the Middle East are distracting all our superiors from this assignment. I can't get anyone's attention, and so, I suppose I am concerned that we may get recalled to Israel!" Anneliese, using her training that had inspired her approach to life, stopped and grasped Carmella's hands. "Carmella, you know, and I know that you can't influence what is going on. If you have no control and, indeed, no chance of gaining control, you must ignore anything beyond your sphere of influence. Don't fall off the road you are on!" Carmella's expression lightened as she thanked Anneliese.

When back around the table, they all began to chatter about all they had heard so far. Anneliese, quite loudly exclaimed, "Let's carry on for a short while. I believe it is essential for you all to study the Wiesenthal file about your own target. You have two days to do that; take any notes, make any copies. At the end of".... Frank interrupted. "What I think Anneliese was about to say was that after two days focused study, I expect each of you to be able to recite, from memory, names, dates, times.... Indeed every important fact. Please, no excuses, no alibi's.... just convincing detail!"

Anneliese stepped back into the arena. "After the two days, I would like all the three files returned to me so I can do the same!"

"In a week's time, I will circulate around you and we will purposefully develop detailed plans to include any intelligence information established by Jerome or supplied by Simon Wiesenthal." Anneliese, as she finished speaking, looked to Frank; then continued! "Once our Action Plans are in place, Frank and I will join you early each morning to review your assignments for that day. That will be the point when we get out and about collecting intelligence that will build us a structure to get us to the top of the pyramid!"

Anneliese grinned as she searched each face. "I will revise that last metaphor to....intelligence that will build us a structure strong enough to support our targets as we lead then to the gallows!" Carmella stood and applauded. The rest followed!

Anneliese then asked if there were any questions or objections. The room fell silent until Albie, with his eyes sparkling, stared at Frank and Anneliese. "With you two leading us, those deranged Jerries' might as well surrender now!"

They all worked 12 hours a day over the next week. They made some time to have enjoyment. They used the cars for their constant visits to areas of Buenos Aires, and were talking carefully to people to extract more information.

Jerome, working mostly alone, turned up some enlightening information on Mengele. He had worked through several sets of public records and had found Mengele's divorce registration documents. Mengele had used his own name, and his address was shown. What was exciting was that he also found Mengele in Company registration documents. Again, in his own name, and with a matching address. He took Anneliese through the information and was so pleased that she recognised the importance. She said it was a great find!

Anneliese called Carmella and Billy in to join them. She began by detailing the documents that Jerome had turned up. "We were just discussing the meetings we had with Simon Wiesenthal in Vienna" said Carmella. "Billy suggested we compare our notes with the latest file tonight, when we return to the Israeli Embassy. One thing I remember is that West Germany tried to extradite Mengele without success. Wiesenthal thought he had disappeared to Paraguay or possibly Brazil. Simon was so incensed by losing him again, he was considering offering a reward for information leading to his capture. When we pick up the trails again, we should use a reward as an incentive with people we question. I'm sure we could persuade MOSSAD and CECD to fund it.

Turning to Jerome, Carmella asked, "Do you know if his company is still trading or operating in any way?" "The papers I searched through showed that the business hadn't traded for over three years." Jerome's eyes moved to Anneliese, as he emphasised that the company continued in registration and had some income from unknown sources, as well as some debts.

"In that case," said Anneliese, "Mengele will probably return at some stage to tie up all the loose ends and settle the business affairs. Even if he is in Paraguay or Brazil, he would need to return to Argentina to satisfy its legal systems."

Scanning across their faces, Anneliese said "Seems to me, this means you have sufficient information to begin the chase. Perhaps visit the addresses Jerome will give you; visit the business premises and find a way to track down employees. As it was a pharmaceutical company, there will be suppliers and medical practices that are worth talking to. You may even conclude you need visits to Paraguay or Brazil. If so, in Brazil, start with Sao Paulo as that seems to be the area that Nazis' gravitated to."

Obviously, pleased with her day's work, Anneliese said, "We now have two teams that can get up and running. Carmella, once you are out hunting, please keep in touch and let us know your whereabouts, and especially, if you need any assistance." Carmella responded saying, "Oh, you have just reminded me! Tomorrow some of our MOSSAD specialists will come here to install a radio communication system. Your cars will also be kitted out. Billy will operate our end and I assume Jerome will take care of you."

"That's great Carmella, thank you so much. I am now going to get with the third team, the sleep team", Anya and Albie!"

69

Old Father Time carried on pushing those hands around the clock face, despite knowing time was against them. Santa would be on the kids' roofs soon, and then the bells would be ringing in the New Year!

Anneliese wanted 1967 to be a very successful year. They had three Nazi's to apprehend and only three years left to do it in. Additionally, it was an important year for Barry and Albie. They needed to start proving to the Commander that they were repaying his generosity, with success! Her personal desire was to complete the assignment within two years; the point when her assignment would end and she would return to Europe. She didn't want to go without Barry, and unless he and Albie provided results, she would have to return without him. They would have to remain to the end of the five year term.

Anya and Albie were sitting by the pool. Anneliese ambled to them and sat down at their table. She connected with their eyes and began by saying, "Shall we talk about your target, Hermine Braunsteiner. By now you will have read the Wiesenthal dossier, so what do you think? Have you got any plans in mind?" Anya spoke first. "Well it seems a certainty that she is living in New York. According to Wiesenthal, she was granted U.S. citizenship only a few years ago. She got married to an American, thinking she would live happily ever after!"

"We've read all the Wiesenthal detail describing her atrocities. She killed women and children by sometimes beating them to death, and sometimes kicking them to death. I don't want to go over that detail, Anneliese. You have read it and so have we. It is sickening!"

Anneliese's eyes opened as her spirit ignited with vengeful thoughts. As her angry expression worsened, her intelligence regained control and composure. Once her mind reached equilibrium, she began to think perfectly clearly again.

She was now ready to export constructive thoughts and direction to Anya and Albie. Anneliese began by saying, "We all have read the detailed files on Braunsteiner. We have more information on her whereabouts than either of the other two Nazis'. Indeed, I don't think you will have much work to do to track her down. She has already been found, according to Simon Wiesenthal. A chance encounter in a Tel Aviv restaurant with someone who had been incarcerated in Majdanek, Braunsteiner's camp. That eventually paved the way to find her in the U.S.A."

"Wiesenthal also provided her last known address in Queens, New York City. The issue we have is this. She has eluded trial as a War Criminal several times already. She is now doing it again in the U.S. and probably sitting there laughing at the bureaucrats and politicians that can't get their act together. Wiesenthal identified her to them as long ago as 1964. He even alerted the New York Times and it went public! But there has been no noticeable action so far."

"My thoughts are these. You should get yourself up to New York. Pin-point her address, locate her and make sure it's her. See her, get her features firmly in your mind's eye. But in the run-up to Christmas, you should spend your time researching U.S. Government Agencies, people, and enlist the help of the CIA. They are supposed to be working with us, CECD, on this assignment. So enlist as much of their influence, help and support as possible."

"Initially, they may not have too much of an appetite for this work, but you will have to use every trick in the book to motivate them. If your efforts seem to hit the brick wall, there are two final options. First, convince the New York Times to go public with an embarrassing exposure with support from European and Israel's Governments. I don't like this one too much, because it may do some damage to political relationships. The second is a direct appeal from the U.K. and Europe to the U.S. Attorney General. The leverage from this potential approach could be used through all extradition stages"

"So, I assume that by Christmas, you will have a plan, and a catalogue of people, agencies and meeting times and dates. After a wonderful Christmas that we will all spend together, you two can get yourselves up to New York for a terrific beginning to the New Year."

"The bottom line to all of this is that you should secure an agreement with the U.S. Government to extradite Hermine Braunsteiner to Germany to be tried as a war criminal."

With each team having an outline of the scope of their plan, things got underway. During the next few weeks, the teams worked within the parameters that had been agreed. Carmella, Ezra and Immanuel focused their investigations in Buenos Aires. Billy did a tremendous job digging deeper into Mengele's business, employees and contacts. He fed information constantly to Carmella over the radio to give her greater direction.

Anya and Albie got a flight up to New York and worked there on the assignment for two weeks. They worked on building trusted relationships with the CIA, U.S. Government Agencies and the New York Times. They confirmed, that Braunsteiner had moved home and were following leads that would, in the end, provide the answers. The end-game was to return to New York immediately after Christmas.

Anneliese and Frank had spent hours discussing and planning their modus operandi. After hours of concerted effort, they had decided to spend the last few weeks supporting the other two teams. They would stay close to the radio and talk to them constantly. At times, they did lose contact with Anya up in New York, but then they just reverted to the telephone. They also spent time with Barry on his element of the assignment up to Christmas.

Both Anneliese and Frank had concluded that Sao Paulo was the place to start, and with luck, may even be the place to finish. The monster they were hunting was like a cat with nine lives. Wiesenthal's Nazi Hunters had raided many properties, but each time found that he had moved on.

Barry had offered an idea! He would map out Sao Paulo, and identify all locations that Wiesenthal had raided. He also would work on areas in Sao Paulo that were strongly Germanic to establish if there were any possible links. He would also investigate the son-in-law that informed on Stangl, to see if he could determine reasons that may be useful to them. Barry would definitely pinpoint the son-in-laws home on the map, because they would need to visit him!

Christmas Eve arrived. The annual excitement arrived! Everyone had returned safely and Christmas jollity and chatter bristled in every corner of the house. Jerome, in two days, had managed to evacuate a 7 foot Christmas tree from a nearby forest. But Jerome, being Jerome, had gone further than anyone could expect. The tree was decorated, mostly with his handmade decorations, as well as the living room!

Carmella and Billy arrived about 7pm. At the outset, Carmella explained that Christmas was not in line with her religion. However, she would love to join them all for Christmas day as an experience, and to enjoy Billy's beliefs. Billy pulled her close, saying "This will be my first ever family Christmas, so thank you my love!"

Christmas day was better than any of them expected. It was more like a family Christmas even though they were over 8000 miles away from home. The food, the drink, the stories about how their work had progressed, and the laughter that reverberated around the house throughout the day, was making this Christmas a splendid occasion. And this wasn't a cold, wet, windy day. The sun was glorious. It was a 30c day. Not too hot but appreciably warm. So there was intermittent swimming, cooling and boisterous drinking fun!

The love and affection and bonding within this group would be very difficult to damage. Their souls, every part of their being, believed that what they were doing, was a righteous crusade!

70

The fine weather continued right through to New Year's Eve. They had all agreed to be together to see in the New Year.... 1967! On the 2nd January they began to set off on their assignments. The hunt would reach a climax as the months' rolled by.

Anneliese and Barry were flying down to Sao Paulo and, as promised, Ezra would pilot them in the Lear Jet. Carmella and Immanuel were also heading to Sao Paulo to attempt to pick up the scent of Josef Mengele, the escape artist! The Lear Jet would fly them all in comfort, and as they would all be in the same city, they agreed on daily contact and to call for assistance, if required.

Anya and Albie were travelling TWA from Buenos Aires Continental Airport to New York, to work on motivating authorities to deport Hermine Braunsteiner to Germany. Jerome and Billy had a cushy job in control of the radio, phones and administration. In Essence, they were the Command Centre.

Anneliese, during the run-up to Christmas, had spent an enormous amount of time preparing all the data; addresses that Simon Wiesenthal had previously identified, the informant son-in-law's address, other Stangl family that may be around the area, bars, clubs and, in particular, known cellar meeting clubs. All these were marked on a map of San Paulo, with most clustered towards the south-east.

Jerome and Barry had worked on all this with Anneliese, making it easily useable with keys to the map areas shown on a small, separate pocket card.

Barry and Anneliese had selected a small hotel in the South-East district, close to the area of interest, shown as a cluster point on the map. It was clean and had reasonable facilities. However, Anneliese saw it only as a place to sleep! She had warned Barry that they would investigate every road in the cluster area, every one of the previous addresses, and carefully question inhabitants, in shops, bars and meeting places. So there may be weeks of arduous, tedious trudging of the streets.

Towards the end of February, they had amassed mountains of street comments, leads that turned out to be negative, and a library of Polaroid photographs. They were both trying their best to maintain morale. Sitting on a small wall, Anneliese, staring into a park opposite, was pushing her analytical mind to its limit. She recalled that the son-in-law had indicated an area where Stangl had made friends and acquaintances, near one of his previous addresses.

They had spent an inordinate amount of time in that district but every rock they turned over, just had moss on it. But there was something eating away at her. Something in her memory that she couldn't put her finger on. As something was breaking through, to put a link in her memory chain, Barry asked "What's going through that brain box of yours, Anneliese? Would you like something? Perhaps a cake or a sandwich from that shop down the road?"

She was about to scream at him for interrupting her thoughts. Instead he had started the bomb ticking!

Anneliese exploded! "Barry, you are a genius! That's what has been bothering me. It's a shop!"

Barry looked stunned. "What is a shop? Where are you talking about? Anneliese pushed her hair back from her forehead and took a deep breath "OK, Barry, I will take this slowly, to get my thoughts organised. We were in the Campano area that had been indicated by the son-in-law as a possible haunt. We went in every shop, bar and premises but nothing turned up. We were going into the last shop before we finished for the day, but it was full, with queues out of the door. So we gave up on the idea, and as we were walking away, I glanced up. It was a Mercado. The name of the place was "Carmel Mercado." I thought of Carmella; maybe it was a sign!"

"Barry, let's get back there. It's only about 20 minutes' walk." Barry tried hard to keep up with Anneliese's quick pace. They stood at the door as Anneliese glanced up at the neon sign "Carmel Mercado."

Anneliese pulled the Stangl picture out of her file and strode into the shop. There were a few people shopping, but as it was late evening, the business was dwindling.

A very cheerful Brazilian shop owner greeted them at the counter. Anneliese used her Spanish, which is similar to Portuguese, to explain she was looking for a family member, un hombre aleman. A German gentleman! She held the picture up for him. He frowned as he studied it. After a few seconds, he said, "Sim Dona, sorry I speak some English. Yes, I will write his address for you. We deliver him papers in the morning; he is a quiet man."

Anneliese smiled that smile that melts every man. "Senor, please, if you see him do not say. It's a surprise!"

The shopkeeper smiled as Anneliese gripped his hand with, "Thank you Senor."

Now in a very buoyant mood, they returned to their car and drove to their hotel. She immediately phoned Carmella, first telling her the story about their luck. Carmella was excited, as Anneliese asked for help. "Tomorrow and possibly for a few days, would you arrange for MOSSAD agents to come with us to see if we can capture him. I will also talk to the CIA, because we may need their help with the Brazilian authorities." Later that evening, Carmella, Ezra and Immanuel visited Anneliese and Barry at their hotel. All three of them were extremely excited with the results of the day. They went over and over the scenario, answering question after question from the Israelis'.

Carmella explained that their MOSSAD officers had studied the map of the area, Stangl's house was on the corner of a road junction. And on the opposite side of the road, about 50 yards along, was a small park with a parking lot facing Stangl's house.

The plan for surveillance involved two cars parked about 100 yards either side of Stangl's corner house, A third car would sit in the parking area opposite. MOSSAD would have two agents in each of the cars, using binoculars, to assist surveillance. Carmella would be in the car in the parking area. Ezra and Immanuel would discreetly wander the area on foot, Radio contact would be used throughout the operation, and would provide contact to the CIA, if and when they were required.

Anneliese commented, "That all sounds pretty water tight." Barry, with an excited expression, asked "What is the timing plan for this?"

Carmella said, "We plan to be in place by 6.30am, but with graduated arrivals, in case he is watching and gets spooked by all the cars arriving at the same time!"

Barry fidgeted for a few minutes, then with a questioning expression asked Carmella "Are your agents confident they could recognise him. Do they have his picture, have they studied it? I hope this doesn't sound disrespectful to your people. I just don't want to discover later that there was a hole in our fence."

Carmella leant across and grasped Barry's hand. "Barry, I know you are putting every ounce of you into this operation and I know you always show us respect. Yes, is the answer! We have all studied his photos and everything about him for years. Capture of this degenerate would mean more to all of us, and the Israeli nation, than I can ever put into words!"

Anneliese then glanced at Carmella and to both Ezra and Immanuel. "I hope you guys will understand, but Barry and I want to be with you in this operation. So my question is, where should we be stationed?"

With a partially shocked look, Carmella exclaimed, "I am so, so sorry! Of course we knew you would want to be part of this. We had planned for two of our agents in each car, such that you could choose which location you would like. You can select any of the three cars, but to be honest, I would love you to be with me!"

Anneliese looked to Barry and both smiled, "Of course we want to be with you, and it's probably the best vantage point."

As the MOSSAD team prepared to leave, adrenalin was at a significant pitch. At the door, embraces were stronger than polite. Barry moved forward and as he shook hands with each of them, he proudly, and loudly, said, "Shalom".

Last to leave, Carmella, turned and said, "Thank you both so much. We will pick you up about 6.00am and let's hope it will be the best day of our lives."

As they left, Anneliese turned and held Barry's face. "I'm so proud of you. All the effort you have put in and without a single complaint. And then to give a sincere goodbye to our Israeli friends in their own language! You have many hidden talents. May I take you to bed?"

Over the next couple of hours, the tenderness of their love-making entwined their souls. It was completely exquisite, breath-taking love!

71

The next morning generated a totally different atmosphere. Both Anneliese and Barry quietly prepared for the day. Stepping into unknown expectancy was creating some stressful feelings. But the arrival of their car seemed to blow the stress clouds away. They were now on the mission. It was real! Not just stressing over what it might be!

They sat in the parking lot, chatting occasionally, but continually watching Stangl's street door. About 8.10am, Carmella's colleague, Jacob, had just said he needed to get out to stretch his legs. As he pulled on the door lock, Carmella said, "Wait!" Stangl's street door was opening. Jacob wanted to rush over to the house, but Carmella said, "No, let's just watch for a moment!"

Franz Stangl left the house, walking toward the Carmel Mercado. Carmella alerted all the agents to go, go, go! Within two minutes he was surrounded and arrested. No arguing, no fighting. Just complete surrender. Carmella immediately contacted the CIA H.Q. They would arrive in five minutes. With them came Brazilian police.

The CIA and Brazilian police jointly took over from the MOSSAD agents. Stangl was handcuffed and taken away. Carmella joined the CIA officers and asked if they would come for a word with Anneliese and Barry. They strolled across to the parking lot in the park.

Carmella introduced them as CECD agents. The senior CIA Officer was very pleased to get acquainted, especially when he saw the beauty of Anneliese.

Anneliese had her questions ready. "Sir, can you assure me that he will not be released and you will have him extradited to West Germany very soon." "Mam," he replied, "I can assure you that procedures already are underway to get exactly that to happen. But you will understand, we are not in the U.S.A; we had already agreed with Brazil that, if we got to this point, they would be very supportive."

"Ok, Sir, sorry, what is your name and position?" "I am Edward Woolton Junior of the Special Skill Group." "Well, Mr Woolton Junior can you give me your assurance that Stangl will, at least, be extradited to the U.S.A. to ensure extradition procedures to West German are progressed. If not, would you please get your Director General on the phone to talk with me. If you are unable to do that, perhaps you would get Mr Richard Helms to call my Commander to satisfy me on the assurances I am requesting."

Mr Woolton Junior appeared impressed by Anneliese's knowledge and approach. "Mam, I sure will try," he said as he strode away to his car. He returned 15 minutes later. "Mam, Mr Helms sends his regards and his thanks for your successful efforts on this CECD assignment. And, you have his word that Stangl will remain in a U.S. penitentiary whilst we work through the bureaucracy to have him extradited to Germany."

Anneliese and Carmella both gave him glorious smiles as they shook his hand. "That makes us feel so much better, Mr Woolton Junior. You have our sincere thanks."

As they left, Anneliese said, "Today will go down in the history books. February 28th 1967. Tomorrow begins a new month where we may hunt down another of the three "most wanted". We will just keep working at it month by month!"

In their car, on the way back to the hotel, Anneliese had a thoughtful expression. As she drove, Barry, seeing her look, asked, "Are you thinking what I'm thinking darling." "What's that Barry?" she replied. "What are we going to do now to move on with our quest to hunt Nazis'?"

Anneliese, turning her head slightly towards Barry said, "You are getting good at reading my mind; I think we should stay here for a while and assist Carmella with the hunt for Josef Mengele. Also, Carmella has stacks of leads to follow up on the trail of the Nazis' that Paulo had assisted to escape down here. After they searched his apartment, she told me that they had good leads on the nine Nazis' he helped to flee, that were all designated "war criminals" So, that's a lot on her plate and we could give her some help!"

Back at the hotel, they were just about ready to go down to the restaurant. Barry was just opening their door when their phone rang. Anneliese turned back and answered it.

It was Jerome. A very nervous Jerome! "I'm so sorry to bother you Anneliese, but it's very important." "What is it Jerome, you sound worried? It can't be as bad as you think?" "Well, it's not too good," responded Jerome. "I've had Albie contact me from New York. There was an incident today. Albie and Anya had been visiting one of those cellar bars, trying to get more information. There were some German types in there and when Anya and Albie left, they followed and attacked them. There were too many, so they gave Albie and Anya a good pasting, all the time shouting, "Do not come here asking about Hermine". Albie is battered and bruised but as he told me, he has had far worse. But poor Anya is in a bad way. They almost kicked her to death.

One of the bastards shouted, "This is from the "stomping mare" as he stamped on Anya. She is tough but she is in hospital, but just for tonight. She has a broken collar bone, but that will mend in a few weeks! They will fly back to Buenos Aires tomorrow evening so they can have time to recover."

"Thank you, Jerome for letting me know. Barry and I will fly back tomorrow to give them every help. Would you please inform Albie?"

Anneliese turned to Barry. "Guess you got the gist of all that. We will need to fly back tomorrow. Suppose we should forget dinner and just get room service later because I need to talk with Carmella."

Picking up the phone and dialling Carmella, she got straight through. She spent 15 minutes explaining the crisis, Carmella was seriously concerned and reacted, with assistance. "I will get Ezra to fly you down to Buenos Aires tomorrow. Tell me what time you want to go." "Carmella, it's not necessary, we can go commercial!" "Don't argue," said Carmella, "it's a quick and easy trip in that Lear Jet!" "Oh alright" replied Anneliese, "if we could take off about 11am, because Anya and Albie won't be back until late afternoon. That will give me time to prepare for her."

Carmella said, "After today, I am having a day off tomorrow. I will pick you up at about 10am. That will give you time for breakfast." "Carmella, you are wonderful" was Anneliese's closing remark.

After a fairly stressful evening, Anneliese turned to Barry saying "Come on my gorgeous fella, I'll buy you a large scotch!"

With a refined model-like turn, Anneliese went for the door handle. Once again the telephone rang. "Blast it" said

Anneliese, "Will we never escape from this room?" Barry tried unsuccessfully to stifle a giggle as he picked up the receiver. "Hello" and a few seconds listening. "Anneliese, it's for you," with a further short giggle. As she took the receiver, Barry, from behind, put his arms around her waist.

It was Simon Wiesenthal calling. "I'm sorry for interrupting your evening, but I've just heard from Carmella. I know we have not spoken before, but I just had to call and thank you. Thank you on behalf of my country and all its bereaved families! Your diligent, intelligent efforts were splendid, and will never be forgotten."

"Carmella and my wonderful partner, Barry, deserve as much praise, Mr Wiesenthal, and I will pass your thanks onto them. Bless you, Simon, God be with you! And I hope we will meet one day!" That was it, they were off to hit the bar in style!

A few drinks later and the bar-tender was kind enough to get them both a colourful salad and some soft, but crusty, bread.

72

As usual, Carmella and Ezra arrived on time. They were walking across the tarmac by 10.30am and taxiing for take-off ten minutes later. Anneliese, Carmella and Barry sat chatting for a few minutes then Carmella jumped up, saying she was co-piloting with Ezra. What a surprising woman Carmella was. She explained later that she was close to gaining her pilot's license and co-piloting was part of her final stage!

The under-carriage lifted and they powered up at a 45 degree angle, through blue sky into the high, but gentle clouds. Carmella returned, asking if they wanted drinks. She had now transformed herself into an accomplished hostess. They all had coffees; even Ezra, who had put the auto--pilot in charge.

Carmella sat with Anneliese and Barry for a few minutes, explaining that she and Ezra would return from Buenos Aires after touchdown. In a day or two, Immanuel would fly the Cessna down to Buenos Aires just in case an aircraft was needed for the CECD team. Ezra and Carmella would continue their search for Josef Mengele around Sao Paulo, to follow up leads on an area called Bertioga. They also had some less-than-convincing information that he may be in Paraguay. They had a location; a very wide location; along the Paraguayan border to Brazil. The suspicion was that he had bought a farm and shuttled back and forth, to throw any hunters off the scent. If this were true, his evasion technique was a master-stroke.

Jerome picked them up from the airport. Arriving back in the San Isidro house, Frank met them at the gates. Anneliese, after the welcoming embraces, bustled in, saying she had to prepare the room for Anya and Albie. Frank and Jerome would head to the Domestic Airport to pick them up in two hours.

They arrived back at the safe house about 5pm. Frank and Jerome were essential to get Anya and Albie out of the car and to help them stumble up the path and through the door. Anneliese became very emotional seeing them staggering into the hallway. Anya was truly a sad and sorry sight! Her beautiful clear white skin was covered in bruises, cuts and abrasions. Her face appeared as if it had been used for football practise; both light blue eyes were about hidden by swelling. She was wearing a figure eight bandage, tightly holding her fractured collar bone in place. Her whole body, legs, arms and torso were peppered with plasters and bandages.

Albie did not look quite so bad. His face and, especially eyes, had been battered and therefore, were suffering swelling. His left arm and shoulder had been bandaged and he had a prominent limp with the left leg.

Anneliese gently embraced Anya, who was trying hard to smile. Tears seeped out slowly from Anneliese's eyes. Although a brave, tough lady, this extreme distortion of Anya's beautiful features was hard to bear.

Sitting in the lounge, on the edge of her seat, Anneliese said she would get them a drink and then they would be helped to bed. Rest and recuperation was the rule for the next several days, so it was stiff drinks all round!

Throughout this time, Barry had been very quiet. Seeing the results of this vicious attack on his loved ones had created a surge in his anger. He had it under control! In his mind he repeated the word RAFT over and over again.

Frank and Jerome had been sitting quietly chatting in the kitchen. These two caring characters decided to head next door to give everyone a chance to ease their noticeable anguish. As they left, shouting, "see you all tomorrow" Anneliese said "They are great fellas.... Giving us some time and space!"

Anneliese's nursing instincts grew, over the next few days, becoming severely acute. Every inch of the house required constant disinfectant. Matron Anneliese's eyes followed everyone's movements and actions. All were required to pitch in and help with laundry, food preparation, medical supplies and applications, and so on. This was Anneliese applying psychology to prevent any of them having time to be melancholy or depressed!

It was definitely getting results. On the third day of Recovery Week, Anya was feeling well enough to call everyone together. She wanted to explain what she and Albie had achieved regarding Hermine Braunsteiner. They had concentrated on lobbying every possible U.S. government department and department chiefs. The CIA were particularly helpful as was the Department of Justice. All had agreed that a concerted effort would be instituted to revoke Braunsteiner's U.S. citizenship, as it could be proved it was obtained with false declarations. Further, the U.S. Government would push hard on the West German Government to initiate extradition proceedings.

She flagrantly used her own name and lived openly in the Mespeth area of Queens, New York City. She had married, but her partner knew nothing of her Nazi history. It was highly unlikely she would try to escape the spotlight! The New York Times had listened to everything Albie and

Anya had to say and would monitor Government progress and continue to lobby and protest until she was extradited. All involved were completely convinced that she would, ultimately, be tried for her War Crimes.

The only potential negative was that this may all take some time. Braunsteiner was a past master at using legalities in her defence. She was already going ahead with lawyers using grounds such as "lack of probable cause" and "double jeopardy". However, Anya had assurances from the U.S Government that extradition to West Germany would be achieved. Nothing more could be done to add to the positives.

Everybody in the meeting applauded Anya and Albie, adding greatly to their well-being and recovery.

That same day, Anneliese phoned Commander Farrell. After Anneliese detailed all they had heard from Anya, he said to tell them both they had done a superb job and he, personally, was extremely grateful. He had already received the same account from Richard Helms, Director General of the CIA.

Next, Anneliese phoned Carmella and, again, gave the same feedback together with the CIA conclusions regarding confidence in achieving extradition.

Carmella was overjoyed. "That's two in one week in the bag," she said. "Well very nearly in the bag! I will pass it onto my MOSSAD superiors immediately. And just to let you know, Immanuel will arrive back with you tomorrow in the Cessna, and I will call you in a couple of days."

Time flew by, Albie began using the swimming pool for physiotherapy. He was almost fully recovered, other than cuts and bruises that were healing. He and Barry, and sometimes, with Frank and Jerome, would amble down to the corner parlour for lashings of take-away ice cream.

Anya and Anneliese were progressively spending more and more time sitting on the loungers in the sun. By the end of the first week, Anya's enchanting nubile features were returning. Her glorious curves were on show again, despite some black and blue areas remaining. And the sensual innocence in her eyes could, once again, excite the male population! Her fractured collar bone would take a few more weeks to recover, but it didn't detract from the beauty of this woman.

Barry and Albie had spent the week like conjoined twins, doing all the tasks set by Anneliese, together. But the drudgery was taking its toll. They both wanted action. Albie was incensed by what had happened to him and Anya and wanted revenge. Barry also!

That Friday evening, Immanuel arrived. They all got together for a dinner that Immanuel cooked for them. An exotic version of chilli-con-carne which hit the spot for everyone. The alcohol began to flow, with everyone discussing the week's events. Immanuel's English improved throughout the evening, and the team made every effort to make him welcome. They all thanked him for his expertise with the food, and as the alcohol gained hold, he joined in the evening chatter and humour.

Although February, the hot sun and humidity woke everyone early. They all gravitated to the garden and sat around having some breakfast. All except Barry who was already in the swimming pool trying to beat his record of fifteen lengths!

The telephone rang; Anneliese left her lounger to answer it, just as Frank and Jerome appeared. The phone call was Carmella. The pleasantries were soon out of the way. Reading Carmella's tone, Anneliese sensed something was wrong. "What's up Carmella, you sound depressed?" "I suppose so," was Carmella's response. "Ezra and I have devoted every ounce of us to this search for Josef Mengele. We've looked into every nook and cranny in Buenos Aires, and every time we think we are getting close, we get feedback that says he has moved again. He moves like a rattle snake being poked with a stick!"

There was a minute's silence, then Anneliese spoke. "Everything we know from the reports we have, is that his main perversion was children. He constantly selected them for his grotesque, depraved operations. Have you thought about staking out some schools? Perhaps selecting some near his previous homes?"

"Anneliese, that's a great idea!" As Carmella spoke, her tone was definitely brighter. "Yes Anneliese, we will start on that tomorrow. But there is another angle that is worrying us. All the digging and delving we are doing seems to keep turning up the same questionable indication. Several surreptitious sources, that probably can't be trusted, keep suggesting that he has a farm or works on a farm, in Paraguay, close to the southern border with Argentina. It may be that we are being fed false information to throw us off the scent, but my concern is that it may be true, in which case Brazil is not the place to be."

"Ok, Carmella, let me go away and think for half-an-hour, then I will call you back." She returned to her lounger, as Barry was standing drying himself. She hardly noticed Barry, as she dropped onto the seat. Her brain was ticking, whirring and twisting as she rolled through all the alternatives.

Barry, standing alongside Anneliese, knew she was grappling with something. "Darling, what's up? You have that perturbed look!" (Barry's vocabulary had come a long way since meeting Anneliese!)

73

nneliese went through the discussion she had with Carmella. Barry listened intently, then turned and slowly wandered around the pool. He stopped at the lounger Immanuel had taken, and stood looking down at him. "Immanuel, shalom." They shook hands as Immanuel sat up. "How long would it take to fly in the Cessna to Paraguay?" Barry, his eyes searching, waiting, whilst Immanuel was thinking. "Two hours or two and a half hours, Barry."

"Thank you, Immanuel. Would you be happy to fly me and Albie up to Paraguay tomorrow?" "Oh yes Barry, Sir, but my boss, Carmella must agree first." "Fantastic Immanuel! Many thanks," as he strode off back to Anneliese.

Anneliese had her eyes closed as he sat on the lounger beside her. "Are you asleep darling?" he whispered. Her eyes opened and she smiled. "Oh no, just thinking how to help Carmella. We got two of those bastards, but now we are out of action and can't help her with the last one! I would go but can't leave Anya to fend for herself, and she needs a few more weeks to fully recover!"

Barry stood, needing to compose himself before he could say what he wanted to say to Anneliese. He knew she would argue, so now it was crunch time.

He made a start. "Anneliese, may I make a suggestion?" She looked up, shading her eyes with her right hand. "Of course, but don't say, let's all have a drink whilst we think." Barry leaned forward and took her hand. "You can be such a comic Mrs Anneliese." She tightly gripped his hand saying, "You just called me Mrs. I've never been referred to as that in such an un-romantic way before!" They both began to giggle as Barry bent down and embraced Anneliese.

"Alright Barry, what's this suggestion? Sorry for distracting you." "It's this" said Barry. "Albie is fine now. You are great caring for Anya, but that will need a few weeks yet. I am sitting around like a spare part, although I am an example of peak physical fitness." Anneliese interrupted. "Barry, quit while you're ahead! If that's true, you will need to prove it tonight! Sorry, carry on!"

"Ok, I will keep this short and sweet. Immanuel will fly me and Albie to the Paraguay border. We will fly as far along the southern border as we can, using the reconnaissance camera to photograph the farms and buildings. I will work on the maps with Immanuel to prepare the best route. That will give Carmella something to work with. If you call her back in a minute, ask if she agrees. Also, ask if there is a town or area along the border we should aim for."

Anneliese could not speak. She remained quiet for a good minute. In her mind, she was searching for a way to keep Barry here with her, safe with her. Then she hit on an answer. "Barry, it's a good idea, but you wouldn't' have a CECD agent with you, which would not meet the Commander's stipulations."

Barry looked to the sky as he noisily exhaled. He went back into the fray. "Anneliese, the Germans broke every single rule of war. That's why we are hunting them, to bring them to trial for war crimes. I'm sure it will be ok for us to bend the rules just a bit. If Carmella gives her consent, and our pilot is her subordinate, we are being supervised! Neither Albie nor I can fly a plane. So we won't be making our escape in it!"

Anneliese chuckled right through to a belly laugh. "I will phone Carmella and talk it through." Barry winked, then tripped off to discuss the whole thing with Albie.

As Barry wandered around the garden, he noticed the skies were blackening in the distance. He stood fascinated by the forming clouds. It was a subject in his school science work that had grabbed his attention.

He watched for a couple more minutes, then shouted, "Hey you guys, we will be getting some really heavy rain in about ten minutes so if I were you, I'd start getting your things inside."

Anneliese and Anya both sat up on their loungers and stared up at the sky. Anya was unconvinced. "Barry, it has been hot and humid for days, I think it will pass!"

"Sorry to disagree Anya, but clouds are one thing I know a bit about. They are Cumulonimbus clouds and they are forming pretty quickly. When the rain comes, it won't last long…. Perhaps an hour. But if it's an aggressive formation, we could get torrents of rain, hailstones and lightning. Sometimes they even whip up tornadoes! The way it's been with long periods of heat and humidity, is the classic preparation for these storms. And I read before we came here that it's not unusual this time of year in Argentina and most of South America."

74

That was it! Clothes, bags, cushions were all being moved inside. Barry and Immanuel walked into the lounge, just as Albie arrived asking what was going on. He had already got out of his trunks and was keen on a stroll to the ice-cream parlour. Barry put his hand on Albie's shoulder and edged him to the rear of the lounge. "Listen Albie," he said …. But a massively loud thunder crack got in first. Both girls bent double with their hands clasping their heads, Barry repeated, "Albie, tomorrow do you fancy flying with me and Immanuel up to Paraguay? We could do some reconnaissance work for Carmella to help her with finding Mengele!" "Yes, of course, I've been getting bored."

Albie turned and shouted back to the others, "Anyone want to come for an ice-cream?" Everybody called back, "Yes please", so there was a queue. Anya, Anneliese, Jerome and Immanuel. "Where's Frank?" said Barry. "He's working in the office, so I'll get him a takeaway." Replied Jerome.

Barry turned to face the queue. Giggling as he spoke, he went on, "Suggest you all get raincoats," as he pulled on his. All together, they replied, "No, we'll be ok!" As Barry opened the door, he smugly said to Albie, "They will come back like drowned rats!"

The heavens opened as they crushed to get out of the downpour into the parlour. They, after half-an-hour, were trying to make their ice-creams last. The rain continued to bucket down. Another 30 minutes and they were all talking about making a run for it. Barry and Albie, in their Boleyn Boys Navy Blue gabardine raincoats, were smiling. Anya and Anneliese were wearing soft cotton summer knee length dresses!

The rain slightly eased and the race was on, but after 20 yards the torrent began again. The girls became banshees as they ran past the security lodge. The security guards, on hearing the screaming and wailing, poked their heads out. They were hypnotised by the two beauties gliding past them with soaking wet see-through cotton frocks clinging to every curve of their anatomy.

Immanuel and Jerome were close behind the girls, with Barry and Albie bringing up the rear, with soaking wet hair. Just like a night out in London!

Whilst they had been in the ice-cream parlour, Barry had tackled Albie again about the trip to Paraguay. "Look Albie, I'm not forcing you. I can get it done with Immanuel. It's only a short flight and you might want to stay with Anya." "Don't' be stupid! I need a break from all this caring stuff and sitting around. I need the adrenalin to kick back in. It will be great!"

Back in the house for ten minutes as they dried off, Jerome went next door to give Frank his chocolate chip tub. A few minutes later, they both quietly emerged; Frank with a disturbed expression. But continuing to spoon-eat his ice-cream.

Frank stood still, under the door encasement. Looking down into his ice-cream tub, he shouted," Barry and Albie, do you have a minute?" They both came and stood in front of Frank. His face raised and they could see he was more than displeased. Whilst still chomping on the choc chip, he slowly spoke. "I've just been talking with Carmella. She tells me you want to fly off tomorrow with Immanuel to Paraguay. Anneliese spoke with her earlier and supports the idea. I applaud your intentions, but as you know, I am your boss. Not Anneliese! Not Carmella! Not even the Commander! If anything goes wrong, it's down to me. Carmella would be extremely grateful and supports you to the hilt. But only if I agree. If I do! She understands the hierarchy. It's about time you did! It's there to protect all of us. Did you ask yourselves, would I want to come with you? No! Did you even think you needed to talk to me first? No! I can forgive you all of that because it's the first time we have had this type of issue. But from now on, always remember I am your boss. I can make or break you. And remember, you are already broken! You are here to repair yourselves. Look, I'm going to soften this a bit. You are my mates. But not when we are working, we are a team! Barry, you were a good footballer, but you could never ever have won a game on your own. When there are many players, someone has to lead, organise and get the best out of them. So at the very least, as your manager, I would have appreciated being consulted. And even though I'm your leader, you may or may not know that whatever we do as a team, I always take advice and counsel from Anneliese. She is clever! She has been trained in psychology. I've not, so I refer to her. That's teamwork! I may be your boss, but I will use your abilities to get the best out of the whole team".

"So I think I have made my point!" Both Albie and Barry nodded. "So yes, you should go on your jaunt up to Paraguay that will, hopefully, give Carmella some worthwhile intelligence."

"My last word, is be careful. You saw the weather tonight and it's active all around us. But I know Immanuel is an experienced pilot, and will take every care"

It was a pretty relaxed carefree evening, with a barbeque and drinks by the pool. Immanuel was staying overnight in the office/house with Frank and Jerome.

Both Frank and Jerome initiated banter, story-telling and jokes throughout the entire evening. Frank never ever held a grudge, and this evening was no exception. As the night wore on, the bonding session became stronger than Marbella sun, and only ended after the lads bombing and ducking session!

Early morning, once again, the rain was thundering down. They all sat around the breakfast table, watching the rain flow down the windows. Albie walked in, still with baby sleep sticking his eye-lids together. Anya proceeded to use wet gauze to pamper and awake his face.

Immanuel, in his fractured English, said "no fly yet, when rain stops!" Albie laughed, "That's good because I need another hour!"

Barry and Immanuel sat for the next hour, studying maps. Carmella had spoken, early morning, with Immanuel and indicated that the intelligence she had, suggested they should fly towards a town called Rosario.

Their flight would take them north-west close to a river near Rosario. That was the best information she had concerning the area where the farm or ranch may be. She had said, do not travel more than 100 miles north or west of Rosario, as you fly parallel to the river.

Immanuel explained, with the flight distance there and back, 100 miles either north or west of Rosario, and with a contingency, they should have 200 miles of fuel in the tank when they arrived back in Buenos Aires.

They eventually arrived at the domestic airport about 11.30am, Albie was now awake! Jerome had driven them. Anneliese also wanted to see them off but Barry had put his foot down. I'm not a baby! This is just a jolly, like a beano to Margate! Anneliese, bothered and bewildered waved!

As they strode across the tarmac, Albie admired the Cessna. "It's a great looking plane. Very streamlined!" Immanuel replied, "Yes, it's the best seller in the world! It's a single engine turbo prop, with four seats, and as safe as you would wish."

75

Immanuel opened the door, pointing Barry and Albie to the rear seats. "Best for photographs" he said, as he passed Barry the camera. "You know how to? It has rapid take!" Barry smiled at Immanuel, as he held the camera up to his face, pretending to take a photo.

The weather now was fine and forecast to get hotter and more humid. They took off to the east then wheeled around, heading north. That turn reminded them both of the waltzer on the Beckton fairground. This was the first thrill, but it didn't end there! Turbulence grew, the further they went towards the border.

About an hour and a half into the flight, the air pressure became erratic. Three times, the Cessna hit air pockets and dropped around 50 feet. Barry and Albie, shouted and laughed, as if it were the fairground ride. Not so Immanuel! As he scanned the cockpit instruments, he turned slightly and shouted "We are flying at 4500 feet, but with this weather it's best to fly below it. So we drop to 2000 feet!

As the Cessna descended, the buffeting from the turbulence gradually eased. Immanuel, always appearing relaxed, turned in his seat saying loudly, "Look, that is Rosario." But then, looking just beyond Rosario, Immanuel noticed a threatening weather pattern forming. Barry and Albie were intent on studying the landscape below. As the plane pressed its way through short bursts of cotton wool clouds, the lads were frantically taking cumulative shots of farms and farm buildings. They were closing in on Parana River.

Immanuel shouted back, "I will turn west. We must stay away from the storm near Rosario!" They banked right, parallel to the river. But the darkening skies kept coming. Their direction, as they turned, was straight into the headwind, so their v-speed slowed. Immanuel decided to descend further, to 1000 feet.

The sky was losing daylight fast. Barry stopped photographing and was now taking interest in the developing weather pattern. "Hey Albie, that's not looking good. Those clouds chasing us are Cumulonimbus. Same as we saw in Buenos Aires yesterday! Just three more minutes, then the Almighty would decide!"

The Cessna's airspeed continued to fall, along with their altitude. The next event was unexplainable, unutterable, beyond description. As if trapped by a tornado, the Cessna began to shake violently. And not just shake; everything became completely uncontrollable. None of them, Immanuel, Barry or Albie even knew which way up they were. They spun and twisted. Objects hit them, from every direction.

Barry grabbed hold of Albie, pulled his head close and kissed his crown; his lips could not withdraw. His arms were locked, totally locked, as they spiralled down. The killer punch was floating above them, deciding if to come, when to come!

A few seconds later, a gigantic lightning strike hit the Cessna, and once again, the whole plane turned over, spinning every which way. The Cessna was totally out of control. Immanuel's cockpit instruments had failed.

The Cessna engine failed. The plane hurtled towards the ground, or possibly the Parana River.

200 feet above ground, the fuselage, with a gigantic ripping sound, shattered and separated from the cockpit. It dropped like a stone into the centre of the fast-flowing river.

The cockpit careered on, then crashed into a Parana Pine tree. It just hung there, like a bat, in the lower branches. Wing pieces rained down, fluttering left and right!

The last thing Immanuel heard was an echoing eerie scream!!! ANNELEEEESA!!!

Then peace! But only for a few seconds! The sky turned grey, as if covered by an old blanket; not caused by the weather, but by flocks of birds, bursting, terrified from the trees along the river-side. With an incredible screeching crescendo of noise, the Gyra Pong birds flew, looping lazily, toward the distant horizon.

The earth fell completely silent, other than the soothing sound of fast flowing water. The sun gradually emerged, its gentle rays picking out the glistening hulk of the silver fuselage as it floated, down river, into the distance.

Convincing confirmation of utter finality was executed by the Red Bellied Parana fish, as they leapt and splashed around the dismembered Cessna carcass.

WHO MADE THIS EARTH, WHO MADE THESE SKIES

IT WAS NOT MAN, WHO LIVES AND DIES!

76

At precisely 3.33pm Anneliese's body shuddered. Her legs trembled uncontrollably. She sat up on her lounger, rubbing her knees as she looked across the pool to Anya, who was peering back at her.

Anneliese stood up and with a determined gait strode round to Anya. Sitting on the edge of the lounger, she asked Anya, "Are you ok?" "I think so," replied Anya. "I was asleep, then, all of a sudden had a sharp pain in my forehead." "Probably lying in the sun for too long!"

Anneliese's intuitive senses became ultra-dominant; she knew she must find Frank. She ran round to the office/house, scrambled through the door, and there was a surprised Frank, sitting at a desk. He turned in his seat, raised his eyebrows, and then smiled at Anneliese. She just stood, arms by her side, as her eyes became moist. Frank's expression became concerned. His brow furrowed as he stood and walked to Anneliese. Putting his arm around her shoulders, he peered into her eyes saying, "What's up my dear. You are shaking! Why? What's happened?"

"I don't know anything has happened, "she replied! There are no facts I can give you, no evidence, just a feeling. An overwhelming feeling! It may sound ridiculous, but some form of telepathic sense collided with my intuition, with serious disturbance to my mental state. Anya experienced exactly the same shock to her system, at exactly the same moment."

"Frank, you know me well enough to know that I'm not easily rattled. I am pleading with you, imploring you, to check on their safety. Are they safe in the Cessna, and on their way home?"

"Of course, Anneliese, I will get onto Buenos Aires Domestic. But calm yourself; go and have a coffee with Anya and try to calm her too!"

15 minutes later, Frank emerged. His face was glum as he slow-walked, head down, around the pool, Anneliese and Anya sensed it wasn't good. Frank wiped his lips with the back of his hand. "I've talked with Buenos Aires Domestic, the Islas Malvinas airport at Rosario, and Ascuncion Airport. They all had them on their radar until about 3.30pm. There was a partial mayday call at that time, but then the Cessna just disappeared off their screens. The Ascuncion conning tower marshaller said the Cessna flew down to only 200 feet before he lost it off the screen. He immediately alerted his air traffic control supervisor who contacted the Paraguayan military. They have four helicopters out, right now, doing an intensive search of the known last location. They will call as soon as they have anything to tell."

Anneliese and Anya sat quietly staring at one another. Frank was joined by Jerome. They both stood in silence. The grief and pain was so difficult to absorb. Their emotions were surrendering to complete numbness!

The phone rang. Only Frank was mentally equipped to move to answer it. The military personnel had rescued the pilot, Immanuel, from the dangling cockpit. He was unconscious and severely injured, but still alive. He had been flown to hospital in Rosario. No further information was available, but they had concluded that the Cessna fuselage had landed in the river. They were searching now!

Anya and Anneliese became totally distraught. It was heart breaking for Frank and Jerome to watch. Anya stood and clutched Jerome, tears streaming down their faces. Anneliese, her whole being racked with anguish, repeated the Lord's Prayer in her mind, over and over again!

The phone rang again! Frank, with a strained expression, listened intently. He did not speak. Not a single question! He slowly turned to face Anneliese and Anya. "Please, please, both gather yourselves. You know you are both strong women, so take a deep breath and let's get this over with. They have found the fuselage in a deep part of the river. They are recovering it now but...." He hesitated... ."I'm so sorry! There is no hope! They didn't suffer. The end was quick! Just like everything else in their lives, they did it together!" Frank couldn't take any more; so strode off to the office. Jerome and Anya were still entwined as they sobbed together. Anneliese sat upright, clearing and cleaning away her emotion! A fixed expression of disbelief invaded her face. She was completely numb.

77

About three weeks later, around the middle of May, Carmella visited. Spirits were lifting. Not exactly in a great place, but they were all in survival mode. Carmella announced that Immanuel was coming home. He had lost his spleen but he would survive without it. His broken leg would be healed in another three weeks, so things were on the up for him.

Then came the crunch. The crisis in the Middle East had worsened and Carmella, Immanuel and Ezra were being recalled to Israel. Well really only Carmella because the other two were still civilians. But they all wanted to go home to protect their country.

The next day, Commander Farrell called Frank and Anneliese. In view of MOSSAD's withdrawal, they also should return to Europe. He stressed that the assignment had been a fabulous success and could not wait for them to return to work with him.

Anneliese and Anya were to have a month's compassionate leave to help with their recovery. Then it would be back to "business as normal."

Initially, they returned to visit Joan and Jess to explain the events of the recent weeks. They stressed that Joan, Jess and Albie's parents, should be extremely proud of the bravery their boys exhibited and how much they had achieved. Obviously, there were tears. And extraordinary emotion; but life has to go on!

Jerome was never going to be left behind. He was appointed as Anya and Anneliese's management support with an increase in salary and a respected Senior Civil Service position. Frank would be continuing as the Commander's Key Secret Service Agent. He loved his job and never aspired to lofty positions in the CECD organisation!

After visiting Joan and Jess in the U.K. Anneliese and Anya settled back in the Amsterdam Red Light District. Subsequently, Anneliese and Anya moved to Tunisia, responsible for the Middle East.

Over the next few years, they followed the news on the "three most wanted" Nazis that had been their targets in South America.

Franz Stangl: 1967	Extradited to Germany June 22, 1967
	Sentenced to life in prison
	Died in prison from heart failure June, 1971
Hermine Braunsteiner:	Extradited to Germany, May 1, 1971
	Remanded in custody in Dusseldorf, August 7, 1973
	Sentenced to life in prison, June 30, 1981
	Died April 19, 1999 after diabetes complications
Josef Mengele:	Never captured.

Constantly eluded capture after moving to Brazil in 1961. Died while swimming off Sao Paulo, Brazil, 1979

So where did life's magical mystery tour take the cast?:

- Carmella and Billy returned to Israel to live on a Kibbutz in Tel-Aviv. Billy almost immediately joined the Israeli armed forces. He distinguished himself during the Israel 6 Day war. With commendations, he was re-assigned to Sayeret Matkal, the Special Reconnaissance forces. Carmella continued her assignment with MOSSAD, eventually becoming a Senior Intelligence Officer. She talked with Anneliese almost every day!

- Billy placed the deaths of Barry and Albie firmly on the shoulders of Josef Mengele. He used his thoughts of revenge to drive him to become one of Israel's bravest, battle hardened veterans. Billy was never ever alone again! Carmella became his loving wife, and they spent the rest of life together.

- Anneliese and Anya, cleverly, quietly and carefully continued their work for CECD. They were settled in Hammamet, Tunisia, responsible for intelligence and counter-espionage across the whole of the Middle East. Their cover was as owners of a travelogue and publishing business. Working constantly with Carmella, they had two notable successes. First, the rescue of 102 hostages from the Entebbe raid in July, 1976. Also, working with Frank, Anneliese secured the release of 26 hostages from the Iranian Embassy Siege; May 1980.

- Frank eventually became a Senior Intelligence Officer with CECD. He had always avoided promotion, but after several commendations and a decoration, he acceded to the Commander's wishes. The Commander became chief Security

Adviser to the Prime Minister. The Honourable Mrs Margaret Thatcher!

- Jerome found that "Everyday went faster than a Roller Coaster." He, after only seven years, was appointed Assistant Director of GCHQ. He never, ever, relented in his love and affection for Anya!

- Joan and Jess were now keeping Central London on the move. They operated on the No25 bus which stopped outside GCHQ every day. At that stop, Joan would always loudly shout "Barry's HQ!" And every so often she would embrace a very special customer, Jerome!. As they pulled away, Jess would honk his horn…. Three times. This was their legacy to the two brave men who had been added to the Mengele death toll.

- Joan and Jess had many nostalgic holidays in Marbella, visiting Café Del Mar. They always stroked the Cruzcampo Beer Pump, displayed proudly on the bar!

- ✪ **The intensity of their loves and friendships had made their lives worthwhile. But as Joan had said, the memories would make their lives complete!**

MAPLE
PUBLISHERS

David R. Dye

Cold War, Hot Pursuit

*A Sequal which follows the under-cover
career of agent Anneliese*

ISBN: 978-1-83538-162-5

**A beautiful woman pursued through
the valley of the shadow of death.**

In the 1960's, an ambitious teenager secures a career position with a prominent vehicle manufacturer. He rapidly climbs the company ladder.

Whilst on business in Amsterdam, he meets a beautiful intelligent woman. To his surprise, by day she works in the same company; by night she works in the Amsterdam sex industry.

Both are extremely driven to access wealth and the rich lifestyle of their dreams. Their relationship strengthens with constant torrid passion and genuine romance. But her secret work in counter-espionage leads them into a dangerous world.

Ultimately, they are pursued by evil forces with potentially devastating consequences. But she eventually achieves a resounding victory, bringing them in for the cold!